MURDER
at the UNIVERSE

★★★★★

A FIVE-STAR MYSTERY

DANIEL EDWARD
CRAIG

A FIVE-STAR MYSTERY

MURDER
at the UNIVERSE

MIDNIGHT INK
WOODBURY, MINNESOTA

FIRST EDITION
First Printing, 2007

Cover design by Ellen L. Dahl
Cover photo © Triangle Images/Digital Vision/Getty Images

Midnight Ink, an imprint of Llewellyn Publications

Cover model(s) used for illustrative purposes only
and may not endorse or represent the book's subject

Library of Congress Cataloging-in-Publication Data
Craig, Daniel Edward, 1966-
    Murder at the universe / Daniel Edward Craig. —1st ed.
        p.   cm.
    "A Five-Star Mystery."
    ISBN 978-0-7387-1118-8
    I. Title.
PS3603.R353M87 2007
813'.6—dc22
                                                    2007012033

Midnight Ink
2143 Wooddale Drive, Dept. 978-0-7387-1118-8
Woodbury, MN 55125-2989

www.midnightinkbooks.com

Printed in the United States of America

To Mom and Dad,
creators of my universe.

Journey to the Center
of the Universe

In my career I have dealt with all types, from old money to new money, blue-blooded to hot-blooded, exceptionally important to merely self-important. I have endured rudeness and condescension, ignorance and obstinacy, verbal abuse and threats of violence. Yet at all times I remain courteous and professional, and rarely do I fail to win over a guest. One might say I kill them with kindness.

Yet I had never encountered the likes of Mrs. Brenda Rathberger.

Mr. Godfrey had debriefed us well in advance. The executive director of the Victims of Impaired Drivers association was highly particular, frugal, and intensely passionate about her cause. In previous years, the conference had been held in a small town, at a moderately priced hotel, attended primarily by small-town folk like Mrs. Rathberger. This year, VOID board members wanted New York City. They wanted a luxury hotel. And they wanted unprecedented media coverage.

In short, they wanted the Universe.

Mrs. Rathberger had lobbied hard against the board's decision. Yet, despite being ultimately responsible for organizing the conference, she had been overruled. And she was not pleased. This morning, a week before the conference was scheduled to begin, she was expected to check into the Universe Hotel to start preparations. Yesterday she had called Mr. Godfrey to warn him that if anything went wrong—*any-thing*—she would go straight to the board to demand an immediate change in venue, taking with her seven hundred delegates, meetings, receptions, and banquets—a total of over $1 million in revenue. The loss would be devastating to the hotel, both financially and in terms of morale. Securing a conference of this size between Christmas and New Year's Eve—a time of year when New York hotels were screaming for business—had been a coup, and competitors were insanely jealous. Moreover, last night, after the staff Christmas party, Mr. Godfrey had informed us that executive bonuses were on hold pending the success of the conference.

Losing it was simply out of the question.

Everything was to be perfect for Mrs. Rathberger's arrival. Preparations were elevated to a frenzy normally reserved for heads of state, royalty, and rock stars. Mr. Godfrey himself, general manager and owner of the hotel, would personally welcome her at the front door, along with a receiving line of management staff. She would be whisked up to her sprawling Supernova suite on the seventy-first floor, and thereafter every wish, whim, or fancy would be granted.

Unfortunately, things did not go quite as smoothly as planned.

To start off, Mr. Godfrey did not show up for the meet-and-greet. This was highly out of character for the consummate hotelier, and a tad unsettling, but there was no time for speculation. In a last-minute flurry of activity, the receiving line regrouped, and I was obliged to step in to replace him. Though not as prepared as I should have been—and suffering the effects of the previous night's rather boozy celebration—I was undaunted.

In a matter of time, I was confident Brenda Rathberger and I would be best friends.

"Welcome to the Universe, Mrs. Rathberger!"

It was 7:23 AM on Sunday morning, six days before Christmas, and I stood on the curb in my best suit, tall and erect, every strand of my sandy brown hair in place, beaming at Mrs. Rathberger as she climbed out of her red Nissan Xterra rental. A stout, pear-shaped woman in her early fifties, she wore an enormous white parka, black tights, and white plastic boots. Her chestnut hair glinted burgundy in the morning sun. The skin of her face was so tanned she appeared to have only narrowly escaped a house fire; in the urbane, sun-starved environs of winter in Manhattan, she looked positively extraterrestrial. With a vague nod in my direction, she went to the rear of the truck, lifted the hatch, and lugged out a large, floral-patterned suitcase.

"Please, allow us to assist you," I said, shooing over George, the doorman.

"Don't need any help, thanks," Brenda said to George curtly.

"But we insist." To allow a guest of this stature to carry her own luggage was out of the question. Yet, whether fiercely independent or simply fearful of having to tip, she put up quite a fight. Eventually, George triumphed, respectfully tugging the suitcase from her grasp. She stumbled backwards.

I reached out to steady her. "We are delighted to have you with us, Mrs. Rathberger."

She turned to regard me as if for the first time. "Who are you?"

I extended my hand, flashing a warm Universe smile. "I'm Trevor Lambert, director of rooms. I'm here to welcome you to the Universe." Her hand felt as cold and stiff as a frozen dishrag.

"I was expecting Willard Godfrey," she said.

"Mr. Godfrey sends his regrets. An urgent matter arose, and he asked me to greet you on his behalf."

"How disappointing," she said, pursing her lips and blinking, as though calculating the hotel's first transgression—and expecting many more to come. "I was looking forward to meeting him."

"And he you," I assured her. "He asked me to apologize profusely for his absence and to tell you that he very much looks forward to meeting you later today."

I was lying, of course; I had no idea where Mr. Godfrey was. The hotel's rules of protocol are meticulously laid out in our staff manual, *An Employee's Guide to the Universe,* in which three Universal Standards of Service are outlined: 1) Smile; 2) Establish eye contact; and 3) Use the guest's name. Not exactly the laws of quantum physics, yet, when combined, these simple rules establish an instant rapport with guests. A fourth, unwritten rule, although nowhere to be found in the guide, is equally fundamental: Lie. Not big lies of the whopper variety, but tiny white lies that preserve the guest's dignity—or that of the hotel—and engender trust and confidence. To wit: At check-out, Mr. Herbert insists that he did not watch the movie *Hot Tub Hotties.* He's lying, of course, and the agent knows it; a quick look into Guest History reveals that, for Mr. Herbert, every stay at the Universe is one big porn fest. But rather than argue, the employee concurs that yes, indeed, an error has been made, and deletes the charge from his bill. Together with smiles, pillow chocolates, and fluffy white towels, lies help foster the Universal Promise: to provide an idyllic escape from the outside world.

"May I escort you in?" I asked Mrs. Rathberger, offering my arm.

She appeared not to have heard. She was eyeing George as he unloaded her belongings onto a luggage cart: two large suitcases, a duffle bag, three file boxes, and a large poster tube. Her eyes searched the entrance area, moving up and down the U-shaped driveway to Avenue of the Americas, as though on the lookout for thieves. The street was quiet, save for a few after-hours club stragglers and an elderly couple taking an early-morning stroll. Up the street, a line of taxis queued for the hotel's Sunday morning airport rush. Seemingly satisfied, she turned to examine the hotel's façade. Her gaze moved up the massive sliding steel doors at the entrance, past the six-foot chrome letters that spelled THE UNIVERSE HOTEL, and up the mirrored glass tower to the giant revolving Glittersphere perched on top. Home to the Observatory, Stratosphere Nightclub, Orbit Restaurant, and four floors of Supernova suites, the Glittersphere resembled the planet Saturn orbiting on a gleaming glass pedestal.

"So this is the Universe," she said, a note of skepticism in her voice.

"Magnificent, isn't it?"

She shrugged. "I'm not much for fancy hotels."

"I see."

Behind us, George slammed the hatch shut and handed the keys off to a valet, then passed the luggage cart to a waiting bellman. "All set, Mrs. Rathberger," he said. "Your luggage is on its way to your suite. Have a wonderful stay." He paused briefly for a tip, but Mrs. Rathberger kept her hands firmly planted in the pockets of her parka, eyeing her luggage as the cart was pushed through the sliding doors and into the lobby. He returned to his post, whistling cheerfully.

Mrs. Rathberger bolted after the luggage cart.

I hurried in after her. "Mrs. Rathberger?" I called out. "May I introduce you to a few of our staff?"

Only then did she spot the twelve smiling employees standing in a row to my right like contestants in a beauty pageant. Muttering an apology, she made her way back. I guided her down the line, introducing each employee. Assembling a lineup of management staff this early on a Sunday morning, particularly after the party, had been a challenge. The director of conference services had managed to drag herself in, looking sheepish after a night of shots and dirty dancing. Next to her, the Galaxy floor manager looked pale and sickly. Fortunately, the robust spa manager followed, then a banquet supervisor, both of whom had missed the party. Next came staff I had recruited as filler: two room attendants, a guest services agent, two banquet staff, and a lobby hostess. Last in line were Gaetan Boudreau, front office manager, and the magnificent Nancy Swinton, duty manager. Both were smiling brightly, looking tremendously competent.

But Mrs. Rathberger bypassed them completely. Her attention was drawn to her surroundings, as if she had only then become aware of the cavernous, circular lobby around her and the atrium above that rose twenty floors through a tunnel of balconies. Suspended in the air on invisible wires above us and embedded on the sleek black marble floor beneath our feet were thousands of tiny halogen star lights, giving visitors the sensation of floating in space. The music of Holst's *Planets* played softly in the background, and the aroma of fresh-baked croissants and Italian coffee wafted from Galaxy.

I thanked the staff members and dismissed them, then joined Mrs. Rathberger. "May I offer you a tour?"

She shook her head and placed her knuckles on her hips. "I'm far too busy for tours. Where is Willard Godfrey? I have a number of concerns I need to address with him at once."

Her words caused a niggle of anxiety in my stomach, as though a school of piranhas had taken residence and were starting to feel peckish. It was a good question. Where *was* Mr. Godfrey? Suddenly I had the distinct feeling that all was not well in the Universe.

"I'm sure he'll be along shortly," I said. "In the meantime, perhaps I can get you oriented quickly? Then we'll get you registered and up to your suite at once." With sweeping gestures, I pointed out Galaxy Restaurant to the left, the Center of the Universe Lounge directly ahead, and the front desk and concierge desk to the right. "The elevator pods are in the center of the lobby," I said, indicating six glass capsules that rocketed into the atrium above. "Jupiter Ballroom is opposite the elevators, next to the curving staircase. One floor up is the concourse level, home to the hotel's administration offices and larger meeting rooms, all named after planets. On the third floor is the business center, the Sea of Tranquility Spa, Shops at the Universe, and smaller meeting rooms, these named after star constellations."

I glanced down and saw that Mrs. Rathberger wasn't paying attention. She was peering at her tanned arm, scratching it with her fingernail, flicking dead skin onto the floor.

"That's quite a tan," I remarked. "You've been somewhere hot?"

"You bet. I was in Maui for two weeks, roasting in the sun like a pig on a spit." She closed her eyes and breathed a long sigh, as though transporting herself back. "It was heaven."

"There's nothing like a sun holiday in the winter."

"Damned right."

"Shall I escort you to the Center of the Universe to get you registered?"

"The what?"

"Our lounge."

She crossed her arms. "I do *not* frequent drinking establishments."

"Not to worry," I assured her. "The lounge is closed until noon. The satellite check-in area is sectioned off from the rest of the lounge. All right by you?" I held out my arm.

Reluctantly, she accepted it. We made our way through a circle of display cases containing various outer space paraphernalia: a replica of the solar system; a model of space shuttle *Endeavour*; an astronaut's suit (remarkably similar, I noted, to Mrs. Rathberger's outfit); props from science fiction movies; collections of moon rocks and meteor bits; and a model of the International Space Station. She stopped to regard a display case in the center of the circle, which contained a replica of the Universe Hotel.

"The hotel complex occupies a half city block in midtown Manhattan," I explained, "from West Fifty-third to West Fifty-fourth and from Avenue of the Americas halfway to Seventh Avenue. When Mr. Godfrey built the Universe he intended to create a city within a city, a microcosm of society that offers everything under one roof so that guests don't have to venture outside if they don't wish to. He thinks New York—and the world in general—is going to hell, and hotels are the last remaining places of refuge."

Her eyes bulged slightly, as though suddenly questioning Mr. Godfrey's sanity. She scratched her chin. "It's been a while since I've been to New York, but wasn't a different hotel here before?"

"Good memory! The Hilton was leveled several years ago to make way for the Universe."

Squinting at the brass plaque fastened to the display case, she read out its inscription. "'This building is dedicated to the late Margaret Bains Godfrey, the center of my universe. With all my love, Willard.'" She looked up. "The wife?"

I nodded. "She died only months before the hotel opened."

She seemed to lose interest and continued on. We circled the periphery of the lounge, passing smiling, purposeful-looking employees along the way. The guest services staff were dressed in form-fitting black Lycra body suits, with gold star nametags pinned to their chests, wireless headsets, and combination wireless handhelds/two-way radios called Universal Communications Devices clipped to their belts. I pressed a button on my own U-Comm to signal our approach.

Mrs. Rathberger turned to gaze up at the great white Christmas tree near the entrance to Galaxy. Rising ten stories into the atrium, it was decorated with nothing but white lights and gold stars.

"Gorgeous tree, isn't it?" I said.

"I'm not much of a Christmas person."

"I see."

We climbed three steps to the VIP satellite check-in area, part of the lounge cordoned off with blue velvet ropes and furnished with lush royal blue carpeting, leather sofas, and Carrera marble cocktail tables.

A young woman whose gold star said Alexandra was waiting. "Good morning, Mrs. Rathberger, and welcome to the Universe!" she said, her voice tinged with a faint Australian accent. "May I offer you a refreshment? I recommend the Astronomical Punch. It's out of this world."

She narrowed her eyes. "Any booze in it?"

"No, but if you'd like we could—"

"No! I'll take it the way it is."

"Certainly, madam."

As Alexandra hurried off, Mrs. Rathberger sat down, sinking deep into the leather sofa, and glanced around warily. A handful of guests occupied the area: a family of five speaking a harsh Slavic language, an elderly woman nodding off into her mink stole, and a young couple cuddled in post-matrimonial bliss. She resumed inspecting her tan.

I took the chair opposite her and searched the lobby for Mr. Godfrey. Brenda Rathberger seemed determined to remain unimpressed, to refrain from engaging in anything resembling friendly conversation.

I desperately needed Mr. Godfrey's help. Few people could resist his charm, his sincerity and unassuming manner. But he was nowhere in sight. I glanced down at my U-Comm; the screen was blank.

An uncomfortable silence descended.

Alexandra returned and set down a champagne flute filled with pink liquid. Mrs. Rathberger took a tentative sip, nodded in approval, then gulped down half the contents. She slammed the glass down and wiped her mouth with the back of her hand, suppressing a burp.

"Is Willard Godfrey a good speaker?" she blurted out.

"Why, yes, he's an excellent speaker, in fact," I replied.

"Good. He's giving the welcome address at our opening reception, and it's an extremely important event. It sets the tone for the rest of the week, and a captivating, inspiring speaker is essential. I normally do it, but the board asked me to sit this one out. We had your mayor confirmed, but then he backed out, citing a 'scheduling conflict.'" She snorted. "Clearly, he's too afraid of controversy. I hope your Mr. Godfrey isn't so flaky. I have enough on my plate this week without having to worry about my speakers."

"He won't disappoint," I assured her. "You've got the right man for the job." Across the lobby, a small choir gathered around the Christmas tree. "It's a shame you have to work over the holidays," I said.

"Makes no difference to me. Don't have much of a family." Her eyes narrowed. She leaned toward me and sniffed. "Have you been drinking?"

"Drinking? Of course not. Why do you ask?"

"I smell booze. I have a nose for booze."

I felt blood rush to my face. "Well, we did have our staff Christmas party last night ... I had a cocktail or two." I was invoking the Fourth Universal Standard here. "Perhaps the odor is lingering."

She pressed her lips tightly together. "I smelled the same stench on a few of the staff members you introduced to me. I trust this won't be a habit. Personally, I find the sight, smell, and effects of alcohol completely abhorrent. Liquor is the devil's elixir. I myself haven't touched the stuff in twenty years."

"Now that's impressive." The choir began singing "Silent Night." "Mrs. Rathberger, I want you to know that I have the utmost respect for your impaired driving efforts."

"My *anti*-impaired driving efforts," she snapped. "I suggest you get the lingo right before the conference begins. My people are highly sensitive to such blunders."

"I'm terribly sorry. I didn't mean to offend."

She grunted and sat back to observe me. "I'm going to be frank with you, Trevor Lambert. I am not a proponent of holding this conference at this hotel." She looked around and sniffed. "Such extravagance sends the wrong message to our delegates, to our donors, to the public. Victims of Impaired Drivers is a not-for-profit organization, built from the grassroots up, and we are not in the business of squandering the generosity of our donors. Our theme this year is 'Society for Sobriety.' VOID's mandate is to eradicate impaired driving from society entirely." She surveyed the expansive lounge, nostrils flaring. "I'm afraid this hotel isn't a suitable environment for advancing this objective. Granted, the tradeshow exhibitors might enjoy it here, as will some of the lawyers, politicians, and media attendees. God knows they found ample time for fun and games in Anaheim last year. I'm more concerned about our members and volunteers, many of whom are pensioners, low-income earners, and students. They won't feel comfortable surrounded by such luxury and pretense."

"I understand your concerns, Mrs. Rathberger, but I assure you—"

"No, *I* assure *you,* Trevor," she snapped, her eyes flashing with anger, "that I will not tolerate any disrespect. So stop trying to woo me with your hoity-toity manners and fancy clothes, and *please* tell your staff to stop calling me 'Madam' like I'm some sort of hooker. I demand reliable, down-to-earth service and respect. At last year's conference, we experienced a number of problems—none my fault, of course, but the board blamed me anyway. This year, my head is on the line. I intend to make this conference the most successful ever. If I don't have 100 percent confidence in your ability to advance this objective, I am perfectly prepared to take my business elsewhere. If need be, I can move the entire conference with only a day's notice." Her eyes and cheeks were bulging. Her tanned face had turned red and blotchy, and globs of spittle had formed at the sides of her mouth.

"With all due respect," I countered, "I believe you have the wrong impression of the Universe. Our employees are accustomed to dealing with all types of people from all walks of life. If your group prefers a more informal approach, then so be it. We too want your conference to be a monumental success. Nothing will go wrong, Mrs. Rathberger. You have my word."

She searched my eyes for a moment, then her cheeks deflated like a balloon. She wiped the spittle from her mouth. "I'll give you the benefit of the doubt," she said, eyes flickering. Then she added, "I don't mean to sound so harsh, but—"

"I understand completely."

Another employee presented himself. "Good morning to you, Mrs. Rathberger! I'm Roberto, manager of the Guest Arrival Experience. Is this a convenient time to register?"

"Good a time as any."

"Splendid." Roberto punched buttons on his Universal Communications Device and it whirred softly, emitting two circular discs, which he tucked into a small folder. "We have you registered for fourteen nights," he said, "departing on Sunday, January 2. Per Mr. Godfrey, we have upgraded you to one of our Supernova suites, which is complimentary for the first five nights, then changes to the special conference rate of $225 for the remainder of your stay."

Mrs. Rathberger snorted. Evidently, $225 wasn't very special in her book, although it was the lowest group rate I'd ever seen at the Universe.

"The nightly valet parking fee of fifty-five dollars will be applied directly to your account," Roberto added.

"*Fifty-five dollars?* That's as much as I usually pay for a room!"

"You'll find things a bit pricier in New York," I told her. "We pride ourselves in offering excellent value. Mr. Godfrey also extended generous discounts on food and beverage items to all your delegates."

She reached for her punch glass and slugged back its contents.

"Mr. Lambert will escort you to your suite," Roberto continued. "Have a wonderful stay, Mrs. Rathberger." He presented the key packet to her with a flourish and hurried off.

Mrs. Rathberger inspected the packet. On the cover was written her room number and the hotel's tagline:

You are the center of the Universe.
THE UNIVERSE HOTEL
Where our world revolves around yours.

She glanced around the lobby warily. "This place doesn't launch into space, does it?"

I stood up, grinning. "Not so far. Shall I escort you up?"

"Can't you just beam me up?"

"Not yet, but we're working on it."

Brenda Rathberger's lips parted into a smile, clearly amused by her own wit.

Delighted to detect a glimmer of warmth under her frosty exterior, I extended my arm. Together we made our way to the elevators.

★ ★ ★ ★ ★

A set of elevator doors opened the instant we arrived, and an elderly couple I recognized as Mr. Godfrey's lawyer and his wife stepped out. "Well, good morning, Mr. and Mrs. Weatherhead!" I said. "And how was your stay?"

"Marvelous, Trevor, thank you," replied Mr. Weatherhead, a tall, distinguished fellow with slicked-back silver hair. His wife, a thin, regal woman with white hair like cotton candy, smiled pleasantly.

"Off to Florida for your cruise, then?" I inquired.

"Indeed," said Mr. Weatherhead. "Have you seen Willard? The old buzzard didn't show up for breakfast this morning. Recovering from the party last night, perhaps?"

"He's off-property," I said with a nervous glance at Mrs. Rathberger. "He's . . . dealing with a family issue, I believe."

Mr. Weatherhead frowned and shook his head sadly. "That daughter will be the death of him. Well, kindly tell him we're sorry to have missed him. We'll catch up in a couple of weeks upon our return."

"Oh, and give him my congratulations," Mrs. Weatherhead chimed in.

"Congratulations?" I asked.

Mr. Weatherhead reached for his wife's hand and squeezed it. "For a successful year," he said quickly, pulling her along. "So long, Trevor! Have a merry Christmas!"

"Bon voyage!"

Brenda Rathberger crossed her arms and turned to me. "Well! He's in bed with a hangover, is he?"

"Certainly not. Mr. Godfrey is a teetotaler."

"Really?"

"Absolutely."

She looked pleased.

As we stepped inside the elevator, a pleasant voice said, seemingly out of nowhere, "Greetings, Mrs. Rathberger. Going to your room?"

Mrs. Rathberger looked around in alarm. "Who was that?"

"Say hello to Mona," I said, "our electronic elevator attendant."

She hesitated. "Hell—hello, Mona."

"Greetings, Mrs. Rathberger. Going to your room?"

"Uh … yeah."

The doors glided shut. "Going up to floor seventy-one. Please hold on."

"Mona scans your disc to identify you," I explained. "Hold on. She likes to speed."

The elevator shot upward, and Mrs. Rathberger lunged for the railing. As we soared through rings of balconies, she turned to look down into the atrium until it disappeared. Seconds later, we came to a smooth stop, and the doors flew open. "Floor seventy-one," Mona announced. "The blue arrows will guide you to your room. Have a pleasant stay, Mrs. Rathberger."

"Thanks," she muttered, stepping into the dimly lit corridor lined with royal blue carpet. A blue neon arrow embedded in the wall at eye level flashed at us, indicating right. More arrows lit up as we made our way down the curving corridor until we arrived at a stainless steel door flashing 7108 in blue neon.

"Be my guest," I said, gesturing to the scanner.

Hands trembling, Mrs. Rathberger waved a disc across the scanner. The door glided open, disappearing into the wall with a swoosh. She turned to me with wide eyes, unable to conceal her delight.

"After you," I said with a smile. We walked in, and the door glided shut behind us.

"My, my!" she exclaimed, gazing around. "I feel like I'm on the set of *Star Trek*!" She was immediately drawn to the window, which comprised the entire outer wall and bubbled out, allowing views in all directions. Her suite was facing northwest, toward Time Warner Center, Central Park, and the Upper West Side, and was slowly revolving eastward, its movement barely perceptible.

"Magnificent view," I observed.

She was quiet for a moment. "I'm not much for cities," she said, turning away.

I wondered if Brenda Rathberger was much for anything. I offered to show her around, but she declined. I lingered by the door; she hadn't yet removed her coat, and I wanted to ensure she was staying before I left. She wandered into the bedroom, where her suitcases and duffle bag had been placed on luggage racks before a king-size bed covered with a lush white duvet, then ducked into the en suite bathroom, furnished with a pedestal sink, glass shower, and crater-sized tub. I heard a cry of delight, likely prompted by the VIP bath amenity basket containing an array of luxury soaps and bath products.

When she emerged her eyes were bulging, but she adopted a bored expression, feigning a yawn. Casually, she surveyed the living room, eyes moving over the black leather sectional sofa, two Swan chairs, Bang & Olufsen stereo, forty-two-inch plasma-screen TV, and bookshelf stocked with CDs, DVDs, and books. A stainless steel door was built into the wall in the corner, and she marched over and pulled it open. Inside was a fully stocked mini-bar.

"The booze will have to go," she said, slamming it shut. "That goes for all the VOID delegates."

"Of course."

She wandered over to the table next to the window, where a set of binoculars sat beside two books: *A Stargazer's Guide to the Universe* and *Universal Values*. She picked up the latter and turned it over.

"Good grief, he wrote a book too?"

"Indeed. It was published two years ago."

"What's it about?"

"He chronicles the challenges of building the Universe and recruiting one thousand staff, then opening only months before the September 11 terrorist attacks. Despite the near collapse of the city's hotel industry, the Universe thrived. He attributes this success to the hotel's Universal Values: commitment, integrity, hard work, dignity, respect, and teamwork. He argues that if we apply these principles to everyday life, we will achieve similar success. All human beings are hoteliers at heart, he says. We welcome people into our life and, if we treat them hospitably, we earn their respect and loyalty. This he calls the Universal Truth."

Mrs. Rathberger shrugged, looking unimpressed, and set the book down. She peeked through the curved alcove on the far right of the living room into an office area furnished with a desk, computer, fax machine, and printer.

"Is everything satisfactory with your suite, then?" I asked, backing toward the door.

She looked around. "It's a little big."

"I can put you in a smaller room, if you prefer." I lifted my U-Comm. "Let me call—"

"No," she said quickly. "I'll make do."

There was a knock at the door, and in walked Flavio from room service, brandishing a gift basket bursting with gourmet delicacies. He set it down on the coffee table and bowed, then departed.

"Good gracious, what's this?" Brenda Rathberger cried, tearing into the cellophane and withdrawing a card tucked inside. "'Dear Mrs. Rathberger,'" she read aloud. "'Welcome to the Universe! I trust you will be comfortable here and look forward to dining in Orbit tonight at 7:00 PM with you and Miss Winters. Warmest regards, Willard Godfrey.'" Her face lit up. "How thoughtful!" She removed a box of Dean & Deluca chocolates from the basket and ripped into it. "But who is Miss Winters?"

"Honica Winters, perhaps?"

She stuffed a square of chocolate in mouth, chewing rapidly. "*The* Honica Winters? Of *Borderline News*?" Her eyes lit up. "What if she wants to do a story on my conference! Imagine, VOID on *Borderline News*! The board said they want more publicity this year ... wouldn't that shut them up!" Her mind racing with the possibilities, she began to remove her coat.

Pleased to see how her mood had transformed, I wished her a pleasant stay and went to the door.

"Oh, Trevor?" she called after me.

"Yes, Mrs. Rathberger?"

"Please, call me Brenda."

"Why, thank you. I will."

"I'm sorry for being a bitch. It was a long flight from Maui, and I'm under a great deal of pressure. I feel better about this place already. I'm sure things will turn out fine."

A smile spread across my face. "They will be flawless, Brenda. I promise."

She smiled back, and a bond of mutual trust and respect, perhaps even a glimmer of fondness, washed over us. Mr. Godfrey would be pleased.

As I stepped out of the suite, I heard her cry out, "Damn! I forgot my purse in the truck."

I turned. "Not to worry. I'll have a valet retrieve it."

"No. I prefer to get it myself."

I hesitated. The parking levels were located underground in the far less glamorous back-of-house, a part of the hotel not meant for the eyes of guests. But Brenda was already putting her parka back on. "Very well. I'll escort you down."

My new best friend Brenda and I retrieved her car keys from the front door and crossed the lobby to the parking elevator. There was no Mona to greet us here. I waved my master disc over the scanner and pressed P4, knowing her truck wouldn't be parked that far down but anxious to avoid P3, where the air was often putrid and stifling, courtesy of the butcher shop and laundry department. I was also curious to see if Mr. Godfrey's vehicle was there. The car jerked into motion, and we began our descent into the bowels of the Universe.

"You're from Colorado?" I asked Brenda over the groan of the elevator.

"Born in Denver, but I live in Colorado Springs now. That's where the head office is. You?"

"I'm from Vancouver."

"Ha! I thought I recognized a Canadian accent. 'Oot and aboot!'" She cackled. "My husband was Canadian. But from the other side, Nova Scotia."

"He didn't want to come to New York with you?"

"Oh, no. He died."

"My god, I'm sorry."

She dismissed my concern with a wave of her hand. "It happened thirty years ago. I kept his name, never remarried. It's not a pretty name, but it's a heck of a lot better than my maiden name, Park. Kids used to reverse it and call me Adnerb Krap." She chuckled, then sighed deeply, shaking her head.

The car bounced to a stop on P4, and we stepped out. I hustled Brenda down a dank corridor lined with stacks of banquet chairs, broken furniture, and piles of soiled linen.

"Sorry about the mess," I said, embarrassed.

Brenda seemed unfazed. "It's a heck of a lot cleaner than my home."

At the end of the corridor, I passed my disc over the scanner and pushed open the door to the parkade. I heard it strike something on the other side. Peeking around the door, I saw a luggage cart rolling down the ramp, spinning in circles. I chased after it and towed it back up the ramp. The hotel's symbol, an iron replica of the Glittersphere, was missing from the top, leaving the four chrome bars hanging loose. Assuming the cart had been left for repair, I unlocked the maintenance repair cage and pushed it in, then locked it back up.

"Shall we?" I asked, holding my arm out to Brenda.

She accepted it, and we started up the curved ramp. The lighting was unusually dim—a light bulb above us was burnt out—but I could make out Mr. Godfrey's yellow Lincoln Continental parked in its usual space to the left.

"Careful," I said, pointing to a streamlet of what appeared to be oil running across the ramp. "His car must be leaking."

She squinted at the Lincoln's license plate, which said UNIVERSE ONE. "Willard is here, then?"

"He must have just arrived. I'll page him when we get back upstairs." As we walked past, something next to the Lincoln caught my eye. "Strange," I said, stopping.

A pile of clothes lay next to his car.

"What is it?" Brenda asked, following my gaze. I felt her grip tighten.

"I'm not sure."

Something told me to keep on walking, but curiosity compelled me to get a closer look. I tried to shake free of Brenda's grip, but she wouldn't let go. We walked over together.

As I drew nearer, I saw what appeared to be a tuxedo crumpled in a heap on the pavement. Mystified, I peered down. Next to the tuxedo was a black patent-leather shoe and...

A foot!

My stomach lurched.

Brenda let out a piercing shriek.

A body was lying on the pavement next to Mr. Godfrey's car. Small like a boy's, its legs were twisted in opposite directions. A gray hand poked from the sleeve of the tuxedo jacket, revealing a starched white cuff stained with blood. My eyes moved up the torso to the face, which was turned in the other direction. The skull was bloody and looked partially crushed. With a cry of anguish, I fell to my knees and peered over to get a closer look. His mouth and eyes were open.

Willard Godfrey was dead.

2

A Bang and a Whimper

Brenda Rathberger was hysterical.

I tried to pull her away from Mr. Godfrey's body, but she collapsed into a heap on the concrete floor, breaking into sobs. I crouched down to offer her comfort, but realized that there were more urgent tasks at hand. Pulling out my Universal Communications Device, I called 911. "This is the Universe Hotel. Something's happened to my boss. I think he might be ... I think he's ..." I glanced back at Mr. Godfrey's pallid, marblelike face. "He's dead." I gave the operator my coordinates, then radioed duty manager Nancy Swinton and briefed her. "Contact hotel security, then go to the front door and escort emergency personnel down. Don't tell anyone what's happened, at least not yet. Okay?"

"You got it, Trevor."

Next, I issued an Emergency Group Page—the numbers 555 on my U-Comm—to alert my colleagues on the executive committee, entering a message to contact me immediately. Returning to Mr. Godfrey's body, I removed my suit jacket and crouched down to place it over him. The frantic *Beep! Beep! Beep!* of a U-Comm made me jump. I reached for my belt but realized it wasn't mine.

I had just paged Mr. Godfrey.

With a grimace, I patted down his stiff body, located his U-Comm in his inside pocket, and shut it off. The EGP would sound Matthew Drummond's U-Comm next, then mine, followed by Sandy James' and Shanna Virani's. I stood up and noticed that the trunk to Mr. Godfrey's car was open. A pile of Christmas presents was stacked inside. Among them was the gift I had given him yesterday, a long, thin box wrapped in gold foil containing a black silk tie decorated with smiling suns, part of a tradition between Mr. Godfrey and me of exchanging ties with an outer space theme.

Gently, I closed the hatch.

Afraid that staff might stumble onto the scene, I walked up the ramp to ensure the gate to P3 was secure, then down the ramp to check the gate to P5. The only other access was through the door Brenda and I had just entered, which required a programmed access card.

I went back to check on Brenda. She was kneeling on the pavement now, her head down, hands over her head. Her shock was manifesting itself in fits of sobbing that, like birth contractions, started out mild and infrequent, then grew in volume and pace, climaxing in a loud, guttural wail. Her sorrow, so instant and intense that it could have been her own husband lying there, was touching and somehow comforting, as though she were grieving for both of us, allowing me to focus on more practical concerns. But it was also distracting. Better to remove her from the scene before emergency personnel arrived.

I helped her to her feet. Her legs trembling like a newborn foal, she rested her weight on my shoulder as I led her to the door and down the corridor to the elevator.

When the elevator door lurched open, Jerome, a supervisor in the security department, rushed out. "Nancy told me to come here right away," he said. "What's going on?" He glanced down at Brenda, who looked like an alien in her great white parka and plastic boots.

"God—"

"What?"

"Mr. Godfrey." My lungs were heaving. "Something happened to Mr. Godfrey. "He's ... dead."

"*Dead?*"

"He's back in the parkade by his car. You might not want to go there—it's not pretty. Whatever you do, don't let any employees go near there, all right? I'll be back down as soon as I can."

"Absolutely, Trevor."

As the elevator door closed, my U-Comm sounded.

"Trevor, it's Matthew. This better be important."

Back in Brenda's suite, I lowered her onto the sofa and placed three pillows behind her back, then turned to leave. But she rolled over like Jell-O, almost spilling onto the floor. I propped her back up and sat down next to her, taking her frigid hand in mine.

"Are you going to be okay?" I asked, anxious to get back downstairs.

She blinked, and her eyes rolled back. Her head lolled in circles. She appeared to have fallen into some sort of trance. Pushing the pillows away, she lowered herself onto my lap, resting her hands over her chest, and gazed at the mural of glow-in-the-dark stars painted on the ceiling.

"When I was a little girl," she said dreamily, "my father put stars on the wall by my bed."

I put my hand on her forehead; it was hot. Reaching for my U-Comm, I called Room Service. "Flavio, it's Trevor. Can you please send up tea service to Suite 7108 as quickly as possible? Charge it to my promo account."

"Right away, Trevor."

Brenda lifted her head. "And a clubhouse with fries," she said, "and a Diet Coke."

Turning to her in surprise, I relayed the request to Flavio. I disconnected and eased myself out from under her. I went into the bathroom to soak a facecloth in cool water and returned to place it over her forehead.

She sat up, suddenly alert. "What happened?" she cried. "Was he murdered?"

The thought hadn't even occurred to me. "Murdered? God, no. It looks like he may have been hit by a car."

"Down there? How could someone have missed seeing him?"

"I don't know. The lighting isn't great."

She stared at me fixedly. "They had to be drunk."

My U-Comm started beeping again.

"Trevor, it's Nancy. I'm on P4 with the NYPD. Matthew just got here. They're asking for you."

"I'll be right down." I knelt before Brenda. "I have to go. Are you going to be okay?"

She gulped. "I'll be fine."

"I'm really sorry about this, Brenda. I had no idea—"

"Of course you didn't, Trevor," she said, patting my hand. "I'm sorry too. Poor old fella. He seemed like such a pleasant man on the phone. Guess I'll never get to meet him."

"We never got your purse."

"No worries, I'll get it later." She let out a small gasp. "The welcome reception! How on earth will I find someone to replace him at such short notice?"

"I'm sure you'll manage," I said. "Now get some rest, and I'll check in on you later."

She collapsed back onto the sofa and moaned, pulling the face-cloth over her eyes.

As I made my way out, it occurred to me that I had just conducted the worst Guest Arrival Experience in the history of the Universe.

By the time I got to P4, a half-dozen emergency personnel had gathered around Mr. Godfrey's body: two paramedics, three NYPD officers, and a youthful-looking Asian man who appeared to be in charge. Matthew Drummond, the hotel's resident manager, was standing off to the side, engaged in an intimate conversation with duty manager Nancy Swinton.

Nancy looked up as I approached. She let her hand drop from Matthew's shoulder. I felt a pang of jealousy, recalling the two of them dancing closely at the party last night. I had admired Nancy from afar for many months now, and though I had resolved not to act on my desires, which would violate the Universal Rules of Conduct, I felt protective of her. She hurried past me, cupping her mouth with her hand, looking as though she might be sick.

Matthew turned to me. "My god, what happened?"

"I don't know. I found him like this about a half-hour ago."

"He's still in his tuxedo."

I regarded his own clothes. "So are you."

He looked down, as if only realizing it then. "I fell asleep on the sofa," he said. "Far too many cocktails." He had moved to the United States from England when he was five years old, yet a faint trace of British accent still lingered in his voice. He looked tired and haggard this morning, older than his forty-two years. His handsome face was unshaven, his jet-black hair unkempt, and there were half-moons like bruises under his eyes.

"You and me both." As though on cue, my head began throbbing.

"I called Cynthia. She's on her way."

I regarded him in surprise. "Should she see her father like this?"

"She insisted."

The Asian man sauntered over, flashing his badge. "Morning, gentlemen. I'm Detective Owen Lim." He wore John Lennon glasses and a long, gray coat over a checkered shirt. His black hair was cropped short.

Matthew and I introduced ourselves.

The detective studied Matthew for a moment, then his eyes flashed in recognition. "Hey, aren't you the astronaut? I watched your shuttle take off on TV. *Endeavour*, right? Late 2000?"

Matthew nodded slowly, a thin, tolerant smile on his face, as though contemptuous of the attention.

"It's an honor," said the detective. "I guess you're in charge here, then?"

"I am."

I bristled. Officially, Matthew was second in command, but he was mostly ineffectual as a manager and was usually content to delegate responsibility to others. Eight months ago, when he was appointed resident manager, the publicity had been tremendous. The story FORMER ASTRONAUT APPOINTED TO HELM OF UNIVERSE ran in newspapers across the globe. But now that the media frenzy had begun to subside, Matthew's inexperience and general indolence had become impossible to ignore. Still, outsiders were drawn to him because of his heroic past and the false impression of competence exuded by his appearance.

"Detective, kindly tell us what happened here," Matthew said.

"Looks like a hit-and-run," the detective replied, walking to the center of the ramp. "He was probably about here when a car came charging up the ramp and *bang!*"—he smacked his hands together—"he was hit about here. The body probably landed here"—he walked a few paces toward Mr. Godfrey's car and stopped, pointing at the ground—"then he crawled—or was dragged—to where he is now."

"Dragged?" I repeated, alarmed. "You mean whoever hit him pulled him out of the way?"

The detective removed his glasses, pulling a blue handkerchief from his back pocket to polish them. "Or the driver kept going and Godfrey dragged himself."

I pointed to a set of tire tracks that cut through the stream of blood and faded down the ramp. "Are those tracks from the car that hit him?"

Detective Lim shook his head. "Whoever hit him was driving *up* the ramp." He fixed his gaze on me for a moment, then withdrew a notepad from his pocket. "When's the last time you saw the victim?"

"Last night at our Christmas party in the Observatory," I replied. "The party ended at midnight. We saw the shuttle buses off, then went back for a year-end toast."

"Who's *we*?"

"Matthew and I, plus Sandy James, our human resources director, and Shanna Virani, our director of sales and marketing. And Mr. Godfrey, of course. We were there for, what"—I looked at Matthew—"a half-hour?"

Matthew nodded slowly. He was rubbing his jaw, eyes fixed on the stream of blood.

"Mr. Godfrey left first," I said. "The rest of us followed about fifteen minutes later."

Detective Lim scribbled in his notebook, then turned to survey the area. "Who parks down here?"

"Only Mr. Godfrey," I said. "Executive staff park one level down on P5, the lowest level. I don't have a car, but Sandy and Shanna park there. And you too, right, Matthew?"

Matthew nodded again. His upper cheek twitched. "My wife and I keep a car there, but it belongs to the hotel and we rarely use it. Godfrey's daughter, Cynthia, parks there sometimes too."

"Did she park there last night?" asked Detective Lim.

I shrugged. "She might have, but she left the party fairly early, long before her father."

"You'll get a chance to ask her yourself," said Matthew. "She's on her way."

"How does one access this level?" asked the detective.

"P1 and P2 are open to the public," I said. "All other levels are restricted to staff and valet vehicles only, and are secured by a locked gate. P3 is restricted to valet parking. The lower levels are used only on busy nights. Our last big function was a week ago, and they've been locked off since. You need a remote control to get through the gates. To get out, you just drive over the hose. To access this level by elevator or stairwell, you need a programmed key disc."

"Is activity recorded?" Detective Lim asked.

"The system monitors all key disc activity," I said. "It records who takes the elevator and stairwells and who passes through that door. But parking activity is monitored only at the main parkade entrance, where all entries and exits via key disc are recorded. Pay booth activity isn't monitored, but a security camera records all activity. The other parking levels are wired for cameras, but they've never been activated—budget constraints."

The detective scribbled more notes in his pad. "Could a couple of joy riders get down here?"

I thought about the question. "People have broken in here before, but it's impossible to get this far down without a remote control or key disc."

Detective Lim whistled to one of the officers. "James, you find any signs of a break-in?"

"Nope. Nothing."

The detective turned back to me. "How did you get home last night, Mr. Lambert?"

"I walked."

"You, Mr. Drummond?"

"I told you, I live here," Matthew replied, a trace of irritation in his voice.

"Who would have driven through here last night?" asked Detective Lim.

I glanced at Matthew uneasily. "I'm not sure."

The sound of a door opening caused us to turn.

Cynthia Godfrey appeared in the doorway. She walked slowly into the parkade, her head down, body hunched over, allowing Jerome to guide her along like a blind person. Last night, she had arrived at the party looking dazzling and glamorous in a floor-length baby-blue gown, her bleached-blond hair woven around her head. This morning, her hair was wild and unkempt. She wore tight bluejeans, a vintage jean jacket, and a black half-shirt that revealed sculpted abs and a pierced belly. Stopping suddenly, she looked up and turned in the direction of her father's body. Her mouth fell open and a short, high-pitched whimper escaped, then she dropped her head again and let her shoulders slump.

Matthew and I hurried to her side.

"Cynthia, I'm so sorry," I said. I wanted to hug her, but she stood drooped over like a marionette; it would have been too awkward. I placed my hand on her back and rubbed softly.

"You don't have to be here," Matthew said.

Seeming to gather strength, she lifted her head again, breathed in deeply and bit down hard on her lip, then marched over. As she approached, emergency personnel parted to let her past. There was absolute silence. She dropped to her knees before her father's body and threw herself over him, wailing. I turned away, unable to watch, as two NYPD officers gently tried to pull her off.

Detective Lim approached Matthew and me again. "I'll need to see those entry and exit reports," he said.

"Not a problem, detective," said Matthew. "I'll have our security department run them at once."

"And I'll want to talk to anyone who has access to this level, anyone who was in the vicinity last night, and anyone who had contact with Willard Godfrey in the past twenty-four hours."

Matthew's eyes widened. "You're not suggesting... you don't think he was... *murdered*?"

The detective pondered the question. "Murdered? Probably not. But a man died here. He was struck down by a vehicle. Whoever did it took off, which is a felony. And I have a strong suspicion that alcohol was involved."

At 6:30 PM that evening I was in the Sea of Tranquility Spa consoling a young receptionist when Nancy Swinton radioed me. "We've got another meet-and-greet due in," she said. "You free?"

I sighed. "Is Matthew around?"

"He went Christmas shopping with Mrs. Drummond about an hour ago."

"You're kidding."

She wasn't. Matthew had been no help all day. The minute Cynthia Godfrey departed, he had holed himself up in his luxuriant bi-level suite on the sixth floor, refusing to answer the pleas for help I issued over my U-Comm. News of Willard Godfrey's death had spread like wildfire, and reaction was swift and intense. I spent much of the day hurrying from department to department, offering what comfort and consolation I could while trying, unsuccessfully, to reach my colleagues for backup. Sandy James hadn't returned my calls, which in itself was unusual. Shanna Virani had returned my Emergency Group Page, but our conversation had been brief: I broke the news, she dropped the phone, and I didn't hear from her again.

"Who is it?" I asked Nancy.

"Honica Winters."

"Yikes. I'm on my way."

A frequent guest of the Universe, Honey Winters was host of *Borderline News*, one of the most popular hourly news programs on television, broadcast Sunday nights on NBC to 10 million viewers. Based in Niagara Falls, New York, near the Canadian border, the show originally focused on issues relating to both sides of the border—hence its name—but over time, it had grown in popularity in the U.S., largely due to Honica Winters' cultlike following. Now it focused almost exclusively on American issues—controversial topics and scandals, in particular. As a hotel guest, Miss Winters was difficult and demanding. She and Willard Godfrey had become quite friendly over the years, and no one could appease her quite like him. As I made my way down the grand staircase, I decided it would be best to escort her to her room, where I could break the news to her in private.

Honica was climbing out of a limousine when I arrived at the front door. To my dismay, I saw that she was carrying her dog, Rasputin, a yappy, scrappy Pomeranian who was notorious for peeing and crapping in guestrooms and suites with abandon.

"Miss Winters, welcome back!" I called out to her. "How wonderful to see you again!"

"Hi there,"—she squinted at my name tag—"Trevor. How ya doing? Where's Will? I'm totally late. We're supposed to have dinner in, like, twenty minutes." Leaving her bags for the doorman, she marched past me and into the lobby like she owned the place. Tall, blond, and striking, she was often compared to a young Barbara Walters, although she was twice as vivacious and about half as smart. On television she looked about forty years old; in person she looked over fifty. Her real age was somewhere in between. Bored silly in Niagara, she spent as much time as possible in New York and had been campaigning NBC executives to relocate her show here. In contrast to her hard-nosed, stone-cold sober TV persona, in person she was an aging party girl, a bit of a lush, and a tireless flirt. Sometimes she went out on the town with Cynthia Godfrey, Willard's daughter, and would stumble back to the hotel in the wee hours, occasionally attempting to lure a luggage attendant or front desk agent to her room.

"May I escort you to your room, Miss Winters?" I asked, hurrying to keep up with her as she sped toward the elevator.

She stopped in her tracks, her heels skidding on the marble floor. "Room? You mean suite, right?"

"Um—"

"Don't tell me I have to go through *this* charade again,"—she looked at my nametag—"Trevor." Rasputin barked at me in support of her. "Are you new? You must be new. I *always* get a suite. Willard *promised*."

Though we had met many times before, she never remembered me. Honica Winters was one of those nightmare guests who were acutely aware of two of the hotel's Universal Principles—#1: The guest is always right, and #2: If the guest is wrong, refer to #1—and never hesitated to use them to her advantage.

"Let's see what we have reserved," I said, unclipping my U-Comm and pulling up her reservation. Although the Universe had excellent negotiated rates with NBC, they were never low enough for Honica. She always made her secretary book the cheapest room available, then, upon arrival, insisted that an upgrade had been confirmed by an agent whose name she never quite remembered. If she didn't get what she wanted, she had a fit. Not long ago, even Mr. Godfrey, despite his endless patience and generosity, became fed up with her antics and flagged her guest profile with the instructions "do not upgrade" and "do not extend special rates or favors." Yet Honica persisted, knowing that if she kicked up enough of a fuss we usually gave in.

"Here we are," I said. "Yes, we have a lovely Standard Queen set aside at the NBC rate of $265."

"*Wrong!* Willard promised me one of those revolving suites up top. I'm doing celebrity interviews and need the space. Plus Rasputin gets claustrophobic."

Rasputin snarled and bared his teeth.

She had used the line before, but the celebrities rarely materialized. "I wish I could, Miss Winters, but all our suites are occupied." (Of course, I was invoking the fourth, unspoken Universal Standard.)

"That's *it!*" she cried. "I'm fed up with this treatment! You people are *impossible*. Let's get out of here, Rasputie. We'll go to the Four Seasons. They appreciate our business there, don't they?"

Rasputin yelped and barked—whether in solidarity or protest, I couldn't be sure—as Honica turned and marched toward the exit.

I watched her go, knowing she wouldn't get far. Recently, my counterpart at the Four Seasons had informed me that Honica had been told in no uncertain terms that she and Rasputin were no longer welcome there. She walked four more paces—five, six—her skinny butt wiggling left, right, left in her snug, lemon-colored skirt. Her pace started to slow. When it became clear that I wasn't about to chase after her and beg her to stay, she spun around and cried out, "*Where* is Willard? I *demand* to speak with Willard! He'll straighten this out."

Her words echoed across the atrium, bouncing off the ears of staff members and guests and restaurant patrons, many of whom turned in shock and stared at us. There was absolute silence in the lobby.

I rushed up to her. "I'm terribly sorry," I said, my voice barely a whisper. "I didn't mean to upset you. I'm sure I can free up a Supernova suite. Please, follow me. We can talk upstairs."

Ten minutes later, Honica, Rasputin, and I were seated on a bright red Ligne Roset sofa in the comfort of Honica's $2400 per night Supernova suite on the sixty-ninth floor of the Universe. I had just broken the news about Willard Godfrey, and a barrage of questions had followed. Not comfortable with providing specifics to a journalist of Honica Winters' reputation, I was as vague and evasive as possible with my answers.

After a while, she grew quiet and pensive. A troubled expression spread across her face as she absent-mindedly patted Rasputin's bottom. She stuck a long, manicured fingernail into her mouth and bit on it.

"I'm in shock. He was *such* a great guy. I'm gonna miss the old dickens."

"Me too."

"What about Cynthia? Does she know?"

"She knows."

"Poor dear must be crushed. I better call her. What did you say happened again?"

"I'm really not sure," I said, deciding it was time to go. "Is there anything you need at this time?"

Chewing on her fingernail, she glanced around the suite. "He usually sends me wine ... And so much for dinner ... Hey, Brenda Rathberger from VOID was supposed to join us. Does she know?"

"Oh, yes," I said. "She knows."

"Willard wanted me to meet her. He had some big idea about *Borderline News* doing a story on the conference and somehow tying in the hotel. But I did some research yesterday, and I'm not sure I like the whole idea. She sounds like a publicity hound, and apparently she's a bit off her rocker."

"Oh?"

Honica nodded. "She used to work with Mothers Against Drunk Driving, but her politics were too radical and they booted her out, so she started up Victims of Impaired Drivers. The two organizations were affiliated for a while, but now MADD won't have anything to do with her. They compete for donations, government support, and media coverage. VOID is like the homely younger sister with an inferiority complex. They tend to be highly litigious. They have all sorts of attorneys in their membership who make scads of money on lawsuits, suing anybody remotely associated with drunk-driving accidents: liquor establishments, distributors, private households, friends, family members. It's a huge business."

"I met her this morning," I said. "She seems passionate about her cause."

"That's an understatement. Apparently her husband was killed by a drunk driver a long time ago, but she refuses to talk about it. VOID has become the 'Act Up' of the impaired driving movement. They have an insatiable appetite for publicity. Over the years, they've evolved from an anti-impaired driving interest group to an anti-drinking *period* group. Last year in Anaheim, Brenda and a few other delegates camped out at a local pub and swarmed drunk patrons as they got into their cars. Her antics almost got her fired."

I wondered if Mr. Godfrey, who had always shied away from politics and controversy, had known this. He had always said that above all else, the Universe was a place for revelry and quiet repose, for dignity and tranquility.

"I admire her work," Honica said, "even if she is a bit nuts. Maybe I'll give her a call." She wandered to the window and stared down at the lights of Times Square. "I think Willard told me he was going to speak at the conference. God, wouldn't it be ironic if he was killed by a drunk driver? Now *that* would make a good story."

I hastened toward the door and punched the exit button. Rasputin leapt from the sofa and scampered to the corner, lifting his leg to pee on the carpet. "Miss Winters—your dog."

"Rasputie, no! Bad dog! Bad!"

"I'll send up housekeeping," I said. "Well, I'm sorry to be the bearer of bad news. I trust you'll be all right?"

"Oh yeah. I'm a big girl. But I could sure use some wine."

"I'll send up a bottle at once."

By the hushed, fear-laden tone of my mother's voice when she answered the phone that night, I knew she was bracing herself for bad news. It was almost 11:00 PM in Vancouver; 2:00 AM in New York.

"What is it, Trevor? What's happened?"

"Willard Godfrey died."

"Oh, no! How awful." She paused. "Who's Willard Godfrey?"

"My general manager—the owner of the Universe. You met him when you were here. Don't you remember?"

"The little man? Yes, of course. My goodness, what happened?"

"He got hit by a car."

"Oh, how dreadful."

"So I'm thinking you'd better postpone your visit."

There was absolute silence.

"Things are going to be chaotic," I said. "Everyone on staff is devastated, guests are starting to find out, we've got a big convention coming in. I'm going to be way too busy to entertain."

There was more silence, the deafening kind meant to allow me time to recant.

"You there, Mom?"

"I don't know what to say."

This was a first. Her voice was heavy with disappointment, almost enough to make me feel guilty, were it not for the hints of skepticism and suspicion that suggested she was not entirely unconvinced that I hadn't made the whole story up—or possibly even killed Mr. Godfrey myself—in order to ambush her trip. I sighed. She had every right to be disappointed, even dubious. Since I moved to New York, I hadn't exactly been the model son.

In five years, I had been back to Vancouver only once, last Christmas, and had worked diligently to maintain New York City as a Lambert-free zone. I lapsed only twice: two years ago, when Mom visited, and this summer, when my two sisters visited. In September, after much guilt-tripping on Mom's part, I had promised to return for Christmas again this year. But then Mr. Godfrey booked the Victims of Impaired Drivers conference and, for the first time since open-ing, the hotel was expected to be very busy over the period between Christmas and New Year's Eve. When I called Mom to cancel in Octo-ber, my words were met with similar silence, followed by a full-frontal assault.

"You're cancelling because of a *conference*? Doesn't that hotel host conferences all the time? What's so important about *this* conference? Can't *anyone* cover for you?"

"No, Mom."

"I think you're inflating your importance, dear. You're only the reception manager."

"I'm the director of the rooms division, Mom." At least she had stopped calling me a receptionist.

"A good manager doesn't covet authority, dear. He trains subor-dinates to be fully capable of running the show in his absence." After two years as head nurse in the pediatrics ward at Surrey Memorial Hospital, she was now a guru of human resources management. "*My* department is the best run in the hospital because *I* empower my nurses to—"

"Your nurses are always on strike, Mom."

"That's not true!"

"Mr. Godfrey asked me to stay. It's a very important conference."

"Does Mr. Godfrey *ever* let you take vacation?"

"Not if he can help it."

Eventually, she accepted it. Then, the following week, I was duped by my own mother. In an email message ominously entitled WONDER-FUL NEWS! she announced, "Darling, I've decided to come visit *you* for Christmas! Your sisters are disappointed"—that part was doubt-ful—"but they've agreed to give me their blessing. I've already booked my flight!" My response was terse: "I told you I have a conference."

Her reply arrived seconds later: "Don't worry about me, dear. I can keep myself busy." Then a PS: "You *will* be able to take a few days off, won't you?" Punctuated with a smiley face.

Mom hadn't always been so irritating. Until I was twelve years old, she had been a carefree, doting, somewhat sedate mother. Then my father died of a ruptured aorta, instantly and unexpectedly, and she turned into a zombie. Her refusal to attend the funeral was, in my opinion, a major error. By depriving herself of this closure, she never got on with her life—at least not for twenty years. In the months following his death, she transformed our household into a funeral parlor. Every day she sat slouched on the well-worn pink velveteen sofa in the living room, swaddled in blankets and sniffling with a cold that never went away, gazing mournfully at the television set as though it were my father's dead body. Occasionally she would speak to my sisters or me, but only to deliver a eulogy about how great our father was and how ungrateful we were or to chastise us for laughing or playing games or demonstrating any form of happiness.

After about a year, she finally stopped crying, stopped eulogizing, and then ceased speaking about him entirely. The word *Dad* was banned from household vocabulary. Broke, she had no choice but to pull herself off the sofa and go back to work as a nurse, working graveyard shifts at Surrey Memorial Hospital. Each morning, as I chased Janet and Wendy around the house to ready them for school, Mom would return from work, pale and stone-faced, and shuffle off to her bedroom with barely a word. In the afternoon, when we got home from school, she'd still be sleeping. I usually made dinner, something simple—tater gems and meat pies, tuna casserole, baked potatoes, frozen fish sticks and fries—and placed leftovers in a pie plate in the oven for Mom. When she emerged from her room and slumped onto the sofa, I would remove the pie plate, add a wedge of orange or a dandelion from the lawn, and place it before her. She ate without relish, pushing pieces into her mouth like unwanted medication, using the remote control to flick channel after channel in search of a show she never seemed to find. Only when the *Mary Tyler Moore Show* came on did she stop flicking. We watched it together, and I would secretly wish that she was Mary rather than depressed, overweight Rhoda. The theme song at the end of the show was my signal to get the girls to bed and Mom's signal to get ready for work. A half-hour later she would emerge dressed in her blue nurse's uniform, peck me on the forehead, and shuffle off to her bus stop. A fun childhood, indeed. Not surprisingly, about three seconds after graduation I moved out. Wendy and Janet followed a few years later, and Mom was left to languish by herself.

Then, miraculously, about three years ago, Mom emerged from her walking coma. I was already in New York by then, and my sisters filled me in on the transformation. It all started with a haircut, they said. One of the gals at the hospital, Penny, convinced Mom to accompany her to the hospital's staff barbecue. She arrived at Mom's house a few hours early armed with scissors, a Miss Clairol dye kit, makeup, an extra summer dress, and a bottle of Chardonnay. She insisted on chopping down Mom's graying rat's nest of hair, dyeing it back to its original auburn color, and styling it. Then she did her makeup and squeezed her into the dress, all the while plying her with alcohol for courage. Wendy dropped by just as they were leaving and almost fell to the floor. "Mom looked better than I've seen her in years," she told me over the phone. "I started crying. That night she got asked out by an orderly ten years her junior! It was like one of those extreme make-over shows on TV."

Until then, Mom had expressed no interest in visiting me or in leaving the house. After the transformation, she became obsessed with the idea of coming to New York. I dodged and thwarted her attempts for months until she finally managed to out-manipulate me. When she arrived, two years ago this July, I almost didn't recognize her at JFK Airport. She had mutated from an overweight, gray-haired, prematurely aging blob of self-pity to a razor-thin, reddish-brown-haired youthful wafer of self-confidence. The new package also came with a dramatic shift in personality. At first I thought she was fantastic, then I found her a bit annoying; by the end of her trip she was virtually unbearable. At fifty-five, Mom had become one of those maniacally ecstatic women from infomercials who swear that life didn't begin until fifty and consider it their duty to spread the gospel.

"Mom, you look amazing!" I cried when I spotted her at the airport that rainy July afternoon.

"I feel *fabulous!*"

"What happened?"

"I got a haircut. You should get one too."

"I don't need a haircut."

"Oh yes, you do."

I soon found out that by "haircut" she meant life makeover. Her transformation was fueled by a book she carried everywhere she went: *Refurbish Your Life!* by Kathy T. McAfee. "Kath," a fiftysomething interior decorator, urged readers to apply the principles of home renovation to life changes. During her visit, Mom quoted extensively from the book; by the fifth day I was ready to set fire to it—and to Kathy T. McAfee, if I could find her. July was one of the hotel's busiest months, and I had only managed to get two days off. On the third night, I arrived home, exhausted, to find Mom all dolled up in a sparkly dress. "Let's go out!" she cried, spinning circles on the floor. "I want to go dancing!"

"I'm really tired, Mom," I said, slumping onto the sofa. "It's been a long day."

"What? It's only 9:00 PM! Let's have fun, Trevor! Oh, please! I want to have fun!"

"I'm too tired, Mom. I've been at work since 7:00 AM."

"But we can't possibly stay in! We're in New York!"

"I *live* in New York."

"Not from what I've seen."

Her words infuriated me. Suddenly *I* was the manic-depressive blob on the sofa and *she* was the fun-loving youth? I missed the old Mom, the Mom with no expectations, not of me or of herself. When it was time for her to leave two days later, I couldn't get her back to the airport soon enough.

Then, to my surprise, not a minute after she disappeared through the security checkpoint, I started to miss her.

"Well, I'm sorry about your boss, dear," Mom said over the phone now, the skepticism in her voice replaced by genuine concern. "What happened?"

I briefed her on the day's events.

"What a shock," she said. "Are you going to be okay, sweetheart?"

"I guess so."

"You were really fond of him, weren't you?"

"Yeah." I had told her once that Mr. Godfrey was like a father figure to me, but then regretted my words, thinking by her silence that they had saddened her.

"I wish I could be there for you right now," she said.

All day I had managed to maintain my composure, keeping grief at bay while all around me people fell apart. Now alone, with my mother actually demonstrating sympathy toward me, I felt my throat constrict.

"Is there anything I can do?" she asked. "Anything at all?"

I looked around at my moldy breadbox of an apartment, so small and rundown and depressing, and felt tears pool in my eyes. "No. It's okay," I said. "I'll be fine. I—" I choked down a sob.

"Poor, *poor* baby!" she cooed. "I wish I could give you a big hug! Is *anyone* there to comfort you?"

I could hear the hopefulness in her voice, and a hint of desperation. This was her way of prying, of asking if I had a girlfriend without seeming too obvious. Nancy Swinton came to mind suddenly, unexpectedly, and I remembered how distraught her sweet face had been that morning as she rushed by me in the parkade. How wonderful it would be to be able to tell Mom that Nancy was my girlfriend. But I had already learned my lesson about falling in love with staff, about misinterpreting a woman's respect and admiration for love. I wasn't about to make that mistake again.

"No," I said, feeling even more sorry for myself. "I'm all alone."

"Oh, no! You really shouldn't be alone at a time like this. I worry about you. What about friends?"

I realized that I didn't have any friends either, that I truly was alone in New York. Work was my life, and now my livelihood, the future of the Universe, lay in doubt. I felt myself begin to cry, and soon the receiver was soaked with tears. Mom listened quietly, offering occasional words of comfort, her voice tender. I found myself longing for her company. I hadn't felt this way since I was a boy.

After a few minutes, I composed myself. "Some bastard just ..." I couldn't say it. "I don't know what I'm going to do! Mr. Godfrey *was* the Universe."

"Things will work out, dear. They always do. It just takes time."

I felt myself choke up again.

"Trevor, baby, I can't possibly cancel my trip. You need your mother at a time like this."

"Sorry?"

"I'm coming out to be with you. I don't care if you're at work. I'll be there if you need me."

Whether she was being sincere or manipulative, I didn't care. She was right; I needed my mommy.

"Okay," I managed.

"Go to sleep now. I'll see you at the airport Thursday. I love you, Trevor. I can't wait to see you."

I gulped and opened my mouth to say "I love you too," but she had already hung up.

3

The Bright Side of the Universe

I was up and out before sunrise Monday morning in anticipation of a long and difficult day. I live on the second floor of a four-story walkup in Hell's Kitchen, on West Fifty-first, just west of Tenth. A few doors down is Barrett's Funeral Home and across the street is St. Vincent's Midtown Hospital and the Sacred Heart Church. I could live my entire life without leaving my street: be born, grow up, get married, become ill, die, and be memorialized—all within a one-block radius.

The cold outside was biting, and a light snow had begun. As I made my way down West Fifty-first, I pulled on my gloves and burrowed into my heavy wool coat. My body was stiff, and I felt anxious and depressed. The death of Willard Godfrey would leave a tremendous void in the Universe. Not all people worshipped him like I did—he was both a visionary and a tyrant at times—but everyone respected him. He was its centrifugal force: the owner, my mentor, my inspiration. I had moved to New York because of him, and now my entire life revolved around the Universe. My colleagues and I had to pull together quickly to restore the balance, or the results might be disastrous.

Fifteen minutes later I reached the rear of the complex, a locked iron gate in a ten-foot spear-headed fence that bordered the hotel gardens. As the gate clanged shut behind me, shutting out the burgeoning chaos of the Manhattan morning, I felt a sense of relief. The gardens were an oasis of calm in the bustling city, a private patch of parkland with trees, grass, flowers, benches, and picnic tables. I made my way down a gravel path lined with hibernating cherry trees and past a labyrinth of trimmed hedges that led to a powerful telescope. The telescope was originally intended for stargazing, but the lights of Manhattan proved too bright, the atmosphere too thick with pollution to permit unobstructed views of the sky. Now it was used primarily for peeping on neighboring office tenants and hotel guests—save for Universe guests, whose privacy was protected by the hotel's mirrored glass exterior.

At the end of the pathway I descended a flight of steps, passed my disc over the scanner, and pulled open the heavy metal door. Bypassing my usual morning walkabout, I hurried down the corridor to the service elevator and went directly to my office.

Before long I was engrossed in my usual Monday morning routine, sorting through paperwork, scanning the weekend managers' log, and reviewing email. I came across an email message that brought the weekend's tragedy rushing back. It had been sent on Saturday evening, at 6:53 PM, just prior to the Christmas party. It was from Willard Godfrey.

It was shocking to see his name onscreen, as though he were sitting in his office at that very moment, banging out his usual barrage of Monday morning questions and commentaries. It was the last message I would ever receive from Mr. Godfrey. Should I cherish it, save it for a time when I was craving his company? But the heading, which was simply entitled THE FUTURE, was too intriguing. I clicked it open.

Trevor—

Kindly mark your calendar for a private
meeting with me at 8:30 AM on Monday, January 3.
General staff meeting to follow at 10:00 AM.

Regards, W.

I scrolled down, but the message ended there, followed by the standard signature line: THE UNIVERSE HOTEL, WHERE OUR WORLD REVOLVES AROUND YOURS. It was unusual for Mr. Godfrey to schedule a meeting so far in advance; he was more inclined to barge into my office and deal with an issue on the spot. Glancing at the calendar, I noted that January 3 was a holiday, since New Year's Day fell on a Saturday this year. But that meant nothing. Mr. Godfrey was oblivious to holidays, weekends, normal office hours; he worked around the clock and expected the same of staff. From day one there had always been a reason to work like a dog at the hotel: first the mad pre-opening phase, followed by the chaotic post-opening phase, then the aftermath of September 11. Now, three years later, New York's hotel industry had been pronounced fully recovered, and business was booming, yet Mr. Godfrey's expectations hadn't changed.

But I never complained. I loved my job, adored my coworkers, and would have done anything for Mr. Godfrey. I had worked with him long enough to know that if he scheduled a meeting, a private meeting, this far in advance, with a general staff meeting to follow, he had an announcement to make. A big announcement. One that concerned not only "the future" but *my* future.

Eight months ago, when Mr. Godfrey surprised us by announcing he had created the position of resident manager and had hired former astronaut Matthew Drummond to fill it, there were rumors that, after almost fifty years in the business, the venerable old hotelier was planning to retire. But little changed after that. Only recently had the rumors resurfaced. At seventy-one, the hotel's sole proprietor remained a fireball of energy, a tireless worker who dedicated every second of his time, every ounce of his energy to his work. Yet in the past few months he had grown more remote, less hot-headed and excitable. He went home earlier, came in later, even took days off. He was either naturally drifting away or deliberately detaching himself from the Universe. As unsettling as the change had been, I was not entirely dejected; I recognized an opportunity for me.

Since my first job in the hotel business eighteen years ago, as a bellman at the Westin Bayshore in Vancouver, I had wanted to become a general manager. I felt an instant connection with hotels—luxury hotels in particular. I loved the optimistic, agreeable staff who populated them and the affluent, successful guests who frequented them. I was passionate about providing great service, and I grew to feel at home within the elegant, formal confines of luxury hotels. Upon joining the Universe, I could not fathom working anywhere else; to become its general manager would be, to me, the greatest possible achievement.

For over a year, save for a brief period during which I mistook Matthew for a threat to my ambitions, I had suspected that Mr. Godfrey was grooming me to replace him. If this were his intention on January 3, the change was coming sooner than anticipated. To move from my current position to general manager would be quite a leap, and I wasn't sure I was ready. Yet Mr. Godfrey had always said that "fit" was essential, and finding the right fit for any position at the Universe had always been a challenge. Universal Culture demanded an entrepreneurial spirit, fierce loyalty, and unwavering dedication. Mr. Godfrey himself told me once that I embodied this culture. Yet he had always been close at hand for guidance and support. The prospect of managing the Universe on my own was daunting. But such speculation was useless, I told myself. The future now lay in the hands of Cynthia Godfrey.

"Ready for the briefing?"

I looked up to see Cassandra James, director of human resources, standing in the doorway. My spirits soared. Sandy was my favorite colleague, a friend, the glamorous sister I never had. She was an eternal optimist; Universal Culture personified. I knew that she, more than anyone, would be devastated by the loss of Willard Godfrey.

"Sandy, good morning! Please, come in."

She stepped partway in but seemed reluctant to enter. Her blond hair was tied back, makeup flawless, her smooth skin the color of ivory. At thirty-eight, with two young children, she was slim and tall and elegant. She was dressed in a stylish navy pinstriped pantsuit and black patent-leather pumps, her only accessories a pair of pearl earrings and her star nametag. She was smiling brightly, and when Cassandra James smiles, her entire face lights up. Like a big hug, it lifts you up, comforts you, and embraces you. But why was she smiling? She hadn't returned my messages yesterday—was it possible she didn't know? Suddenly I was sick with the prospect of having to break the news.

"Oh, god, Sandy," I said, rising to pull her into my office, "I have some terrible news."

"It's okay, Trevor. I know. I talked to Matthew last night."

"You did? Then why are you smiling?"

Her smile vanished. "I am not."

"You were."

She reached up and touched her mouth. "God, I didn't even realize. Sometimes I forget to turn it off."

"An occupational hazard," I said to reassure her. Close up, I could see cracks in her flawless exterior: her bright blue eyes, which always sparkled, looked pale and lifeless, as though the flame inside had been extinguished, and there was a tightness around her lips I had never seen.

"I was up the whole night," she said.

"Me too." We regarded one another in silence, unable to find words to articulate our feelings. I saw a tear pool in her eye and opened my arms to hold her. Her head fell onto my shoulder. I stroked her back, feeling her body convulse, her lungs heave. A sweet, subtle citrus fragrance emanated from her. She pulled away, looking embarrassed, as though we had just sneaked a secret kiss. I reached for a box of tissues from my desk and handed one to her.

She accepted it, dabbed her eyes, and used it to polish her nametag. "Do they know who did it yet?" she asked, sniffing.

"I'm not sure. I don't think so."

"How could *anyone*...?"

"I've been asking myself the same question."

She sat on the edge of my desk and picked up the paperweight beside her, turning it over in her hands and regarding it thoughtfully. It was a gift from Mr. Godfrey, an iron replica of the Glittersphere. Suddenly she let out a gasp and dropped it. It landed inches from my foot. She turned over her hands and stared down at them. On either palm was a large, open wound, with patches of dried blood and shredded skin.

"My god, Sandy, what happened?"

"Nothing." She hid her hands behind her back. "I had a little fall."

"That looks really painful."

"I'll be fine. We better get to the briefing."

I wanted more time with her. I wanted to ask her if she had driven home after the party or if she knew if Shanna had. But she was already out of the office and halfway down the corridor. I caught up with her at the main reception desk, which opened onto three corridors, the first leading to the sales and catering offices, the second to the offices of Willard Godfrey and Matthew Drummond, and the third, from which we had just emerged, to the human resources and rooms division offices. She pulled open a set of glass doors embossed "Administration Offices" in gold letters and hurried across the concourse.

"Are you limping, Sandy?" I asked as we descended the staircase to the lobby.

"No."

"You're walking funny."

"I scraped my knee."

"I'd hate to see the other guy."

A former Miss Teen Utah and high-school cheerleader, even with a limp Sandy still walked like a beauty queen: tall, poised, and graceful, a perennial smile on her face. After high school she retired her pleated skirt and pompoms for a polyester suit and synthetic scarf as a front desk agent at the Sheraton Salt Lake City. From there, she moved through various positions—cocktail server, reservations supervisor, front desk manager—before settling into the personnel department. Along the way, she became friendly with one of the hotel's regular guests, Jack James, a New York artist who lectured at the College of Fine Arts, and secretly they began dating. Two years later he asked her to marry him, and they moved to New York.

In New York, Sandy held positions at the Sheraton Manhattan, the Palace, and the Four Seasons, then took a few months off to give birth to her son before joining the Universe as director of human resources. The hotel's third employee after Mr. Godfrey and his secretary, Susan

Medley, Sandy had been charged with the recruitment and training of over one thousand employees. When I joined two months after her, we became instant friends. Together we worked around the clock to prepare for the opening, writing policy and training manuals, developing orientation programs, collaborating with Mr. Godfrey to establish Universal Standards of Service, Universal Values, and Universal Rules of Presentation. Three weeks after we gave birth to the Universe, Sandy gave birth to her daughter, Kaitlin.

Although her cheerleading days were long over, in spirit Sandy never let go of her pompoms. She was an eternal optimist, quick to commend and reluctant to condemn. Yet her sweet exterior could be misleading; she was a tough-as-nails interviewer, had zero tolerance for misconduct, and did not hesitate to terminate recalcitrant employees. I have observed her haul an employee into her office, fire him for misconduct and march him off-property, then return to greet a candidate for the same position with a dazzling smile. Everyone respected her, including many of the people she had fired.

"Did you get my messages last night?" I asked as we crossed the lobby.

"I did, but it was late, and I thought you'd be in bed. Jack and I were upstate all day. We took the kids to see Santa, then had dinner with his parents."

"Sounds like fun."

"It was hell."

We crossed the Center of the Universe and climbed three steps to a circular glass gazebo that housed an oval silver-laminated table and twelve black-lacquered throne chairs. I put my hand on the faux-ivory door handle and hesitated, turning to Sandy.

"This is going to be difficult."

She nodded slowly, a determined expression on her face: jaw clenched, eyes fixed in steely resolve.

I pulled open the door and gestured for her to enter first.

"Thanks, Trevor!" she said with a bright smile. She limped in.

Every weekday morning at 8:00 AM, the five senior executive staff of the Universe Hotel gathered in this boardroom for the morning briefing. Dubbed the Cosmic Bubble for its domed glass exterior, the room was raised several feet above the rest of the lounge, its glass walls tinted dark to allow us to observe the lobby without being observed ourselves. When the hotel first opened, Mr. Godfrey, a huge fan of all things science fiction, had insisted on calling the room Command Central, but the rest of us couldn't say it with a straight face. At times we worried that he truly believed the hotel was a massive starship hurling through space. Last summer, when the Universe hosted the annual *Star Trek* fan convention, the hotel was overrun with Leonard Nimoy lookalikes, Borgs, Vulcans, and Starfleet cadets, alien abductees and William Shatner himself. Mr. Godfrey was giddy with excitement. On the first day of the conference, as we gathered for the briefing, we spotted him descending the staircase dressed in a red and black Captain Picard uniform. Alarmed, we quickly huddled to decide what to do. Conventioneers might be amused, but what about other guests? Clients? The media? An intervention was required. Shanna Virani was appointed spokesperson.

"Be subtle," Sandy warned. "We don't want to embarrass him."

"I wouldn't think of it," said Shanna.

Willard entered with a foolish grin on his face, clearly thrilled with his costume. Before he could utter good morning, Shanna shot up from her seat. "Willard, you look absolutely ridiculous in that costume. The hotel's dignity is at stake, not to mention your own. You must change at once." Mr. Godfrey's eyes bulged. He turned to the rest of us, but we looked away, embarrassed. He nodded slowly, then touched two fingers to his chest as though activating a teleporter device and marched out. Twenty minutes later he returned dressed in his usual conservative three-piece suit and tie, and not another word was said on the issue.

The term "briefing" was a bit of a misnomer. The meetings could be painfully protracted, sometimes lasting into the afternoon, occasionally through dinner. Their purpose was to review occupancy and revenue statistics, to discuss incoming groups and VIPs, and to address issues of Universal Importance. But Mr. Godfrey tended to go off on tangents, ranting about breakdowns in communication, shortfalls in service, and the predatory tactics of competitors. Originally attended by ten department heads, over the years the meetings had been pared down to five, mostly because of Mr. Godfrey's impatience. First he relieved the director of food and beverage of the obligation to attend, then the director of catering, the director of conference services, and the director of public relations (who was also relieved of her job). Last came the controller. "If I have to listen to one more goddamned financial analysis, I'll shoot myself," he explained. "Or I'll shoot him." His passion lay in service, in cultivating business relationships, and in courting the media; everything else he found painfully dull.

Upon entering the Cosmic Bubble, I noticed that Matthew Drummond had seated himself at the head of the table in the chair normally occupied by Mr. Godfrey. By the sharp intake of Sandy's breath, I knew that she too was shocked by his audacity. Matthew's face was buried in the *New York Post,* and he did not look up. I took my usual seat on the right, halfway down the table, where I could keep an eye on the front desk and lobby. Sandy sat opposite me, flashing me a reassuring smile. She smoothed her hair, then reached for a teacup from the silver tray at the center of the table. Again I caught a flash of red welt on her palm and wondered what happened. A fall, no doubt, on gravel or pavement. Her hands trembled as she sipped her tea. She saw me staring and frowned, setting the cup down and hiding her hands beneath the table.

"Jesus!" Matthew cried suddenly, flinging the newspaper across the table. "Have you read this garbage?"

"Not yet," I replied. I avoided newspapers and news in general, finding it too depressing; it was more pleasant to pretend that the world outside was as peaceful and harmonious as inside the Universe. But Matthew was blinking and twitching madly, as though an irksome fly were buzzing around his head, and curiosity compelled me to reach for the paper. A headline ran along the top of page three: RENOWNED HOTELIER KILLED IN HIT-AND-RUN. There was a photograph of Willard Godfrey standing in front of the hotel dressed in an ivory-colored business suit and grinning ear to ear, arms open wide like Ricardo Montalban on *Fantasy Island*. How incomprehensible it was to me that this man, so full of life in this photograph, could be dead. I began to read the article, but Matthew snatched it back.

"Can you believe this nonsense?" he cried. "'… struck down following a boozy staff Christmas party …'; '… found in a gated underground parkade restricted to the hotel's executive staff …'; '… police investigating the possibility that an employee may be responsible.'" He looked up, eyes blazing. "What sensationalistic bullshit!" He looked over to Sandy, who was sitting with a pleasant smile on her face, zoned out. He sighed and turned back to me. "Where the hell is Shanna?"

I looked into the lobby and spotted her descending the stairs. "Here she comes," I said.

We turned to watch the hotel's brassy director of sales and marketing strut across the lobby, the muffled tap-tap of her heels echoing in the atrium, her tiny shoulders punching the air, arms swinging back and forth with the cool confidence of a supermodel. Shanna Virani's entire demeanor screamed wealth, beauty, height, and power—none of which she possessed to a remarkable degree, but perception is reality in the hotel business. Remove the heels and flatten the big, black hair, and she stood no taller than five foot two. Her features were striking but severe—dark, smooth skin; high cheekbones; exotic black eyes—softened with expert makeup, tailored suits, and haute couture accessories. Her age was as volatile as her moods; she professed to be anywhere from thirty-nine to forty-eight, depending on what she felt she could get away with at any given time; according to her personnel file, she was fifty-three. Raised in poverty in a village in a small community in Pakistan, she left for England as a teenager and now spoke with a regal British-Pakistani accent. Fluent in six languages, she conducted herself with impeccable manners, cultivated over what she herself termed as "a thousand years in the business." Frequently guests mistook her for one of their own—a Pakistani princess, perhaps—but to staff, her identity was never mistaken. They called her Queen of the Fucking Universe.

"Sorry I'm late," she said as she flung open the door, her tone suggesting it was anyone's fault but her own. She rounded the table and took a seat in the queen's throne opposite Matthew, a cloud of exotic perfume trailing in her wake. I watched her closely as she poured herself a cup of coffee and gulped it down without a flinch, then collapsed back in her chair with a heavy sigh.

"I cannot believe he's dead," she said, fanning herself.

We nodded our heads in commiseration, and a moment of troubled silence ensued.

"Well, we'd better get started," said Matthew. "We're all deeply distraught, I realize, but as the hotel's senior management team we need to keep a stiff upper lip. Employees will be looking to us for leadership. Guests will expect the usual levels of service and professionalism. We need to put forward a brave face."

Shanna's nostrils flared. "You suggest we just forge onward as though nothing occurred?"

"That's not at all what I meant," said Matthew. He was easily riled by Shanna, who had a great deal more experience and did not hesitate to remind him of this. "Perhaps if you had shown up yesterday, you might have witnessed all the grieving that took place. Trevor and I spent the entire day counseling staff."

I turned to him and opened my mouth to protest, but decided to let it go.

"I agree, Matthew," said Sandy. "This morning I did a quick tour of the property, and everywhere I went employees were displaying outward signs of grief. At the front desk, Alexandra was literally bawling in front of a guest. Mr. Godfrey would have been mortified! Guests pay hundreds of dollars a night to escape from reality, not to witness tears and sadness. We need to ask ourselves what Mr. Godfrey would want. I think he'd want us to keep on smiling."

"Exactly," said Matthew. "We need to keep this ship on course."

Shanna groaned. "You can shake your pompoms all you like, Sandy, but the reality is, without Captain Picard at the helm, this starship is going to crash like the *Enterprise*."

"Why, Shanna," Sandy cried, "aren't you being a bit cynical? I firmly believe that—"

"Guys," I said, interrupting. "Can't we get along for a minute? I don't know about you, but I'm not ready to forge ahead. I feel like crawling under this table and curling into a fetal position."

"Impressive leadership instincts," Shanna said, with an exaggerated nod in my direction.

"Why, thank you."

Shanna sat back and examined her exquisite nails. "This reminds me of an incident while I was at Claridge's in London. One evening, our general manager was enjoying a pleasant dinner of roast pheasant in our restaurant in the company of his wife and two Austrian diplomats. Suddenly, he clutched his chest and keeled over. His wife, a strapping Nordic type and a dreadfully stupid woman by all accounts, rushed to his aid, mistakenly believing he was choking, and performed a rather overenthusiastic Heimlich maneuver. As it turns out, he was having a mild heart attack. Her efforts did little to improve his chances. In fact, we suspect she killed him."

Sandy gasped. "How terrible!"

"It being Britain," Shanna continued with a half-smirk, "everyone pretended nothing occurred. The corpse was dragged away, along with the blubbering wife and the mortified Austrians. The table was reset, and a group of unwitting diners was seated. Incidentally, they all ordered pheasant. Two weeks later, a new general manager was installed, and we went about our business as though nothing had occurred."

"A riveting story, Shanna," said Matthew. "But how does it pertain to our present situation?"

"It's simple. This isn't Britain, it's America. We need to respond with openness and compassion."

"And exactly who will provide us with these qualities?" asked Matthew.

"Certainly not you. Nor me, for that matter. Sandy and Trevor are the compassionate ones."

"Shouldn't we determine who's in charge first?" I said.

Matthew folded his arms in a look of defiance. "There's nothing to decide. I'm second in command. I'm in charge."

"What makes you think you're entitled?" asked Shanna.

"Oh, please!" Matthew said. "It's no secret that Godfrey was grooming me for general manager. In fact, I have an email from him requesting a private meeting on January 3 to formalize the appointment."

"He scheduled a meeting with me, too, Matthew," I said. "Mine was for 8:30 AM. How do you know...?"

"Mine was for 9:00," said Sandy.

"And mine was 8:00," said Matthew. "Which clearly means he planned to offer me the position first, then inform the three of you, then announce it at a general staff meeting." He turned to Shanna.

"He didn't schedule a meeting with me," said Shanna.

"How intriguing," Matthew said, stroking his jaw, his tone implying that the exclusion was deliberate.

"I didn't need a meeting," Shanna snapped. "I had dinner with Willard on Friday night, along with Cynthia and Roger and Katherine Weatherhead, and he told us exactly what he was planning. He—" She stopped talking suddenly. She placed her elbows on the table and buried her face in her hands. "Forget it. It doesn't matter anymore."

Sandy got up and went around the table to comfort her.

"Can we assume Cynthia has inherited the Universe?" I asked.

Shanna lifted her head. "She's the sole benefactor of the estate, as far as I know. There's no one else."

"How convenient that her father died only a few months after he cut her off," Matthew said, raising an eyebrow.

"He didn't cut her off," said Shanna. "He sharply curbed her allowance. She still gets everything."

Sandy's eyes grew wide. "You don't think she...?"

"I wouldn't put it past her," said Shanna. "She's a—"

"People, *please*," I said. "The poor girl just lost her father."

"What if she decides to step into his shoes?" Sandy said.

There was a collective gasp in the room.

"Cynthia Godfrey run this hotel?" Shanna cried. "The girl can't even run a vacuum."

The room fell silent. Around us, the everyday sounds of the Universe seemed to amplify: the rumble of luggage carts on the marble floor; the clatter of silverware in Galaxy; guests exchanging morning greetings. Cynthia was the antithesis of her father: she was spoiled, temperamental, and unrefined. Partying was her full-time career. A constant fixture on Manhattan's social scene, she hobnobbed with other heiresses, supermodels, and celebrities, her photograph appearing frequently in gossip columns and fashion magazines. Two years ago, in a desperate attempt to straighten her out, Mr. Godfrey had hired her as a "management trainee." But she quickly demonstrated little aptitude for hospitality and was passed from department to department, generating an unprecedented number of guest complaints.

"We need to keep her as far away from this hotel as possible," said Matthew.

Shanna nodded. "I think that's one issue on which we all agree." She stood up and stretched, as though the meeting had been adjourned, then collapsed back down in her seat. Her hand moved to her temple. "My *god*, I've had a headache for two days. What were those vile little concoctions the bartender created?"

"Big Bangs," I muttered, feeling her pain.

"How appropriate. I didn't get out of bed yesterday."

"I think we all had a few too many," I said.

"*I* didn't," said Sandy.

We turned to her, surprised by the uncharacteristic vehemence in her tone—and the audacious claim.

Shanna chuckled softly. "From what I recall, Sandy dear, you were sucking drinks back like oysters."

"That is *so* not true!" Sandy shouted, rising in her seat.

"Ladies, I caution you to choose your words carefully," Matthew said. "Yesterday, the detective had many questions for Trevor and me. He was most interested in who drove home from the party. He'll want to speak with both of you today."

Shanna's hand flew to her heart. "Us? Why?"

"We might have been the last to see him," said Matthew. "The circumstances are a bit disturbing, to be quite honest. He was found on P4 and, as you know, only a select few of us have access to P4."

"You're not suggesting...?" Shanna's voice trailed off, as if the question were too inconceivable.

Suddenly, we were sneaking glances at one another, our eyes flickering with paranoia and suspicion. I felt a perceptible drop in the temperature of the room. Could one of us be responsible?

"I wouldn't worry," I said to ease the tension. "Some teenage joy riders probably broke into the parking lot. The detective intimated as much. But while we're on the topic, we might as well clear the air. Did either of you drive home after the party?"

Shanna glanced at Sandy and cleared her throat. "Well...I drove," she said. "But I was completely sober by then. I didn't see Willard or anything out of the ordinary as I left. Sandy, you must have driven out shortly after me. I saw your husband's truck parked next to mine."

We all turned to Sandy.

She did not look up. She was fidgeting with her hands under the table, like a little girl coveting a field mouse.

"Sandy?" Shanna said. "Did you drive?"

Her expression anxious, Sandy lifted her hand and rubbed it against her forehead. When she pulled it away there was a smear of blood above her brow; the wound had opened.

"My goodness, Sandy, what have you done?" Shanna cried, pointing to her hand, which was now dripping blood onto the table.

Horrified, I reached for a napkin from the tray and tossed it to her.

Sandy looked down at her hand and let out a cry. She took the napkin and dabbed her hands and face, then cupped it in both hands. "I—I left the party right after you, Shanna," she said, her voice almost inaudible. "I stopped by my office to pick up my coat and purse."

"Did you drive?" Matthew asked impatiently.

Sandy hesitated. "Yes, I drove. I shouldn't have, but yes, I did."

"Did you see Willard?" asked Shanna. "Did you see anything?"

We leaned closer, holding our breath, eyes riveted on her.

"No," she replied. "I didn't see anything."

We all breathed a sigh of relief.

"That settles it, then," said Matthew. "We have nothing to hide. Godfrey was run over by delinquents. Let's hope they catch the little bastards quickly. In the meantime, we had best get on with our business."

After the briefing, determined to continue with my usual routine, I embarked on a property inspection, starting on P3 and working my way to the upper floors, checking on every department under my responsibility: housekeeping, laundry, security, reservations, front desk, bell desk, and switchboard. On the guest floors I inspected five guestrooms at random, running my finger along picture frames, pulling out televisions sets, lifting sofa cushions, and making note of every speck of dirt, smudge, and stain. Even the most minute of flaws rarely escaped my scrutiny, which had earned me the nickname Eagle Eyes. In the bathroom I sat on the lid of the toilet to observe from a guest's perspective, then verified that the hotel logo was imprinted on the toilet paper rolls, that bathroom floors were heated to ten degrees above room temperature, and that complimentary Voss water and fruit had been placed in every arrival room.

After my inspection, I went back down to the basement and stopped by the Milky Way staff cafeteria for a coffee. It was 10:20, break time for housekeeping staff, but the usual spirited chatter of a dozen languages had been replaced by virtual silence. At least twenty room attendants had gathered around a newly constructed shrine bearing a large framed portrait of Willard Godfrey, surrounded by flowers, cards, handwritten notes, rosary beads, candles, and religious figurines. They knelt before it and prayed, crossing themselves, gripping one another's hands.

At the far end of the room, the television on the wall caught my attention. Coffee in hand, I wandered over. A tape was playing, and I recognized a scene from the Christmas party; the footage had been taken by Susan Medley, executive secretary. I turned up the volume and watched for a moment.

Onscreen, Mr. Godfrey was finishing his speech, his voice charged with emotion. "And, from the bottom of my heart, I thank you all for everything you do to make the Universe Hotel *the best goddamned hotel in the world!*" There was thunderous applause. People rose to their feet, thumping chairs, whistling, and cheering.

My heart swelled.

The camera followed Mr. Godfrey as he climbed down from the stage using his cane. Behind him, the band started up and the dance floor began to fill. The camera left Mr. Godfrey as he reached his table and searched the crowd, darting from one grinning face to another, before coming to a halt at the portable bar near the Observatory's outer window. I recognized Shanna, Sandy, Matthew, and myself standing in a circle, clinking shot glasses and tilting our heads back, swallowing Big Bangs.

Oh. My. God.

I glanced over my shoulder. A few faces were turned in my direction, but no one seemed to be paying attention. I pushed the *eject* button and discreetly tucked the cassette into my pocket, then shut off the television and turned around, assuming a pleasant smile.

"Mr. Trebor! Mr. Trebor!"

Suddenly a half-dozen housekeeping staff surrounded me. They hugged me, tugged at my arms, and placed their heads against my chest and back, reaching up to touch my face.

"We very sad today," said Ezmerelda, assistant director of house-keeping.

"So am I, Ezzy," I said. "So am I." I reached down to wipe a tear from her cheek. "But we have to be strong, all right? Mr. Godfrey would want us to keep on smiling, wouldn't he? He loved you all very much." I felt a rush of emotion. "Let's make him proud, okay?"

Heads nodded all around. "Okay, Mr. Trebor. We be strong."

I had always insisted that staff members call me by my first name, but for many it was a show of disrespect; their compromise was to call me Mr. Trevor—or "Mr. Trebor" in Spanish and Tagalog.

"You be next general manager, Mr. Trebor?" asked Milagros.

"I don't know, Mila," I said. "That's up to Cynthia Godfrey."

"We vote for you," said Ezzy. "All of us, we want you."

Heads nodded all around.

I was deeply touched. "Thank you, thank you all. That's so very kind."

A bell clanged, ordering them back to work. Within seconds they had deserted me, leaving the cafeteria empty. Alone, I went to the shrine to pay my respects, staring at Mr. Godfrey's grinning face for a long time, until more employees, mostly shift engineers and restaurant staff, started filing in. I left the cafeteria, taking the back stairwell up to the service corridor that ran the periphery of the lobby, and stopped at a door that opened onto the lobby, the crossing point between the back of the house and the front of the house. A full-length mirror was mounted on the wall below a red stop sign that read:

STOP! YOU ARE ABOUT TO GO ONSTAGE!

DO NOT OPEN THIS DOOR UNLESS
YOU ARE IMPECCABLE.

REMEMBER THE UNIVERSAL RULES OF PRESENTATION:

SMILE! EYE CONTACT! GUEST NAME!

THIS IS NOT A REHEARSAL!

Sandy and I had posted this sign on the hotel's first day of operation. These days, most employees ignored it, but only because its message was ingrained in our minds. Sandy liked to use an outer space analogy to describe the functioning of the hotel, but to me it was like a Broadway show: guests were the audience, back-of-house staff were crew, front-of-house staff were performers. Every morning, as I burst through this door and joined the choreographed staff movements, I experienced a surge of adrenaline. The star lights shone down like spotlights, the piped-in music provided the score; the Universe was a hit show that played to a packed house every night. As director, it was my responsibility to ensure the troupe executed a flawless performance.

Makeup and wardrobe were critical. It astounded me how hotels spent thousands of dollars on physical décor—ornate marble lobbies, grand crystal chandeliers, massive floral bouquets—yet paid little attention to staff, allowing them to dress in cheap polyester suits, ugly ties, wrinkled shirts, and scuffed shoes. At the Universe, employees were required to be as scrubbed and polished as the silver spoons in Orbit. Facial hair, tattoos, piercings, and accessories of any kind save for simple earrings and watches were strictly forbidden. Hair had to be squeaky clean and conservatively styled, with minimal product. Bad dye jobs, braids, beads, hooker hair, frosted tips, and trailer-park perms were in direct violation of the Universal Rules of Presentation. Bad hair was a particular source of vexation for me; in addition to Eagle Eyes, I had also been dubbed the Hair Police by staff for my zero tolerance policy. Even smiles were regarded as an essential part of uniforms; more than one employee had been dismissed simply for not smiling enough.

For the most part, employees respected the rules. There was a palpable sense of pride in working at the hotel, and it was felt at all levels, from part-time houseman to senior executive. Like Mr. Godfrey, I knew virtually every employee by name, as well as the names of their children, spouses, siblings, parents, and even pets, and where they lived, where they came from, and which schools they had attended.

Today, however, as I made my entrance into the lobby, I detected a dramatic shift in the atmosphere of the Universe. The lobby star lights seemed dimmer, the atrium music more somber, even the temperature seemed colder. Employees I passed looked sad and defeated, as though having grown tired of this performance. There wasn't a guest in sight.

Had our hit Broadway show run its course?

Granted, the circumstances surrounding the weekend's incident were enough to give one pause: a suspected drunk-driving death on hotel property, possibly involving an employee, on the eve of the arrival of seven hundred militant anti-impaired driving activists, the irascible Brenda Rathberger leading the charge. And now, Honica Winters, the queen of controversy, was nosing around. Suddenly, our treasured guests threatened to become our worst enemies. Judging by their behavior at this morning's briefing, my colleagues were too busy protecting their own interests to pull together as a team and protect the interests of the Universe. It would be up to me, I realized, to honor the memory of Willard Godfrey, to protect the dignity of the hotel, and to get this show back on the road.

I wondered if Mother might reconsider postponing her visit.

4

Sparkle Factor

After my rounds, I went to the executive offices to see Susan Medley. The executive secretary was perched at her desk, running her computer workstation like a NASA mission-control operator, leaning forward and frowning into the screen while typing furiously on her keyboard, all the while barking into her headset in a thick, though exceedingly polite, Bronx accent.

"Thank you fuh cawlin' Executive Offices, Susan Medley speaking, how may I help you? ... I'm sorry? ... Yes, yes, sadly, it's true ... Thank you for kind words.... Well, we're coping as best we can ... No, I'm not aware of any discounts or special offers ... One moment, please, I'll put you through to Reservations ... Thank you for holding, how may I—Pardon me? ... I'm sorry, Mr. Godfrey is ... unavailable at this time. May I assist you or have someone return your call? ... That would be Mr. Matthew Drummond, our resident manager ... No, I'm sorry, Mr. Drummond is not available at this time ... Certainly, one moment, please ... Thank you fuh cawlin' Executive Offices, Susan Medley speaking ..."

By the determined look on her face, I could tell she was fighting to hold herself together. She had been Mr. Godfrey's faithful assistant for more than fifteen years, having accompanied him from New

York hotel to New York hotel before settling down at the Universe. This morning, the chubby, cherubic-faced thirty-three-year-old was dressed in her typical off-duty nun attire: long black polyester skirt, plain white blouse, and dowdy gray wool sweater with pink roses stitched around the neck. Her face, framed by a halo of curly brown hair and huge, burgundy-rimmed glasses that jutted out a full inch on either side, was pale and devoid of makeup.

"I'm sorry, ma'am, Mr. Drummond is *still* not available ... Yes, I did tell him it was urgent ..."

As I waited for her to get off the phone, I examined the curved walls of the waiting area. They were crowded with photographs of Mr. Godfrey posing with famous people who had stayed at the Universe, an eclectic group that included the Dalai Lama, the Aga Khan, Bill and Hillary Clinton, Stephen Hawking, Jennifer Lopez, Brad Pitt, and Sharon Stone. Photos of virtually every cast member of *Star Wars, Star Trek,* and their various spin-offs were also displayed. A number of real-world astronauts were there too; since opening, Mr. Godfrey had provided complimentary accommodation to anyone from any-where in the world who had traveled in space. Since he was a boy, he had dreamed of traveling in space; as he grew older and the odds of becoming what he referred to as "the oldest fart in space" diminished, he settled for the next best thing: he built the Universe and invited astronauts to stay for free.

To the right of Susan's desk, the door to Mr. Godfrey's office was closed, the lights off. I half expected him to come rushing out like he always did when he heard my voice, full of vim and vigor, quick with a smile, a handshake, a slap on the back. "Trevor, ol' boy," he would say. "How are you this fine morning? Keeping guests happy, I trust!" He rarely spent time in his office, preferring to rove the floors on a never-ending site inspection, stopping to pick up garbage along the way, to empty ashtrays, to polish smudges, and to chat with guests. Often he held spot quizzes with staff to test their knowledge of in-house VIPs and groups, hours of operation, and Universal Values, and would send them to their managers for retraining if they did poorly. Every morning he stopped by the kitchen to sample daily features, giving the thumbs-up or thumbs-down, and dropped by banquet rooms to inspect setups. His favorite post was the front door, where he spent hours welcoming guests upon arrival and wishing them a speedy return upon departure. Always willing to help, he parked cars, carried suitcases, and bussed tables. He never tired of conducting tours, whether for a pair of senior citizens from Akron, Ohio, or the Queen of England herself (this occurred a year after opening; she stayed for three nights and proclaimed her experience "truly out of this world"). The Universe was Willard Godfrey's one-thousand-room home; employees were his beloved family, and guests were his treasured visitors.

"Of course we'll honor the gift certificate Mr. Godfrey donated to your winter ball, Mr. Jeffries," said Susan, still on the phone.

To the left of Willard's office, Matthew's door was closed. I put my ear against the door but couldn't hear a peep inside. I glanced at my watch: 11:30 AM. Too early for his afternoon lunch-and-nap session, too late for his morning coffee break. He often disappeared for hours, and on evenings and weekends staff were forbidden to disturb him except in the event of an emergency, in which case "there better be blood." Considering his role as resident manager, his behavior was extraordinary; in most hotels, his position required a round-the-clock presence.

But Matthew was content to leave that to the rest of us.

"Hi, Trevor."

Now off the phone, Susan Medley had removed her headset and was regarding me with a sad expression. Sensing she needed a hug, I hurried over to her.

"Susie, how are you? You doing okay?"

"I miss him."

I took her in my arms and stroked her curly hair. "Me too, Susie, me too. Sounds like you're doing a wonderful job of being brave. Mr. Godfrey would be proud." I allowed her to cry in my arms for a few minutes, then extracted myself, withdrawing the videocassette from my pocket and handing it to her. "I had to take this out of the Milky Way."

She looked down at it, then up at me, eyes blinking behind her thick glasses. "Why?"

"I don't think staff are ready to see it quite yet, Susie. I'm afraid it might upset them. Let's put it away for a while, then maybe we can take it out again when things aren't so raw. Okay by you?"

She nodded, seeming to understand, and opened her desk drawer, dropping the cassette in. "I thought it might cheer them up. The police took the original away this morning, but I made a copy first."

"The police were here?"

She nodded. "They spent some time going through Mr. Godfrey's office, then they interviewed a few employees in the Mercury board-room. They spent a *really long time* with Mrs. James." She pursed her lips, eyes bulging. "A *really long time.*"

"Why did they want the tape?" I asked.

She shrugged. "Evidence, I guess. They spent a *really long time* with Mrs. James."

"I heard you the first time, Susan." I wasn't about to indulge her gossipy nature. "Is Matthew in?"

"Yes, but I wouldn't bother him. He's in a really bad mood. He refuses to take calls or see anyone."

"So ... a typical day?"

"Pretty much."

I marched over to Matthew's door and knocked. When there was no answer, I opened it and peeked inside. He was leaning back in his chair, hands folded behind his head, staring off into space. The only light in the room came from the pale glow of gray sky from the window behind him.

"Matthew, you got a sec?" I asked.

He started. "Trevor! I didn't hear you. Come in. I was just going to call you."

I stepped inside and closed the door against Susan's prying eyes. Large by New York standards, Matthew's office was stark and sparsely furnished, a deliberately inhospitable environment meant to discourage visitors from lingering. The only place to sit was to the left, where two orange designer chairs shaped like eggs sat by the door, as far away from Matthew's desk as possible. His desk, a sheet of mirrored glass, was spotless except for a pen, pad of paper, flatscreen monitor, telephone, and a silver-framed photograph of his wife, which was lying facedown—whether it had fallen over or been deliberately pushed, I couldn't be sure. The large window behind him overlooked the hotel gardens.

"Have a seat, Trevor," said Matthew. "I need your advice." He gestured to one of the egg chairs but remained seated where he was, at least twenty feet away.

Lugging an egg chair closer to his desk, I sat down and glanced around. On the wall to the right of Matthew's desk were framed documents and photographs from his previous life as an astronaut: a Masters of Science in aviation systems from the University of Tennessee;

Navy Flight Training certification; NASA Space Flight medal; and a congratulatory letter from then-President Bill Clinton. A series of four photographs chronicled his one and only space flight, as mission specialist on Space Shuttle *Endeavour STS-97*. In the first, taken November 30, 2000, Matthew posed in an orange jumpsuit with fellow astronauts at the Kennedy Space Center just prior to takeoff. He was grinning ear-to-ear and giving the thumbs-up, his chest puffed out, helmet tucked beneath his arm, looking handsome and heroic and brimming with confidence. In the next, *Endeavour* blasted into the night sky amidst a cloud of smoke and fire. The third photo was famous, having made the cover of *Time* magazine, accompanied by a story entitled SPACE WIVES: WOMEN WHO LOVE MEN WHO WORK IN SPACE. Marline Drummond and two other crew wives were watching the launch from an observation deck nearby, the reflection of the shuttle captured in the glass, juxtaposed with their anxious faces, glowing orange in the glare of burning jet fuel. In the fourth and final photograph, Matthew and his fellow astronauts were disembarking the shuttle eleven days later. Matthew's expression was decidedly less heroic: he looked gaunt and shell-shocked, like a little boy stumbling off his first—and last—roller-coaster ride.

Turning to observe Matthew now, I noted striking similarities to his expression in the latter photograph. "Is everything all right, Matthew?" I asked, concerned.

He blinked several times. His upper cheek twitched. "*All right? This is a fucking nightmare, Trevor!* News of Godfrey's death is everywhere, and now *everyone* is calling—media, guests, employees, former employees, suppliers, politicians, Donald *Fucking* Trump, the goddamned *paper boy*—and they all want to speak to me."

"What do they want?"

He threw his hands in the air. "How should I know? I haven't taken any calls. But I don't need to. I know what they want. They're calling to pry, to scavenge, to collect morsels of gossip to savor like butterscotch and spread around. They're vultures, all of them!"

"I wouldn't be so quick to assume the worst," I said. "I'm sure they're simply upset by the news and looking for answers, for a bit of comfort and reassurance."

"Comfort and reassurance? How can I offer comfort and reassurance when I myself don't have a clue what's going to happen? Who's going to comfort and reassure *me*?"

I raised an eyebrow. These were hardly the words of a fearless leader, but I wasn't surprised. In the eight months since he joined the Universe, Matthew had demonstrated little flair for—or interest in—the hotel business. Though highly intelligent, he wasn't exactly a "people person"; he lacked warmth and charisma and, in fact, I suspected he harbored a secret loathing for people in general. Shanna once told me that Mr. Godfrey had considered a number of candidates for the resident manager position prior to hiring Matthew, including a former Miss Universe, a reigning Mr. Universe, and a chimp who had traveled in space. The chimp—Mr. Godfrey's first choice, she insisted, a mischievous smile spreading over her lips—turned it down in favor of something more intellectually challenging.

She was being facetious, of course, but there was truth in her words: in the past few months, Matthew's role had been relegated to little more than figurehead. Whether things had evolved this way because Mr. Godfrey had refused to relinquish authority, as Matthew claimed, or because Matthew was an arrogant slacker was the subject of great debate. His only significant contribution was Stargazers Nights in the Observatory, his monthly lecture on astronomy and space travel that had proven enormously popular. Besides this, the only reason I could fathom why Mr. Godfrey had continued to employ Matthew now that the media frenzy following his appointment had subsided was the close friendship between Matthew's wife, Marline, and Willard Godfrey's late wife, Margaret, to whose memory he had been fiercely loyal.

With few responsibilities, Matthew and Marline lived a life of leisure in the lap of luxury, residing in a luxurious bi-level suite on the sixth floor and enjoying a generous expense account, health club and spa privileges, daily housekeeping and laundry services, and a sparkling new gold BMW 7 Series.

"What can I do to help?" I asked Matthew now.

"I don't need your help," he snapped. "I'm perfectly capable of handling things on my own. What I need is your support. I'm concerned about Cynthia Godfrey. We should all be concerned about Cynthia Godfrey. I called her this morning to inquire about her intentions, and she was vague and noncommittal. I don't trust her. I'm afraid she'll put the hotel up for sale. If Ritz Carlton or Four Seasons or some other odious hotel chain snaps it up, we'll all be thrown out on the street."

The prospect was alarming. "What makes you think she would sell?"

"Would *you* want to run this place if you were as clueless as she? She's cash poor. Her father cut down her allowance drastically a few months ago. She has no interest in working. If she sells, she'll make millions, and she can spend the rest of her life shopping in Paris with her supermodel friends." He stood up and made his way around the desk, towering over me. "Trevor, we need to convince her that if she retains ownership and allows us to run the show, she'll be able to sit back and spend the profits. I intend to ask her to appoint me as general manager immediately. If you endorse my candidacy, I might consider promoting you as my number two. I might even consider giving you a juicy little title like 'executive assistant manager.'" He reached down to slap my arm in a gesture of fraternity. "How does that sound, my boy?"

"I don't think so, Matthew," I said.

There was a soft knock at the door, and Susan Medley peeked in. "Mr. Drummond, will you be taking calls anytime soon? Honica Winters is on the phone again."

"I'm still busy, Susan." He returned to his desk and slumped into his chair.

"I tried to tell her that, but she won't take no for an answer. She keeps asking me all these questions."

"What kind of questions?"

"About Mr. Godfrey. About what happened."

"Jesus! Tell her it's none of her goddamned business!"

Susan's eyes grew wide. "It's Honica Winters! I could *never*—"

Matthew slammed his fist on the desk. "I don't care if it's Barbara Fucking Walters! Tell her to go fuck herself!"

Susan gasped. "Goodness, there's no need to swear!"

"Matthew," I said, "that's hardly appropriate."

He sprang from his desk, fuming. "Why isn't it appropriate? If she's being an asshole, why can't I tell her to go fuck herself? Why is everyone in this place so bloody concerned with appearances? It's like living in a goddamned Jane Austen novel! No one ever says what they really think!"

"Matthew, for god's sake!" I glared at him, as though warning a dog to stay, then turned to Susan. "Sorry, Susie, we're just under a bit of pressure here. Kindly tell Miss Winters we're in a meeting at the moment, but I promise to contact her this afternoon and will be happy to answer her questions then."

Susan thanked me, scowled at Matthew, and pulled the door closed.

I stood up and went to his desk. "What was that all about, Matthew? How can you expect me to get behind you—and anyone to respect you—when you act like this? Swearing at staff, insulting guests, refusing to speak to them! This isn't how the hotel industry operates. After eight months, I would think you'd have figured out the basics at least. Did you *ever* see Mr. Godfrey behave like this?"

Matthew sat down again and ran his fingers through his hair. "I'm sorry, Trevor. I don't know what's come over me. I feel a tremendous amount of pressure, and quite frankly, I don't know what to do. I'm still getting my bearings in this business—never really had to do much or say much. Suddenly, overnight, I'm in the spotlight! Everyone wants to talk to me! They never used to want to talk to me. It was always Willard Godfrey."

"Then why are you so eager to become general manager?"

"I feel a sense of duty to Willard. If not me, who else?"

"Well, let me think … maybe *me?*"

He looked up. "You?"

"Yes, Matthew, *me*. Listen, there's too much at stake right now for us to get into a power struggle, and quite honestly, I'm far too distraught. Let's focus on damage control first, then we can worry about succession. I'm more concerned about Honey Winters than Cynthia Godfrey. I spent some time with her last night. She's in town to do a story, and I'm afraid that Mr. Godfrey's death has inspired her to do some digging around. Likely she won't be the only journalist to smell a story. We're going to need a cohesive strategy for dealing with the media. Have you contacted our PR agency?"

"As a matter of fact, yes. They politely informed me that Godfrey fired them two months ago."

"Right. I forgot about that. Mr. Godfrey has been handling the media on his own since then. What about you? You do interviews all the time."

"To be honest, Trevor, I can't stand the media. Up to this point, my interviews have been easy—upbeat and always positive. Even at NASA, the tough questions were left to administration. I don't have enough experience in this business to handle a topic as potentially controversial as this one. As for Honica Winters, I simply refuse to speak to that horrid woman. She interviewed me after my *Endeavour* flight and almost ruined me."

"Really? What did she—?"

"It's not important, Trevor."

"Handling the media isn't rocket science. It's pretty basic. After 9/11, Mr. Godfrey put a few of us through media training. We learned the three Cs of crisis communications."

"The three Cs?"

I tried to recall them. "We *care* ... we're *concerned* ... and we're ... "

"Cooked? That must be it. We're *cooked*."

"No."

"Catatonic?"

"Be serious, Matthew. We're ... *committed*—that's it. Simply tell them we *care* about what happened to Mr. Godfrey and its impact on his family, friends, and colleagues. We're *concerned* about the circumstances surrounding his death. And we're *committed* to safety for all employees and guests."

"That's good, very good. You seem to have a knack for this type of thing." He became pensive for a moment. "Trevor, as a test to see if you're ready to become executive assistant manager, I'd like to appoint you the hotel's official spokesperson."

"Me? No way. I'm not good on camera. I get nervous."

"You'll do fine."

Susan knocked on the door again. "Mr. Drummond, your wife is on line five."

"I *told* you to tell her I'm not here."

"I did, but she saw you coming in as she was leaving the spa."

He sighed. "The downfalls of living at work." He pressed the speakerphone. "What is it, Marline?"

"Darling, it's about our New Year's Eve party. People keep calling to ask if it's still on. What should I say?"

Matthew sighed. "I haven't had time to think about parties, my dear. You may recall I'm in the midst of a crisis?" He reached for her photograph and held it in front of him, frowning as though trying to recall who the woman was. In a glam shot taken from her acting portfolio, a wistful-looking Marline was resting her mousy chin on a knuckle, her thin lips parted to reveal a row of tiny childlike teeth, crow's feet airbrushed away, complexion rendered flawless. At the bottom she had signed in black felt, "To my darling Matthew, Yours Forever, Marline Drummond"—as though Matthew were not her husband but an anonymous fan, perhaps. In the biography that accompanied her portfolio, which she had painstakingly taken me through over lunch one day, Marline described herself as "a star of stage and screen." Yet, according to Matthew, since moving to New York she had appeared in only two B movies, a Staples commercial, and a handful of *off*-off Broadway plays. The rest of her time was dedicated to entertaining friends and family on Matthew's expense account.

"I'm perfectly aware of that," Marline snapped. "*Everyone* is talking about it. It's like 9/11 all over again."

"I hardly think you can compare the two, my dear."

"One of those Indonesian chambermaids was just up here cleaning, and she was going on and on and *on* about Willard. At one point she stopped making the bed, plopped her fat behind down, and started bawling! I hid in the bathroom until she left. You should speak to her supervisor." She stopped talking, and there was a chewing sound.

"Are you eating, Marline?" asked Matthew.

"You know I don't eat, darling. I'm chewing this horrid nicotine gum. It's actually working. I have no desire for a cigarette right now." She chewed loudly, as if to demonstrate its effectiveness. "So what is it? Party: on or off?"

Matthew looked at me inquiringly. Each year, Mr. Godfrey hosted the Gods of the Universe party on New Year's Eve and invited our biggest clients, our most frequent and high-profile guests, and a host of local celebrities, businesspeople, and politicians. It was one of the city's most exclusive parties, and people clamored for invitations. The party was hosted by Mr. Godfrey and held in the suite now occupied by the Drummonds.

"It's probably not the best timing for a party," I said. "Especially considering the host is dead."

"Did you hear that, Marline?"

"Who was that? Do you have me on speakerphone, Matthew? I told you I hate it when—"

Matthew picked up the receiver.

Deciding it was an opportune time to leave, I got up and backed toward the door.

Matthew covered the mouthpiece. "Wait, Trevor. I need you to write a nice little tribute to Mr. Godfrey for this afternoon's general staff meeting."

"Sure. I'd be happy to say a few words."

"Not *you*. *I'll* do the talking. I need you to *write* my speech."

"Sorry, Matthew. If you're speaking, you should write it."

"Marline, will you pipe down for a second? *Please*, Trevor? You knew him so much better than I."

"Sorry." I pulled the door shut behind me.

"Trevor, wait!" I heard him shout through the door. "Come back!"

I looked over to Susan, who was rolling her eyes.

"He already asked me to write his speech," she said. "Hey, do you think we should play the Christmas party video?"

"Probably not a good idea."

"Suit yourself. Oh, Sandy James was looking for you."

Sandy's office door was open. She sat swiveled around in her chair, her back facing the door, speaking quietly into her headset. I cleared my throat, but she didn't seem to hear.

"I don't *care* what it costs, Jack," she was saying, her stern voice lacking its usual singsong tone. "Just get it fixed. *Today* ... What? God, I don't know. 8:00 PM? 9:00 PM? It's pure chaos around here. Early as possible, I promise ... Love you too. Bye." She disconnected and spun around. "Trevor! I didn't hear you."

"You were looking for me?"

She looked down at her watch. "Got time for a quick lunch? I'm buried, but I need to eat something before I pass out."

"Sure."

"Great." She stood up and grabbed her purse, then went to the full-length mirror on the wall and began reapplying her lipstick. "Where to?"

"Galaxy?"

She stepped back and smiled at herself in the mirror. "Perfect."

As we walked down the corridor, I noticed that Sandy's hobble looked even more pronounced. She seemed determined not to acknowledge it; she kept her head high, body upright, and swung her arms exaggeratedly, as though it was all part of a sexy new walk.

"I heard the NYPD interviewed you," I said.

"Hmm? Oh yes, that's right. They did."

"How'd it go?"

"Terrific!"

"Terrific?"

"Well, as good as one could expect. It was all very routine."

"So no arrests?"

She either didn't hear me or didn't think it was funny. As we descended the stairs, she kept her eyes fixed directly ahead. We crossed the lobby to Galaxy without a word.

Clarence, one of the shift managers, led us to a quiet table.

"Thank you so *much*, Clarence!" Sandy gushed as he held out a chair for her. She watched him with a fond smile as he returned to his post, then turned to me. "Such a dear boy! One of my best hires, I think. Oh, I've been meaning to tell you, I interviewed an outstanding candidate this morning."

"You held an interview this morning?"

She covered her mouth with her hand in an *oops* gesture. "It was too late to cancel. It was worth it, though, believe me. The young man was amazing. He's the ideal candidate to replace Nancy Swinton."

My heart lurched. "Nancy *quit?*"

Our waiter, Michael, arrived just then to take our orders, and Sandy turned to him without responding. She hemmed and hawed over the menu, chatting amicably with Michael and asking for his advice on various items. My mind raced. Could Nancy really have quit? Why wouldn't she talk to me first? The prospect of losing our star duty manager was almost too much to bear. Nancy Swinton demonstrated the rare combination of diligence, sweetness, and discipline essential to her position as one of the hotel's troubleshooters. She could appease any guest, no matter how irate. Her virtues had rendered me completely enraptured. The thought of no longer seeing her every day was profoundly distressing.

"Sandy, I'd like to get back to work sometime today," I said.

"I'm sorry, Trevor, how inconsiderate of me!" She finally settled on coffee, a fruit bowl, and two fried eggs. "Sunny side up, please."

I glanced down at the menu and chose the first thing I saw—Shrimp Neptune—then turned to Sandy as soon as Michael was out of earshot. "*Please* tell me Nancy didn't resign." My mouth was so dry I could barely get the words out.

"Don't worry, she didn't," Sandy replied, to my utter relief. She frowned down at her palms, which were now covered in bandages. "I'm just thinking ahead. We had a heart-to-heart a week ago, and she confessed she's feeling bored. I fear it's only a matter of time."

"*Bored?* How could she feel bored? She has one of the most exciting jobs imaginable."

"Believe me, I know. I think she'd be crazy to leave."

I huffed. "I can't believe she never said anything to me."

Sandy blinked. "Maybe she feared you'd overreact."

"I'm not *overreacting*, Sandy. I just can't believe she would…" I grew silent, annoyed by her knowing expression. "Whatever. I don't care. If she wants to quit, fine."

"She hasn't quit, Trevor. Are you okay?"

"I'm fine," I said, crossing my arms.

"Anyway, as I was saying, the young man I met with, Jordan, is assistant front office manager at the Ritz Carlton Battery Park, and before that he spent three years as guest services manager at the Millennium.

He's a graduate of Cornell—with honors. He's friendly but assertive, has great hair and—*la pièce de résistance*—a fantastic smile."

"Sparkle Factor?" I asked, only half-interested.

"Way up there: 9, maybe 9.5 with a bit of training. Potential for 10."

Sparkle Factor was a term Mr. Godfrey had introduced to me on my first day on the job, in early May, almost five years ago. I had arrived in New York only two days earlier and was still adjusting to my new environment. Compared to Vancouver, which was so clean and fresh and green, Manhattan seemed filthy, gray, and suffocating. Yet I was ecstatic about my new adventure, and my escape from what I had considered a life sentence to mediocrity in Vancouver.

Still under construction, the Universe was slated to open eight months later (in fact, construction delays pushed the opening back another two). I reported to the pre-opening office at Madison and East Fifty-third. Mr. Godfrey introduced me around—the entire staff body was comprised of Susan Medley, Sandy James, and Shanna Virani, at the time—then told me to follow him out the door. We headed north on Madison Avenue, passing swarms of pedestrians, fleets of taxis, ubiquitous high-rises, and sidewalks worn by millions of footsteps. I found the incessant honking, the roar of traffic, and the buzz of thousands of voices both dizzying and invigorating. At Central Park South we turned left, where I was relieved to see flowers and budding trees along the periphery of Central Park. We stopped before one of New York's most venerable hotels.

"Whaddya think a dis place?" Mr. Godfrey asked, a lifetime in New York apparent in his accent.

"It's magnificent," I said, regarding its weathered façade in awe.

"Piece a shit," he proclaimed. "Guests pay a small fortune to stay here, but rooms haven't been renovated in a century, service is crappy, and employees are miserable. Management doesn't know it yet, but we're gonna steal their best staff—if there are any worth taking. Then we're gonna steal their guests. Won't be hard."

He marched toward the entrance, and I scrambled after him. The doorman ignored us, and we pushed open the door ourselves. "That surly son-of-a-bitch was here thirty-five years ago when I was chef concierge," Mr. Godfrey said. "Today he's got the same job, the same grotesque uniform, the same bad attitude. He won't lift a finger unless it involves a tip. Makes over two hundred grand a year in gratuities alone. Sonofabitch owns three houses in Jersey and an apartment building in Williamsburg."

Having started my career as a bellman, I was well aware that bell staff, and doormen in particular, were some of the highest-paid employees in luxury hotels, sometimes earning—when tips and tax evasion were considered—more than the general manager. Their income was rivaled only by cocktail waitresses; Sandy had told me stories of taking home over five hundred dollars in tips on a single shift.

Godfrey gestured around the lobby. "Whaddya think?"

To me it was grand and opulent, but this time I was more cautious. "It's okay."

"It's a fucking abortion!" His words boomed across the lobby, causing guests and employees to turn and stare. "Look at this cracked, shoddy marble—look at those gaudy chandeliers! And all this dust! And brass, my god, who said hotel lobbies have to have all this hideous brass? And look at those tacky flower arrangements! Those paintings of dead people!" He held his hand to his ear. "Listen. They're playing fucking Vivaldi! This place is one big tired cliché. We're in fucking Buckingham Palace!"

He reached up to grip my shoulder, staring at me intensely. "Trevor, my boy, the Universe is the antithesis of this hotel. Forget this old-school masturbatory bullshit about 'pampered indulgence' and 'refined elegance' and 'your business is our pleasure.' My hotel will be contemporary and stylish, understated and minimalist. There will be a sense of warmth and freshness everywhere. Materials will be the finest granite, sparkling chrome, stainless steel, and sleek black marble. There will be bold colors, modern art and music, sensuous curves, great open spaces, and warm, intimate places. Wait 'til you see it! It's magnificent!"

"I can't wait."

"If those lazy construction assholes ever finish, that is."

He promenaded me around the lobby, stopping first at the front desk and gesturing to the two clerks standing there. "Why so glum? Where are we, Siberia?" He pointed to a tall, angular man behind the concierge desk. "That sonofabitch runs a racket so corrupt it rivals the Mafia. Drugs, hookers, after-hours clubs, gambling, rent boys—you name it, he'll get it, as long as there's a big fat tip in it for him." He turned to me again and gripped my arm. "If you hire *anyone* like that, even *one person,* you're fired. Understand?"

I gulped. "Yes, sir."

He winked, and his face broke into a grand smile. His teeth, so perfect they couldn't possibly be his own, gleamed in the light of the dusty chandelier. At five foot two he was almost a foot shorter than me, but stature, warmth, and charisma oozed from him. "I know you never will," he said. "I saw the people you hired in Vancouver. I saw how well they were trained. They were superb! That's why I hired you."

"Thank you, sir."

"Don't call me sir! This isn't the army. Call me Mr. Godfrey."

I had met Mr. Godfrey nine months earlier while I was director of rooms at the Park Harbour Hotel in Vancouver, a six-hundred-room,

Four-Star, Five-Diamond property on the waterfront. He and Margaret stayed for three nights before boarding an Alaska cruise. Mr. Godfrey was quirky and funny, and Margaret was handsome and elegant. She was also shockingly thin; only later did I find out she was dying. On the day of their cruise, their luggage was stolen from the hotel entrance while awaiting transfer to the cruise ship. Mortified, I took them shopping to replace their items, insisting the hotel pay. They were most impressed. After the cruise, they stopped by and invited me to lunch. Mr. Godfrey told me about the hotel he was building, his eyes wild with passion, while Margaret looked on, looking half-amused, half-alarmed. I promised to visit them in New York but never really expected to see them again. At the time, I was experiencing major issues at the hotel; disillusioned and depressed, I was planning to leave the industry.

A month later, I left the Park Harbour to take a job in Vancouver's booming film industry as an assistant director on a local production. Before long, however, I discovered that film industry workers weren't quite as concerned with optimism and good manners as hotel workers. My cheerful disposition made them suspicious. Unable to survive the transition, I quit after three months and enrolled at the University of British Columbia to finish my bachelor's degree. I learned to loathe university life even more than the film industry: I couldn't concentrate, resented the time and effort required to study for exams and write papers, and hated being broke. I missed the hotel business. So, when Willard Godfrey called to ask if I might be interested in interviewing for the position of director of rooms at his new hotel, I leapt at the opportunity. Six weeks later, I moved to New York.

Days later, as I regarded this peculiar old man ranting at me, I was beginning to wonder if I had made the right decision.

"Trevor, you're going to hire the best goddamned employees available in this disaster of a city," he said. "We're looking for very special people, people with a twinkle in their eye." He led me to an ornate guild-framed mirror on the wall. "See how my eyes twinkle?"

I peered into the mirror. Indeed, they did have a glint about them.

"Your eyes twinkle too," he said, pointing through the mirror.

I opened my eyes wide and decided that yes, they did.

He reached up and shoved his hand in my hair. "What's this gunk?"

"Um ... thickening lotion."

"Makes you look like a woman. I don't want to see it again. Now smile for me." I complied. "You have a perfect smile, Trevor Lambert. You're a bit generic looking, but your smile lights up your entire face. We need smiles like this at the Universe. I don't want the fabricated, assembly-line smiles of chain hotels, the obsequious grins of the cruise lines, or the plastic smiles of Disneyland. Forget derisive French smirks and frosty German scowls and retentive British sneers. Give me genuine smiles, resplendent smiles, American smiles! Smiles so disarming you can't help but smile back no matter how pissy you might feel! Give me *Universe Smiles*!" He flashed his dentures in the mirror and winked.

I couldn't help but smile back.

"I'm writing a book, Trevor. It's called *Universal Values*. It's about the tremendous success one can achieve by simply applying the rules of hospitality to everyday life. Eye contact, name usage, smiles—it's as simple as that. Add a dash of hard work, integrity, and respect, and you've got the formula for success. Wouldn't you agree?"

"Sure."

"Let's get the fuck out of this dump." He pushed me toward the exit. "Smiles aren't everything, of course. Universe staff must also have immaculate grooming, excellent posture, impeccable manners, proper diction, and a can-do attitude. I call the whole package Sparkle Factor. I don't give a hoot about experience. We'll train. There are some things you can't teach: sunny optimism, warmth, positive energy. We're going to be more than a five-star hotel, Trevor, we're going to be the hotel of a thousand stars. Sparkle Factor will illuminate the Universe brighter than any hotel in the world. Got it?"

"Yes, Mr. Godfrey."

That night I lay in my hotel room wondering if Willard Godfrey was a complete lunatic. Although my theory had never been fully disproved, I quickly grew to respect him, then to admire him, and finally to worship him. His passion for the hotel business was contagious. When the steel doors of the Universe finally slid open for the first time, his vision had become a reality: the hotel was populated by a constellation of star employees from all walks of life, all cultures, and all levels of experience, with one thing in common: Sparkle Factor.

"So I'll send you his résumé this afternoon," said Sandy, jolting me from my thoughts.

"Sorry?"

She wrinkled her brow. "You okay, Trevor? You seem off."

I gave her a look of incredulity. "I *am* off, Sandy. Are you in denial or just completely insensitive? Mr. Godfrey *died* yesterday." An elderly couple at the table next to us turned their heads, and I lowered my voice. "I can't bring myself to just go on about my business as though nothing happened. Unlike you!"

She looked hurt. "We talked about this. We agreed to set our grief aside for personal times and forge onward like Mr. Godfrey would have wanted. Guests don't need to suffer along with us. The Universe is a happy place." Her face contorted suddenly and a tiny sob escaped from her mouth, then instantly she regained her composure and smiled.

"Sandy, did you just—?"

"Yes, Trevor?" She cocked her head, still smiling, and blinked.

"Oh, nothing." Was I crazy or had I just witnessed a three-second breakdown? She was sitting with her elbows on the table, smiling through her arched fingers, her palms pressed so tightly together I could see blood seeping through her bandages.

"Did something happen to your car?" I asked.

She gave me a puzzled look. "No. Why do you ask?"

"I thought I heard you on the phone…" Her smile was flashing on and off like a faulty light bulb. "Oh, nothing." I glanced around, shifting in my seat. "Sure is busy in here."

"'Central orbit to the worlds of shopping, theater, and business,'" she said, quoting the hotel brochure. She leaned back in her chair and started air smoking, a nervous habit she had acquired after quitting smoking while pregnant with Kaitlin, claiming that going through the motions kept her from doing the real thing. Resting her elbow on the back of her hand, she touched two fingers to her lips and inhaled, then tilted her head back, closing her eyes languidly as though savoring nicotine. A clump of hair had escaped from her tight chignon and was blowing at her forehead, propelled by one of the hotel's mysterious wind channels. No doubt, Sandy was out of sorts. Her behavior was bizarre and unsettling.

"Your mom in town yet?" she asked.

"Thursday night. But I'm thinking of calling her again and insisting she cancel. It's too crazy here."

"I don't blame you. Mine lives in Salt Lake and I haven't seen her since Kaitie was born. Sometimes I get so busy I forget she exists. Is she staying here?"

I nodded. "Mr. G comped her suite for the week."

"Nice." Our meals arrived, and Sandy stabbed a knife into her egg, watching the yolk bleed yellow. "Trevor, I need to talk to you about something." She hesitated, gathering her thoughts. "I feel guilty scheming so soon after ... you know ... but I'm worried that if we don't act quickly, it might be too late. I'm pretty sure I know what Mr. Godfrey had planned for us. In fact, he stopped just short of telling me last week over lunch. He asked me what I envisioned for the future of the Universe. He seemed to really like my ideas. I'm sure you can guess what I said."

I looked up in mid-chew, my heart warming. "Probably," I said. At least I had Sandy on my side.

"We've earned it, haven't we?"

"We?"

She lifted her napkin and dabbed the corners of her mouth. "Me as general manager, you in the newly created position of director of operations."

I almost choked on my Shrimp Neptune. "*You* want to be general manager?"

"You sound surprised. I've wanted this for a while now, Trevor. I've got it all figured out. I'm certain that Mr. Godfrey intended to let Matthew go in the New Year, so I have no problem following through with his wishes. He's not happy here anyway. Maybe NASA will take him back. Matthew and Marline will move out, and Jack, the kids, and I will move in. I'll promote you to director of operations, and the two of us will run the show. Doesn't that sound fantastic? We'd make a great team, wouldn't we?"

"But—but I thought Jack was pressuring you to spend less time at work, not more."

"Ironically, living here would allow me to spend more time with my family. Jack freaked when I told him. 'You want our kids to grow up in a *hotel*?' he cried. 'In *Manhattan*?' Better than a suburb in Jersey, I said. And this isn't just any hotel. What an incredible environment in which to raise kids! It's cosmopolitan and safe, in a good neighborhood, with a constant influx of intriguing people. It's like a miniature city, a microcosm of everything that's good in society. Plus, of course, the perks wouldn't hurt. Jack hasn't sold a painting in over a year, and money hasn't exactly been flowing lately. I still haven't had the heart to tell him our Christmas bonuses were put on hold pending the success of the VOID conference. We bought presents on spec this year, assuming I'd get the same amount as last year or more." She leaned toward me. "There's nothing to worry about, right? I mean, preparations for the conference are on track, and you managed to charm Brenda Rathberger into submission?"

"Well, not exactly," I said. "She's quite volatile, possibly even unstable. Things were on track, then I escorted her down to P4 and introduced her to a cadaver. She fell to pieces. I've tried to call her, but she doesn't answer her phone, even though the motion sensors tell me she's in her suite. Besides, even if the conference is a success, how do we know for sure that Cynthia will follow through on her father's promise and distribute our bonuses?"

"She wouldn't dare!" Sandy cried, her expression transformed by the dire possibility. She pushed her plate away, her meal only half-eaten, and sat back to resume air smoking. "All the more reason to secure our positions before she makes any stupid decisions. So, what do you think? You and me, a team?"

I bobbed my head up and down enthusiastically, concealing my disappointment. I loved Sandy, but did I want to relinquish my own ambitions for hers? I didn't think so. Suddenly, three of us—Sandy, Matthew, and I—were pitted against one another for the same position. Our fate lay in the hands of Cynthia Godfrey, who, I suspected, had designs of her own for the future of the Universe.

After lunch, Sandy and I went to Jupiter Ballroom for the general staff meeting. We positioned ourselves at the entrance, standing on opposite sides of the ballroom doors to welcome staff. Just prior to 1:00 PM they began pouring in, kitchen staff in starched white uniforms and chef hats, guest services agents in lycra body suits, restaurant staff in tuxedo shirts and bow ties, banquet staff in black vests and dress pants, chambermaids in white blouses and black skirts, and sales and administration staff in business attire. Many stopped to chat with us, sharing heartwarming stories about Mr. Godfrey, shedding tears, hugging us, and crying on our shoulders. At 1:30 PM we closed the ballroom doors.

Eight hundred chairs had been arranged in precise linear rows facing a podium on the stage at the front, where a large portrait of a smiling Willard Godfrey rested on a chair surrounded by flowers. Sandy and I parted ways, taking seats on opposite sides of the aisle. I sat down a few rows from the front and turned to survey the room. Hundreds of sad faces stared back at me. Across the ballroom, employees were reaching across chairs to hug one another, some weeping openly, others sitting quietly and dabbing their eyes, still others standing before the portrait to pay their respects. The grief in the room was almost palpable. How ironic, I thought, that this beautiful ballroom built by Mr. Godfrey had been transformed into his funeral parlor.

There was something beautiful in all this sadness, a sense of camaraderie among colleagues who had worked so hard to make the hotel a success and now assembled to pay final respects to our leader. I began to worry that Matthew wouldn't be able to speak to the grief and expectation in the room. I wondered if I should have helped him with his speech after all.

At that moment, the ballroom doors were flung open, and Matthew appeared. Tall and erect, arms swinging, he marched down the aisle as though an orchestra of trumpets had signaled his arrival. Eyes fixed on the wall ahead, he ignored the stares of people around him and went directly to the stage. How unlike Mr. Godfrey he was, who had always worked the room like a politician.

Onstage, Matthew paced back and forth, head down, and muttered to himself. After a few minutes, he stopped pacing and approached the microphone. "Would everyone please take your seats," he said, his voice booming across the room. Like a cat waiting to pounce, he followed them with his eyes, head unmoving, as they scurried to their seats like frightened mice.

Someone started shushing, and the room fell silent.

Matthew's face was twitching. His knuckles were white against the podium. "Thank you all for coming," he said. The microphone screeched, emitting ear-piercing feedback. He swatted it, as though a bee had stung him. It screeched even louder.

We had to cover our ears.

The feedback settled after a moment, and Matthew began. "Today ... today is a sad day in the Universe. By now, you all know that Willard Godfrey was killed in a hit-and-run accident early Sunday morning."

There was a chorus of gasps, as though people had heard the news for the first time.

Under the heat of the star lights above, beads of sweat were forming on Matthew's forehead. He took out a handkerchief and mopped his brow. "We are, of course, very upset by the news," he said. "We will miss him dearly. But Christmas is in five days, and after that we have an important conference due to check in. Then it's New Year's Eve, our busiest night of the year. So we must keep our chins up, our upper lips stiff, our noses to the grindstone, and soldier on. We must, as Cassandra James likes to say, *keep on smiling.*"

People squirmed in their seats. I glanced over at Sandy, who looked mortified.

Matthew added quickly, "Of course, this will be most difficult, since Mr. Godfrey's death is a tragedy of immense proportions." He stared into the crowd and blinked stupidly. "I want you all to know that ... we *care* ... we care about ... what happened ... and how it may impact your employment here at the Universe."

There were more gasps, whispers of alarm.

"We're also *concerned.* Yes, we're very *concerned* about the suspicious nature of Willard Godfrey's death, since it occurred on hotel property as he was leaving our staff party. Needless to say, we're offering the New York Police Department our full cooperation. We're also c—co—ca—cu..."

I regarded Matthew in disbelief. He was behaving like a blathering fool! How could he screw up so badly? *Committed!* I wanted to cry out. We're *committed* to ensuring the Universe runs just as beautifully as it did when Mr. Godfrey was alive! But he stood frozen behind the podium, mouth open, eyes panicky, searching the ballroom as though looking for cue cards. He stepped back and mopped his brown again, hands shaking.

There was absolute silence in the ballroom.

I sat on the edge of my seat. Should I rush up and rescue him? What would I say? I glanced over at Sandy, who was sitting rigid in her seat, her mouth open in a look of shock. Behind her, Shanna Virani was staring down at her nails, a mildly bemused expression on her face. Neither looked prepared to assist. I turned back to Matthew. His eyes moved to the exit, and for a moment I feared he would bolt from the room. He scanned the crowd again, his gaze halting a few rows behind me. His eyes glazed over, as though he might faint. I turned in my chair to see what had caught his attention and spotted Nancy Swinton sitting primly in his direct line of vision, a faint smile of encouragement on her face. Next to her sat Gaetan Boudreau, front office manager. Matthew seemed to have locked eyes with Nancy.

Feeling a pang of jealousy, I coughed loudly.

The spell was broken. Matthew tore his eyes away. He inhaled deeply, and a high-pitched, anxiety-ridden whine escaped from his throat. "I am so very sorry," he said. "I had hoped to be more eloquent. This is very difficult for me. Willard Godfrey was a colleague and dear friend. I, like so many of you, am shattered by his death ... I regret that I have failed to convey the admiration and respect I have for this great man."

There was a collective sigh in the room. Heads nodded.

"We have arranged for grief counselors in the Uranus and Neptune suites this afternoon between 2:00 and 5:00 PM. I urge you to see them, and to take as much time as you need. Your managers will ensure your work is covered. I myself will be first in line."

The crowd chuckled softly.

Matthew seemed to be regaining his confidence. "I spoke with Cynthia Godfrey only a few minutes ago and extended heartfelt condolences on behalf of all of you. I told her how much we loved her father and will miss him dearly. She was most grateful. She had one simple request, something she knew her father desired deeply, and I promised to grant this request. She wanted me to share this news with all of you today, which she hopes will give you comfort and reassurance at this difficult time."

The crowd leaned forward in anticipation.

Matthew straightened his posture and adjusted his tie, then, lifting his chin and puffing out his chest, as though anticipating applause, he announced, "Cynthia Godfrey has appointed me general manager of the Universe."

5

Not the Brightest Star in the Universe

It was a sleepless night. I tossed in bed, tormented by my thoughts, the clanking and hissing of the radiator seeming to vocalize my anxiety. Until now, my world had revolved around the hotel. Like a planet circling the sun, I had made work life the center of my universe, using Mr. Godfrey as a source of inspiration and encouragement, as a means of keeping me grounded. Now that he was gone, it felt like the center of gravity had melted away, and I was spiraling out of control with no direction or purpose.

The prospect of working at the Universe without Mr. Godfrey, with Matthew Drummond in his place, was unappealing. But what alternative did I have? The hotel had sponsored my green card to allow me to work in the United States. Another hotel might be willing to sponsor me, but that could take months; in the meantime, I would be forced to return to Vancouver, where I had floundered in my career, where I had grown increasingly distant from family and friends, where no one understood me. I had no desire to take that step backward in time, which left me little choice but to remain at the hotel and find my place in the new order, at least for now. More than anything I wanted to restore the balance, to recapture that comfortable place in life that Willard Godfrey had helped me to create. If that meant vying for the number two position under Matthew Drummond, then so be it.

Was I really ready to settle? Did I have to accept a decision dictated without consulting me or the others without a fight? If, as Matthew claimed, Cynthia was merely following her father's wishes, I felt used and betrayed by him. Mr. Godfrey had sold me out. After years of hard work and unwavering dedication, I had earned this promotion. While simultaneously courting me, dangling the possibility of promotion before me, inciting me to work even harder, it appeared that he had dangled the same carrot before Sandy, possibly even before Matthew as well. How could he have been so ambiguous? Or had he deliberately pitted us against one another in order to maximize our output? It didn't seem like Mr. Godfrey, but I was beginning to question many of my assumptions about the old man.

If only there was a paper trail that documented his plans. But Mr. Godfrey wasn't one for business plans, for contracts or flow charts or even letters. He disdained anything that required writing and reporting; his preferred mode of communication was verbal. He was highly secretive about certain aspects of the operation and was wary of documenting sensitive information. Even so, there had to be something—a letter, a computer file, a few notes scribbled on a pad—that alluded to his plans. If I was able to produce evidence that Mr. Godfrey intended to promote me rather than Matthew, would Cynthia reconsider?

It was worth a shot. I threw off my covers and headed for the shower.

★ ★ ★ ★ ★

It was just past 6:00 AM when I passed my disc over the scanner at the entrance to the Executive Offices. There was a soft click, and I pushed the door open. I saw a beam of light shining beneath the door of Willard Godfrey's office and made my way over, thinking Susan had left a light on.

Halfway there, I stopped in my tracks.

There were noises coming from inside Mr. Godfrey's office. Drawers being opened and slammed shut, papers rustling, items being shifted around. An overzealous night cleaner? Not likely. My pulse quickened. Taking a deep breath, I slowly turned the doorknob. Then I stopped. What if it was Willard Godfrey? I envisioned him flinging open the door and standing before me as I last had seen him: face ghostly white and streaked with blood, the side of his head caved in. "Trevor, ol' boy!" he would cry. "How would you rate my Sparkle Factor *now?*" I almost turned and fled.

But a voice stopped me. "Fucking hell!"

It was a familiar voice, a female's, but I couldn't quite place it. I put my ear against the door. An item crashed to the floor. How dare she—whoever she was—rifle through Mr. Godfrey's office! That's what I was there to do. Emboldened by indignation, I banged on the door.

"Hello? Who's in there?"

All sounds ceased.

Suddenly the door flew open, and Cynthia Godfrey was standing before me. "What the fuck?"

"Cynthia! I'm terribly sorry. I didn't know it was you."

"You scared the hell out of me!"

"I thought you were a prowler."

"Do I look like a prowler?"

I looked her up and down and decided that no, she didn't look like a prowler. She was dressed in a tight black sleeveless turtleneck that stopped just above her pierced bellybutton, faded low-rise blue-jeans, and a large white leather belt with a silver buckle decorated with rhinestones that spelled RICH CHICK. At twenty-eight years old, she had a thin, delicate face—quite pretty, in fact, save for a voluminous nose that, according to Shanna Virani, had already been downsized twice. Her boobs were so big and bouncy and fake they almost touched her chin. Her hair was long and feathered and bleached platinum, revealing an inch of black roots at her part that matched her thick black eyebrows. These features, combined with an upper lip that curled into a perpetual sneer—the result of a collagen treatment gone wrong—gave her the overall appearance of an eighties-era porn star.

Glancing past her shoulder, I saw files and papers strewn all over the floor. Chairs were overturned, drawers open. Mr. Godfrey's office was trashed. "My god, what are you doing in here?" I asked.

"Going through my father's stuff. Got a problem with that?"

"Of course not," I said quickly. I tried to conceal my irritation. Cynthia was foul-mouthed, crass, and confrontational. She dispensed with the niceties on which the Universe was built—the please-and-thank-yous, the sorry-to-bother-yous, even the hellos and good-byes—and blurted out thoughts and demands like a three-year-old child. She was universally disliked at the hotel, save for Matthew Drummond, perhaps, who once remarked, "Her bad-ass attitude is positively refreshing amongst all the lackeys and ass-kissers." I myself felt more sympathy for her than anything. I suspected that her behavior was deliberate. In an environment so concerned with decorum and politesse, her candor attracted attention—far more attention than her workaholic father was at liberty to provide.

"Can I help you find something?" I asked.

"I'm looking for momentos," she said.

"Momentos?"

"Photos and letters and stuff. I'm putting together a collage for the memorial service."

"Oh, you mean *mementos*." I felt shame wash over me. Here I was, breaking into her father's office to pilfer private documents to advance my career, only to find his poor, grieving daughter searching for items by which to remember him. "I'm so sorry to disturb you," I said. "I'll leave you to it." I turned to leave.

"I don't mind," she said.

There was a hint of desperation in her voice, like she didn't want to be left alone. I regarded her pale blue eyes, half-crazed, pupils enormous, as though in a permanent state of shock. It was an odd time of day to encounter Cynthia Godfrey, who rarely surfaced before noon. I wondered if she was so distraught she had been up all night. In fact, she was dressed as though having just arrived from a club. A faint smell of cigarettes and stale alcohol lingered in the air. My heart melted. The poor girl probably couldn't sleep.

"Do you want me to stay?" I asked.

She shrugged, as if it were inconsequential, but stepped aside to allow me to enter.

I walked in and looked around. Mr. Godfrey's office was identical in size and shape to Matthew's, but far more cozy and welcoming. The furniture was contemporary but comfortable, and there were many places to sit: a semi-circular mohair sofa, three blue Swan chairs, four Mirra chairs, and a faux rabbit-fur chaise longue. At the far end of the room, an oval table finished in silver laminate served as a desk; next to it was a matching armoire. On the floor, a computer monitor had been overturned, its screen cracked. Behind the desk, a wall of windows overlooked the hotel gardens. The walls to the left and right were crowded with framed awards and accolades: three AAA Five-Diamond Awards, two Mobil Four-Star plaques, a Hotelier of the Year award, an honorary master's degree from Cornell, and a platinum imprint of the cover of *Universal Values,* Mr. Godfrey's book.

"So, my dear," I said, turning to Cynthia. "How are you holding up?"

"I'm okay."

"I didn't expect to see you so soon—thought you'd lay low for a while."

"Yeah, well ... it's not much fun moping around at home."

"I guess not." I crossed the room, slipping on a piece of paper along the way and almost tumbling to the floor. "Mind if I tidy up a bit?" I asked, stooping down to gather up papers. Cynthia watched me for a moment, looking like she might tell me to stop, then began helping me. Each paper I picked up I scanned furtively, then stacked in a pile on Mr. Godfrey's desk. There was little of interest to me—countless reports, articles printed from the Internet, guest correspondence, copies of *Hotelier* magazine, *Omni,* and *Astronomy.* Within a few minutes I could see the carpet again, but I had found nothing.

I stood up and eyed a stack of papers crammed into a folder on the far side of the desk. Cynthia seemed to be guarding them, buzzing around them like an angry bumblebee anytime I got close. The folder did not appear to contain "momentos," but letters and documents. I tried to put it out of my mind; I could come back for it later.

"Cyndy," I said, dusting off my hands and taking a seat in one of the Swan chairs, "I want you to know how much I loved your father. He was a great man. I've never met anyone like him who—"

She held up her hand. "Trevor, please. Don't. I'll cry."

"I'm sorry. I didn't mean to upset you."

"Yeah, well, don't flatter yourself. I seem to burst into tears every three seconds." She crossed the room to the armoire and opened its doors, crouching down to dig around, her search punctuated by grunts and curses. After a moment she let out a cry of triumph and stood up, holding up a dusty bottle of Johnnie Walker Black Label

Scotch. "I was hoping it was still here." She pulled an ice cube tray from the mini-refrigerator, found two rock glasses and filled them with ice, then poured each glass half-full. She handed one to me.

I made a face. "I couldn't." It was barely 6:30 AM, and I wasn't a Scotch drinker at the best of times. But she looked hurt by my refusal, and I decided it would be only polite to accept. I peered down at the tawny liquid, my stomach lurching.

"To my father," she said, clinking her glass against mine.

"To your father."

I took a sip. It felt like fire ripping down my throat and scorching my belly, yet the sensation was not entirely unpleasant. I took another sip and grinned conspiratorially at Cynthia. Drinking before sunrise on a Tuesday morning. I had hoped that my company would give her comfort; in turn, I was surprised to find her presence a comfort to me.

"I love Scotch in the morning," she said, rounding the desk to take a seat in her father's chair. She kicked off her shoes and curled up in the seat, sticking out her tongue to lap Scotch from the glass like a kitten drinking milk.

I pulled my chair closer. "Tell me, Cyndy," I said, emboldened by the Scotch, "have you given any thought to the future of the Universe?"

She licked the side of her glass. "Nope."

"I see." I paused. "Do you intend to make Matthew's promotion permanent?"

"What promotion?" Her voice betrayed only passing interest; she seemed far more intrigued by the Scotch. She stuck her finger in her glass, swirled it around and licked it.

"His promotion to general manager," I said.

"Who promoted him?"

"You did!" My mouth dropped open. "Are you saying you didn't?"

She scrunched her face up, as though trying hard to recall. "Oh, yeah. I think I asked him to keep things running yesterday."

"Keep things running? That's a far cry from promoting him to general manager! He announced to staff that you asked him to take over! Can you *believe* his audacity?"

She shrugged. "Relax, Trevor. Don't go getting your knickers all in a knot. I can't remember exactly what I said."

I swallowed hard, recalling how infuriating her lackadaisical attitude had been during her stint as an employee of the Universe. On a number of occasions I had been overcome by the urge to throttle her.

"Somebody's gotta run this place while I figure things out," she said. "Might as well be Matthew."

The glass was shaking in my hand. I took a generous swig. "What do you mean 'figure things out'?"

The image of Cynthia Godfrey seated in her father's chair was unsettling enough without having to listen to such nonchalance. Was this a peek into the future? I shuddered to think it. Who would be worse as general manager, Cynthia or Matthew? It would be a close competition, but no doubt Cynthia would win. She would move her office up to Stratosphere Nightclub and hire all her Rich Chick friends to replace us, turning the Universe into her private nightclub, running it into the ground in a matter of weeks.

"I hope *you* aren't planning to take your father's place?" I blurted out, unable to help myself.

"Trevor, you moron. You of all people know I fucking hate the hotel business. Remember how useless I was when I worked here? I couldn't even figure out how to answer the switchboard after two weeks of training. You're the only asshole who had the balls to tell me straight that there was no hope. I may be dumb, but I'm not so dumb that I think I could run a hotel. Daddy worked his butt off here. I don't like working. It's too hard. Working is, like, too much work." She giggled at her own wit.

I breathed a sigh of relief. "For the record, you weren't *completely* hopeless."

She raised an eyebrow.

"Okay, maybe you were." In fact, Sandy and I had attempted to rate her Sparkle Factor and came up with the number zero—for the first time ever. "I realize it may be too late, Cyndy, but I'd like to put my name forward for consideration as general manager."

She scrunched up her face. "You?"

"Yes, *me*. Your father had been mentoring me to take over for years. He told me once that I possessed all the key qualities required of a gen—"

"What do you do here again?"

"Pardon me?"

Her eyes widened when she saw my outrage. "Front desk manager?" she ventured.

I gritted my teeth. During her employment at the hotel, Cynthia had reported directly to me—or at least she did after every other department head had run screaming in the other direction. Unlike the others, I had gone to great pains to try to shape her into something worth keeping, to eke out even the slightest glimmer of competence. First I tried her on the front desk, which proved disastrous (among other things, she refused to look people in the eye). I moved her to reservations, where she refused to quote anything but full rates and argued with callers when they didn't want suites. Next I installed her at the switchboard, where she insisted on calling guests by their first names. Finally, I shipped her off to housekeeping, where one day I found her not making a bed but lying in it. Each move drew her further away from direct guest contact.

Though clearly hopeless, I knew she wasn't quite as stupid or rude or incompetent as she pretended to be; she simply had no interest in working, and resented her father forcing her. Over a period of three months I persevered, giving up only when she simply stopped showing up for work. And how did she repay me? She couldn't even remember my position.

"I'm the director of rooms," I replied icily.

"Right." Her tone implied that she knew all along and was only testing me, but clearly she had no concept of the position. "How old are you, anyway? Like, twelve?"

"Much older than you. I'll be thirty-seven in March."

"You seem really young."

It didn't come across as a compliment. "Listen, Cyndy. Your father was planning big changes when he died. He was going to retire, and I'm positive he was going to appoint me general manager. Didn't he discuss his intentions with you?"

"My father didn't tell me anything except that I was a failure. I don't know what you're trying to pull, Trevor. Matthew already told me Daddy was going to appoint *him* as general manager, not *you*."

"Matthew is a *liar*! Your father was planning to fire him! He's a useless twit!"

"*I* think he's very intelligent, and pretty damned hot for an old guy. If he can fly a rocket to space, he can run this hotel."

"Matthew was a *passenger* on that shuttle, Cyndy, *once*, and he was never invited back." I told her about the email message I had received from her father requesting a meeting. "I'm sure there's documentation around here somewhere to prove his intentions. If we have a quick look around, maybe—"

"Nobody's going through my father's things but me."

"It's a little late for that," I snapped, feeling mean-spirited. "The police went through everything yesterday."

Cynthia sat up in her chair. "They were *here*?"

"Yup."

"Fuckers. No wonder I can't find anything."

"I doubt they would have taken photographs and personal letters or 'momentos.'"

She sighed, as if suddenly I was boring her.

"I assume you know about the bonuses he promised," I said. "I myself was up for at least—"

"Matthew already told me that too, so save your breath. I intend to honor my father's intentions."

"Oh. Good. Well … thank you." I hesitated. "Does that include retaining ownership? Matthew seems to think you plan to sell the hotel. You realize if that happens we'll all be fired?"

"Don't worry your pretty little head, Trevor. I have no intention of selling." She tilted her glass and licked the last drops of Scotch, then got up to pour more.

"Whatever you decide, Cyndy, I want you to know that you can count on me. If you give me the opportunity to run this hotel, I promise I won't disappoint. I may be young, but I've always dreamed about becoming a general manager, and the Universe—well, it's the best in the world. It's not about age, it's about experience, and attitude, and Sparkle Factor, and—"

She looked up from the Scotch she was pouring. "You're Canadian, aren't you?"

"Yes. What does that have to do with anything?"

She made a face. "Thought so."

"What's that supposed to mean?"

"Nothing." She held up the Scotch bottle. "More?"

"No, thank you. No one works harder than me, Cyndy. I'll make you proud—and rich, very rich! I started in this business fifteen years ago, back in Vancouver, and I've worked in virtually every department in a hotel. I'm great with guests, and I always make sure I—"

"Jesus, Trevor, this isn't a job interview. We haven't even buried my father and you're trying to push your way into his job! Have you no shame?"

My face burned with embarrassment. "I didn't mean to be insensitive. I just worry about—"

"Let's see how Matthew does, okay? If he fucks up, then we'll consider the alternatives." She carried the Scotch bottle over to me and poured more in my glass. "Sound fair?"

I sighed, watching the glass fill up to near the rim. "Sounds fair."

She looked up at me. "Fucking asshole."

By the fond expression in her eyes I assumed this was a term of endearment. "I'm sorry," I said. "I'm very passionate about my work. I'm concerned about the future of the Universe."

"'The future of the Universe,'" she mimicked in a mocking tone, putting the Scotch bottle back in the armoire. "What a stupid name for a hotel. My father had such grandiose ideas. What a goddamned egomaniac! An egomaniac *and* a nutcase."

I bristled. "*I* think the name is brilliant. It captures the essence of—"

"Blah, blah, *blah!*" she shouted, silencing me. She went to the window and set down her glass, then picked up a silver-framed photograph of herself posing arm in arm with her father and mother at Niagara Falls. She held it up to the light, frowning like it was a crossword puzzle. "I remember when this was taken," she said, lowering her voice to a whisper. "It was about six years ago. A stranger took it, and I was terrified we were all going to topple backwards into the falls.

Might as well have happened. We should have all died then and gotten it over with. Christ, if we had known all the misery that lay ahead, we would have jumped. First Mom died, then Daddy. It's just me now." She flipped the photograph over and showed it to me. "See us smiling? See how happy we look?"

I nodded slowly.

She turned it back over and caressed her father's image. "Daddy was always smiling. No matter what was going on, no matter how bad things got, he always smiled. Ever notice that?"

I nodded again. My lower lip began to tremble.

Her tone grew angry. "No matter how completely *fucked up* everything was, he still smiled." She lifted the photograph and flung it across the room. It smashed against the armoire and fell to the floor in pieces. She turned to me, eyes fierce. "Did you see him down there? Did you? Lying dead on that cold cement? He was smiling, Trevor, *fucking smiling!* Stone cold dead, yet he was smiling as though everything was *just fine*. A fitting end to that fucking bastard! I hope they burn those falsies with him."

Alarmed, I stood up and went to her. "Cynthia, I'm sorry."

She pushed me away and stormed over to the armoire, kicking at the broken glass. Throwing her hands in the air, she slammed her fists against the armoire, then cried out in pain. Her eyes scanned the room ferociously, as though in search of something to pounce on—something softer and more pliable. Frightened, I backed toward the door.

Then, as quickly as her tantrum had begun, it ended. She fell onto the chaise longue, folded her arms over her chest, and started to cry.

Slowly, I made my way over, intending to sit down beside her.

"Get out of here, Trevor," she said.

"Are you sure? I can stay."

111

She sat up and wiped her eyes. "I'm leaving too. I can't stand to be in this place for another second."

"Okay. I'll walk you out."

She stood up and grabbed her coat, then went back for the folder of papers, tucking it under her arm.

"You parked on P5?" I asked her as we walked down the corridor.

She shook her head. "Police have it closed off. I'm on P1."

"Right. Tell me, did you park down there the night of the party?"

"Yeah. Why?"

"Just curious."

"I left a long time before my father, you jerk. So don't get any ideas."

As we descended the staircase, I heard a commotion in the front lobby and looked over to see Matthew Drummond and Honica Winters engaged in a heated argument. As I drew nearer, Matthew spotted me and signaled me to hurry over. Cynthia trailed behind me. On my right I saw Honica's crew, a group of five men, sprawled in the Center of the Universe, surrounded by equipment and a large camera.

"Hiya, handsome," Honica said, turning as I approached. She appeared much calmer than Matthew, who was glaring and twitching madly.

"Good morning, Miss Winters."

"Call me Honey! Everyone else does. Except my exes, that is. They call me the Antichrist." She guffawed.

Once again I was struck by the contrast between Honica Winters' tough-as-nails TV persona and her real-life persona as a goofy, older Chrissy Snow from *Three's Company*. This morning her appearance was as striking as ever: bright yellow blazer over a low-cut black blouse and a short black skirt that revealed her long, shapely legs. Her face was heavily made-up and camera-ready. Under the atrium star lights, her platinum hair glowed like it had its own light source.

"Trevor," Matthew said, gritting his teeth, "will you kindly inform 'Honey' that it doesn't matter who gave her permission to shoot here, I am in charge now and the answer is no."

"Actually, Matthew," Cynthia said, coming up from behind, "I gave her permission."

Matthew turned to her in surprise. "You did?"

"She's doing a story on my father. I thought a little filming would be harmless."

"Cyndy, how *are* you?" Honica gushed, stooping down to air-kiss each cheek. "It's so *good* to see you. How *are* you holding up, you poor little dear? Now, tell me you've changed your mind about an interview!"

Cynthia shook her head. "My father loved the camera, not me."

Honica stuck her lower lip out. "I'm disappointed, but I understand. How *are* you doing, anyway?"

Cynthia closed her eyes for a moment, as if asking herself the same question. "Okay, I guess."

"I'm glad. Well, I better get to work before my crew dozes off." Honica stuck her fingers in her mouth and whistled loudly. "Let's get a move on, boys!"

I cringed. The whistle likely woke up a half-dozen guests in the balcony rooms above.

"Thanks so much, Cyndy," Honica said, grasping both her hands and smooching them. She turned to me and glanced at my nametag. "Lovely to see you again, Trevor. Thanks again for the suite. I love, love, *love* it! Rasputin couldn't be happier." She turned to Matthew, her nostrils quivering as though detecting a bad smell. "Matthew," she said curtly, then spun around and clipped across the lobby.

Matthew was seething. "With all due respect, Cynthia," he said, his tone suggesting that little respect was due, "I request you refrain from compromising my authority like this in the future."

"Relax, Matthew. She's harmless."

"Harmless? The woman is a hyena. She rips her victims open, exposes their insides, and eats them alive on national television!"

"Drama queen," Cynthia said with a smirk.

"I'm serious! She interviewed me about a year after *Endeavour* and within minutes she had reduced me to tears. Thank *god* NASA forced the network to kill the story." He looked down at the file folder she was holding. "What brings you here this morning?"

"I'm collecting momentos for a collage."

"Momentos?" He gave her a puzzled look.

I noticed that Cynthia hadn't removed anything from the office but the file folder.

"Have you set a date for the funeral?" Matthew asked.

Cynthia nodded. "Friday at 1:00 PM. Church of St. Ignatius Loyola on the Upper East Side."

"On Christmas Eve?" I said, surprised.

She nodded. "It was the only available time. The church is a few blocks from my townhouse, and Daddy and I went there together a few times. Matthew, can I ask you to say a few words?"

Quite clearly she hadn't heard Matthew's speech yesterday.

"Of course," he replied, swelling with importance—though his expression looked anxious.

"I'm having him cremated," Cynthia said, looking away, as though overcome with emotion. "I'm storing his ashes for a few months. He stipulated in his will that his remains are to be sent into space on a rocket. Everything is prearranged."

"You're not serious," said Matthew.

"I am."

I smiled inwardly. At last, Mr. Godfrey would fulfill his lifelong desire to travel in space.

A loud clomping sound caused us to turn toward the elevators, where a stout, pear-shaped woman wearing a huge white parka, green knit hat, and white plastic boots was making her way across the lobby.

"My god," Matthew muttered, "how do these people get in here?" If it were up to him, only rich, attractive, and stylish people would be allowed into the Universe.

"That's Brenda Rathberger," I said, "head of the VOID conference. You should meet her, Matthew."

"Must I?" he whined.

I looked over to Cynthia, hoping she had picked up on his attitude—yet another reason why he was unfit to run the hotel. But she too was regarding Brenda with trepidation.

"That woman is *stalking* me," she said. "She's called five times in the past twenty-four hours. She desperately wants *me* to speak at her conference in place of my father."

Brenda Rathberger spotted me and lumbered over.

"What in god's name is she wearing?" Matthew hissed. "Is she heading out to the slopes?"

"I'm getting out of here," said Cynthia.

"Me too," said Matthew.

"Oh, no, you don't," I said, gripping Matthew's arm. "You need to meet her. It's hotel protocol."

"Cynthia Godfrey? Is that you?" Brenda called out. "Why, yes indeedy, it is! I recognize you from the papers. Saw you at the airport the other day too." She held out her hand, panting heavily. "Brenda

Rathberger, Victims of Impaired Drivers. Pleased to meet you. Did you get my messages?"

"Uh … no."

"Strange. Well, on behalf of VOID, I'd like to tell you I'm very, *very* sorry about your father. Never met him, but we spoke over the phone many times. He was quite a gentleman."

"Thank you," said Cynthia, her expression wary.

I noticed that Brenda's face looked more tanned than ever. The colors were a bit uneven and patchy, as though she had done a poor job of applying sunscreen or tanning cream. "Brenda," I said, "I'd like to introduce you to our acting general manager, Matthew Drummond."

"How do you do." Brenda shook Matthew's hand limply, but kept her eyes trained on Cynthia.

"How's everything with your stay?" I asked.

She glanced up at me and sighed heavily, shaking her head. "Not good, I'm afraid."

"Well, I gotta run," said Cynthia.

"Me too," said Matthew.

I regarded them in astonishment. They were like rats bailing ship at the first sign of trouble.

"Wait a sec," Brenda said, her hand clamping onto Cynthia's wrist. "I want you to know that if you need support to help you through this difficult time, VOID is here to help. Counseling, lawsuits, legal questions, a sympathetic ear—you name it. In fact, soon this place will be swarming with our members."

"Thanks," Cynthia said, looking cagey, "but I really don't need your help."

"I mentioned in one of my messages that I'm willing to consider you to replace your father at our welcome reception. No guarantees—

I've got quite a lineup to choose from—but I thought we could sit down for a few minutes and discuss."

"I'm really not in any frame of mind to give speeches," said Cynthia, wrenching her arm free of Brenda's grip. She turned to me, eyes pleading.

I stepped forward. "Cynthia is going through a lot right now, Brenda."

"I am fully aware of that," said Brenda, her eyes flashing me a warning to back off. She turned back to Cynthia. "A few minutes is all I need. Your father was planning to speak about recent anti-impaired driving initiatives in the hotel and restaurant industry. I thought you could talk about the tragedy of losing your father to a drunk driver. It's bound to have quite an impact."

Cynthia's mouth dropped open. "What makes you think my father was killed by a drunk driver?"

Brenda chortled. "I hate to break it to you, young lady. Believe me, I know how much it hurts. But I've been in this business long enough to know that when an accident takes place in the wee hours of the morning, especially on a weekend, alcohol likely played a role."

"Brenda," I said, "perhaps you and Cynthia can chat when she's a little less distraught?"

"That's a wonderful idea," said Brenda. "I'll call you tonight. Can I count on you Monday night?"

"No!" Cynthia cried, backing away. "You can't call me, and I won't speak at your conference! How dare you, you pushy cow!"

Brenda held up her hand. "Just asking, that's all. Remember, I'm one of the good guys. Perhaps when things settle you'll consider doing some volunteer work for us? We have two chapters in New York, one in Queens and another in Brooklyn, but I'd like to see one in Manhattan.

Donations are always appreciated too. Perhaps you'll consider a little endowment in your father's memory?"

With a huff of indignation, Cynthia turned and hurried toward the parking elevator. I watched her punch the call button repeatedly, then rush inside the moment the door slid open.

"Charming girl," said Brenda without a trace of sarcasm. "But a temper, *sheesh*! I saw her at the car rental counter at the airport Sunday morning, recognized her from the tabloids. She was taking a strip out of a poor young agent. At least I think it was her."

"Could well have been," said Matthew. "She probably drove the Weatherheads to the airport."

"Brenda," I said, "what exactly has gone wrong with your stay?"

She opened her mouth to say something, then snapped it shut, her eyes bulging suddenly. She pushed her face toward me and sniffed. "Have you been drinking? Again?"

I covered my mouth. "No! I, uh—"

"Good grief, it's not even eight in the morning!" Brenda cried. "What kind of place is this, anyway? Managers drinking at all hours. How despicable! I'm going to be honest, Trevor Lambert, I'm even less comfortable now than when I first arrived. It didn't help that I had to pay thirty-three dollars for breakfast yesterday, even with my discount. Truth is, I'm *very* concerned about that incident this weekend and how VOID will be perceived holding a conference under the very roof where a man was run down by a drunk driver! It won't sit well with delegates or donors, and I fear bad publicity may result. I am *very seriously* considering moving the conference out."

I gasped. "You can't be serious! This late in the game?"

"As I told you before, the success of this conference is paramount. You've been very kind, but I really feel like I have no choice."

"I'm sure we can make things right for you, Brenda," I said. "Give us a chance and—"

But Matthew interjected. "What a bunch of horseshit," he said.

We both turned to him in shock.

"Willard Godfrey was run down by joy riders, you silly woman," he said. "We can't be held responsible for that. Go ahead, pull your conference out. We'll sue you for every penny."

"Matthew, please!" I cried, turning to Brenda. "He didn't mean that. We are fully committed to—"

"Why, I *never!*" Brenda cried, her hand flying to her chest. "All of you, you're nothing but pretentious, pompous jerks! And a bunch of drunks at that! This settles it! I'm pulling the conference out!" She turned her back on us and marched off, clomping back across the lobby to the elevator.

I turned to Matthew, furious. "*What* were you thinking? You just lost the entire conference! Do you realize it's worth over a million dollars in revenue?"

"She's bluffing."

"She is not! I know her by now, and she's dead serious."

An expression of remorse crept over Matthew's face. He blinked several times. "Why—why would we want a group like this anyway? They're the wrong fit for this hotel. They have no money. They won't buy anything, and they'll dispute every little charge. And what if they all dress like that? It'll be the *Star Trek* convention all over again. Now that Godfrey's out of the picture, we need to be more selective about the people we allow in."

"We don't exactly have other groups banging our door down this time of year. We need the revenue desperately! Our bonuses are tied to this conference!"

"Well then, I guess you better make up with her quickly."

"Me? You're the one who messed things up."

"You're the one who has booze on his breath. That's what set her off. Besides, she likes you, I can tell. Take her up to Orbit for an expensive meal and get her tanked. That always works. Just don't bore her to tears like you do everyone else."

"She doesn't drink."

"Then take her up to a room and fuck her."

"Matthew!" I looked around, hoping no one had heard us.

"We better get to the briefing." He turned and marched toward the Cosmic Bubble.

I hurried to catch up with him. "You can't just dump this problem on me!"

"It's your call, Trevor. Do whatever you feel is necessary. Just remember, your pal Cynthia won't be pleased if she finds out you lost this conference. It might affect your ambitions to become number two. In fact, it could very well affect your future employment."

6

Lost in Orbit

"Do you think I'm boring, Shanna?"

She didn't answer. She was too preoccupied by the goings-on in Orbit. We had arrived thirty minutes earlier and, for the fifth time in as many minutes, Shanna raised herself from her seat to check the entrance for Brenda Rathberger. She glanced at her watch, sighed heavily, and splayed her long, lavender nails out before her to admire them, then turned to check her appearance in the window. Clearly, she was agitated, and her fidgeting was driving me crazy.

The longer we waited, the more fearful I was that Brenda Rathberger would not show. She could be checking out of the hotel at that very moment and taking the entire conference with her. Since the incident with Matthew yesterday morning, she had refused to speak with me. Only late this afternoon, after cornering her in the Sea of Tranquility Spa and using no small amount of obsequiousness, did I manage to convince her to join me for dinner to discuss the future of the conference. Matthew insisted that Shanna join us—"to provide a sales and contractual perspective," Shanna claimed, to which Matthew added, "And to make sure you don't bore her to tears." The remark had taken a while to sink in, and now my mind was whirling with neurotic thoughts.

It was Wednesday evening and Orbit, one of New York's finest restaurants, was as jammed full as ever. Located on the seventy-third floor, the restaurant occupied the band of steel and glass that bisected the Glittersphere like a ring around Saturn, its outer walls, floors, and ceiling comprised of glass, allowing views in all directions and giving the sensation of floating in midair above Manhattan. Décor in the restaurant was simple and elegant; virtually everything was white—linen, candles, flowers, china. The menu, prepared by celebrity chef Marco DeSoltis, was contemporary and audacious, a fusion of cultures and flavors that surprised, provoked, and sometimes outraged, yet consistently garnered rave reviews.

At the center of the dining room, a tall Afro-American woman dressed in a glittering white gown stood next to an ivory grand piano, crooning soft, bluesy music that mollified the sounds of conversation and laughter around us. An army of male service staff worked the room, their posture perfect, manners flawless, dressed in black from head to toe, stopping to pour fine wines from crystal decanters, setting down enormous plates containing tiny morsels of food, and standing at attention on the periphery of the room.

At least two dozen people with confirmed reservations were waiting in the lounge for tables. Three tables over, deep into the dining room, Mayor Bloomberg and his girlfriend Diana Taylor were dining with press secretary Ed Skyler and Senator Hillary Clinton. They hadn't managed to secure a window table. Barbra Streisand sat at a table next to them with her son, Jason Gould, and husband, James Brolin—nor had they managed to secure a window table. Nor had Donna Karan and the three very thin, very fashionable women accompanying her. The waiting list for Orbit was two months long; for a window seat it was four months. And absolutely no one jumped the list.

Except for Shanna Virani. She *always* got a window seat. Who could be more important to the Universe than her clients? she had argued to Mr. Godfrey shortly after the restaurant opened. Who drove millions of dollars in revenue into the hotel each year? How could she *possibly* entertain at an inferior table? Tonight, in consideration of the business at stake, we had been reserved the best table in the house. A half-dozen service staff hovered around, awaiting our VIP guest.

"Shanna?" I said again. "Do you think I'm boring?"

She turned to me, squinting slightly, as if emerging from deep thought—or trying to remember who I was. "Pardon me?"

"Matthew said he was afraid I would bore Brenda to tears. Is that why you're here?"

She smirked, her expression betraying either derision or fondness, or a combination of both. "Of course you're not boring, my darling. You're absolutely delightful! You have a wonderful, gentle nature that wins guests over every time."

"Sounds pretty boring to me."

"The problem is, if I may be frank—" she hesitated, carefully selecting her words—"you have little to offer beyond pleasantries and idle chitchat, remarks about the weather and staff and hotel operations." She pondered a moment. "No, boring isn't the right word. Vapid—that's better. You're a bit vapid, Trevor."

"Vapid? I am not *vapid*." I slumped back in my chair and huffed.

"I'm kidding! So sensitive! You are far from vapid, my dear. There's a simplicity about you, a naiveté, that I find enviable. Such a hardworking, dedicated fellow you are! You're a machine. I really don't know *what* we would do without you." She glanced down to her right, through the glass floor and onto the street below, where hundreds of taxis inched along Seventh Avenue.

Through the gap in her arm I could see the lights of Times Square. I looked up quickly. I found window seats in Orbit vertiginous and mildly terrifying; I feared the glass would give way and we would plummet seventy-three stories to our deaths.

Shanna was touching her hair now. She had arrived in a whirlwind of silk fabrics and French perfume, having surrendered her usual corporate garb—upon my advice (to help put Brenda at ease; I myself had removed my tie)—for a long, flowing, crimson dress like a sari. A black shawl was thrown over her left shoulder, gold bangles dangled from her wrists, and a large ruby was fastened to her neck with a silk choker. Her black, luminescent hair was so big and stiff with hairspray that it looked like a freeze-dried explosion.

Regardless of the purpose of Shanna's presence, I was happy to have her along. As director of rooms, I was rarely obligated to entertain guests and was happy not to. To spend so much time in such an intimate environment, two strangers sharing a meal only inches away from one another, made me ill at ease and edgy. I always struggled to carry the conversation. Shanna, on the other hand, could converse for days. A life of travel and adventure, of working in luxury hotels in a dozen countries, had provided her much fuel for conversation. But she was intensely private about her personal life and preferred to focus on her guests, taking a keen interest in their comfort and satisfaction, feigning fascination at their stories, connecting with each person in a unique and special way. Her popularity had helped to make the Universe one of the top-performing hotels in New York, attracting conventions, high-profile groups, and famous guests away from competitors like the Mandarin, the Ritz Carlton, and the Peninsula, and making them green with envy.

Shanna was also a clever marketer. After recruiting her from Claridge's in London, Mr. Godfrey had worked closely with her to develop the Universe Hotel's brand identity. Along the way, they hired and fired a dozen advertising agencies, until Shanna, fed up with their incompetence, appropriated the creative work for herself. She coined the phrase "a hospitality experience light years ahead of its time." When Galaxy underwent construction last year to increase seating capacity, she had a sign made up that read THE UNIVERSE IS EXPANDING ... WE APOLOGIZE FOR THE CHAOS. A recent press release she wrote was entitled "When Godfrey Created the Universe." Of all her work, in my opinion her current advertising campaign was the most brilliant: a series of advertisements featuring striking photographs of the hotel's interior accompanied by one of three simple phrases: "Living Space," "Working Space," and "Breathing Space."

Yet Shanna was not so gifted when it came to staff relations. Virani Rages were legendary in the hotel. If she received poor or inattentive service while entertaining clients, she would return after the client had departed to tear a strip out of the offending employees, often reducing them to tears. Her tactics were in blatant disregard of Universal Values, yet Mr. Godfrey, held hostage by her brilliant sales results, demonstrated more tolerance for Shanna than any other employee. She effectively drew a line in the sand only a month after the hotel opened, when a Virani Rage prompted two employees to resign on the spot. "There's something you should know about me," Shanna explained to Mr. Godfrey at the briefing the following day. "I am not a nice person. On a good day, I can conjure up maybe eight hours of niceness; on a bad day, less than two. Would you rather I reserve it for employees, who are paid for their work, or for clients, who bring in the business?" From that point forward, the Queen of the Fucking Universe was virtually untouchable.

"Where *is* that silly woman?" Shanna said. "I'm dying for a drink." It was hotel policy not to order anything, not even a glass of water, prior to the arrival of guests.

"She's not going to show," I said.

"Oh, she'll show, all right," Shanna said with a confidence I found reassuring. "I took the liberty of highlighting a few clauses in her contract and slipping it under her door."

"Did you review the group résumé?" Shanna was not a details person; she was notorious for not reading group résumés, even though they were generated by her department. Instead, she preferred to "shoot from the hip," using her magnanimous personality to get by, which occasionally got her into trouble.

"I read the contract," she replied. "That's all I need to know. I'm ready for her."

At that moment, the maitre d' presented Brenda at our table. With a sigh of relief, I stood up to greet her. "Brenda! How wonderful to see you again!"

"Trevor," Brenda said curtly, casting a vague nod in my direction.

"I'd like to introduce you to Shanna Virani, our director of sales and marketing."

"How *lovely* to meet you!" Shanna gushed. "I've heard so much about you! Here, let me take this." Brenda seemed reluctant to let go of the enormous wicker purse draped over her shoulder, but Shanna managed to extract it anyway. Setting it down beside the table, she took Brenda's hands in hers, coveting them like precious jewels. "I've been *so* looking forward to meeting you! I have enormous respect for your work. Why, look at you! What a darling little outfit!"

Brenda was wearing black stretch pants, white sneakers, and a pink sweatshirt with the words *Maui Island Mama* written across her bosom in rhinestones. I was certain that Shanna was, in fact, horrified by the outfit; had she not been our guest, she would have been refused at the door.

"My, what a marvelous tan you have!" Shanna exclaimed.

I flashed her a look to tell her to bring it down a notch, but she was too enthralled by Brenda. I glanced at Brenda, who seemed to appreciate the compliment.

"Thanks," she said. She lifted her arm to admire the tan herself, then scratched at it, flicking dead skin onto the glass floor. Only then did she appear to realize that she was standing on a sheet of glass seventy-three floors above the street. She gasped. Her eyes rolled backwards, knees buckling, and she almost fell to the floor.

I lunged forward to steady her, my heart leaping, fearing that if she fell, the glass would break.

"Goodness, all this glass," she remarked, easing herself into the chair the maitre d' held out for her.

"Isn't it marvelous?" Shanna said. "It's like we're floating above Manhattan."

This didn't seem to comfort Brenda much. "I'm not much for heights," she said.

"We can move to another table, if you wish," I offered, ignoring Shanna's reproachful stare.

"I'll be fine."

Shanna and I sat down too. I looked up through the glass ceiling. The sky was black and clear, dotted with stars that twinkled faintly.

The head waiter, Dominic, arrived at our table brandishing menus and a basket of breads, presenting them with great ceremony. He filled our water glasses.

Brenda opened her menu and licked her lips. "I'm starving."

Shanna flashed her a magnanimous smile. "Shall we dispense with business first, so we can enjoy an exquisite meal without distraction?

I understand that you're contemplating taking the conference else-where, Brenda. I must tell you now that such a movement is *completely* unacceptable."

I tensed at her words. Such an aggressive stance so soon?

But she continued, "We love you too much to lose you! I under-stand that many of our staff have taken quite a shine to you already." This was a stretch; I had received nothing but complaints about her rude behavior and outrageous demands. "Your conference is far too important to jeopardize its success with such a major last-minute change, don't you agree?"

Brenda shook her head. "I'm sorry, but my mind is already made up." She slapped the menu shut and helped herself to a wedge of fo-caccia from the bread basket, smearing it with basil-garlic butter. "I've been approached by a number of other hotels, many of which have offered substantial incentives like lower room rates, complimentary meeting space, sharply discounted food and beverage prices, compli-mentary Internet usage and local calls, and free parking. One hotel even offered to pay for our opening reception."

"How very generous of them!" said Shanna. These hotels could expect a nasty call from her in the morning. "I *do* wish we could offer such concessions, but I'm sure you understand that it's simply out of the question. Already you're getting the best hotel in New York for a fraction of the normal cost." She frowned, biting her thumbnail, as though deeply confused. "Forgive me, but I didn't think this was about money. I understood you were more concerned about the weekend's incident?"

Brenda was chewing rapidly. "As I've told Trevor, I have a number of concerns, not the least of which are the circumstances surrounding Willard Godfrey's death. I'm *also* concerned that delegates won't feel comfortable here, and that hasn't changed since the day I arrived. The other hotels are much more modest."

Shanna nodded slowly. She glanced up at Dominic, who had approached our table, and gave him a hand signal, shooing him away. "Did you have the opportunity to review the contract I sent to your room?" she asked Brenda. "I might just have a copy with me." She reached for her briefcase and withdrew a red folder, handing it to Brenda. "Correct me if I'm wrong, but I believe that's your signature at the bottom?"

Brenda gave it a cursory glance. "Yes, and the other signature belongs to Willard Godfrey. Correct *me* if *I'm* wrong, but I believe he's dead."

Shanna's mouth dropped open. Her eyes flickered. For a moment I was afraid she might burst into tears. But instead she clenched her jaw and turned to me with a half-smirk. "Perhaps, but I do believe he was alive when he signed this, was he not, Trevor?"

I nodded. "He was."

"Which makes it a legal, binding document. By my calculations, Brenda, if you withdraw your conference today, a cancellation penalty of approximately $225,000 will apply. This adds up to a lot more than a few complimentary phone calls at some substandard hotel, wouldn't you say?" Her tone remained light and cordial, as though she were discussing the pros and cons of switching laundry detergents.

Brenda's tone was much less conciliatory. "I've consulted with my lawyers, and they believe we have a solid case for cancelling without penalty. But wouldn't it be a shame to have to go to court? Trials can be so costly. Fortunately, VOID keeps a generous reserve for this very purpose, and we have a number of attorneys willing to provide work pro bono. In my experience, a judge is far more likely to be sympathetic to a humble not-for-profit organization than a fat-cat corporation like a luxury hotel. The outrageously rude treatment I received yesterday from your resident manager might be sufficient to declare this contract null and void; it certainly violates your promise that 'our world revolves around yours.' Further, not a half-hour after I arrived, Trevor here led me directly to a dead body! I was traumatized by the experience, and I'm not sure I'll ever recover. My attorneys recommend I sue for emotional suffering. I don't want to be difficult, but ..."

While Brenda ranted, her lips moving staccato-like, making the situation seem increasingly hopeless, Dominic arrived at our table brandishing a magnum of Dom Perignon. To my utter shock, he placed three champagne flutes down and proceeded to uncork the bottle. There was a loud pop, causing Brenda to start.

"Champagne!" Shanna cried, clasping her hands in rapture. "How wonderful!"

"Uh, Shanna ..." I said. Had she read the group résumé, she would have known that Brenda was not only a teetotaler but vehemently anti-alcohol. "I don't think ..."

Brenda's hand flew to her chest. She eyed the magnum as though it were a loaded gun. "I *certainly* won't be having any of *that*," she said.

"You can't *possibly* refuse good champagne!" Shanna cried. "Why, it's a crime!"

Brenda's lips tightened. "May I remind you that I'm here for an anti-impaired driving conference?"

"Darling, *please!*" Shanna said. "None of us are driving tonight, are we? I don't know about you, but I've had a horrid few days. Let's forget our troubles and enjoy some champagne. Then we'll resolve our differences. We can toast the memory of Willard Godfrey and the success of your conference." She pushed Brenda's glass toward the waiter. "Fill it to the brim, Dominic, I insist."

Dominic complied.

"No!" Brenda shouted, her voice silencing the dining room. As she shoved the glass away, it toppled over, and the stem snapped. Liquid flowed onto the tablecloth and fizzled.

"*Shanna*," I said between my teeth. "Brenda doesn't drink."

Shanna turned to me, her eyes widening. "Oh, dear."

"Dominic, can you please bring Mrs. Rathberger something non-alcoholic. A Diet Coke, perhaps?" I turned to Brenda, who nodded. "I'm so very sorry," I said to her.

"And I as well," said Shanna. "I didn't mean to offend."

"My husband died because of alcohol," Brenda said, her voice almost a whisper. She wrapped her arms tightly around herself and rocked back and forth in her chair like a swaddled mental patient, staring down at the broken glass as though her dead husband were lying there.

"Oh, dear," Shanna said, looking even more mortified. "I'm so sorry."

I squirmed in my seat as the waiter mopped up the champagne and carried the glass fragments away, then returned a moment later with a Diet Coke for Brenda. The three of us sat in embarrassed silence.

After a moment, Shanna placed a tentative hand on Brenda's shoulder, as though testing its temperature. "Do you want to tell us about it?"

Brenda sipped her Diet Coke, her eyes fixed on the table. "There's not much to tell. It was a long time ago, over thirty years. It happened the night of our first wedding anniversary. Frederick and I were driving home from dinner, and Frederick was behind the wheel. Another vehicle struck us head-on. He was killed instantly. It was a girl's fault, a stupid, drunken teenage girl. That's all there is to tell."

Shanna's hand massaged her throat like she was having trouble breathing. "How very tragic," she said, her voice raspy. "I'm so sorry for your loss, Brenda."

"Me too," I said. I felt sick to my stomach.

Brenda blew her nose into her napkin. "I'm not here to celebrate, people. I'm here to organize one of the year's most important conferences. If you treat me with such insensitivity, I can only imagine how you will treat my delegates. You think my story is sad? Wait until you hear the stories of other VOID delegates. Some of our members have lost entire families."

I glanced at Shanna. We couldn't have managed this meeting more poorly. There was no hope of saving the conference now.

"Normally, I'm not so insensitive," Shanna said. "But it's been a terrible week. We've lost someone we loved dearly. I'm sure you understand."

Brenda's eyes flickered, but she said nothing.

"As for your personal loss," Shanna went on, "I can certainly relate. I too lost my husband."

I turned to Shanna in surprise. I knew she was divorced, but I recalled Sandy saying that her ex-husband and their two children had moved from London to California after the divorce. Was there another husband? It amazed me how little I knew about many of my colleagues, despite seeing them every day.

Brenda seemed to soften. She looked at Shanna. "Is that right."

It was Shanna's turn to nod sadly and stare down the tablecloth.

Brenda reached for the bread basket but found it empty. She drained her Diet Coke and wiped her mouth with the back of her hand. "Can we order now? I'm starving."

"You still have time for dinner?" Shanna said, looking up in surprise. "I assumed you'd need to get busy coordinating the move. I suppose your programs must be reprinted, all delegates contacted, media notified. There must be a thousand details to take care of."

Brenda's brow wrinkled with worry. "Yes, there is lots to do. But I'm sure I have time for a quick bite."

Dominic approached our table. "Are we ready to order?"

"Yes, I'll have the Grilled *Venus*on," said Brenda, "and—"

"I'll need a few more minutes," Shanna informed Dominic, cutting Brenda short. Dominic excused himself, and Shanna picked up her menu and glanced through it languidly. "Now let me see... It's always so hard to choose."

Brenda's eyes followed the plates of food servers were carrying across the dining room. She licked her lips. Clearly, Shanna was deliberately delaying dinner, trying to starve Brenda into submission. It was an interesting tactic; I myself thought she might be more compliant on a full stomach.

"Well, if it isn't the handsome hotel manager!"

Honica Winters had presented herself at our table, towering over us in a tiny black cocktail dress.

I stood up. "Miss Winters, how lovely to see you!" I introduced Shanna and Brenda.

"Why, what a coincidence," said Honica. "I've been meaning to call you, Brenda. You and I were supposed to have dinner Sunday night with Willard Godfrey."

Brenda gazed up at Honica with wide eyes, seemingly starstruck. "So we were!"

"I'm having dinner right now with his daughter, Cynthia," Honica said, indicating another table down the curved window. We looked over, and Cynthia lifted her hand half-heartedly and fluttered her fingers, her trademark sneer exaggerated in the dim light of the dining room. "Listen, Brenda," said Honica, "I'm hoping I can interview you tomorrow. I'm doing this story on"—she sneaked a glance at me, then Shanna—"uh, drunk driving, and I need an expert to provide statistics. Maybe you could talk about your conference."

Brenda's face lit up. "Why, I'd be delighted to! In fact, I was thinking of calling *you*. I thought you might be interested in speaking at my welcome reception on Monday night."

Honica frowned. "I'm afraid I can't. I need to head back to Niagara for Sunday night's show."

Brenda looked crestfallen. "Could you fly back on Monday? The reception is at 6:00 PM. VOID will cover all travel costs, including paying for your room here in New York."

Honica pondered the proposition. "The show is breaking for a couple weeks ... and I never pass up an opportunity to get out of Niagara. In fact, I'm planning to come back for New Year's—maybe I'll fly down a few days early." She looked over to me. "But only if Trevor promises me a Supernova suite again."

"Unfortunately, you won't be staying here," Shanna said. "Brenda's decided to move the conference to a more moderate hotel."

"*What?*" cried Honica. "You're *not* leaving the Universe." Brenda opened her mouth to speak, but Honica interjected. "Deal's off, then. I love love *love* this hotel! I couldn't imagine staying anywhere else. This is my dog Rasputin's favorite hotel, and he is very discriminating about where he stays."

But not where he pees, I thought, wondering what little Rasputie was up to at this very moment.

"I was only contemplating moving it," said Brenda quickly. "But I've decided to stay."

Shanna and I exchanged looks of surprise.

"It's a deal, then," Honica said. "You give me an interview tomorrow, and I'll speak at your conference on Monday. I'll give you a call tomorrow. Bye guys, have fun!"

"Well!" said Shanna, breaking into an enormous grin as Honica bustled off. "I'm famished! Shall we order?"

An hour later, I escorted Brenda to the elevator and returned to the table to say good night to Shanna, only to discover that Dominic had uncorked a second bottle of champagne for her.

"Well, I'm exhausted," I said with a yawn.

"Not so fast, young man. It's still early. Sit down."

"You're not afraid I'll bore you to tears? That I'll be too vapid?"

"Stay and keep me company, Trevor. I'm not ready to go home."

She was cradling the champagne glass in her hand like a baby. In the light of the candle, her features appeared softer, more peaceful, even a bit vulnerable. I wondered if Shanna was a lonely person. It occurred to me that I wasn't in much of a hurry to get home either. I sat down.

Shanna lifted the flute and drained the contents as though guzzling a yard of beer, then reached for the bottle to replenish hers, then mine.

"You barely touched your meal tonight," I said, watching her consumption warily, thinking that a little food might be wise.

"Ugh, all this rich food. I'm so *sick* of it! I'm craving a peanut butter sandwich."

"You should make one when you get home. Otherwise you're asking for a hangover."

"I don't cook. Haven't cooked in twenty years."

"Um … you don't have to cook a peanut butter sandwich."

She held up her glass. "Here's to the end of a dreadful few days."

We clinked glasses. "You weren't your usual charming self tonight, Shanna. I've never seen you so easily riled—at least not with clients."

"I couldn't stand that horrid woman. Her cause is admirable, but her tactics are reprehensible. She manipulates people with guilt. I knew she was bluffing, simply trying to wrangle more concessions."

"I think she was serious," I said. "She never wanted to be here in the first place. She was looking for an excuse to convince her board to let her move the conference. We provided her several to choose from."

"The important thing is she's staying. Although I'm starting to wonder if we should have fought so hard to keep her. She's going to be a royal pain in the ass. Maybe we should have let her go."

"And give up so easily? That's not like you."

Shanna was silent for a moment. "I've run out of patience. I don't care anymore. I'm so tired of it all. I've been in this business for over a quarter century. My god, I'll be fifty soon!"

I knew she had turned fifty-three in November, but I let it go. I looked around the dining room, which had thinned out considerably. Honica and Cynthia were gone, and so were all the famous people. Only Shanna and I remained, and a group of Japanese businessmen.

"I'm teetering toward perpetual bitterness, Trevor. Do you know how many meals I've sat through in this restaurant? Hundreds. You know that saying, 'If cocktails and dinner isn't your idea of a pleasant evening, you probably work in the hotel industry'? It was written for me. Some of the people I've had to entertain here have been so dull I've wanted to hurl myself through this glass. Others were so obnoxious I wanted to hurl *them*. I don't have the patience anymore. Certainly not this week. If we weren't all in the same boat, Trevor, I would have taken a week or two off to recover, but circumstances have forced us to work through this horrid time, to be functioning mourners. A three-hour dinner with Brenda Rathberger was the last thing I needed. I'm drained." She sighed heavily, her eyes almost closing. "Everything is so different now. There seems to be no point."

Until now I hadn't realized how hard Shanna had been hit by Mr. Godfrey's death; she had simply seemed angrier than usual. Now I saw that she too was devastated. Yet her defeatist attitude was unsettling. "I've had a bad couple days too," I said. "But you don't see me compromising my values as a hospitality professional."

Shanna threw her head back and burst into laughter. "Listen to yourself! *'You don't see me compromising my values as a hospitality professional.'*" She stuck out her two front teeth as she said this, mimicking me in a highly unflattering manner. "You and Sandy, such little suck-ups. Willard's little stars. 'Sparkle Factor 10!' Do you know what stars are made of? Hot air and gas, light that burned out eons ago. Nothing of substance."

"I guess that makes you a comet," I said. "Solid ice."

"I prefer to think of myself as Venus." She touched her upper breast with two fingers and made a sizzling sound. "Hot!"

I couldn't help but smile. The champagne was dulling my irritability. "I guess I'm disappointed, Shanna. It's like you've given up. Mr. Godfrey would have wanted us to—"

"Godfrey, Godfrey, *Godfrey!*" she cried. "Enough! Godfrey is *dead*, Trevor! Let it go. You and Sandy worshipped him like some sort of god, toting around *An Employee's Guide to the Universe* like a Bible, devotees of the Church of Godfrey! When you deify someone like that, you're bound to be disappointed. Life is full of disappointments, Trevor."

"Can't you be more sensitive?"

"Me, *sensitive*?" She burst into laughter again. "I know what you people call me: Queen of the Fucking Universe. I don't care. I have to be a bitch to ensure my clients are taken care of. I used to care what people thought of me, wanted desperately for everyone to like me, but I don't care anymore. It's a product of age, I suppose. As long as I work hard, do a good job, and maintain my integrity, it doesn't matter what people think. It's what *I* think that matters. I come from a long line of bitches. Compared to my mother, I'm Julie Andrews. In Pakistan I grew up in the equivalent of a trailer park, except there was no trailer and no park, just a ramshackle hut in a field of dirt beside an open sewage ditch. My brother was killed by the army when I was eleven. When my father came to break the news, my mother and I were sewing dresses for the rich ladies across town. He was sobbing so hard we could barely understand him. He left us to go tell the others, and I started to cry. My mother looked at me with hatred. 'Wipe away your crocodile tears, silly girl,' she said. 'But my tears are real, Ami,' I told her. But she only spat at me and resumed sewing. I tried to compose myself, thinking she was disappointed by my weakness, and dried my eyes on the dress fabric. 'See, Ami?' I said, reaching up to take her hand and pressing it against my eye. 'No tears. I am strong like you.' 'You are not strong!' she cried, slapping my face. 'We do not cry because we cannot cry. We have no emotions. Strength lies in having emotions and controlling them. You and I, we have no heart.' I believed her. When she died ten years later, I did not cry."

I was saddened by the story, but also confused. Was she saying she was *like* her mother—void of emotion—or *unlike* her? I waited for her to explain, but she remained silent, her eyes growing distant. She was staring past my shoulder and up through the glass ceiling. I turned to follow her gaze and saw the moon in the night sky, almost full, shimmering behind a thin veil of clouds as though submerged in water. In the distance, a great chasm of darkness marked where the Twin Towers once stood.

"I never knew you lost your husband," I said.

Her eyes flickered. "I didn't. I was invoking the Fourth Universal Standard."

"You *lied?*"

"I stretched the truth a bit. I was desperately searching for a way to connect with her. For god's sake, the woman was dining in the same room as Hillary Clinton, Michael Bloomberg, and Barbra Streisand, and she barely batted an eye! She was far more interested in the bread basket. Anyway, I wasn't lying. I did lose my husband—to an adolescent Iranian trollop with breasts and lips so bloated by silicone it has seeped into her brain and rendered her mildly retarded. Ramin is as good as dead to me. He's been holding my son and daughter hostage in LA for ten years, filling their ears with propaganda about what a terrible mother I was."

"You're kidding. What a jerk."

"No. He's right. I was a terrible mother."

"Maybe if you'd cooked more than once in twenty years."

"Maybe."

"So what will you do for Christmas?"

She closed her eyes for a moment. "Who knows? Maybe I'll come into work. I did have plans, *grand* plans, but they fell through." She reached for her champagne. "Things were going far too well, Trevor. I was actually happy! But I've learned that happiness is fleeting for me, an unnatural state. Misery is much more comfortable in my company. Thank god for this job. It's all I have left."

I decided I preferred the sassy, brassy Shanna to this lonely, pathetic woman. "Did you ever consider putting your name forward for general manager?" I asked.

"Me? Oh, god no. In fact, I want the opposite. I had planned to take early retirement, but with Willard out of the picture I may have to stick around a while. I suppose you're upset by Matthew's promotion."

I shrugged, concealing my true feelings. "I would have loved the opportunity, but I'm not going to lose sleep over it."

"Take some advice from an old hag like me: lose your ambitions and get out of this business. From the outside, hotels look glamorous, and they are—but for guests, not for employees. Running a hotel is far too consuming to live a normal life. Hotels never close. You can never be a truly good hotelier *and* a good spouse, a good parent, or a well-rounded human being. You, Trevor, you're still young. Go back to school. Travel. Raise a family. Make new friends. Join a soccer league. If I could afford it, I'd get a job folding sweaters at Gap, then enroll in a fine arts program at NYU."

"But I love this business. I couldn't imagine doing anything else. It pisses me off that Matthew doesn't even like it here, yet *he* gets the job. I have a hard time believing that this was Mr. Godfrey's intention."

"Believe me, it wasn't. Matthew is lying through his teeth."

"How do you know?"

"Trust me, I know exactly what Willard had up his sleeve."

I reached for the champagne bottle and replenished her flute. "What exactly did he tell you?"

She opened her mouth to speak, then closed it. "It doesn't matter anymore, Trevor."

"Come on, you have to tell me! Why bottle it all up inside?"

"Stop it, Trevor. I don't want to talk about Willard Godfrey."

"Was he going to promote Sandy?"

"Sandy has too much on her hands right now to worry about taking on more responsibility."

"What do you mean?"

Shanna regarded me as though trying to assess if I was serious. "Isn't it obvious? Besides me, she was the only one who drove out of that parkade around the time Willard was leaving. She's been hobbling around the hotel as though she's missing all her toes, has two enormous welts on her palms, yet she's pretending nothing is wrong! The police were here again this afternoon. They didn't want to talk to anyone but her, then they took her away in a cruiser."

"*What?* She was arrested?"

"Not *arrested*—not yet, anyway. Police had come to see her vehicle, but she's been taking the train all week, so they drove with her back to Jersey. According to Matthew, they were quite perturbed to find that her husband's truck is in the shop getting damage to the front bumper fixed."

I remembered the telephone conversation I overheard. *I don't care what it costs, Jack. Just get it fixed. Today.* But Sandy had insisted she hadn't been in an accident. "You don't think ..."

"I don't know, Trevor. I love her to death, but I fear that our little Sandy Sunshine might be in trouble. The thought of her running down poor old Willard and taking off is sickening to me. I'd prefer not to think about it."

"Come on, Shanna, Sandy isn't capable of such a thing. She's far too upright and honest. She would never just take off like that. She'd seek medical attention for Mr. Godfrey and turn herself in."

Shanna raised an eyebrow. "Even if she was drunk?"

A chill ran down my spine. "Yes."

She sat back in her chair and sighed. "You're starting to bore me now, Trevor. Please go. I want to finish my champagne and wallow for a while in private."

"Fine," I said, rising from my seat. "I'm going to do a quick walk-around first. Want to share a cab?"

"I have my truck."

"You're not driving?"

She glanced at the empty champagne bottle. "Of course not. But you go ahead. I'll get my own taxi."

I pecked her on the cheek and made my way out.

★ ★ ★ ★ ★

A half-hour later, as I exited the front door and crossed the parking ramp to West Fifty-third, I was almost run down by Shanna's yellow Chevy Blazer. She honked and waved, then lurched left onto Avenue of the Americas.

Shaking my head, I turned down West Fifty-third and headed home by foot.

It was just after 11:00 PM, and the temperature was unseasonably warm. As I walked down the street, I passed people carrying bags of Christmas presents, gift wrap, poinsettias, groceries, and liquors for entertaining. I couldn't help but smile, feeling melancholy and festive from the champagne. I thought about previous Christmases with my family before my father died, when things were happy and normal. There was never much under the tree, but gifts were always appreciated and much needed. After Dad died, Christmas became a funereal affair. Mom began to schedule herself for double shifts, and my sisters and I created our own secret Christmas, furtively exchanging gifts and hiding stockings under our beds. Now, years later, living in New York, where Christmas was impossible to ignore, I understood why Mom had preferred to work. I found myself missing my sisters and mother. It cheered me to think that I wouldn't be spending it alone this year. Next year, I told myself, maybe I'll go home for Christmas, and we can all celebrate together.

When I arrived in my apartment I collapsed on the sofa, exhausted. The TV remote was sitting on the coffee table, a few inches from my grasp, but I couldn't muster the energy to reach for it. On the coffee table before me was a pile of magazines, issues of *Men's Fitness, Time,* and *Omni,* all unread, covered by a thin layer of dust. Next to the coffee table a shelf teemed with books, fiction on the top shelves and non-fiction on the bottom shelves, most dating back to my short-lived college days. I had stopped buying books after arriving in New York, growing tired of seeing them laying around unread. Now, I wondered if was time to cancel the magazine subscriptions.

My apartment was tidy, mostly due to sparseness. It desperately needed a paint job, a thorough cleaning, and a few homey touches. With its light wood, monotone furniture, and simple, symmetrical appointments, it resembled an IKEA showroom—or a hotel room. In fact, most of the furniture had been purchased at hotels' retired furniture sales. When I found this apartment so close to the hotel, even though it was drab and rundown I was delighted, having previously lived in a tiny room much farther away in the Lower East Side. Determined to make it a home, I took a week off from work, agonizing over the right paint colors, appropriate accessories, proper positioning. But my week was cut short when I was called back to work for a minor hotel emergency. Now, years later, the paint tins were still stacked in the closet along with the crown molding, the prints still leaning against the walls where I had intended to mount them.

A year ago I bought a kitten to keep me company and named him Little Sparky. But I became so wrapped up in work I kept forgetting about him, remembering only when I pushed my key into the door late at night and heard his desperate, starving mews. Six months later, a computer crash at the hotel forced me to spend three consecutive nights away. I came home to find Little Sparky sprawled in the bathtub, his little head poised beneath the tap to catch each droplet of water as it fell. I nursed him back to health, then took him to work and gave him to a room attendant who promised a better home. I retained visiting rights, but still hadn't gotten around to dropping by.

Abandoned, just like the books and magazines and decorating. Now, the last surviving life form in my apartment—besides the mold that grew in the bathtub—was dying: my three-hundred-dollar cactus stood doubled over in the corner, soon to collapse forever. Of all things, I had allowed a cactus to die of thirst.

I thought about Shanna and how sad and defeated she had seemed. Her words were those of an aging, lonely, bitter woman, I decided, not the brassy, high-powered executive she used to be. I would never let myself go in that direction. After everything settles down at the Universe, I told myself, I'll organize my books and magazines, start reading again, and buy a new cactus, more plants, and some homey things from Crate and Barrel. Then I'll paint the walls, put up the crown molding, and mount the prints. Then I'll find a girlfriend. We'll get married and have two kids. It will all be so simple and seamless and perfect.

Maybe, one day, I'll even move back to Vancouver.

7

Universal Values

Early Thursday morning, I stopped by the Milky Way on my pre-briefing rounds and was floored to find Matthew Drummond there. He was sitting alone at a table, clutching a mug of coffee and reading a copy of the *New York Post*. Not only did Matthew avoid the back of the house at all costs for fear of having to fraternize with staff, but he rarely made an appearance on-property prior to the 8:00 AM briefing.

"Are you lost, Matthew? Sleepwalking?"

"Very funny, Trevor."

Only a few employees occupied the cafeteria, all of them seated at the opposite extreme of the room. A few tables over, the shrine to Willard Godfrey had doubled in size, and flowers were spilling to the floor. I put two slices of bread in the toaster, poured a cup of coffee, and took a seat across from him. He was dressed sharply in a tailored navy suit with gold pinstripes that matched his tie. The flecks of gray in his thick black hair seemed more pronounced this morning. He kept his face buried in the newspaper, ignoring me.

"Anything about Mr. Godfrey today?" I asked.

He looked up. "Only a photo on page five of Cynthia Godfrey partying it up at an art gallery opening Tuesday night. The poor girl is really suffering."

"I wouldn't be so hard on her. She told me she can't stand being alone. This is probably her way of coping."

"Apparently partying is her answer to everything."

My toast popped up. I got up and smeared it with peanut butter. "All ready for Christmas?" I asked.

"I despise Christmas. And I despise that question even more."

"Does anyone like Christmas anymore?"

"My wife does. She's been shopping since July."

I walked back to the table and sat down. "We should pair her up with my mother. She keeps asking if I've bought tickets to the Rockettes' Christmas Show at Radio City Music Hall yet. I'm running out of excuses."

"I couldn't imagine anything more repugnant."

"Nor could I." I stuffed a wedge of crust in my mouth and washed it down with coffee. "Anything in particular bring you down here?" I asked, still baffled by his presence.

"I wanted to see if the coffee is as vile as people say." He lifted his coffee cup and swallowed what was left. "It's worse." Setting aside the newspaper, he watched me eat, a faintly contemptuous look on his face. "Truth is, Trevor, I've turned a new leaf. Godfrey's death made me realize that I'm too detached from operations. I intend to spend more time on the front lines, get better acquainted with staff."

"You realize they're the ones in uniforms? The ones sitting as far away from you as possible?"

"It'll take some time, of course. I've canceled this morning's briefing to attend a housekeeping department meeting instead. I did such a lousy job at the staff meeting that I'm going to each department to apologize personally."

"Impressive."

"*I* thought so. How did dinner with Brenda Rottweiler go last night?"

I exhaled loudly through my teeth. "Shanna butted heads with her. It was touch-and-go for a while. Ironically, it was Honica Winters who saved the day." I told him about Honica's visit to our table.

"*Honica Winters* is speaking at an anti-impaired driving conference? What, is she giving a demo?"

A trio of female reservations staff passed our table. Matthew looked up and smiled at them, but his expression came out as more of a leer. They crossed the room hurriedly and joined the others.

Matthew leaned closer me. "Did Honica talk at all about the story she's working on?"

"Not really. She asked Brenda if she could interview her. That's about it."

"She's been traipsing all over this place with that camera crew. I'm certain she's not producing the tearful tribute to Willard Godfrey that his daughter expects. How did your interview go with her, anyway?"

"My interview?"

He rolled his eyes up at me, his mouth falling partway open. "You promised to call her Monday afternoon."

"I did?" I had completely forgotten. "When I saw her with you on Tuesday morning, I assumed you had taken care of it. She doesn't seem too interested in talking to me, anyway. She wants the astronaut."

"I appointed *you*, Trevor. As general manager, I need to distance myself from scandal."

"*Scandal?*"

"Honey Winters didn't make her name narrating wildlife documentaries. Damn it, Trevor, can't I depend on you for anything? I gave you an opportunity to prove yourself, and you screwed up. You better find her before she checks out today. Otherwise, god knows what kind of conclusions she'll draw."

"Can't we just hire a new PR company?"

"No. We need a representative of the Universe to speak on our behalf, not some ditzy PR person."

I opened my mouth to protest further but could tell by Matthew's determined expression my words would be futile. "Fine," I said. "I'll do it." It would be good practice for my future as a general manager, I decided.

Matthew looked around and leaned toward me, lowering his voice. "If she asks about Sandy, just play dumb. You're good at that."

"What do you mean, play dumb?"

"Exactly. That's very good."

I felt my blood starting to boil. Clearly, Shanna and Matthew had been talking. "Sandy is innocent, Matthew," I said. "She could *never... and just take off like that."

"I don't want to believe it either, Trevor," he rasped, looking genuinely distraught. "I spoke with Detective Lim yesterday. The officious little prick refused to tell me anything, but he did confirm one important fact: the time of death was approximately 1:00 AM. I asked security to run another activity report for that period. Between 12:45 and 1:15 AM, aside from Willard, only Shanna and Sandy accessed the lower parkade. Their activities are recorded at three access points: elevator, parkade door, and parkade. As difficult as it is comprehend, we have no choice but to face the facts: it was either Shanna or Sandy. This week, Shanna has been cool as a cucumber, whereas Sandy has been hobbling around with bleeding hands and a smashed-up truck like some sort of smiling Lady Macbeth on Valium. Who looks guiltier to you? I was afraid she was going to be arrested yesterday when police dragged her off, but she's back at work this morning, humming in her office like a delusional lunatic."

"Please, Matthew, show a bit of respect." I rested my elbows on the table and squeezed my temples hard. "You really think she did it?"

He sighed. "I don't know. If she can come up with a satisfactory explanation, I'd be willing to reconsider. I'd much prefer to have Shanna hauled off to jail." He looked instantly remorseful. "I didn't mean that. I sincerely hope neither of them had anything to do with it. We'll need their help getting through this nightmare."

After Matthew's despicable behavior this week, it was heartening to see a glimmer of humanity. "I still think it was some stranger. I refuse to contemplate Sandy or Shanna." I got up to put my dishes away, then headed for the exit. At the door I turned.

Matthew was crossing the room to the table occupied by catering and reservations staff. He stood before them with hands in his pockets, looking awkward and sheepish, mouthing a few words I couldn't hear. They looked confused for a moment, then they smiled and slid down to make room for him.

Matthew was making new friends.

At 9:00 AM I went to the operations meeting, then straight to my office to call Honica. There was no answer in her room. I left a message to contact me as soon as possible. Then I went looking for Sandy.

I caught up with her as she was descending the staircase to the lobby. "Sandy! Good morning! Still limping?"

"I'm *not* limping, Trevor."

"If you say so. Listen, is everything okay? I hear police have been badgering you."

She stopped on the stairs and turned to me, a perplexed, slightly irritated look on her face. "Badgering me? Detective Lim has been a perfect gentleman. I don't know where you're getting your information, Trevor, but it's a little tainted." She resumed her descent, picking up the pace.

"Hold on a sec," I called after her, catching her arm at the bottom of the stairs. "Then tell me one thing, Sandy. Why did you tell me you didn't get in an accident this weekend when clearly you did?"

A flicker of anxiety passed over her eyes, then her expression turned blank. I had never seen her so expressionless; she was always smiling or looking interested or nodding in enthusiasm. I noticed tiny lines around her eyes and mouth.

She turned away, rubbing her arms and shivering as though a cold breeze had brushed past. "I'm sorry for lying, Trevor. I was so embarrassed, I couldn't bring myself to tell anyone."

"Tell anyone what?"

"Shhh!" She looked around and lowered her voice to a whisper. "I *did* get into a little accident on my way home Saturday night. Nothing serious, just a little fender-bender. Nobody was hurt. After it happened, I was so distraught I tripped while climbing out of my truck. That's how I got these." She turned her hands over. "And these." She lifted her skirt a few inches, revealing bandages on each knee. "I told Jack to get the truck fixed right away because I wanted to erase the entire incident from memory, especially considering what happened to Mr. Godfrey. I felt so ashamed."

I blinked. "That's it?"

"Yes. You expected more?"

"I'm just so relieved."

Her eyes narrowed. "Don't tell me *you* thought I had something to do with Mr. Godfrey's death?"

"Of course not."

"I should hope not." She studied my face for a moment. "It's been a brutal week so far, hasn't it? Hey, your mom arrives tonight. I saw her name on the arrivals list. How fun! Are your sisters coming too?"

"God, no. Mom is enough."

"I really liked those girls! So down to earth."

At the foot of the stairs, I spotted a cigarette butt and stooped down to pick it up. I rolled it into my handkerchief, which I stuffed into my pocket. If Sandy weren't so genuine, I would have thought she was making fun of me. My sisters had behaved like small-town hicks when they visited last May, shuttling back and forth from the lobby to their suite toting shopping bags from H&M, fake designer handbags bought from street vendors, and bags of Burger King, the stench of Whoppers and Biggie Fries trailing in their wake. Nightly they staked out the Center of the Universe Lounge on a sharp lookout for celebrities, all dolled up in tight angora sweaters and acid-wash jean skirts, sipping rum and Cokes, giggling like school girls and swearing like long-haul truckers. Yet all the while they had the audacity to make fun of *me* for my formal attire, to mock my diction, my walk, and my refusal to let loose on hotel premises. By the time they left, I was deeply relieved. As much as I loved them, it had become painfully clear how far apart we had grown. Yet a few days later, I was surprised to find myself missing them. Now, I wished they were coming to visit too.

"Why don't you bring your mom over for Christmas dinner?" Sandy suggested. "Jack bought a turkey the size of an elephant. The kids would love to see you."

"I'm sure they'd love to see you, too," I said.

"Hey, be nice! I'll have you know I went home early yesterday."

"Yeah, under police escort. We'd love to come, Sandy. Thank you."

"Terrific. I'll let Jack know. Oh, did Nancy Swinton find you?"

"No. Why?"

"She resigned this morning." She sighed.

My heart leapt. "She didn't."

Sandy nodded gravely, but by the determined look in her eyes I could see she was already scheming to have her replaced; as director of human resources, she never let herself get too attached to any employee. "It's going to be hard to trade up on this one," she said, referring to our policy of treating every resignation as an opportunity to find someone even better. "I'll send you the résumé of that young man I met on Monday. He's definitely got the potential." She turned and limped away, humming to herself like an injured bird determined not to let a broken wing dampen her spirit.

As I watched her go, the full effect of her words sunk in. Nancy was leaving me. Suddenly I couldn't breathe, as though all the oxygen in the Universe had begun to deplete, and soon I would suffocate and collapse to the floor. First Willard abandoned me, now Nancy... who was next?

By 2:00 PM, a full hour after check-out time, Honica Winters still hadn't checked out of her suite nor had she returned my messages. I had received a report that she and her crew were filming in Brenda Rathberger's suite, but by the time I got there everyone was gone. Fortunately, a housekeeping check confirmed that her bags were still in her room. I reprogrammed her key to lock her out. If she wanted her bags, she wouldn't be able to escape without coming to me first.

At 2:45 PM, Matthew paged me. "Honica is filming in front of the hotel. Now is your chance."

I hurried downstairs and found her standing at the southeast corner of the complex taping a segment, the UNIVERSE sign hovering in the backdrop. She wore a tan trench coat with a red scarf wrapped around her neck. Her blond hair was blowing wildly in the wind. A crowd had gathered to watch.

She was holding up a sheet of paper I recognized as Universe letterhead and shouting into the camera over the roar of traffic. "—crucial question is, how did the drinkers get home? And what led to the tragic death of the man who footed the bill for this extravagant affair?"

The camera operator lowered his camera. "We're done!" one of the crew called out.

Honica handed a crew member her microphone as a crowd of admirers descended upon her.

I watched for a moment, waiting for the best time to approach. But the crew was packing, and her last few words were too disturbing to miss this opportunity. I pried my way through the crowd, silently arranging thoughts in my head for the interview. "Miss Winters?" I called out.

She looked up from the crowd and squinted over. "Why, it's the handsome hotel manager! You probably want your suite back, don't you? I promise I'll be out as soon as I can. You better not charge me!" She stuck her lower lip out in a pout, then lifted a pen to sign an autograph.

"I won't charge you, but I need to talk to you."

"Hey mister, wait your turn!" someone yelled, jabbing an elbow into my ribs.

"Can I steal you away for a minute?" I shouted to Honica. "It's important."

She nodded and signed a few more autographs, then apologized to the rest of the group and made her way over. "What's up, doll face?"

"Miss Winters, I know that you're producing a show on the Universe or on Willard Godfrey, and that you tried to reach Matthew Drummond to interview him. I apologize. I was supposed to call you Monday, but it's been a busy week. I'm here to answer any questions you have—on camera, if necessary. I've worked at the hotel since day one, and I knew Mr. Godfrey well. I could give a nice little tribute to him."

Honica bit on her fingernail. "I wanted to interview the astronaut. Is he around?"

I shook my head. "Matthew's tied up all day. He asked me to speak on his behalf."

She crossed her arms, unconvinced. "Were you at the Christmas party?"

"Yes."

"Were you part of the group that stayed behind with Willard after the others left on shuttle buses?"

It seemed a strange question, but I was determined to convince her to interview me. I didn't want to face Matthew if she turned me down. "I was. In fact, I was one of the last people to see Mr. Godfrey alive."

"Okay," she said, turning to whistle at her crew. "Guys. One more quick one!"

"Sure thing, Honey."

First I was relieved, then suddenly I was very nervous as the crew busied around me. A crowd began assembling again to watch. I shivered. The air wasn't particularly cold, but it felt damp, and the gloomy sky above threatened rain.

A crew member started to remove my nametag. Without thinking, I pushed his hand away.

"He can leave it on," Honica said, flashing me a reassuring look.

I tried to smile, but my mouth was too dry. I took a deep breath and tried to steady my heartbeat. *Remember the three Cs,* I told myself.

"Ready?" Honica asked as the cameraman lifted the camera and pointed it at me over her shoulder. She plucked a piece of lint from my lapel. "Look at me, not the camera."

I nodded and tried to shut out the expectant gazes in the burgeoning crowd. Honica's face was attractive and pleasant to look at. Her smile inspired confidence and trust. I started to breath easier.

"Rolling!" said the cameraman.

Honica stuck a microphone in my face. "Spell your full name and title." She was standing extremely close.

My voice trembled as I spelled my name and title.

"Mr. Lambert," Honica asked, assuming an authoritative tone, "how have staff of the Universe Hotel reacted to the news of Willard Godfrey's death?"

"We're absolutely devastated," I replied.

"Tell me about the conference your hotel is hosting next week."

"Conference? You mean VOID? Of course." My mind went blank. "Uh, it starts next week, and … it's about drunk driving." I stopped, unable to think of anything else. The microphone jerked in Honica's hand, urging me on. "It's a fairly large conference, though, uh, certainly not the biggest we've had …"

"Mr. Lambert, do you think it's ironic that Willard Godfrey was struck down and killed by a suspected drunk driver only days before he was slated to speak at this anti-impaired driving conference?"

My eyes bulged. It was a loaded question, and certainly one I had not anticipated. I tried to decide how to respond appropriately, but found it difficult to think clearly with the camera only inches from my face. Honica was glaring at me, and hundreds of eyes were ogling from the street.

"Ironic?" I said. "How so?" Hadn't Matthew instructed me to play dumb? In that regard I was performing brilliantly.

Honica seemed to decide on another approach. "Tell us about the Universe Hotel's Christmas party."

"Well, it was held in the Observatory, which—not that I have to tell *you*—is on the top floor of the hotel. We have it every year. This year close to eight hundred staff attended."

"And the booze was free?"

I blinked and sneaked a glance at the camera. "Well, yes, it was."

Honica nodded slowly. "In your opinion, did excessive drinking take place at this party?"

"Excessive drinking?" I realized I'd better regain control of this interview at once. "Absolutely not."

"Did you have a lot to drink?"

"Me?" I gritted my teeth. "No. I had, um, a drink or two, that's all."

"How about your fellow executives of the Universe Hotel? Did *they* have a lot to drink?"

"I really can't comment on their behalf, Miss Winters. It was a Christmas party. Staff were encouraged to let loose, but rest assured, no one drank excessively, and nothing irresponsible took place. In fact, complimentary transportation was arranged to take all staff home in safety."

Honica jabbed the microphone at me accusingly. "Did all staff take the shuttle buses?"

"As far as I know, yes."

"Even executive staff?"

I'd been set up! If I said yes, I'd be exposed as a liar on national television. If I told the truth, I would be ratting out my colleagues. "*I* walked home. I can't speak for the others."

"Sources tell me that some of the hotel's executive staff drove home after the party," Honica said. "How do you think this reflects on their judgment?"

I opened my mouth in protest, then closed it. I shifted on my feet. How bad would it look if I turned and fled up the driveway, taking refuge in the Universe? "I suppose it would depend on whether or not they were intoxicated," I said at last.

"Let's say they *were* intoxicated."

"Then it would be irresponsible, I suppose. But to my knowledge, nobody drove home intoxicated."

"Mr. Lambert, there is speculation that a Universe Hotel employee may be responsible for Willard Godfrey's death. How do you respond to that?"

Why, the little bitch! "No comment."

"No comment?"

"It's a ludicrous proposition. Impossible! A nasty rumor with absolutely no truth." I was seething now. "Miss Winters, we run a first-class hotel here. My colleagues and I are highly responsible, law-abiding citizens. We are role models for hotel staff—and, I believe, for society in general. The Universe Hotel operates in accordance with Universal Values, as written by Willard Godfrey and elaborated on in his book by the same name. Our behavior is guided by the principles of respect, integrity, and accountability. We *care* very much about what happened to Mr. Godfrey, and our thoughts and prayers go out to his family. We're *concerned* for the safety of all staff, guests, and patrons." I stopped and tried to recall the third C. All I could hear was Matthew saying, "We're cooked! We're catatonic!" I stared at the microphone. At last it came to me. "And we're *committed* to ensuring an accident does not occur on hotel property again. I must say I resent your innuendo. We are still recovering from the loss of Willard Godfrey and kindly request that you leave us to mourn in peace. My colleagues and I are assisting the New York Police Department in every way possible to ensure the perpetrator is caught promptly. Now, if you don't mind, I must get back to work." Pushing the microphone out of the way, I stormed past Honica.

"Bravo!" someone shouted in the crowd.

I turned and saw Shanna Virani standing with a few other employees, all of them applauding loudly.

Honica placed her hands on her hips and huffed.

I passed through the steel doors and into the hotel, feeling a sense of relief as they slid shut behind me, cutting short the clamor of New York life and leaving the horribly stressful interview behind me. As I passed the front desk, I instructed Gaetan to charge Honica Winters for late check-out if she wasn't out of her suite by 3:00 PM.

"You bawled her out on camera?" Nancy Swinton exclaimed, regarding me with her big brown eyes.

"Yep."

"You weren't even nervous?"

"Nope." We were standing in the bedroom of Suite 2112, where I had caught up to her on her afternoon rounds. So far I hadn't said anything about her resignation, and I wasn't about to bring it up; secretly I hoped that Sandy had somehow got it wrong, that it was all a terrible misunderstanding.

"Wow! So did you say lots of nice things about Mr. Godfrey?"

I pondered the question. Had the subject even come up? "A few things," I said. "But it was a very quick interview." Suddenly I wasn't feeling very triumphant anymore. Honica hadn't seemed interested in hearing me sing the praises of Mr. Godfrey. Judging by her questions, instead she must have been focusing on some sort of scandal. "Well, I should get back to work." I went to the door, pausing to stretch, allowing Nancy time to stop me. "I'm heading to JFK in a couple of hours to pick up my mother," I added, hoping she'd be impressed with my attentiveness to my mother, which might make her fall in love with me and decide not to quit.

"Trevor, do you have a minute? I need to talk to you."

My impulse was to run away, but bravely I turned around. My heart was racing. "Yes, Nancy?"

There was an anxious look on her face, an expression that made her only more beautiful. She was wringing her tiny hands, her full lips pressed together, and wrinkling her narrow, slightly turned-up nose. A lovely floral scent always emanated from her; not perfume, but something from her hair, which was dark and thick and impossibly lustrous. In accordance with Universal Standards of Presentation, it was tied into a bun, but I had seen it set free on a few occasions—at the Christmas party, once when I ran into her on the street, and another time when she came to pick up Gaetan on her day off—and it was magnificent. Nancy was magnificent. More than her appearance, however, I was attracted to Nancy's work performance: her ethic, her diligence, her smile, the way she disarmed upset guests like a trained assassin.

Sparkle Factor 10.

She sat down on the bed and patted the space beside her. "Come here, Trevor."

I swallowed. The thought of sitting so close to Nancy—on a *bed*—was electrifying. For many people, hotels are intensely erotic. It's a well-known fact that couples make love more frequently in a hotel room than in their own bedrooms; for many, it's the first thing they do after checking in. On the road, people have more time to think about sex, to engage in sex, to recover from sex. Hotel rooms are built for sex: they are equipped with lockable doors and privacy signs, extra towels, sheets that are changed daily, and mini-refrigerators stocked with booze and intimacy kits. Solo travelers also spend an inordinate amount of time on the road thinking about sex—just ask a handsome bellman or a pretty cocktail server how often they're hit on, or ask a prostitute why she hangs out in hotel lounges. Lonely, far removed from daily lives and commitments, travelers feel liberated, anonymous, and uninhibited on the road. They encounter strangers at meetings and conventions, over dinners and drinks, in an environment where the risks of an affair are sharply reduced because eventually, everyone must go home.

Hotel employees aren't always innocent bystanders. I have known colleagues to slip into rooms for quickies with guests or other staff. Besides being constantly propositioned by guests, some employees are flashed, others seduced, many harassed. The accidental dropping of the towel by female guests in front of wide-eyed luggage attendants has played itself out in hotel rooms time and again. Sometimes employees go on secret dates with guests; occasionally, like in Sandy James' case, they even marry them.

The only guest I'd ever dated was Melanie Coffey, a young woman who stayed at the Universe three times, and only because she was relentless. First she hit on Gaetan Boudreau at the front desk, but then found out he was gay, so she went after the next tall, single employee she found: me. Over several visits I dodged her overtures, until one day she called me up from the Mercer, asking if we could go out now that she wasn't a guest anymore. She was pretty hot and seemed pleasant enough, so I accepted.

I thought the date went well—save for the part where she drifted off to sleep over dessert while I was babbling about work. But a few days later, I still hadn't found the right time to call her, so she took the liberty of calling me—in the form of a nasty message on my voicemail. In it, she accused me of treating her like a hotel guest: dinner in Orbit, drinks in the Center of the Universe, overnight at my place, breakfast in bed, and an escort to the front door, where I hailed her a cab. I thought I was being a gracious host; she said I made her feel like a prostitute. I sent her flowers. She never called again. One unhappy ex-Universe guest, courtesy of me.

For me, the hotel is anything but erotic. It's my place of work and no sexier than a cubicle, a corner office, or a cash register. A bed in which a different person sleeps every night, sweating and drooling and doing god knows what else, is not terribly appealing. People come to hotels to recover from illnesses, to visit sick people, to attend funerals, to fire employees, to close down offices, to do drugs, to escape reality, and sometimes to kill themselves. To me, a hotel is about as sexy as a hospital.

Of course, there are few places of employment where a meeting can take place on a bed. As I regarded Nancy's lovely, beckoning figure perched on the edge of the bed, my view of hotel rooms started to become decidedly less antiseptic. I stood frozen where I was.

"Don't be shy now," she said. "I really need to talk to you."

Did I detect a tremor in her voice? Cautiously, I made my way over, sitting down on the far edge of the bed. She smiled up at me. I looked down and noticed that her skirt was riding up her leg, exposing a few inches of nyloned thigh. I felt myself becoming aroused. I looked away and tried to think about nonsexy things like arrivals reports and Little Sparky's starving mews and Brenda Rathberger's thighs. I tried to pull the lapels of my jacket over my lap.

"Trevor, I'm leaving the Universe. My last day is in ten days." She added quickly, "But I can stay longer if you want."

"That won't be necessary," I said, my voice rising an octave higher. I could feel heartache and rejection wash over me like a cold shower. "I'm sorry to hear it, Nancy. You've served us well. I wish you the best of success in the future." I stood up to shake her hand, wanting to get out of there as quickly as possible, but realized my crotch was face level with her face. And I was tenting. Quickly I sat back down and folded my hands over my lap. "Are you going to another hotel?"

She looked hurt. "Oh, no. I'm going to take a few months off and just chill for a while. I want to start the New Year fresh. Read, travel a bit, hang out, think—you know."

I stared at her blankly.

"I'm planning to go back to school in September," she added.

"For hotel management?"

She laughed. "I'm going back so I *don't* have to work in a hotel. I plan to take fine arts."

I felt offended by her remark. Why did I feel like I was being dumped? On the carpet near my foot was a short piece of white thread, and I picked it up, winding it around my forefinger.

"Eagle Eyes," she said, smiling.

"You could do a lot worse than this career, Nancy. I tried college a few years ago. It was a complete waste of time."

"Really? Why?"

I shrugged. "I already had a great career in the hotel business, but I abandoned it because my mother convinced me I was worthless without a degree. I hated school. I couldn't understand why I had to memorize information that was completely irrelevant to the outside world. Fortunately, Mr. Godfrey rescued me with this job."

She regarded me with a bemused expression. "You take your job really seriously, don't you?"

"Of course I do." I noticed that her nametag was lopsided and wanted to reach out and fix it. "You're so good, Nancy. You could be a department head in a year or two. A general manager someday."

"I don't want to be a general manager. Don't get me wrong, I love working here, but it's not fulfilling enough for me. I need more. Don't you ever feel like you're missing out?"

"On what?"

"On life."

"Oh, I tried another career once. Just before I went back to school I worked in the film industry. I loathed every second of it. People are so much nicer in the hotel industry."

"On the surface, maybe. Hotel people are better at hiding their true feelings."

I sighed and stood up again, glancing down to ensure all was safe. It was; Nancy's words were sobering and upsetting. "Well, I suppose you should experience another career to find out if the hotel industry really is your thing. You'll be back, I'm quite sure."

"Sit down, Trevor," she said, grabbing my hand and pulling me down. She moved closer to me on the bed and stared at me fixedly. "Do you think we'll ever see each other outside of the hotel?"

I regarded her in surprise. Was I crazy, or did I detect a glimmer of hope in her eyes? It occurred to me that there was an upside to Nancy leaving the Universe: I could ask her out on a date without fear of violating my professional integrity or of being charged with harassment. Was this what she was hinting at? Suddenly I was incapacitated by the possibility. "Uh, well, sure, if that's what you want," I stammered.

A flicker of annoyance passed over her. "I don't want to force you to do anything, Trevor. I just think you're a nice guy, and it wouldn't hurt you to get out of this place once in a while. It's my thirtieth birthday on the fourteenth of January, and G—uh, the guy I live with—is throwing a party for me. You should come."

"You live with a guy?"

She closed her eyes slowly in affirmation. "I thought you knew, but I guess not. It's been almost three years. We decided not to—"

I stood up abruptly, cutting her off. I didn't want to hear about her boyfriend. "I'll try, Nancy, but the hotel will be very busy around then, so I can't make any promises." I wandered toward the door, dejected, feeling like a fool. I had read her completely wrong. She didn't like me; she felt sorry for me. I had to get out of there before she saw how devastated I was. At the door I turned to her and said, "Well, thanks for telling me. I guess I'll see you around over the next ten days."

She was staring at me with her mouth open.

I bolted from the room.

★ ★ ★ ★ ★

There are reasons why I'm so hopeless with women, why I'm ruled by fear around them. Aside from the usual rejection experienced by tall, gangly, geeky guys in high school, the real damage occurred while I was at the Park Harbour Hotel, when I learned a harsh lesson about the dangers of office romances. What started out as a small, harmless crush snowballed into disaster.

Rosa Roberts started in the business center in January. She was plump and rosy-cheeked, always smiling, and I found her delightful. She was also highly flirtatious. Over the course of several months, I grew from thinking she was a real cutie to becoming hopelessly infatuated with her. But it wasn't one-sided; she encouraged my attention and appeared to harbor similar feelings toward me. Every day I made up new reasons to visit her in the business center—*Look, more photocopying! More faxing! Another document for word processing!*—

and Rosa always smiled coyly and watched me as I worked or let me watch her as she worked. She wasn't particularly good at her job or hardworking, and her manager often complained to me about her performance. But I saw potential that no one else did. Rosa told me she wanted to move to the front desk, and I promised to help her. I spent many hours schooling her. She would listen intently, eyes riveted on me, both of us pretending we were actually thinking about five-diamond check-in procedures and not about me throwing her onto the photocopier and lifting up her skirt. Although flirtatious, our relationship was highly professional and businesslike, developed exclusively within the hotel and without so much as laying a hand on one another, aside from the occasional brush of our bodies as we navigated our way around the small business center. We engaged in a kind of reverse Tantric sex—orgasms without touching, though of course the orgasms took place in my mind.

After about six months, I worked up the courage to ask her out. As director of rooms, it was against my better judgement, but Rosa seemed receptive, and I was confident that she wouldn't tell anyone. Over dinner, after too much wine, I broke down and confessed my love, something I had been dying to do for weeks. Then I waited for her to reciprocate. Instead, she shifted in her seat a great deal and drained the contents of her wine glass. After much hemming and hawing, she informed me point-blank that I had misread her feelings, that dinner was a mistake, that she was not interested in me that way.

I, of course, was shattered, humiliated, and semi-suicidal.

A week later, Rosa's manager came to me and said she was fed up with Rosa's piss-poor performance and wanted her fired. As head of the department, the deed would be up to me. I was panic-stricken. If I fired her, she would think it was because she had rejected me. Worse, I might never see her again, and I had convinced myself that, in time, Rosa would fall in love with me. I told the manager to give her another chance, but she returned the next day with four other managers—an intervention.

The meeting with Rosa lasted three minutes, although I desperately wanted it to last longer, knowing I might never see her again. I would take her on any terms, even loved her while I was firing her— loved her even more, in fact, and wanted the meeting to last a lifetime. But she wasn't quite as enthralled by the meeting as I; she sat very composed, listening to me quietly, then got up and walked out. A week later, I was served with a notice from the Human Rights Tribunal that Rosa was suing me and the hotel for sexual harassment and wrongful dismissal. We hired a lawyer, who came to interview me.

"Is it true you spent hours in the business center photocopying pages of the telephone book just to be close to her?"

"Uh, yes."

"Is it true you sent facsimiles of blank pages from the business center in front of her?"

"How did she—? Um ... maybe once or twice."

"Did you intentionally jam the photocopier and leer at Rosa Roberts while she fixed it?"

"Absolutely not!"

The case was resolved in a settlement meeting, from which Rosa walked away with the equivalent of a half-year's salary. Whether she had truly liked me at first, then changed her mind, or had deliberately manipulated me, or had retaliated for being fired, or had truly felt harassed, I would never know. The damage was done. My reputation was ruined. Management supported me, but somehow news spread throughout the hotel, and in the following months I worked under a cloud of shame. All joy for work was gone. During this dark period, I met Willard and Margaret Godfrey; soon after, I quit the hotel for the film industry job.

I therefore had good reason to avoid Nancy. I was not prepared to jeopardize my employment or my integrity, or to risk misinterpreting her feelings and make her feel uncomfortable or harassed. Up to this point I had conducted myself around her with complete professionalism, content to admire her from a distance, to glance at her briefly, taking a snapshot of her in my mind that lasted for days. For a brief moment this afternoon a window of hope had opened—she was leaving, we could go on a date—only to be slammed shut by her live-in boyfriend of three years. It was for the best, I decided. How could I be with someone so dismissive of the hotel business, a career my life revolved around? The best place for a love affair, I decided, was in my mind, where love lasts forever and no one breaks your heart.

When I reached the end of the corridor, I pushed the elevator call button frantically, afraid Nancy might catch up with me. A car arrived within seconds.

"Good afternoon, Mr. Lambert," came Mona's cheerful, dutiful voice. "Where may I take you?"

"Lobby, please."

"Going to lobby level. Please hold on."

As the elevator plunged downward, I thought about Mona, the talking elevator. She was so friendly and efficient, so reliable and professional. Maybe I should start dating her.

Christmas was everywhere in New York. Despite the unseasonably warm weather, there were enough fake snowflakes, fake sleighs, fake trees, and fake reindeer to make it look like an authentic northern holiday. Despite a harrowing week and a depressing day, I was in surprisingly good spirits as I rode to JFK in the back seat of the hotel's shimmering black Bentley. I felt wealthy and accomplished and important, as though the car, the driver, and the sprawling suite at the Universe awaiting my mother all belonged to me.

The driver waited outside the terminal while I went in to find her. She was standing at the baggage carousel, struggling with a heavy red suitcase. "Allow me to help you with that, ma'am," I said.

"Trevor! Sweetheart!"

She dropped the bag and we embraced. I felt a rush of emotion. I really did miss my mommy. Stepping back to regard her, I saw that she looked more terrific than ever: radiant and rail-thin, blue eyes shining, hair dyed a light auburn with blond highlights and cut short in a modern-day twenties style that suited her thin, angular face. It amazed me how women underwent so many transformations in life, constantly rejuvenating and reinventing themselves, while men suffered a gradual and unrelenting descent into old age and irritability.

"It's lovely to see you, dear," Mom said. "I've missed you so much!"

"I've missed you too, Mom." I had to hug her again.

"The girls send their love. Wendy's pregnant!"

"Again? What is this, her twelfth?"

"Third. You look terrible, dear. If I didn't know better, I'd think you were pushing forty. You've been working too hard, haven't you?"

The end of our joyous reunion clocked in at just under one minute. "I've had a rough few days, Mom."

"I know you have. The story even made the *Vancouver Sun*! I clipped it for you. Are things getting back to normal yet?"

"Slowly, but they won't really settle down until they find the perpetrator."

She took my arm as I pushed a luggage cart containing her two suitcases toward the exit. "You'll have to tell me *everything*. I *love* a good mystery."

But during the ride into Manhattan I barely got a word in. Mom chattered excitedly, updating me on family and friends, telling stories about aunts and cousins and neighbors I swear I'd never heard of.

"Aidy will be six in February."

"Who's Aidy?"

There was a sharp intake of breath. "Aiden is your nephew, Trevor. Your sister Janet's second son."

"Oh, *Aiden*. Of course I know Aiden."

"By the way, Claire Bentley says hello."

"Claire…"

"You remember, the girl down the street when we lived on Cumberland? Richard and Maxine's daughter. She's in my acting class."

"Right, Claire." I decided to postpone asking about the acting class until later. Or maybe never.

"Well, *she* graduated last year with her doctorate in pediatrics, and no less than *four hospitals* offered her a job! Everyone calls her Dr. Malciewski now—she married Ted Malciewski a few years back, he's the owner of a thriving wholesale coffee bean business! Claire's taking acting lessons to help her bedside manner, which colleagues have told her is too gruff. I hope she's a better doctor than she is an actress! But what a bright girl! Almost as smart as you, Trevor. Of course, she did something with her brains."

"*Mom.*"

"Look at this traffic! Honestly, I don't know why people live in this city." She was quiet for a beat, allowing time for her comments to sink in. "I've always wanted to see New York at Christmastime. But I didn't expect rain! I might as well have stayed in Vancouver. Oh, Aunt Germaine sends her regards. Yesterday, she said, 'What on earth is Trevor doing in New York that he can't do here?'"

"For starters, I'm not working on a farm."

"I don't understand why you didn't stay with the Park Harbour. Such a lovely hotel! Oh, did you hear the news? Shangri-La is building a hotel on Georgia Street, and there are rumors of a ValuLuxe hotel going in up the street from it. You should give them a call." Another beat. "Wait 'til you see how your nieces and nephews have grown! They really liked you, Trevor. *Everyone* misses you."

My last visit had started off pleasantly enough. At a gathering of extended family at the home of my dad's sister, Aunt Germaine, I was treated like a celebrity. Mom had been out for a visit that summer and had talked up the Universe to anyone who would listen, sounding much more enamored with it than during her visit. I held court in the living room, perched on an overstuffed green pleather sofa, relating stories to over thirty relatives and partners gathered around. Relishing the attention, I revised the stories to embellish my importance. It was me and not Gaetan who broke up a celebrity couple's spat and was almost taken out by a lamp hurled across the room. My audience begged me to tell them who it was, but I was coy, explaining I had to protect their privacy, though rest assured they were Big. I told them about a famous, never-to-be-revealed teenage pop star who, terrified of fires, fled from her suite during a fire alarm in nothing but a bra and panties, taking refuge in my office (it was actually Sandy's), and watched in amusement as perverted grins broke out around the room. I told them about the young woman I talked out of leaping off the eighteenth-floor atrium balcony while we waited for the NYPD to arrive (in fact, Nancy did most of the talking). I didn't tell them that three months later, a drunken, twenty-two-year-old Argentine man fell from the twelfth floor while performing stunts for his new wife, landing on a seventy-three-year-old New York society gal and killing them both. When I told them about evicting the Russian president from the lounge for drunken and lewd behavior (a true story, but Godfrey did all the talking), they began to lose interest; they were much more interested in pop stars in their panties.

"Did your hotel get all blown on September 11?" one of the boys blurted out.

I winced. Although over three years had passed, it was still a sensitive topic, and this was the wrong venue, the wrong atmosphere, and the wrong context. "No," I replied quietly. "My hotel is in midtown, quite far away. We were lucky. Wait 'til you hear about the Arkansas flight attendant who—"

"Did ashes from burnt-up bodies fall on you?" the same boy asked.

I was horrified by the question. Everyone I worked with knew someone or someone who knew someone who was killed in the attacks. Sixteen of our staff lost loved ones. Yes, ashes had fallen on me; they had fallen on all of Manhattan. We knew it was debris from the towers, but it felt like a giant crematorium was showering ashes on the city, covering it with a blanket of human snow. After the attacks, we had evacuated the Universe, fearing that, as one of Manhattan's tallest buildings, it might be a target. When we returned, the hotel became a refugee camp for displaced souls. We did everything we could to help, but most of the damage was done, and there was nothing we could do to change it.

"No," I said quietly, "no ashes fell on me. Did I tell you about the Japanese businessman who checked in with six Amazonian-sized hookers?"

The boys giggled. But after a while, the television, Wendy's tarot cards, and Aunt Germaine's buffet table proved to be stronger draws, and one by one my audience deserted me. In the days following, my family treated me differently, with a mixture of indifference and contempt, as though they feared I considered myself better than them. I didn't; I just felt different. Surrounded by babies and toys, Wal-Mart clothing and permed hair, no-name beer and instant mashed potatoes, I had little in common with them anymore. I couldn't wait to get back to New York.

"Here we are," I said to Mom as the car rolled up to the hotel driveway.

The doorman opened the door for Mom. "Mrs. Lambert, welcome back to the Universe! It's wonderful to see you again."

As we crossed the lobby to the elevator, Mom continued to chatter away, paying little attention to her surroundings. "I hadn't seen Bruce and Ann for *at least* a year. The first thing Bruce says to me is—"

"See the tree?" I asked, pointing over.

She gave a cursory glance in that direction. "Pretty. So Bruce says, 'Evelyn, you look twenty years younger! I've never seen you look so good nor seem so happy! What's your secret?' 'Well, Tom,' I said, 'when you take a twenty-year nap you're bound to come out looking rested.'" She laughed heartily.

As we stepped inside the elevator I thought about introducing Mona to Mom as my fiancée, but decided she wouldn't find it funny. As the elevator soared upwards, Mom continued talking without turning to admire the view of the lobby below.

When we arrived in her suite on the fifty-first floor she was still talking. "So Bruce says, 'Why don't you come with Ann and me to the opening? We have a friend we'd like you to meet...'"

"See the view, Mom?"

She went to the window, which rose sixteen feet to the ceiling. "It's really quite extraordinary, isn't it? But look at this crowded city." She turned to me. "I was hoping for a view of the Hudson."

"I'm sure the Mandarin could arrange that for $1500 a night."

"I don't mean to sound ungrateful, Trevor, but it's a little depressing facing this gap in the skyline."

"What gap?"

She pointed through the window. "Where the Twin Towers used to be."

"You could never see the Twin Towers from here—from some of the upper floors, yes, but not from here."

"Really? I suppose it's psychological, then. You still sense the loss."

She turned to observe her surroundings. "It's lovely, Trevor. But I hardly need all this space. I don't intend on spending a lot of time here." Seeing my hurt expression, she rushed over and took my hands. "But I'm so happy to be here with you! Tomorrow is Christmas Eve and we're in New York City! How exciting! What will we do? See the lights at Rockefeller Center? Go ice skating? Take a horse and carriage ride through Central Park? Shop on Fifth Avenue? That reminds me, did you get those Rockettes tickets?"

"Uh, not yet."

She frowned. "I hope they're not sold out! We don't want to miss it." She picked up the bottle of red wine from the table and examined it, then sniffed the cheese platter. "What else do you have planned for us?"

I realized I hadn't planned anything yet. "Well … there's the funeral tomorrow," I said with a sheepish grin.

Mom did not look impressed.

8

Farewell to the Sun

As the taxi charged up Park Avenue to the Upper East Side, I gazed out the window and watched the busy streets, so crowded with last-minute holiday shoppers. The sun shone blithely on the buildings we passed, warming the cool Christmas Eve in New York. At East Fifty-seventh, a tall, skinny Santa stood on the corner ringing a bell, unnoticed by the hundreds of anxious shoppers that hurried past.

My mom had expressed dismay with the funeral falling on Christmas Eve, thinking it cast a shadow over an otherwise festive day, but to me, considering my somber, solitary Christmases past, it felt perfect.

She was sitting quietly beside me, dressed in black from head to toe, looking pensive. "Do you think about your father much?" she asked as the taxi stopped at a red light.

I turned to her in surprise. "Not really," I said. "Do you?"

"No."

I assumed this would be end of the conversation, that we had filled our annual quota on the topic. But she went on. "I used to think about him all the time. He was the center of my universe, Trevor. When he died, I couldn't function. For years I pined for him. I went through the motions, but I wasn't really there."

"From what I recall, you barely went through the motions."

She turned to regard me. "You were really crushed when he died. I felt so sorry for you, more so than the girls because they were too young to really understand. I wanted to comfort you, but I couldn't. I felt like I was mired in quicksand, slowly sinking, unable to reach out and help you as you stood on the edge and cried out my name because I was afraid I'd pull you in too. I hated myself, but I couldn't help myself. Do you remember when I asked you to take care of your sisters just before I left for that nurses' conference? You thought I meant for a couple of days, but in my mind I went away for a lot longer than that."

"About twenty years, by my calculation."

She smiled sadly. "I'm back now, Trevor. I've pulled myself out from the quicksand, washed myself off, and I feel better than ever. Never again will I build my world around one person like that." She turned to me again. "Now it's time to pull you out too."

The taxi rolled into motion again, accelerating to make the most of a span of open road. I watched the streets fly by, one after another. They all looked the same to me. All these people on the street, so determined, so full of purpose, were they simply going through the motions too?

"I'm happy for you, Mom, but I don't need your help." I glanced over to her. She was looking out the window now, where glimpses of a frozen, hibernating Central Park flashed at each intersection.

"You don't remember much about your childhood, do you?" she asked.

"I remember a great deal of resentment."

"Toward your father?"

"Toward you. I couldn't understand why you bitched at him and complained about him all the time while he was alive, acting like you resented his presence, then when he died he became a saint."

Her eyes grew wistful. "Your father and I fought a great deal in the months leading to his death, but beneath the nicks and scrapes in our relationship was a solid foundation of love. It was a stressful time. He lost his job at Scott Paper after fifteen years. We almost lost the house. I understand now that he was depressed, but I didn't know it then. After the car accident, when he complained about chest pains, we thought it was stress. Even the doctor said it was stress. How could we have known that the seat belt had ripped his aorta and it was slowly bubbling out like a balloon?" Her voice broke, and I reached over to squeeze her hand. "When the bubble burst, all the ill feelings, all the resentment and petty annoyances just vanished. All that remained was love, the purest, most heart-wrenching and all-consuming love you can imagine. I was overwhelmed. I thought the world was such a cruel place, and I withdrew from it. Does that make sense, Trevor?"

"I guess."

"I'm sorry I was such a bad mother."

"Was?"

She smiled. "I didn't recover on my own. I got help. Have you ever considered counseling?"

"Me? Why?"

"We all could use a little counseling. I don't think you've dealt properly with your father's death. I think you've shut everyone out. You're afraid to let people get close."

I sighed. The morning was stressful enough without her needling me.

"Counseling really helped me," she persisted. "That and the Good Book."

"The Bible?" I should have guessed that Mom's next phase would be evangelical Christianity.

"No. *Refurbish Your Life!*"

"Right." I was relieved to spot the church up ahead. "We're almost there."

My father died on a Tuesday morning, on December thirteenth, three days before school was out for Christmas break. I was twelve years old. I remember the morning clearly, not because anything unusual happened but because it was the same as every other morning in our household. Mom chased my sisters and me around the house to get us ready for school, and Dad sat in his usual place at the table reading the newspaper and drinking coffee. "Your father is sick again this morning, kids," Mom announced with a long-suffering sigh. He looked the same to me, except his face was a bit pale and he kept pressing his palm against his chest like he was having bad heartburn. As we were leaving, he called out, "'Bye, kids!" but didn't get up. We scrambled into Peter Graham's mom's station wagon, joining a half-dozen neighborhood kids, and backed out of the driveway. I looked for Mom and Dad at the doorstep to wave goodbye, but they weren't there. Before long, I was too embroiled in high-level negotiations with Peter to coerce him to trade his Wagon Wheel for my bruised banana to worry why.

My school day ended three hours later. A grave-looking secretary knocked on the door of my classroom, consulted with my teacher for a moment, then called out my name. All eyes were on me as I walked to the door. I heard a few snickers. My classmates assumed I was in trouble, but I thought I had been singled out for something great. I had aced my math test and was identified as a child genius; they were sending me straight to university like that thirteen-year-old boy in Ontario. Only when I saw Janet and Wendy sitting in the principal's office did I consider that the news might not be good. Janet looked frightened. Wendy was bawling. Whereas ego had ruled my moment, intuition had ruled theirs.

The principal shut the door and paced back and forth before us, jangling the change inside his pocket. Sometimes when he visited our class he asked us to guess how much was there, and if someone got it right he handed it over. I was trying to guess when he kneeled before us and took little Wendy's hand in his. "Kids, I have some bad news. Your father passed away this morning. They think he might have had a heart attack. Your Aunt Germaine will be here to pick you up as soon as possible."

After that, my classmates treated me differently; not with the compassion and sensitivity one might expect, but with mockery and taunting. I became the handicapped kid in class—not missing a limb, but missing a father.

The taxi slowed at Eighty-fourth Street and let us out at the main entrance to the Church of St. Ignatius Loyola. Clusters of people dressed in black were gathered out front. I took a deep breath to quell my anxiety. My father's funeral had lasted almost a year in our household. I feared that Willard Godfrey's might be similarly drawn out. I climbed from the taxi and took my mother's hand. We hurried down the steps to Wallace Hall in the basement of the church.

The room was beautiful: an eight-thousand-square-foot Gothic chapel with a soaring vaulted ceiling, thirty-foot stone columns, and stained-glass windows. Already at least five hundred people crowded the room, and more were pouring in. As we made our way down the aisle, I nodded to several staff members present. My eyes darted across the aisles in search of Nancy Swinton until I realized she was on duty at the hotel. I recognized a number of others: general managers and staff of other hotels; Mr. Godfrey's fellow board members from NYC & Company and the Rose Center for Earth and Space; and a number of regular guests and clients of the Universe. At the front of the hall, a large portrait of Mr. Godfrey sat on a silver easel, flanked by two massive bouquets of white flowers.

"Trevor! Yoo-hoo! Over here!"

Marline Drummond was beckoning us over to a row near the front. Reluctantly, I pulled Mom over and made introductions. Beside her, Matthew looked up briefly to shake Mom's hand, then resumed studying a damp, crumpled piece of paper he clutched in his hands, silently mouthing words. Mother and I squeezed past him and took a seat to Marline's right. We sat in silence for a moment, taking in all the sights and sounds. I stared at Mr. Godfrey's smiling portrait and tried to comprehend what had happened, tried to step outside of myself and see things in perspective, but it all seemed unreal and dreamlike. I was going through the motions but not truly feeling the experience.

Beside me, Marline couldn't keep still. She kept turning toward the door to see who had arrived. Unable to sit still any longer, she jumped up and squeezed past Matthew, hurrying up the aisle.

I looked over to Matthew. "That your eulogy?" I asked.

"Yes."

"Must have been tough to write."

"It was."

"Can I see it?"

"No."

"Are you the only one speaking today?"

"Cynthia's going to say a few words."

"Really. I thought Roger Weatherhead might."

"He's still on his cruise. Trevor, if you don't mind, I'm trying to concentrate."

"Sorry." Recalling his performance at the staff meeting, I decided it was best to leave him alone.

Beside me, Mom was sitting perfectly still, hands folded in her lap like a little girl on her best behavior in church. I squeezed her hand and she looked up at me gratefully. She was a comfort to have around, particularly when she wasn't speaking. Behind me, the hall was beginning to overfill, and people were squeezing down benches to make room. I saw Rudy Giuliani and Judi Nathan walk in. Behind them came Sarah Jessica Parker and Matthew Broderick. Marline was chatting in the back of the chapel with Ronald Perelman and Helen Gurley Brown. Next to them stood Donald Trump and his wife Melania. So many acquaintances, I thought, but how many of them did Mr. Godfrey call friends? I had always found it difficult to draw a distinction between Willard Godfrey's life and his work. Was work his life or was life his work? He never seemed to have much going on that wasn't somehow associated with the hotel.

Brenda Rathberger arrived, looking unusually elegant in pearl earrings, a pearl necklace, and a black dress. Her expression was sorrowful and respectful as she squeezed down the aisle and seated herself halfway down. I wondered how many funerals she had attended in her career; she looked like a professional mourner.

Marline made her way back down the aisle, walking in tandem with the organ music as though part of a bridal party, her sleeveless dress exposing her sinewy, Boxercised arms. She assumed an expression of pure anguish, a tortured stoicism that proclaimed her life had been shattered by Willard Godfrey's death, but she was doing her best to maintain a stiff upper lip. She stopped at our row and turned to stare into the crowd.

"Marline, will you *please* sit down?" Matthew snapped. "You're driving me crazy."

"In a moment, dear." She opened her arms in a stretch, then placed her hands on her upper buttocks and arched her back, her tiny breasts pointing at Matthew accusingly. "I need a cigarette," she said, reaching for her purse and withdrawing a stick of nicotine gum. She popped it into her mouth and threw her head back, emitting a great sigh. Then she squeezed past Matthew and sat down next to me.

"Don't look now, but here comes Cynthia," she whispered.

I glanced over my shoulder. Cynthia was making her way down the aisle by herself, wearing a simple black dress, shiny black belt, and black patent-leather pumps with straps that crisscrossed their way up her ankles, halfway to her knees. I lifted my hand to wave at her, but her eyes remained fixed on the portrait of her father at the front of the room. Her expression was anxious but brave as she passed. At the front pew she stopped and sat down, its sole occupant. I looked around the room for her collage, her collection of "momentos," but it was nowhere to be seen. Perhaps she had saved it for the wake.

"Is there a wake after this?" I asked Matthew.

He shook his head. "I offered to host one at the hotel, but Cynthia said she wasn't in the mood for socializing. Ironic, I know. She says she'll do something in a few months, after his ashes are sent into space."

"*Sandy James* is here," Marline said out of the side of her mouth, as though on surveillance, her tone hinting at scandal. "Somebody should tell her this isn't a beauty pageant, she can stop smiling now. Is that her husband? Now there's a hunk! Matthew, you never told me Sandy's husband was such a hunk. Oh, there's Shanna. She shouldn't wear so much rouge, she looks like a Hindu vampire."

"Marline," said Matthew, "will you please stop judging people?"

"I'm not judging, I'm simply observing." She crossed her arms sulkily.

Nikki Hilton and actress Virginia Madsen came to the front of the room to pay their respects to Cynthia, then took a seat on the opposite side of the aisle, a few rows back. The chapel had now reached capacity, but Cynthia's row remained empty. It made me feel sad for Cynthia, having to suffer through her beloved father's funeral all by herself. I considered going up there with my mother to console her, but worried that she might prefer to be alone.

The organ music stopped, and a tall, thin reverend with dark circles under his eyes approached the podium, placing a pair of round spectacles on his nose. He spoke in a quiet, gravelly voice. "Ladies, gentlemen, family, colleagues, friends, and neighbors, we are here today to pay our final respects to Willard Godfrey, to mourn the passing of a dear man, a beloved colleague, and a loving father. But we are also here to rejoice in the miraculous gift of life that almighty God bestowed upon him, a gift we must never take for granted..."

Over the next twenty minutes the reverend, who apparently had never met Mr. Godfrey, talked about his life, his family, his career, and his tragic end. Once finished, he summoned Matthew to the podium.

As Matthew stood up, Marline rose with him, for no apparent reason other than to attract attention to herself. She held her arms out beseechingly as he made his way up the aisle, as though offering her husband as a sacrifice to the altar.

I prayed that Matthew would be better prepared this time.

At the podium, he cleared his throat and looked around the room. "Willard Godfrey was a wonderful man," he began.

A chorus of sobs broke out across the room, as though on cue, and continued throughout his eulogy. Matthew's words were peppered with clichés and mixed metaphors, and contained more anecdotes to glorify him and his wife than Mr. Godfrey, but overall it was a significant improvement over Monday's speech, and the audience showed their gratitude with nods of remembrance, knowing smiles, tears, and cries of grief.

"And I know in my heart that no star in the universe—save perhaps for the sun—shone as brightly as Willard Godfrey," Matthew concluded. "Though this light is now extinguished, we retain within ourselves a flame of love, admiration, and respect for this brilliant man, a flame that will burn for eternity. As we bid him a final farewell, we thank him for his warmth, his energy, and his enlightenment."

Matthew stepped down triumphantly, as though expecting applause.

Beside me, Marline dabbed her eyes and gripped my hand. "Wasn't that beautiful?" she said.

I nodded solemnly.

"I wrote it," she said, nodding her head up and down and pursing her lips.

Cynthia Godfrey was at the podium now. "Thank you for those kind words, Matthew," she said.

The presence of Willard Godfrey's orphaned daughter prompted renewed displays of grief across the chapel. On the opposite side of the aisle, I spotted Susan Medley sitting with her face buried in her hands. Behind her, Brenda Rathberger was weeping openly. Shanna was seated a few rows back, her head down, hair concealing her face, body rocking with sobs. Sandy sat in the same row, leaning her head on her husband's shoulder, her face contorted with grief.

I thought of Matthew's comment yesterday: *We have no choice but to face the evidence: it was either Shanna or Sandy.* Could one of these beautiful, grief-stricken ladies be responsible for this funeral? I pushed the preposterous notion from my head, refusing to contemplate it. It had to have been a stranger, I reassured myself. Somehow, someone broke into the parkade and escaped without detection.

As Cynthia began to speak, I felt tears well in my eyes. Her voice was smooth and strong, but void of emotion. She spoke without notes.

"I have to agree with Matthew," she said. "At times my father was as bright and warm as the sun. But he had another side that few people saw. He could be as cold and distant as the moon. Sometimes I felt light years away from him."

People shifted uncomfortably in their seats.

"In a way, my father died many years ago, right after my mother died. He couldn't bear to be alone, so he immersed himself in the Universe. He always had people around him, yet he never let anyone get too close. Today, I look around at all these sad people and wonder if any of you really knew my father. I didn't.

"I think Daddy gave up hope of ever being happy after my mother died. Instead he concentrated on making other people happy through his work, through welcoming people to his hotel and making them feel safe and comfortable and pampered, through being the best hotelier he could possibly be. Those of you who have stayed at the Universe or have worked there have benefited from this dedication." She turned to observe her father's portrait, growing quiet for a moment. "Goodbye, Daddy," she whispered, blowing a kiss.

She stepped down from the podium and walked down the aisle and out of the church.

The organ music recommenced. The audience remained still and silent, confused and disturbed by Cynthia's short speech and its abrupt conclusion. Marline was the first to move. "Only three more shopping hours 'til Christmas!" she announced to me with a wink, too loudly for my comfort. She squeezed past Matthew and fluttered down the aisle.

Soon after, everyone stood up and followed.

After the funeral, Mom went shopping and I went to the Universe to check on things.

The hotel was quiet and somber. Occupancy had plummeted to its lowest point of the year, business and leisure travelers having gone home for the holidays. Yet the calm would be short-lived: in two days, VOID delegates would begin to arrive and occupancy would ramp up as the week progressed, culminating in a full house on New Year's Eve. But tonight, there was little reason to stay around.

Still, I somehow got home late. I had arranged to meet Mom at my apartment at 7:00 PM, but it was after 8:00 when I arrived. She wasn't there. By 9:15, I was starting to worry, when I heard her key in the door.

"Hi, dear! Sorry I'm late!" She was dressed in a new faux-fur sable coat and faux-Versace scarf. Her cheeks were flushed.

"Where've you been, Ma?"

"I got tired of waiting, so I went out for a drink. I found this delightful little place just down the street."

"Down the street? Where?"

"I think it was called Posh."

"Posh? Mom, that's a gay bar."

"Of course, I know that." She removed her coat and sat down beside me on the sofa. "Well, I didn't know at first. I peeked through the window and it looked so cozy and inviting. Only a few boys were there when I arrived, then the place started to fill up, and before I knew it I was surrounded by handsome men! I chatted with a group of boys from Dallas. Such gentlemen; they didn't let me pay for one drink! I told them all about you, and they're quite keen to meet you."

"Mom, I've told you this before. I'm not gay."

"I know that, dear. But it wouldn't hurt you to make a few friends, gay or straight." She got up and went to the refrigerator, pouring herself a glass of white wine. She sipped it and looked around the room. "This place is so depressing, dear. Why don't you fix it up? You've been here for over three years now."

I reached for the remote and turned on the TV. "I'm planning to paint."

"You told me that last time I was here." She sat down beside me again. "I'm not a doctor, but I have a pretty good idea that cactus is dead."

I glanced over. The cactus was doubled over in its planter like an outlaw that had been shot, its green skin turning a sickly shade of brown. "I don't know, Mom, I think its best years might still be ahead."

"So what are we going to do tonight?"

"Tonight? It's 9:30 on Christmas Eve. There is nothing to do." I glanced at her flushed face. "Haven't you had enough fun for one night?"

"One can never have enough fun in New York City. We could go back down the street for a pint."

"I'm not going to a gay bar. Certainly not with my mother."

"If you're going to be such a stick in the mud, I may go back there by myself."

"Be my guest."

"I *am* your guest. And you're certainly not being very hospitable. You seem to have a lot more time and energy for your hotel guests—a bunch of strangers!—than for your own mother."

Life had been so much simpler alone. I flicked channels on the remote control, staring intently at the TV set.

"Well, I guess I'll go back to the hotel, then," Mom said. But she didn't move. She pretended to watch TV with me.

I started to feel guilty. Maybe I should take her out, even for a walk. But I was so exhausted I couldn't move, and soon I drifted off.

When I woke up a few hours later, she was gone.

9

A Parallel Universe

Mom called me at eight the next morning and insisted on coming over to my cramped apartment to spend Christmas morning rather than staying in her roomy suite at the Universe. "I've had the heat cranked since I got here but it's still cold," she complained. "All these windows and that high ceiling! I thought we should be somewhere cozy."

She arrived in a taxi promptly at 9:00 AM, her arms loaded with bags of wrapped gifts and snacks, a grinning taxi driver behind her carrying even more bags. He set a small suitcase down by the door, wished us a merry Christmas, and left.

I regarded the suitcase warily.

"I brought my jammies!" Mom explained. "I thought it would be fun to change into our PJs for old times' sake."

I couldn't recall a Christmas where we had ever sat around in pajamas, but I played along. "How about sweatpants and a T-shirt?"

"Whatever makes you comfortable."

When I emerged from my room, I found that she had stacked a half-dozen wrapped gifts around the twelve-inch fir tree that I had bought at a corner store on Ninth, dwarfing it. We sat on the floor, sipped coffee, ate cinnamon buns, and opened our presents. Once again I felt content, but I was also a bit on edge, suspicious of her unusually cooperative and compliant behavior. We were like enemies during a cease-fire.

"This is for you," I said, handing her a gift I had purchased and wrapped at Saks after the funeral yesterday.

"You shouldn't have!" She peeled off the silver foil and withdrew a tiny jewelry box. When she lifted the lid, her eyes bulged at the diamond studs that glittered back at her. "My goodness!" she exclaimed, looking up at me in shock. "They're gorgeous! But dear, how extravagant!"

I was delighted that she liked them, having spent a small fortune, although I had justified it because I rarely spent money on myself.

She put them on and marched back and forth behind the sofa as though on a catwalk. "Hot or not?"

"Definitely hot. This is for you, too."

She accepted the next gift almost reluctantly and unwrapped it carefully, sliding a copy of Willard Godfrey's book from the paper. "Oh," she said, her eyes fluttering as she turned it over. "*Universal Values.*"

"I thought it might help you appreciate my work. He autographed it inside."

"So he did. Well!" She sighed and put the book down, reaching for one of her gifts and handing it to me with great ceremony. "Your turn!"

I tore the wrapping off. It too was a book, a copy of *Refurbish Your Life!*

Touché, mother, I thought. Not wanting to reveal my irritation as blatantly as she, I opened it enthusiastically and flipped to the first page, reading aloud. "'Too often we approach change in our lives the same way we might approach a home renovation. Either we want to gut the whole room and start over or simply paint over the problem.

But true change requires getting to the root of the problem and truly understanding it before we start reconstruction. Sometimes we strip away that weathered surface and discover a whole lot more needs fixing than we bargained for. Other times we find a beautiful original finish that should never have been painted over. Whatever the case, within all of us is a solidly built foundation that's worth preserving. Seldom is a full renovation required; usually a few simple changes— sealing a few cracks, replacing outdated furniture, a bright new paint color—is all we need. And that's what this book is all about. Drawing from my own experience as host of a hit home-makeover series and my battles with depression, cancer, and loss of a loved one, I'm going to show you how to *Refurbish Your Life!*'" I flipped the book over and regarded the photo of a smiling Kathy T. McAfee, looking fresh from the beauty parlor—or plastic surgeon. "Hmm, thanks, Mom. Can't wait to read it."

"And I yours."

We were squaring off. Our books might as well have been called *My Agenda,* with each of us the respective authors. I set the book down on the sofa and opened her other gifts. They weren't quite as manipulative: a forty-eight-pack of Royale three-ply toilet tissue, a flat of Campbell's tomato soup, and an enormous box of no-name lemon-fresh laundry detergent. In recent years Mom had developed an obsession with bulk products, the bigger the better, as though terrified of running out of things. It was likely the result of my upbringing; after Dad died, we ran out of things regularly—little things like food and clothing and money.

"Thanks, Mom," I said, wondering where I'd find room to put this stuff.

"Oh, and this last one is for you, too."

I unwrapped it and found a shimmering silver shirt inside the box. I thought it was a mistake, that it was a New Year's Eve blouse meant for Wendy. I held it up. "What is it?"

"It's a club shirt. All the boys wear them now."

"But I don't go to clubs."

"You can wear it to parties too."

"I don't go to parties."

"How about New Year's Eve? It's very festive."

"I'll be working on New Year's Eve, and I certainly won't be dressed in a strobe light."

"Then wear it to the goddamned grocery store, for all I care!" she cried, her eyes flashing with rage.

I regarded her warily. "Maybe I'll try it on." I carried the items into the bathroom, placing the enormous package of toilet paper on the toilet and the detergent into the bathtub, the only places they would fit; the cabinet beneath the sink was still overflowing with the bulk cleaning products she had sent for my birthday. I squeezed into the shirt. The sleeves were so short and tight they cut off the circulation to my arms; if I wore it for more than a few minutes amputation would be inevitable. I glanced in the mirror. I had to admit, it made me look kind of buff. I flexed my arms, puffed out my chest, and sucked in my gut. Whatever happened to last year's resolution to start working out? One of the perks of my job was free membership to the gym at the Sea of Tranquility Spa, one of the best gyms in the city. I desperately needed a tan, too. Maybe a winter vacation in January? I hadn't gone anywhere since I moved to New York; last year, Mr. Godfrey had paid out about six thousand dollars' worth of unused vacation time to me. It was still sitting in the bank.

"Let's see!" Mom called from the living room.

I walked out.

"Look at you!" she cried. "So strong and handsome! You look like a rock star."

"Yeah, Barry Gibb." I returned to the bathroom and pulled it off, putting the T-shirt back on.

"So what are we doing for dinner tonight?" Mom asked when I came back.

"Didn't I tell you? Sandy James invited us to dinner."

"Who?" I saw hope flicker in her eyes. A girlfriend?

"Our human resources director. You met her last time you were here. Don't you remember?"

She made a face. "That smiley woman?"

"I thought you two hit it off. She really liked you."

"I recall her being a bit vacuous."

"She is not vacuous! She's very intelligent."

"Intelligent isn't the first adjective that came to mind when I met her."

"I adore Sandy, Mom. She's like a sister to me."

"Pardon me? You *have* two sisters."

"Like a third sister," I added quickly, "like my glamorous New York sister."

"As opposed to what? Your frumpy Vancouver sisters?"

"That's not what I meant."

"She struck me as a bit phony. All that smiling! I don't trust people who smile a lot."

"Mom, that's one of the most ridiculous things I've ever heard."

She began fussing around the room, folding the wrapping paper for reuse, tidying up the sofa cushions, and going to the closet to withdraw a broom. "It's true, Trevor. No one's that happy all the time. People who smile that much are desperate for you to like them. Either that or they're hiding something. Smiles are meant to be cherished, to be dispensed frugally, to be used at times of joy or mirth. Otherwise they're gratuitous and sycophantic."

Clearly she had given the subject a great deal of thought. I glanced at the book I had just given her, which argued, among other things, that smiles could heal all wounds. Perhaps it was best she didn't read it. It would only make me vulnerable to more ridicule, to more of her infuriating theories.

"Smiles happen to be one of the most basic tools of my profession," I said.

"So I noticed. I've been meaning to tell you, dear, that people smile far too much at your hotel. I passed the front desk this morning and all three clerks looked up at me and grinned in unison for no reason whatsoever. They looked like a bunch of half-wits. I was tempted to give them the finger."

"Jesus, Mom. Don't you dare! They're still recovering from Janet and Wendy's visit."

"Yes, well, Janet and Wendy are still recovering, too."

"What do you mean by that?"

"Why don't you ask them? You might want to rethink how that hotel is run now that Mr. Godfrey's out of the picture. People don't want all this fussing about and obsequiousness. They want simple, efficient, unobtrusive service. Just hand me my bloody key and I'll let you know if I need anything."

"Clearly you're not our target market. Next time, I'll book you into some fleabag motel in the Bronx."

She was on her knees now, sweeping under the sofa, extracting items I hadn't seen for ages. I bent down and snatched up a copy of *Penthouse* and secreted it into the bedroom, hiding it under a pillow.

"Can't we just go out for a nice dinner?" she asked, her voice whiney.

"It's too late to cancel, Mom. Besides, you'll love Sandy's husband. I don't think I've ever seen him smile. He's one of those tortured artist types who's angry all the time. The two of you will get along famously."

Mom put the broom down and squatted down at the table, removing her earrings and placing them into the box. "Don't you spend enough time with people from work? The gals at the hospital are always asking me to join them for various silly activities like bowling and lingerie parties, but they're the last people I want to see in my free time. Don't you have a lady friend, Trevor?"

Finally, the question that had been burning inside her since the moment she stepped off the plane. I had to admire her for holding off this long. Immediately I thought of Nancy, and my heart soared; then, upon recalling our last conversation, it deflated like a wayward balloon. "No, Mom, no 'lady friend.'"

"Anybody special at all?"

"Will you please stop insinuating that I'm gay?"

"I was doing no such thing! I was simply saying that—"

"You're disappointed that I'm not gay, aren't you?"

"Sometimes you say the most ludicrous things. No, I am not disappointed that you're not gay. But it wouldn't matter to me either way. Your Uncle Thomas has lived a wonderful life without the burden of women and children. That man really knows how to live. Oh, he gave me a list of Broadway shows he says are just fabulous. Apparently there's a place you can buy same-day tickets for half price. Maybe that's what we could do tomorrow night. He recommends *Hairspray*."

"I hate Broadway."

"How you've become such a curmudgeon at such a young age, I'll never know."

"I am *not* a curmudgeon. Listen, I promise we won't stay long at Sandy's. Her kids go to bed early."

"Kids?" She wrinkled her nose. "I'm not much for children, Trevor."

"So I gathered from my upbringing."

"I mean other people's children. I *love* Aiden and Tate and Jordan and Quinn and Emily. Those are your nephews and nieces, in case you were wondering. I was hoping to spend time exclusively with adults on this trip—with *you*, dear. We see so little of one another." She was silent for a moment. "What about that girl from the Park Harbour Hotel you told me about a while back? I believe her name was Rosa. What ever happened to her?"

"She sued me for sexual harassment."

"Oh, right, I forgot. Well, I guess it wasn't meant to be."

That evening, Mom and I took a train to Hoboken, New Jersey, then a taxi from the train station to Sandy's house, located on a nondescript street among a row of identical houses.

When Sandy opened her door, she broke into a huge smile. "Well, if it isn't Evelyn Lambert," she cried, throwing both arms open wide, "producer of the finest director of rooms in New York! How lovely to see you again! Merry Christmas! Oh, you shouldn't have! What a *lovely* poinsettia!"

Before entering, I turned to sneak another look at the '96 black Ford Ranger parked in the driveway and tried to imagine it plowing into Mr. Godfrey. *Impossible.*

"You coming in, Trevor?" asked Sandy.

I walked inside and gave her a hug. She looked like a beautifully wrapped Christmas present in a festive red dress and shiny gold belt, with a corsage of holly and red berries pinned over her breast. She took our coats, and we made our way up the stairs to the living room.

The smell of turkey wafted from the kitchen, and Karen Carpenter was singing "Christmas Song" on the stereo. A fire burned in the fireplace.

"Why, isn't this cozy!" said Mom, eyes nervously scanning the room for children.

Sandy fussed around us almost maniacally. "Make yourselves at home! Jack is so looking forward to meeting you, Evelyn. Can I offer you a cocktail? Perhaps a glass of rum and eggnog? My, what a gorgeous dress! What a slim, lovely figure you have! Jack, darling, come and say hi!" In the few times I had visited Sandy's home, I was surprised to see that she maintained the exact same persona at home as at work: she was always impeccably groomed, full of smiles, and exceedingly gracious. Yet her home was modest, much more so than I would expect, the furniture plain and monotone, floors scattered with toys. A faint smell of cat litter lingered in the air, although I had never seen a cat. Somehow I had expected a more glamorous home environment, and each time, although I could not say why, I felt disappointed.

Mom was drawn immediately to the artwork on the walls, an abstract series of splotches of color framed in stainless steel, most of them—to my eye, anyway—indistinguishable from one another. She stopped to examine a particularly disturbing smear of dark colors.

"Aren't they beautiful?" Sandy said, coming up from behind. "Jack painted all of them."

"Stunning. This one's a landscape, right?"

"Very good!" Sandy pointed to a black smudge in the upper right-hand corner. "That's the sun."

"How intriguing."

Jack came round from the kitchen, wiping his hands on an apron. "Merry Christmas," he said. He was dressed in a loose vintage T-shirt, tattered jeans, and flip-flops. His thick, dirty-blond hair was mussed.

He was a handsome, rugged man, a former college football player who had quit sports to pursue the arts.

"Hey, Evelyn, good to meet you," he said, his shy, casual manner a contrast to Sandy's gushing formality.

As I anticipated, Mom seemed to take a shine to him immediately. She spent the next ten minutes raving about his artwork.

"Kids!" cried Sandy. "Come and say hi to Trevor and Mrs. Lambert."

I saw Mom visibly wince.

There was no response.

"They got video games for Christmas," Sandy explained. "We might not see them all night."

Mom broke into a smile. Jack served cocktails, then clattered about the kitchen, emerging every once in a while to offer hors d'oeuvres and to replenish our drinks. He was pleasant but quiet and unsmiling. I wondered how he was taking all the trauma and drama Sandy was experiencing at work.

About an hour into the evening, Jack carried Kaitlin and Wesley in and plopped them down on either side of Sandy, then returned to the kitchen. They both looked pissed off.

"Evelyn," said Sandy. "These are my two children, Wesley and—" she hesitated for the slightest moment. The little girl stared up at her with enormous eyes, sucking her thumb. "Kaitlin. Kaitie is three, and Wesley is four."

"Five," said Wesley.

"Five."

"Nice to meet you," Mom said, flashing a fake smile that likely didn't fool the kids.

The children snuggled up against their mother, clinging to either arm as though afraid she might escape, and stared at my mother with a mixture of curiosity and fear. As Sandy chattered away, Mom listened politely, likely clicking an imaginary counter every time she smiled—which happened often. Yet Sandy's smile was different tonight; it seemed unnatural and forced, even more so than I had observed at work this week. Whenever Jack made an appearance he avoided eye contact with her, even when they exchanged words. I sensed that things were not good between them and wanted to ask Sandy if she was okay. But I knew it would be pointless; even if she wasn't, she would never admit it.

Mom drank three rum and eggnogs before dinner and seemed to be having a wonderful time. When we sat down for dinner, Sandy asked her about her job as a nurse, then said, "I myself always wanted to be a nurse. I remember visiting my aunt in the hospital when I was six years old. She was terribly ill with rheumatic fever. A huge, matronly nurse kept coming in to perform various nursely duties, taking her temperature, giving her medication, and fluffing her pillows. I was so impressed with her efficiency. The next time I saw my aunt, she was fully recovered, and I attributed the recovery entirely to the nurse. At the time, I thought it was the doctors who played the supporting role."

"In many ways, they do," said Mom.

"I never went to nursing school, but I did stay in the hospitality profession."

Mom tilted her head. "I never thought of nursing as hospitality."

"But isn't it exactly that?" Sandy persisted. "I mean, we both work in a place full of rooms with beds, where people come to sleep, and it's our job to take care of them. A hotel is like a hospital, but with more comfortable beds and better food." She burst into laughter.

Mom smiled pleasantly.

Dinner was hearty and down-home, though somewhat bland, and certainly not of Universe caliber.

Mom raved and raved and *raved* about it. "Such a pleasant change from all the rich food at your spaceship hotel," she said. "Rich food gives me gas."

"I guess that makes you a comet, then," said Sandy. "Full of gas." She burst into laughter again. By now she had consumed the better portion of a bottle of sparkling wine.

"Sandy uses a space analogy to describe how the hotel functions," I hastened to explain. "She likes to categorize people according to where they fall in the solar system, kind of a mix of astrology and astronomy."

As Sandy launched into an explanation, I got up to help Jack with dessert: pumpkin pie he had made from scratch. In the kitchen I made several attempts at conversation, but he gave one-word answers.

Later, when Mom was in the kitchen helping with dishes, I pulled Sandy aside. "Is everything okay?"

"Of course! Why?"

"I sense tension between you and Jack. He seems angry."

"Jack always seems angry, but he's a big ol' teddy bear. Things couldn't be better!"

"I'm glad," I said, not believing her.

"While you're here, Trevor," she said, hushing her voice, "I should probably tell you what I plan to do when we get back to work on Tuesday. I've been so distraught about how things are going at the hotel. I think Cynthia has made a terrible mistake promoting Matthew, and I'm going to do something about it."

"Oh?"

"I've decided to pitch Cynthia on promoting me to general manager," she said. "I'm going to divulge our plan, including promoting you to director of operations. I hope I can count on your support."

In the kitchen I heard Mom shriek with laughter.

By the steely resolve in her eyes, I could tell she was dead serious. "Why don't we discuss this on Tuesday," I said, "when things have settled down."

"Fine," she said. "But my mind is already made up."

10

Cosmic Shock Wave

The next day, Boxing Day, Mom convinced me to take the morning off to go shopping with her, but she failed to mention it would involve being hauled out of bed at 6:15 AM so we could stand in the freezing cold outside of Lord & Taylor in a line of bargain hunters a mile long. She had scoured the *New York Times* for sales, mapping her day of shopping with the cunning and precision of a military invasion, organizing her route not geographically but in order of maximum discount advertised.

At 7:20 she stormed out of Lord & Taylor in a huff, hands empty. "Even with 70 percent off, it's overpriced," she muttered, charging onto Fifth Avenue to hail a cab.

We went to Borders at Union Square next (50 percent off), then back uptown to Saks Fifth Avenue (also 50 percent off), down Broadway to Macy's (40 percent off), and uptown again to Burberry (30 to 40 percent off). Once she started buying she couldn't stop, and soon my arms were weighed down with bags.

"This place looks expensive," I said as we arrived at Burberry.

"Nonsense. They're having a huge sale. I need a dress for New Year's."

I opted to shiver in the cold on Fifty-seventh Avenue rather than brave the artillery inside. A half-hour later she emerged, grinning ear to ear, handing me a checkered Burberry bag and rushing into the street to flag a taxi. I peeked inside the bag and saw an expensive-looking burgundy silk dress and a pair of leather gloves.

"Trevor, come on! Hurry!" She was holding open the door of a taxi.

"Where are we going now?" I asked as I climbed in.

"Soho."

"We just came from downtown! Do you realize you've spent more on cabs than you've saved on sales? Ever consider the subway?"

"With all these bags?"

In Soho Mom checked out what I estimated to be over 1,500 stores. She shopped with killer instincts and surgical precision, first lurking around the display window outside to determine if the store merited her attention (invariably, it did). Once inside, she dodged even the most tenacious retail clerk, pistol-whipped regular-price racks out of her way, and launched a full frontal assault on heavy-discount racks and bargain tables. In seconds she weeded out the junk and snatched up anything of value, holding it up to perform a quick cost-benefit analysis. If it measured up, she tucked it under her arm and charged for the cash register. On several occasions I witnessed her flagrantly butting to the front of the line; on one occasion a young guy protested, but relented when she pretended to be a confused, doddering old woman. Emerging from the store, eyes rabid, she would hand me her kill, already scoping the street ahead.

She went into three RiteAid outlets. Whether she didn't realize they were the same store or was searching for something the other outlets were out of, I couldn't be sure, and I knew better than to question.

"This is for you," she said, handing me a bag as she exited the third outlet.

I peered inside. "Minoxidil?"

"It's a generic brand of Rogaine."

"*Rogaine?* I'm not balding."

She glanced at my scalp and pressed her lips together. "Let's call it a preventative measure. Your grandfather was bald by the time he was forty. He had one long strand of hair that he coiled around his head. Mother hated it so much she shaved it off one night while he was sleeping." She was walking so fast I could barely keep up. "Your Uncle Thomas asked me to pick some up for him, and I thought I'd get some for you too. It's cheaper here in the States. And stronger—just like the cocktails. God bless America."

For the rest of the day I obsessed over my hair, checking every mirror and window we passed for bald spots or signs of thinning.

Next on her list was Century 21. It was a bloodbath. Alarmed by the size of the opposing army, I decided to accompany Mom inside to help shield her and was almost flattened on more than one occasion. Soon I lost patience and grabbed Mom by the arm, forcing her into a full-scale retreat. She agreed on a cease-fire, and we stopped at Balthazar for lunch.

"I bought presents for your sisters and all your nieces and nephews," she said over a croque monsieur. "There might even be a surprise or two for you."

"What, more Rogaine? Maybe some Viagra too?"

"Trevor, please."

"Where are you getting all this money, anyway?"

"I'll have you know I make a decent earning at the hospital. I'm not going to defend myself for a little harmless consumerism. I barely spent a dime on myself for twenty years. I'm still catching up. Besides, this is my holiday. I have every intention of shopping and drinking excessively, and your miserly ways are not about to get in the way." As if to prove the point, she ordered a glass of merlot.

After lunch, I left her to continue shopping alone and took her bags home. When she showed up three hours later, she rummaged through her bags and presented me with a twelve-pound box of laundry detergent, a two-gallon container of Palmolive, a twelve-pack of Bounty paper towels, and an eight-bar package of Dial Mountain Fresh soap.

"No wonder my arms are killing me," I said. "Where am I going to put all this?"

"In your kitchen cupboards."

"No way. They're jammed."

"Not anymore."

I went to the kitchen and opened the cupboards. They were almost empty, and spotless. "When did you do this?"

"The other night, while you were sleeping."

"What did you do with everything?"

"I threw most of it away. It wouldn't hurt to check expiry dates once in a while, dear. Cereal doesn't last three years. Nor does peanut butter. Oh, that reminds me." She searched her bags and handed me three netted pouches containing wood chips and dried flowers. "These are for you."

"What are they?"

"Potpourri sachets. Your apartment smells musty."

I sniffed them. "They smell like an old lady's perfume."

"Better than sweaty jockstraps." She searched through more bags and pulled out a pair of bluejeans. "Here, try these on."

They were Diesel jeans, tattered and worn, faded at the front and back, with patched holes on the behind. I didn't own any jeans like this; I knew they cost over two hundred dollars. I went into my bedroom and pulled them on. They fit nicely, although a bit loose around the waist, but nothing a belt wouldn't fix.

I came out to model them. "Wow, Mom. These are great. Thanks."

"Oh, they're not for you, they're for your Uncle Thomas. I wanted to see how they fit. They do look good on you. You should buy a pair too."

"I have enough jeans, Mom."

"No one under forty wears Levi's 501s anymore, dear."

"*You* bought them for me!"

"Ten years ago."

I went to my bedroom to remove them and handed them back to her. "I booked you for some treatments in the Sea of Tranquility Spa tonight at 6:00 PM. Massage, manicure, pedicure, and facial. How does that sound?"

She scrutinized my face, as though suspicious of my motives. "Sounds divine! We can have a late dinner afterwards. I asked your concierge to book us at a hot new restaurant. He reserved us at Ono at 9:00 PM. It's a swank little restaurant in Hotel Gansevoort in the Meatpacking District. I read up on it in *New York Magazine*."

We agreed to meet at the front door of the hotel at 8:30 PM.

I hung around at home for a while after she left, but I was restless, so I decided to go to the hotel early to check on things.

All was quiet in the Universe. I stopped by the front desk to casually inquire as to the whereabouts of Nancy Swinton and was disheartened to learn that she had worked a morning shift; Gaetan was working the evening shift. I spent an hour doing rounds, drifting listlessly from department to department, and at 8:00 PM I stopped on the seventy-fourth floor, at Stratosphere, which was closed for the evening.

One of the city's most popular nightclubs, Stratosphere was located in the upper hemisphere of the Glittersphere; like the other floors, its outer walls were comprised of mirrored glass, and the room completed one full revolution each hour. From Monday to Saturday, club-goers flocked to Stratosphere for the spectacular laser shows and celebrity sightings. The ceiling and dance floor were embedded with tiny star lights to emulate a futuristic nightclub floating in space. Five tiered levels of banquettes and cocktail tables descended to a dance floor at the center of the room, its inner walls mounted with large screens for videos and graphics.

I flicked on the lights and made my way to the window, which was facing the southeastern edge of Central Park and the Upper East Side. Through a gap in the skyline, I could see a sliver of the East River and the lights of the Queensboro bridge. It was raining, and great globules of moisture were exploding on the glass, blurring the glow of city lights below. I checked all three bars to ensure they were tidy and locked up, then verified that the bathrooms were clean and the manager's office was secure. Satisfied, I headed for the exit. As I was passing the coat check, my Universal Communications Device sounded. I pulled the device from my belt and peered into the blue fluorescent window.

EGP 555—CALL GAETAN BOUDREAU.

An Emergency Group Page. Quickly, I punched in the code.

Gaetan answered immediately. "Are you near a TV?" he asked.

I looked down at the dance floor and the enormous video screen before it. "Kind of. Why?"

"*Borderline News* is about to start. They've announced a story on the Universe."

I disconnected and went to the bar for the remote control. From the middle of the dance floor I flicked on the television and found NBC. On the enormous screen before me, a swirl of colorful graphics morphed into a map of North America, the words "*Borderline News*" forming the border between the United States and Canada. A deep, masculine voice announced, "From NBC's *Borderline News* studio in Niagara Falls, New York, here is your host, Honica Winters."

The map faded and a silhouette of Honica Winters appeared. She was sitting on a stool in her studio. The lights slowly brightened, revealing her striking face, her blond hair tied back. She was dressed in an opal-colored satin blouse, cobalt blue blazer, and a short black skirt that revealed her long, slender legs. She looked stern and seasoned.

"Good evening," she said, "and welcome to our special holiday edition of *Borderline News*."

Her image rose before me to twelve feet in height, an amazon of legs and breasts and hair. Her voice was thunderous. I stumbled away from the screen and scrambled for the remote to reduce the volume.

"This holiday season," she said, "as the U.S. economy continues to recover and corporations report greater third-quarter profits than any quarter since September 11, across America the lavish office Christmas party returned with a vengeance. Nowhere was this more evident than in New York City, where for three years a rattled population has shied away from conspicuous displays of corporate excess in favor of more modest celebrations or no party at all. This year, New York hotels and catering companies reported increases in holiday party spending of between 20 percent and 100 percent.

"Along with this renewed enthusiasm for celebration came behavior that has made office Christmas parties legendary: excessive drinking, bad judgment, and career-limiting conduct. These celebrations also prompted a spike in the most dangerous holiday pastime of all: drunk driving."

Honica paused and fixed her stare into the camera. "Every year, seventeen thousand people in the United States are killed in alcohol-related traffic accidents and over a half a million people are injured. The holiday season alone accounts for over fifteen hundred of these fatalities. Every year it's the same story: people go to parties, get drunk, and drive home, sometimes with tragic consequences.

"Tonight, *Borderline News* takes a sober look at the attitudes and behaviors of North Americans toward drunk driving. The focus of our story is Manhattan's swanky and futuristic Universe Hotel, where this year function rooms and restaurants were sold out months in advance. Last week, Willard Godfrey, owner of the Universe Hotel and author of the best-selling book *Universal Values,* was struck down and killed by a vehicle in the hotel's underground parkade only minutes after leaving the hotel's staff holiday party. The perpetrator fled the scene and no arrest has yet been made, but circumstances suggest a tragically ironic scenario: Mr. Godfrey, a teetotaler and a supporter of the anti-impaired driving movement, may have been killed by a drunk driver—perhaps by one of his own staff who could very well have been intoxicated by alcohol paid for by him."

"Oh god," I said under my breath. My pager went off, but I ignored it, unable to take my eyes off the screen. I backed into a banquette on the edge of the dance floor and sat down.

Honica swiveled in her chair and faced another camera. Behind her, a photo of a smiling Willard Godfrey appeared above the caption INTOXICATED UNIVERSE. "Willard Godfrey's death occurred on the eve of the arrival in New York City of fifteen hundred delegates of the Victims of Impaired Drivers conference, commonly known as VOID. The host hotel for seven hundred of these delegates? The Universe. In fact, Willard Godfrey was slated to speak at the conference's opening reception tomorrow night. His death has left conference organizers scrambling to find a replacement."

The lights in the studio faded, and Honica reappeared on Avenue of the Americas below the Universe Hotel sign. I recognized her tan trench coat; she was in the exact spot she had interviewed me. I covered my eyes, afraid to look, but peeked at the screen through my fingers.

"I'm standing before the formidable edifice of the Universe Hotel," Honica shouted over the din of traffic, "one of New York's most famous modern landmarks. Since the massive steel doors behind me glided open almost five years ago, the hotel has hosted heads of state, royalty, celebrities, rock stars, and astronauts. Built to resemble a futuristic space colony, the Universe houses a remarkable combination of astronomy, technology, and hospitality under its glittering glass sphere. Celebrities love it, scientists and astronomers praise it, and thousands of tourists and New York residents flock to it every year.

"This year, Willard Godfrey threw a lavish staff holiday party in the hotel's Observatory, located on the top floor of the hotel, seventy-five floors above the city streets." The camera moved up the glass tower to the Glittersphere and back down to Honica. "Almost eight hundred staff members attended the party, from chambermaids to busboys, room service attendants to line cooks, dishwashers to executive staff. For one special night, these hardworking employees experienced the five-star service they are more accustomed to providing: gourmet cuisine, vintage wines, and sumptuous desserts.

"This year, the menu was typical of the hotel's five-star Orbit Restaurant," Honica continued as the camera scrolled down the menu. "A sumptuous buffet featured gourmet dishes like steamed Atlantic lobster, filet mignon, wasabe mashed potatoes, snow peas, and grilled asparagus. For dessert, there was Grand Marnier soufflé, chocolate Frangelico mousse, Indian Ginger crème brûlée, and a selection of gourmet ice creams and sorbets. To drink? Sparkling wine upon arrival, a selection of wines for dinner, liqueurs for dessert, and a host bar all evening.

"I have a copy of the party's liquor bill," Honica shouted, holding up a sheet of paper that rippled in the wind. "The total came to over *fifty thousand dollars* for alcohol alone, almost half the party's budget, an average of approximately six drinks per person. Getting drunk is no crime, of course. In fact, for many in our nation it's a holiday tradition. The crucial question is, how did the people who had too much to drink get home? And what led to the tragic death of the man who footed the bill for this extravagant affair?"

I breathed a sigh of relief as Honica reappeared back in her studio. I was off the hook—for now.

"Willard Godfrey arranged for complimentary shuttle bus service for staff to ensure they got home safely that night," said Honica. "But *Borderline News* has learned that not all hotel staff took advantage of this service. When we come back, we'll find out exactly who took the bus and who drove home. We'll also talk to the executive director of the Victims of Impaired Drivers conference to find out just how much of a problem drunk driving is in America."

Honica faded from the screen and a commercial began.

I stood up and paced the room. My U-Comm went off again. Disregarding it, I climbed up the stairs to the bar and used my master key to unlock the liquor cabinet, pouring a generous glass of Scotch. By the time I got back to my seat, *Borderline News* had recommenced.

Brenda's corpulent figure was onscreen now. She was sitting in a Swan chair in her Supernova suite, facing Honica, elbows resting on the armrests, fists clenched. A silver tray of tea and scones sat on the coffee table beside her. Onscreen appeared the caption BRENDA RATHBERGER, VICTIMS OF IMPAIRED DRIVERS.

"Mrs. Rathberger," said Honica, "how many drinks does it take to become legally impaired?"

Brenda's face filled the screen. She looked confident and authoritative, and seemed to have a great deal of makeup on. "Each person's tolerance level varies," she replied. "It depends on body type, gender, health, and other factors. For most people, it takes only one or two drinks to reach the legal limit of .08 percent blood alcohol content set by most American states and Canadian provinces. Contrary to popular myth, once you reach that limit, while it will make you more alert, a cup of coffee or a cheeseburger is not going to lower your blood alcohol content."

Honica nodded, her lips slightly pursed, a purple-polished fingernail propping up her chin. "You've seen the bill for alcohol from the Universe Hotel's Christmas party. Do you think it's excessive?"

"Yes, I think it's excessive, but I'm more concerned about how the impaired people got home and how a man ended up dead. Whether there's a connection I cannot say but, as they say, where there's smoke, there's fire. In the majority of cases where traffic accidents occur late at night on weekends, especially during the festive season, alcohol plays a factor. It's the responsibility of the party host, whether it's a small business, a billion-dollar corporation, a bar, or a small house party, to ensure guests get home safely."

"But it's not always easy to monitor how much our guests have consumed. How can we tell if they're impaired?"

"The signs of impairment are easy to recognize: bloodshot eyes, impaired speech, poor balance. Intoxicated people tend to respond inappropriately to questions, to behave erratically. Some experience a feeling of invincibility and, as a result, they think they are fine to drive home. This sense of invincibility compels them to drive faster and more aggressively. Alcohol is a depressant; it dulls the senses and impairs reaction time, concentration, coordination, judgment, information processing, and visual awareness."

"Not the best conditions for driving."

"The worst conditions for driving," said Brenda. "A drunk is the last person who should be making a decision whether or not to drive."

Honica flipped her hair back. "How common is drunk driving?"

"Drunk driving is the nation's most frequently committed violent crime. Alcohol is responsible for over 40 percent of traffic fatalities. One life is lost every thirty minutes to an alcohol-related automobile crash. As far as VOID is concerned, there is no difference between a loaded gun and a loaded driver. In fact, almost three times as many people are killed in impaired driving crashes in America than are murdered." Brenda was blinking furiously now. "Impaired drivers are guilty of the most serious, most deadly, and most costly crime on the continent."

Honica nodded slowly. "The theme of your conference is 'Society for Sobriety.' Is drunk driving a social disease?"

"Alcohol is society's oldest and most popular drug. As long as it is socially acceptable to drink and drive, it will continue to be a social disease."

"Is drunk driving on the increase or on the wane?" asked Honica.

"On the wane, I'm happy to say, for a number of reasons. The efforts of organizations like Victims of Impaired Drivers have ..."

My U-Comm sounded again. I muted the TV and answered it.

It was Matthew Drummond. "Are you watching this abomination?"

"Yes."

"I thought I told you to straighten Honica out!"

"I tried to! She must have decided not to show my interview."

In the background I could hear Marline ranting, "How will I ever face my friends again?"

"Will you *pipe down*, Marline!" Matthew cried. "Trevor, you better hope Cynthia Godfrey isn't watching this. She'll be furious! How could you let this happen?"

"Me? It's not *my* fault. Cynthia's the one who gave Honica permission to film in the hotel."

"You should have known she was working this angle. I warned you about this and told you to put a stop to it. You've really messed up, Trevor. God knows what's coming next."

I looked up at the screen and almost fell over. A twelve-foot version of my face filled it. "Oh god," I said. "I gotta go." I disconnected and turned up the volume.

"... rest assured, no one drank excessively," I was saying to Honica. The footage jumped to the end of my interview, where my face had assumed a decidedly less cordial expression. "Miss Winters, we run a first-class hotel here. My colleagues and I are highly responsible, law-abiding citizens. We are role models for hotel staff—and, I believe, for society in general. The Universe Hotel operates in accordance with Universal Values, as written by Willard Godfrey and elaborated on in his book by the same name. Our behavior is guided by the principles of respect, integrity, and accountability." My face faded from the screen.

Honica was back in her studio. "Is Trevor Lambert telling the truth? Are he and his colleagues the responsible, law-abiding citizens he claims? Are they really 'role models' for other staff? To help us better understand what really went on at that night, *Borderline News* obtained exclusive video footage from the Universe Hotel's holiday party."

Uh-oh. I fumbled for my Scotch and gulped it down.

The screen came alive with footage from Susan Medley's video. *How on earth...?* I suddenly recalled how smitten Susan had been with Honica, how eager to please. She must have given her the video! A clip of Sandy, Shanna, Matthew, Willard, and me appeared; we were standing at the front door of the hotel receiving staff as they climbed out of the shuttle buses. We were dressed in our finest, looking glamorous, dignified, and very sober. The footage jumped to later in the evening. Matthew and Sandy were standing at the bar, sipping drinks, as Mr. Godfrey gave his speech. Shanna Virani appeared, sneaking a generous gulp of red wine as she watched him speak. Matthew appeared next, whispering into Sandy's ear. Someone bumped him from behind and red wine flew out of his glass, landing on Sandy's bosom. She looked down in alarm, then the two of them burst into laughter. The music of Gene Autry's "Rudolph the Red-Nosed Reindeer" began playing in the background, and Matthew's face filled the screen again, his nose looking rather rosy. He lifted a glass of beer and drained it while Nancy Swinton and Gaetan Boudreau looked on. Gaetan was grinning in amusement, and Nancy was resting her hand on his shoulder as if to steady him.

The next clip showed a conga line forming on the dance floor, an improbable Shanna at its lead. As it snaked around the periphery of the Observatory, the city lights in the backdrop, people pushed their faces into the camera, sticking out tongues and making foolish expressions. I appeared last in line, grinning ear to ear like a complete fool, wearing a napkin around my head and kicking my legs in a can-can.

I cringed at the image. I looked more absurd than I could possibly imagine. Fearing I might vomit, I pushed the glass of Scotch away.

The clips grew shorter and faster. Every one depicted my colleagues and me sipping, slurping, guzzling, and spilling drinks as names and titles flashed onscreen. The most disturbing shot came last. It was taken near the end of the evening, just before we went down to the front door to see off the last of the shuttle buses, the same clip I had seen in the staff cafeteria: Sandy, Matthew, Shanna, and I standing around the bar, swallowing Big Bangs.

The footage ended and Honica Winters reappeared in her studio. "Clearly," she said, "footage from the Universe Hotel's Christmas party suggests that these hotel executives were not as sober as Trevor Lambert claims. But can they be faulted for having a few drinks with their fellow staff? Certainly not—unless, of course, they chose to drive home inebriated. *Borderline News* has obtained exclusive video footage that tells a much different story from that told by Trevor Lambert, the Universe Hotel's director of rooms." A gritty black-and-white video image appeared behind Honica. "Tape recorded by the hotel's parkade camera captures the license plates of three vehicles leaving the hotel shortly after the party, all registered to hotel executives. The first is the 2004 yellow Chevrolet Blazer owned by Shanna Virani, director of sales and marketing." An inset image of Shanna Virani swallowing a Big Bang appeared onscreen and zigzagged to the upper left corner. "Minutes later," Honica said, "a 1996 black Ford Ranger registered to Jack James, husband of Cassandra James, the hotel's director of human resources, is recorded driving out." The security camera showed Sandy's truck. A screen shot of Sandy sipping red wine appeared and zigzagged to the upper right-hand corner of the screen, juxtaposing Sandy and Shanna like a police lineup. "Seven minutes later," Honica said as the parkade footage fast-forwarded and slowed, stopping on a car speeding out of the parkade, "a 2003 gold BMW 7 Series registered to Matthew Drummond, the hotel's resident manager, is recorded driving out."

Matthew? I jumped to my feet in shock.

A photograph of Matthew spilling wine on Sandy's dress appeared and zigzagged to the top center of the screen between Shanna and Sandy. Said Honica, "Of course, positive identification of these drivers can only be determined by the New York Police Department, who have been extremely tightlipped about their investigation. Autopsy reports and forensic samples taken at the scene of the accident, due for release this week, are expected to provide more clues about who ran down Willard Godfrey."

Honica swiveled in her chair. "The hotel executives in question refused to be interviewed, as did Willard Godfrey's daughter, Manhattan socialite Cynthia Godfrey, who, according to parkade activity records, drove out well before her father was run down." Honica paused and stared fixedly into the camera. "*Borderline News* has uncovered one last shocking piece to this puzzle. Less than twenty minutes after Cassandra James' vehicle was recorded driving out of the hotel parkade, she was involved in an accident at the corner of West Thirty-fourth and Joe DiMaggio Highway in Manhattan."

A photo of Sandy filled the screen. She was sprawled on a patch of pavement next to her Ford Ranger, her party dress soiled and stained. Beside her, the left headlight of the Ranger was smashed, the fender dented. A police officer was shining a flashlight on her. She was gazing into the camera, mouth open, shielding her eyes from the glare.

Said Honica, "According to witnesses, Sandy James, wife of New Jersey artist Jack James and mother of two young children, veered into the oncoming lane as she turned left onto Joe DiMaggio Highway, striking another vehicle head-on. Fortunately, the other driver was not injured, and Mrs. James suffered only minor injuries. Police arrived on the scene immediately. Witnesses report that as Mrs. James climbed from her vehicle, she tripped and fell to the pavement. Seconds later, this photo was taken by a passerby.

"Mrs. James was taken to a local precinct and tested for blood-alcohol content. According to police records, her reading indicated a blood-alcohol level of .15 percent—almost *twice* the legal limit. She was charged with impaired driving and reckless driving and is due to appear in court early in the New Year."

A mug shot of Sandy filled the screen. She was wearing her wine-stained dress, staring wide-eyed into the camera. And smiling.

"When we come back," said Honica, "Brenda Rathberger of Victims of Impaired Drivers shares some tips on ensuring your holiday guests drink responsibly."

I fumbled for the remote and shut the TV off. I had to find Sandy.

11

The Search for Intelligent Life in the Universe

Of the six messages left on my U-Comm, none were from Sandy, the person most likely to be devastated by the *Borderline News* segment. Two were from Gaetan Boudreau, who had called in a panic when the switchboard lit up the instant *Borderline News* ended. The third was from Matthew, to whom I'd already spoken and wasn't about to call back.

The last three were from my mother, whom I'd completely forgotten about.

In the first message, she sounded cheerful and patient: "Hello, dear, it's 8:40 and I'm at the front door. Come down when you're ready." In the second, she sounded irritated but still upbeat: "8:50 and still waiting! Come down as soon as you can!" In the third and final message, her tone was frosty but still tinged with hope: "Well! I guess I've been stood up by my own son! I'll be at Ono if you care to grace me with your presence."

I glanced at my watch. It was 9:05 PM.

I ran out of Stratosphere and down the corridor. In the elevator, I instructed Mona not to stop on any guest floors, then radioed Gaetan as the car plummeted to the administration level, briefing him on how to best handle inquiries. "Tell people as little as possible," I said. "Advise them we simply cannot comment on rumors and innuendo, that the investigation is in the hands of the police and it's business as usual at the Universe."

"Got it," he said. He hesitated. "Did Sandy really do it? Did she run down Mr. Godfrey?"

"Of course not, Gaetan. *Nobody* on staff ran down Mr. Godfrey."

"That's what I'm hoping."

Next I tried to contact Sandy, but there was no answer. I envisioned her at home, hiding under her bed and moaning, in a fetal position. My heart went out to her. As I hastened down the corridor to my office to pick up my coat, I noticed the light on in Sandy's office. The door was partly open. I stopped to shut it, but heard the rustle of papers inside and the sound of … humming.

I pushed the door open. "Sandy?"

She was sitting at her desk, busily organizing files into color-coded stacks of red, blue, green, and yellow. When she heard my voice, she stopped humming and looked up. Her eyes brightened. "Trevor, what a lovely surprise! What brings you here at this hour?" She was fully made up, hair tied back, dressed in a very corporate olive green pantsuit with a white pashmina scarf draped over her shoulder—as though it were Monday morning.

"*I'm* heading out to dinner with my mom," I said. "What are *you* doing here?"

"Honestly, the work never ends." She sighed in a breezy manner that indicated she didn't mind the work at all. "I thought I'd get a head start on our annual personnel file review. Oh, I have some files for you that need updating." Swiveling in her chair like a girl on a swing, she kicked out her heels and reached for a stack of yellow files behind her, handing them to me. "I've made notes on the inside fold-ers so you'll know what's missing. Thanks a bunch!"

I looked down at the stack of files, then back to her. Clearly she knew nothing about *Borderline News*. Still, her behavior was strange, almost *too* happy—even for Sandy. I closed the door and took a seat in the leather chair across the desk from her.

"I'll pick these up on Monday, okay?" I said, sliding them back to her. "Right now, we need to talk."

She accepted the files good-naturedly. "Sure, whatever works for you." She resumed her work.

I hesitated, searching for the best way to break the news. The leather armrests beneath my hands were well worn, prematurely aged by thousands of tense, sweaty hands that had gripped them during interviews. Sandy's techniques were legendary: she interviewed can-didates with the warmth and patience of a kindergarten teacher, set-ting them at ease with seemingly innocuous, often ditzy-sounding questions punctuated by smiles, compliments, and remarks about the weather. Yet she scrutinized every word uttered, every flicker of the eye, and every change in tone with the thoroughness of a grand jury and the intolerance of a Spanish Inquisitor. At the outset she always informed candidates that the interview would be "a preliminary ten-minute get-to-know-you session" so that if they weren't the right fit—and she usually knew this within about fifteen seconds—she could cut the interview short without making them feel they had failed. Ninety percent of candidates didn't last the full ten minutes. Those who did were kept on, sometimes for an hour or more, depending on the level of the position, while Sandy slowly and unwaveringly peeled away lay-ers and exposed the true measure of their potential: Sparkle Factor.

"Sandy," I said, feeling the angst of a thousand failed candidates, "*Borderline News* just aired an episode on drunk driving. The focus was the Universe, and somehow they got hold of Susan's Christmas party video. They showed pictures of you, of all of us, drinking excessively, then Honica revealed that—"

"I saw it, Trevor," Sandy said without looking up.

I blinked. "You saw *Borderline News?*"

She nodded. "When I got Gaetan's EGP, I went up to a guestroom and watched it there."

I searched her face for signs of distress, but she seemed perfectly calm. "Did you see the whole show?"

"Yes."

"And?"

"I thought you did a wonderful job in your interview! You looked so clean-cut and handsome, almost angelic. You came across as a true professional, Trevor. I was so proud!"

"You think?" I swelled with pride. "It didn't seem like I was exposed as a liar?"

"Absolutely not! You were marvelous."

"Wow, what a relief. I really did try my best, but she edited out most of the good stuff. I was afraid people might think..." I stopped, realizing that Sandy was flattering me, deflecting from the issue at hand: her drunk driving charge. I leaned forward in my chair, intent on turning the tables so that I was the ruthless interviewer and she the nervous interviewee.

She resumed her work, pulling a red folder from the stack to her left to inspect its contents. She drew a big check mark and happy face on the inside flap and placed it on the stack behind her, then lifted a yellow folder to repeat the process. She began to hum again.

"Sandy."

She looked up, as though surprised I was still there. "Yes, Trevor?"

"Aren't you upset?"

She thought about it for a moment. "No."

"Did you and I watch the same program?"

"I believe so."

I wanted to rise from my seat and shake her. "Is it true? Did you get a DWI after the Christmas party?"

She slapped the file shut. "*Holiday* party, Trevor. How many times do I have to tell you to stop calling it a Christmas party? It's an insult to our non-Christian staff. As a senior manager, you should be more thoughtful."

"Okay, *holiday* party," I said, relieved to see some fire in her. "Sandy, do you want to talk?"

"No." She was opening and closing files frantically now, their contents sliding out, spilling to the floor.

"Please, Sandy. This isn't healthy."

"Everything is *just fine,* Trevor!" she cried, rising in her seat. "Everything is JUST FUCKING FINE!" In one fell swoop she cleared the desk, sending files, pens, and paperclips flying in all directions. Then she collapsed onto the desk and broke into sobs.

I stood up and hurried around the desk, placing my hand on her back and rubbing softly. "It's okay, Sandy. Everything's going to be okay." I looked down at her, shocked to see her fall to pieces before me, and wondered if she was in far more trouble than I had ever imagined. All week, while I had staunchly defended her to our colleagues, she had been deceiving me. What else was she hiding? For the first time, I began to seriously contemplate the horrifying possibility that she *had* run down Mr. Godfrey.

She lifted her head and dabbed her eyes. "Can we go for a drink?"

"Of course. Somewhere private? Rudolph's across the street?"

"No. I can't bear to leave the Universe."

The Center of the Universe was quiet save for about a half-dozen occupied tables. I led Sandy to a remote corner, hoping she hadn't noticed the group who turned and stared at her as we passed, then huddled together, gossiping and sneaking furtive glances at her.

We sat down at a table for two and ordered double Scotches—my new favorite drink, thanks to Cynthia—the only remedy powerful enough to dull my overactive senses. When the drinks arrived, Sandy reached for hers and gulped it down. I glanced warily at her and asked timidly, "You're not ... driving tonight?"

"Of course not." She set her glass down and tilted her head back, staring at the atrium star lights above. "I should never have driven that night, Trevor. You have no idea how many times I've regretted that foolish decision. I'm so ashamed."

"Why didn't you tell me? You know you can tell me anything."

"I could barely admit it to myself. I tried to block out the entire evening, to pretend it never happened. The truth is, I wasn't entirely surprised when I watched *Borderline News*. Honica called me a half-dozen times this week, but I never took her calls or returned her messages. I had a pretty good idea of what she was up to, but I had no idea how vicious she would be."

"Nor did I."

"Where's your mother?" she asked. "I saw her in the spa earlier tonight."

My mother! I glanced at my watch. It was 9:30, but I couldn't leave Sandy now. "I'm meeting her later for a drink," I said. "So will you tell me what happened?"

She sat back in her seat and began to air smoke. "I had no intention of driving, Trevor. I asked Jack to drive me to the party. Depending on how late it went, I planned to either call him for a ride or take a cab. But by the time I was dressed and ready to go, Jack was still out with his brother and the kids. They were buying a Christmas tree. So I called a taxi, but a half-hour later it still hadn't arrived—you know what it's like trying to get a cab this time of year. I knew Mr. Godfrey would be upset if I wasn't there to greet the first of the shuttle buses, so I hopped in the truck and drove, intending to either stay sober or take a cab home. Then the party started, and I got swept away. It was so much fun." Her eyes sparkled in remembrance. "I loved seeing everyone all dressed up. The room attendants looked like Hollywood starlets on Oscar night in their beautiful gowns. Maintenance men looked like heartthrobs in their tuxedos. We all work so hard, and it's been such a difficult few years. This was *our* night. I wanted to celebrate."

I thought back to all the laughter and carrying-on. It had seemed so harmless at the time. "So did I."

"My sobriety plan went out the window within about a half-hour. Things get a little foggy as the night progressed. I remember going down to the front door with you and the others to see off the last of the shuttle buses, then going back to the Observatory for our year-end toast. That's when things went sour. Mr. Godfrey gave that cryptic speech, telling us our bonuses were on hold, and I was crestfallen. And furious. We *earned* that bonus, Trevor, and at the eleventh hour he changed the rules! Jack and I needed that money desperately. I don't remember much after that, until..." She trailed off, burying her face in her hands. "Oh god, Trevor, why was I such a fool? How could I let this happen?"

I gulped, feeling a confession coming on. Did I really want to hear it? Wouldn't it be better to simply go about our business and pretend nothing happened, that everything was as perfect as it had been before the party?

But Sandy was determined. "I don't think I even thought twice about driving," she said, her lips trembling. "I was so distraught. I took the elevator down to P5, climbed into Jack's truck, and drove out. That's all I remember—until the accident."

I reached for my Scotch and sipped it. "Did you see him before you hit him?"

"Him? It was a woman."

I hesitated. "God—"

"*Mr. Godfrey*?" She cried. "You think I ran down Mr. Godfrey?"

"I just thought—"

"Christ, Trevor! I thought you of all people would stand by me!"

"You can't blame me for having doubts. You haven't exactly been honest this week."

"No, but I haven't outright lied, either. I've simply withheld information—information that's nobody's business but my own." Clearly perturbed, she held up her glass and rattled it at the server, indicating another.

"Is it possible you blacked out and don't remember?" I ventured bravely.

She gave me a blank stare and said flatly, "I think I'd remember running someone down, Trevor."

"Of course."

"Do you want to hear my story or would you prefer to tell it yourself?"

"I'm sorry. Please, continue."

She resumed air smoking. "I took my usual route home, down West Thirty-fourth to Joe DiMaggio. As I was turning left, the steering wheel slipped in my hands and I veered into oncoming traffic, clipping a blue Volvo. Thank god the driver wasn't hurt. I pulled over immediately. I hadn't even gotten out of the truck before the NYPD arrived. Right away, I knew I could be in big trouble. I remember digging around in my purse for gum to mask the smell of booze, but all I could find was a bottle of Chanel. I pulled it out and sprayed it all over me, all over the cab, then into my mouth."

"Into your *mouth*?"

"I was desperate." She made a face. "I don't recommend it. I gagged and almost vomited. The officer was banging on my window by then. He was very young, and handsome, and really polite, with a thick blond moustache and a goatee. I remember thinking he had a lot of Sparkle Factor—until I discovered how officious he was. He asked where I'd been. I didn't want to admit I'd been at a party, so I told him I went to a movie. My mouth was really dry, and my words were probably slurred, and I remember thinking that I sounded like Jodie Foster in *Nell*. He asked me which movie and all I could think of was *Nell*, of course, which played in theaters over a decade ago. Finally, recalling a billboard I'd seen that day, I said '*Meet the Fokkers*.' 'Really?' he said. 'I thought that didn't open until next week.' I told him it was a preview, but he didn't look convinced. He stood with his arms folded and scrutinized me, his eyes boring into me, making my skin turn inside out like salt on a slug. I could hear my wedding ring rattling against the steering wheel. He asked me if I'd had anything to drink, and I told him no. To my alarm, he stuck his head into the cab of the truck and sniffed. 'Smells like a duty-free store in here,' he said. 'Okay,' I said, 'I had a glass of wine after the movie.' He started laughing, and said, 'I meant the perfume.' I was relieved, thinking he had a sense of humor, that it all was going to be fine. But I was wrong."

Sandy's second drink arrived. She paused to take a sip, then inhaled deeply from her imaginary cigarette. "The woman whose car I hit was standing a few feet away, staring me down, looking angry and impatient. I was too afraid to get out of the truck. My legs felt paralyzed. The officer kept staring at my breasts, which I found offensive, but I wasn't above suffering through a bit of lasciviousness to get out of trouble. Only when I looked down did I realize that he was staring at the big red wine stain on my dress."

I nodded and winced. "Yeah, I saw Matthew do that to you on *Borderline News*."

"You and everyone else in this country," she said, her face grim. "I remember thinking it looked like a gunshot wound. The officer seemed to make his mind up then. He told me to step out of the truck. I knew I was doomed. I tried arguing with him, tried to explain that I was a law-abiding citizen, an executive at a very respectable hotel, but he wasn't interested. I had no choice but to push open the door. It was freezing outside. He stepped back and folded his arms, watching me closely as I swung my legs out and looked down at the pavement. I was wearing the most un-sensible pumps you could imagine, and my dress was so tight it wrapped around my legs like cellophane. 'Ma'am,' he called out impatiently, 'will you *please step out of the vehicle.*' I jumped.

"I remember it in slow motion. Like a gymnast off the balance beam, I threw my arms out wide on the dismount, but my right hand struck the truck door. When I hit the ground, my pumps skidded on the pavement. I felt myself falling backwards. I lunged forward, but overcompensated, and my entire body fell toward the pavement. I threw my hands out to break my fall, which is how I got these." She lifted her hands. The bandages were gone, and her palms were healing nicely, but the flesh was still pink and sore-looking. "And these huge scrapes on my knees. I remember lying on the pavement with my eyes squeezed shut, praying I would open them and find myself at home in bed with Jack. When I did open them and saw the officer's black boots only inches from my nose, I contemplated rolling into traffic and ending it right there. I could hear people hooting and hollering and I looked across the street, thinking there must be a party there. A crowd had gathered, and they were watching me, laughing and yelling things like 'Smooth move, ex-lax!' and 'Have another one, lady!' There was a flash in the air like lightning, and I realized someone had taken my picture."

"The photo that appeared on *Borderline News*?"

She nodded, looking mortified. "The officer helped me to my feet and pushed me into his car, talked to the other driver for a while, and then drove me into the precinct. As you now know, I failed the blood-alcohol content test. They put me in a cell with a bunch of hookers. I was scared out of my wits, but I refused to let them call Jack. I couldn't bear the thought of his reaction, his outrage, his sanctimonious response. Finally, they let me go, and I took a cab home. In the morning I told Jack I had a little fender-bender, and we went together to pick up the truck. He didn't ask questions, and I didn't volunteer much."

"That mug shot of you—it looked like you were smiling."

She grimaced. "I don't remember. My attorney told me it's not that uncommon. People smile reflexively when a camera's pointed at them."

"I don't know what to say, Sandy. I'm sorry for your troubles, but I'm relieved they aren't any worse. You could have hurt someone or yourself."

Her hand moved to her brow and pressed down on it. "I know. I'm determined not to let this get to me, Trevor. If it gets through, I'm afraid I'll implode and crumble to the floor in a heap of powder. I can't let that happen."

"You can't live in denial either. It's out in the open now. Do you have a good lawyer?"

She nodded. "He seems pretty sharp. I'm a little concerned by his obsession with the Chanel I sprayed into my mouth. He's getting the bottle analyzed for alcohol content. He thinks I might be able to use it in my defense, to say it was the Chanel that sent my blood-alcohol content over the limit."

"You're not serious."

She nodded slowly. "Maybe I need another lawyer. I'm prepared to face the consequences of my actions. I just don't want to go to jail." Her eyes clouded with worry.

"They're not going to send you to jail," I said, hoping I was right. I reached over and took her hand. "I'm really sorry, Sandy. I wish I could do something to help."

"I wish you could too." Her hands moved to her temples, as if to quell a sudden migraine. "God, why did I drive home?" she shouted. "Why didn't I stay here? Over one thousand beds in this place, and I had to drive home to my own. Everything is such a mess! I'm a bad, bad person, a bad wife, a bad mother!"

"You are not, Sandy. You made a poor judgment call. People drive drunk all the time. You got caught."

"Somehow that doesn't make me feel better."

"Then how about Honica's revelation that Matthew was caught on tape driving out of the parkade that night?" I said, suddenly remembering. "That must make you feel better. He lied about not driving! Clearly he's got something to hide. This takes a bit of heat off you."

"But where do you think he drove?"

"Who knows? When I think about it, though, of all people Matthew is probably the most capable of doing something awful like running down Mr. Godfrey and not confessing, allowing innocent people like you to take the blame. Don't you think?"

Sandy shook her head. "I refuse to accept that anyone I know could do such a thing. I won't speculate. I'll leave that up to the police."

"I guess you're right," I said.

"What time are you meeting your mom?"

I looked at my watch. It was just after 10:00 PM. "Now." I stood up and waved to the server for the bill. "Sorry, Sandy, but I better run. Do you want to share a taxi? I can drop you off at Penn."

She shook her head. "I'm not going home."

"You're not?"

"Jack kicked me out. I'm staying here in the hotel."

"My god, Sandy, I had no idea! Are you okay?"

She forced a smile. "Believe it or not, I *am* doing okay. I miss my kids, and Jack, but I'm a big girl."

"I can stay for a while longer."

"No. Go to your mother."

I signed the bill and handed it to the server. I pecked Sandy on the cheek and hurried across the lounge. At the exit, I turned back to check on Sandy. She was sitting back in her seat, eyes distant, a brave but melancholy look in her eyes, looking light years away.

When I pushed open the door to Ono, I assumed Mom would be either long gone or sitting by herself at a table in a quiet rage. But as I passed through the lounge I spotted her perched on a barstool, surrounded by a circle of people about my age and whooping it up.

I stopped to observe her. She was holding court before three men and two women, all leaning toward her, seemingly enthralled as she regaled them with one of her stories. Once again I tried to reconcile this social butterfly before me—arms outstretched, wings flapping, uttering something that made the group howl with laughter—with the despondent larva I grew up around, wrapped in a cocoon on the sofa for twenty years.

"There he is!" she cried upon spotting me. "It's my errant son!" As I made my way over she crossed her arms in a show of mock anger, but grinned from ear to ear, apparently too happy—or too sloshed—to be mad. "Come meet my new friends, darling!" She opened her arms wide to embrace me, air-kissing both cheeks in a gesture I had never seen her use before—part of her new New York persona, I guessed. She looked youthful and stylish in a retro paisley blouse and black skirt.

"Trevor, this is Brett, Kayla, Rod, Leanne, and—no, don't tell me"—she held up her hand and closed her eyes like a soothsayer—"Robert! No, Richard. Randall? Yes, Randall!"

The group cheered.

"This is my son, Trevor, the one I was telling you about."

They reached out in turn to shake my hand, smiling with amused expressions as though Mom had told a number of embarrassing stories about me.

"Nice to meet you all," I said. I turned to Mom. "I'm sorry I'm so late. You want to get a table?"

"In a moment, dear." Evidently, Mom wasn't finished holding court. "Now, my Trevor has a very, *very* important job at the space hotel uptown," she informed her new friends in a singsong voice. "This hotel is so *important* it's called the Universe." She held up her finger like a professor, teetering precariously on the barstool. "Everyone smiles there, *everyone!* It's such a happy place that my son works there day and night and doesn't even mind. Isn't that wonderful?"

The group held their smiles, eyes darting from Mom to me, unsure whether to laugh or feel sorry for me.

"Trevor is a *Big Shot* in this *Universe*," Mom continued, her words slurred and squished together. "He's the ... *director* ... *of*..." She looked over to me and raised an eyebrow.

"Rooms," I said quietly.

"Rooms! Which means he's responsible for the upkeep of *one thousand rooms.* Yet he can't seem to take care of his own apartment! Isn't that ironic? His place smells like a locker room and looks like a college dormitory!"

"Mom."

"As director of rooms at this spaceship hotel," she continued, "Trevor is responsible for the Guest Experience. Yet, ironically, *I'm* his guest, and so far my trip hasn't been much of an experience. The highlight of my visit so far has been a funeral!"

"*Mom.*"

The woman named Kayla winced and shot me a look of sympathy. The other woman, Leanne, tittered, lifting her hand to cover her mouth. The guys remained silent, eyes trained on my mother.

"The *whole world* revolves around the Universe," Mom went on, "and Trevor spends so much time there he hasn't had much time for his mother, who's visiting him from the other side of the content." She stopped and frowned. "Did I say content? I meant continent. Well, at least I didn't say *in*continent!"

Everyone laughed.

Suddenly I needed a drink. I lifted my hand to get the bartender's attention. I had a burning desire to silence my mother by muzzling her with both hands but sensed that she needed to get this out. Although she wasn't looking at me, I knew she was firing her words in my direction like missiles.

"I traveled all the way from *Ca-na-da,*" she said, as though it were some obscure foreign country, "and tonight Trevor is over two hours late for our one and only dinner date."

"I said I was sorry. I had an emergency."

"An emergency, dear?" Her hand flew to her chest dramatically. She turned from me to her audience, as though performing a vaudeville routine, her tone expressing the utmost concern. "Whatever could have happened? Did one of your guests run out of foot cream?"

There were a few nervous chuckles.

"Perhaps someone's pillows weren't fluffy enough? Did you have an emergency pillow-fluffing situation, dear?"

"Okay. You've made your point."

"Was someone's toilet seat heater malfunctioning?"

This prompted hysterical laughter all around.

Mom broke into a grand smile and grew quiet, nodding her head slightly as though bowing after a performance. For a woman so disdainful of fake smiles, she was being extraordinarily hypocritical.

"Mom," I whispered into her ear, "it's Sandy. She's in trouble."

"What!?" Mom cried. "Sandy's in trouble? The poor dear, did all that bleach she uses on her teeth seep into her brain?"

More laughter.

I was seething now. I had had enough.

Someone tapped me on my shoulder from behind. I turned to see a hefty, mustachioed man seated at the bar behind me.

"You work for the Universe?" he asked, his eyes fierce.

I nodded.

"You see *Borderline News* tonight?" His foul breath made my nostrils quiver. "That hottie blond executive, did she really run the old guy down?"

I gritted my teeth. "No, she did not." I turned away.

The man jabbed his finger into my shoulder. "But Honica Winters said she got really drunk and—"

I turned back to him, suddenly furious. "Mind your own fucking business, asshole!" I cried.

I turned back to my mother and her friends, who regarded me in alarm.

"Why, Trevor!" mother exclaimed, her expression betraying a mixture of admiration and disdain. "That's hardly hospitable of you. I'm quite sure those words aren't listed in your *Universal Values* book." She must have seen the pain in my eyes because her tune changed suddenly. She put her arm around me and pulled me close, her hands rubbing my back. "I'm sorry, dear. I was just having some fun. Let's get you a drink. Randall, what are these lovely drinks called again?"

"Blue Moons."

"How fitting!" She signaled the bartender. "Two more Blue Moons, please!"

"Mom, haven't you had enough? Have you eaten?"

"Of course not. I was waiting for you. Besides, food kills a good buzz."

"I think you better eat."

"I'm not hungry anymore. We've been stealing olives when the bartender turns his back, haven't we, Kayla?" She winked at Kayla conspiratorially.

"Your mother is *amazing*," said the woman called Leanne, who was petite and raven-haired and had pert little breasts that were pressed tightly together inside a mauve shirt. "What an awesome attitude! And hot! I'd be happy to look half as good when I'm her age."

I tried to smile politely but couldn't quell my irritation—with my mother, with the guy with bad breath behind me, with this obsequious woman who thought my mother was fabulous.

Mom giggled girlishly. "Leanne's a designer with Donna Karan, and she's *single*." She covered her mouth and pretended to whisper this into my ear, but spoke loud enough for the entire restaurant to hear. "She says she's a bit of a Miranda—you know, from *Sex and the City*. Kayla's a Charlotte, and Randall is a self-professed Big!" Mom leaned toward Randall to allow him to kiss both cheeks, then grasped his hand, eyes fluttering. "Such a handsome young man!"

The bartender placed an aqua-colored martini before me. I lunged for it. "So who does that make you, Mom?" I asked, instantly regretting the question. I preferred not to even know she watched the show.

All together her friends shouted "Samantha!" at the same time and burst into laughter.

Mom pretended to demur, but by the mischievous look on her face I could tell that the comparison had originated from her. I swallowed three-quarters of my martini.

"Brett here works for Goldman Sachs," Mom said, "and Rod works in the marketing department at Pfizer. Leanne recently became single and is mostly heterosexual. Right, Leanne?"

Leanne nodded and smiled at me.

"Kayla used to be a lesbian but she's currently feeling disillusioned with both sexes. Randall was just telling me about a date he had with a woman *twice his age* a few weeks ago…"

For the next half-hour Mom related every minute detail she knew about these people, as though I would be fascinated. I pretended to listen, nodding every few seconds with a bemused smile on my face, laughing when they laughed, looking attentive when they looked attentive, but I was completely preoccupied.

Poor Willard Godfrey would roll in his grave if he knew half the things that had occurred this week. The scandal surrounding his death and the resulting embarrassment would have crushed him; he had always been preoccupied with appearances, with dignity and professionalism, with maintaining a pleasant, controlled demeanor no matter how bad things got behind the scenes. Suddenly, his treasured executives had been thrust into the spotlight, exposed as lying, reckless, irresponsible drunkards.

I knew I shared responsibility, and this made it all the more difficult to bear. I was at the party and could have stopped Sandy and the others from drinking so much and from driving. Which meant, if one of them did run him down, that *I* was partly responsible for his death. The prospect made me physically ill.

Things weren't likely to settle down soon. Tomorrow, the bulk of VOID delegates were scheduled to arrive for the conference, and the welcome reception was to be held tomorrow night. How would they react to tonight's show? If Brenda were speaking the truth, they would be outraged. Brenda herself would probably be ballistic, having almost pulled out the conference when things weren't half as scandalous.

And still, the question remained: Who killed Willard Godfrey? Based on *Borderline News'* revelations, and assuming Sandy was telling the truth, Matthew suddenly looked like the guilty one. Why had there been no record of him leaving the parkade? Or at least that's what he had claimed. I realized I hadn't seen the reports myself.

"Trevor, darling, pay attention!" said my mother, jolting me from my thoughts. "Leanne's offering to buy you another Blue Moon."

Leanne was leering at me, her purple lips resting on the edge of her martini glass, her tongue darting suggestively at a maraschino cherry. For a fleeting moment I envisioned myself throwing her over the barstool and pulling her skirt down. By the look in her eyes I sensed that she was thinking similar thoughts. But I was far too preoccupied to think about casual sex. Besides, my mother was three inches away from me and, judging by the way her hand rested on Randall's knee, things were about to get really weird.

"Thanks," I said, "but I have to go. You coming, Mom?"

"I think I'll stay with my friends for one more Blue Moon."

"Fine."

I pecked her on the cheek, said good night to her friends, and went out to the street to hail a cab.

12

VOID in the Universe

When I called up to Mom's suite late Monday morning, for the first time since she had arrived she sounded her age. "Are you *still* sleeping?" I asked.

"Ugh. What time is it?"

"11:00 AM."

I heard a big yawn and stretch, then the smacking of dry lips. "I had a late night."

"How late?"

"It ended a few hours ago."

"You're kidding."

Her voice regained its youthful tone. "But it was so much fun! You should have come with us, Trevor! After you left we went out *dancing*, then Leanne took us to an after-hours club, and one thing led to another, and we all ended up back here. Hold on a sec, dear." I could hear her cover the phone and speak in a muffled voice. A male voice replied.

"*Mom?* Are they all still with you?"

"What was that, dear? Oh no, the others left. It's just Randall. Randall, you remember my son, Trevor? It is Randall, isn't it? Oh, thank god! Trevor, do you want to say hi to Randall?"

"No!"

"Randall, Trevor says hi. 'Hi, Trevor,' says Randall."

"Randall is *my* age, Mom."

"Oh, I don't think he's *that* old," she giggled. "I think we'll pop down for a late breakfast. Will you join us?"

"No, I won't join you. Besides, I'm busy with work."

"You're working today? Isn't today a state holiday? Christmas was on Saturday."

"Things don't work the same here as at your hospital. Most of the delegates of the VOID conference are arriving today, and so far it hasn't gone too smoothly. There were a dozen no-shows last night, and today there have been last-minute cancellations, errors with reservations, and delegates showing up without reservations. The organizer is blaming us for everything, flagrantly exploiting our 'guest is always right' policy to cover her own butt. She's flagged every second delegate as VIP and I've been doing meet-and-greets all morning. Matthew, Shanna, and Sandy all took the day off, so that leaves *me*. So, no, I won't be able to join you and Junior for breakfast."

"Too bad. Are you still free for dinner tonight?"

"Only if it's just the two of us. Or maybe you want me to bring along one of our busboys?"

"Darling, be nice." She dropped the phone and burst into a fit of giggles. "Stop that, Randall, please! I'm trying to talk to my son. No!" More giggles.

"Mom. I've got to run. I have to check in on the VOID welcome reception around 6:30 tonight, so let's plan to meet in the lobby at 7:00 PM. I promise I won't be late this time."

"Sounds like a wonderful plan. I'll ask the concierge to make reservations."

After hanging up with Mom, I went to the security office and asked Jerome to run parkade and elevator activity reports for the night Mr. Godfrey was killed.

"Sorry, Trevor, but Mr. Drummond forbid us from releasing this information," said Jerome.

"That rule doesn't apply to me," I said.

"But he specifically named you."

"Step aside, Jerome," I said impatiently. "I don't need your help anyway." The security department fell under my responsibility, and I had administration passwords for all computer systems. Jerome didn't put up much of a fight as I elbowed my way into his seat and began typing on the computer. He stepped back and folded his arms, sighing and shaking his head, likely drumming up an excuse in case Matthew found out.

Within a few minutes, I had the stairwell activity report onscreen and was scrolling through it. No activity was recorded below P3 between 9:00 PM Saturday and 5:00 AM Sunday, so the stairs were ruled out. I pulled up the elevator activity report next. Only five trips were taken below P3 during that time period: Cynthia Godfrey at 10:16 PM; Willard Godfrey at 12:38 AM; Shanna Virani at 1:04 AM; Sandy James at 1:09 AM; and finally Matthew Drummond at 1:16 AM. I remembered that Matthew had told me only Shanna, Sandy, and Willard were named on the report, but ran it until only 1:15 AM. Clearly he had deliberately excluded his own departure. *The scoundrel.* The approximate time of death had been reported as 1:00 AM. Could Mr. Godfrey have died closer to 1:20 AM? How deftly Matthew had extracted himself from suspicion in the eyes of his colleagues. Yet he likely wasn't as successful with the NYPD. Surely they would have demanded to see activities beyond 1:15 AM, in which case Matthew would be considered a suspect. I scrolled down the screen. Matthew's name appeared again at 7:58 AM, taking the elevator up this time and stopping on the sixth floor—to his suite, I assumed.

7:58 AM? Where had he been for six-and-a-half hours?

The next activity was mine, at 8:03 AM, when I escorted Brenda Rathberger down to P4. Little had I known that Matthew had driven in only minutes earlier. I remembered the tire tracks through the streamlet of blood and realized they must have belonged to Matthew. Why hadn't he noticed Mr. Godfrey's body? I had almost missed it myself, I recalled. A bulb was burnt out on that level. Also, the body was partially hidden by Mr. Godfrey's car and could easily have gone unnoticed by someone driving through the parkade. I scrolled through the remaining elevator activities, which documented the flurry of activity that followed the discovery of Mr. Godfrey's body: Jerome coming down, me up, Nancy down, Jerome up, Matthew down, and so on.

I pulled up the parkade exit reports next. Only four vehicles had exited the parkade using parking passes during the same time period, each registered to the same individuals who had taken the elevator, in the same order, and with similar intervals: Cynthia at 10:23 PM; Shanna at 1:08 AM; Sandy at 1:13 AM; and Matthew at 1:20 AM. If one of these people ran down Mr. Godfrey, clearly he or she did not linger. Matthew was recorded reentering the parkade at 7:53 AM. Aside from these, no other pass activity was recorded. The remaining movements would have been guests, visitors, and valets using the pay booth, which did not require a scanner and therefore was not recorded other than by camera, and none of these individuals would have access to the lower parking elevators.

I pushed my chair away from the computer and folded my arms, staring at the screen. To my dismay, there was no record of a mystery passenger in the elevator or stairwell, no mysterious vehicle recorded leaving the parkade. And, according to police, there were no signs of break-in on the parking levels. Which narrowed the possibilities to three people: Sandy, Shanna, or Matthew. My heart sunk. All along I had desperately hoped it wasn't one of them, but now it was becoming extremely difficult to think otherwise.

How come police hadn't made an arrest yet? Wouldn't they have found paint fragments at the scene or on Mr Godfrey's clothes and been able to match them with one of the suspects' vehicles? Wouldn't there have been damage to the vehicle? Were they incompetent, lazy, or apathetic? It had been over a week since Mr. Godfrey's death, yet still no arrests. Either they were stumped or they were being extremely careful.

Whatever the reason, it seemed to be a pretty simple case. It was likely only a matter of time before one of my colleagues was arrested. I had to prepare myself for that reality.

I went looking for Brenda Rathberger next and found her sitting at the VOID Welcome Center, flanked by two young female volunteers. Dressed in a big floral muumuu and white tennis shoes, she munched on a cinnamon bun as she distributed registration packages to a line of delegates. Behind her, a number of delegates were gathered in the lounge area set up in the Venus room.

I stopped to watch her work for a moment, and it occurred to me that there were two significant misnomers in VOID conference arrangements. The first was Brenda's title as organizer and executive director. The terms *dis*organizer and executive *dictator* seemed more fitting. Many of the delegates she dealt with experienced some sort of problem: no registration package to be found; no room reservation; no record of payment. Yet she deftly deflected blame, muttering things like "*Damn* this hotel!" and "Not *again*? Jeez Louise! I told them three times!" With huffs of indignation, she dispatched her volunteers to fix the problems. The second misnomer was the name Welcome Center. In fact, little "welcoming" seemed to be taking place. Brenda was grouchy and abusive, berating delegates for forgetting confirmation slips, for not signing up for educational sessions, or for declining to purchase one of the green "Ribbons of Hope" she was hawking for twenty dollars.

Yet, despite her approach, which went completely counter to Universal Values, I couldn't help but admire her. People seemed perfectly willing to accept her abuse, to agree with her misplaced blaming, and to fulfill her commands. Her volunteers treated her with humility and deference and fussed around to make things right. There was something practical and efficient about her tactics. With the power of such a worthy cause behind her, she could bypass the niceties of tiptoeing around people and expend all her energies on getting things done.

Eager to test the waters after *Borderline News*, I made several attempts to approach her, but she seemed to be doing her best to ignore me. I had every reason to be upset by her appearance on *Borderline News*, which had so viciously attacked the Universe, but Brenda Rathberger was a guest, an important client, and protocol required me to conduct myself with the utmost professionalism. So I swallowed my hostility and stood to the right of her desk, trying to catch her attention. But each time I tried to talk to her between delegates, she held up her hand to stop me, without actually looking at me, and called for the next delegate. When it became abundantly clear that she was not going to speak to me, I went away, feeling humiliated.

I went to the front office to discreetly check Nancy's schedule. She was leaving the hotel and she had a live-in boyfriend, but I was determined to see as much of her as possible before she left in order to have a store of images in my mind from which to draw on lonely nights in the future. Nancy was due in at 3:00 PM.

On my way past the front desk, Gaetan Boudreau stopped me and took me aside in confidence. "There's a two-hundred-dollar mini-bar charge to Sandy's room from last night," he said. "Should I apply it to her credit card?"

"Two hundred dollars?" I had forgotten that she had taken residence in the hotel. "No, write it off," I said. The image of Sandy cleaning out the mini-bar by herself was deeply disturbing.

Gaetan seemed relieved. "Thanks, Trevor. Will do."

I went to my office next and tried calling Sandy's room, but there was no answer. She didn't answer her U-Comm either. I hoped she was at home visiting her children and reconciling with her husband. After hearing her story last night, I was once again convinced of her innocence—innocence in regard to Mr. Godfrey's death, that is; clearly, she was guilty in other respects. The questions that now burned in my mind were: 1) Where did Matthew Drummond go after the party? and 2) Why did he lie and say he didn't drive? I was determined to find out the answers. Unfortunately, I was unable to ask Matthew directly, since he didn't show his face on-property all day.

At 6:45 PM I headed for Jupiter Ballroom to check on VOID's welcome reception. As I cut across the Center of the Universe Lounge, I was surprised to see a mass of platinum hair at the bar: Honica Winters was perched on a stool, by herself, dressed in a clingy tan dress and white leather heels. Hands buried in her hair, she was frowning down at a stack of papers as though cramming for an exam. A martini glass, almost empty, rested next to her elbow.

I assumed that she had already given her speech and was disappointed. I had been curious to hear what she had to say and wanted to be there to witness any slander she might direct toward the hotel. I hadn't seen her since I watched *Borderline News*, and I was tempted to march over and swat her off the chair. For years we had coddled her, upgraded her, slashed her rates, and tolerated her prima donna-like behavior, and this was how she had thanked us. Better to ignore her.

Averting my eyes, I walked past her and opened the door of Jupiter Ballroom.

The VOID welcome reception was buzzing, with at least three hundred delegates in attendance. It was a standup reception, with nonalcoholic beverage service and canapés until 8:00 PM. Speeches had been scheduled to begin at 6:30 and were expected to last approximately one-half hour, yet apparently they had ended early.

Glancing around, I realized it was my first look at VOID delegates en masse. They were an eclectic bunch, from very young to very old, an even split between male and female, dressed in everything from three-piece suits to leisure suits. Their badges announced their names, organizations, and hometowns; they came from across the continent, most from the United States and Canada, the others from Europe, Asia, and South America. They seemed to be enjoying themselves; many were smiling and laughing, others were hugging one another and sharing stories. A few looked at me and smiled pleasantly as I passed. For the most part, they looked like typical conference attendees, yet pain and suffering was evident in several of the faces I passed, and anger and steely resolve in others. A few delegates were in wheelchairs. I remembered Brenda telling me that her own drunk driving tragedy paled in comparison to that of some of her delegates, and I wondered what kind of horrors they had endured, whom they had lost, and how they were coping.

Halfway across the room, someone thumped my back. "Trevor?"

I turned around.

Brenda Rathberger's round, red face was glaring at me, her upper lip glistening with perspiration. She had changed into another floral dress, this one of fine silk, and wore white satin shoes. Her hair looked freshly permed and highlighted, and her tan seemed darker than before, less blotchy, as though she were wearing a generous amount of bronzing cream or foundation. A green ribbon was pinned over her right breast.

"Brenda! Don't you look nice! How's the reception going?"

"Have you seen Honica Winters? That bloody bimbo was supposed to be here a half-hour ago! My delegates are getting impatient, and I'm starting to look like a fool."

"She hasn't even spoken yet? I just saw her in—"

A petite, girlish-looking Afro-American woman elbowed between us. "Well, if it isn't Brenda Rathberger! Great to see you again!"

Brenda eyed the woman suspiciously.

"It's Judy! Judy Gordon! I volunteer for the Chicago chapter. Remember? We did a workshop together in Dallas last year."

"Oh yes—of course. Judy. How are you."

"Couldn't be better! I love this hotel! It's about time we stopped holding the conference in those fleabag suburban motels. Everyone is raving about this place!"

Brenda nodded. "I thought it would be a nice change of pace."

"You were fantastic on *Borderline News*," Judy gushed. "I was so proud! *Imagine,* I thought, *our little organization on national television*! We've come a long way, haven't we? I just called the office and apparently the phone's been ringing off the hook. People are falling over themselves to give donations. Bravo, Brenda, *bravo!*"

Brenda swelled with pride.

Judy was clutching a wine glass filled with orange juice and sipping it like a cocktail. She leaned closer to Brenda. "Are we going to get started soon? The natives are getting restless."

"Yes, very soon." Brenda searched the room again, her face anxious.

Judy turned to me, and her eyes flashed in recognition. "Hey! You were on *Borderline News* too, weren't you?" Her pleasant expression changed instantly, as though a terrible smell had enveloped her. "You're the guy who tried to cover everything up."

I felt blood rush to my face. "I wasn't *covering up*," I said, trying to contain my indignation. "I was simply setting the record straight. *Borderline News* wasn't exactly telling the truth when—"

"Where is she?" Brenda cried out, cutting me short. "Judy, I need your help finding my guest speaker. She's gone AWOL."

"She what? Oh my god! Who's going to speak?"

"Brenda," I said, "I tried to tell you—I saw Honica in the lounge a few minutes ago."

Brenda's eyes bulged. "In the *lounge?* What on earth is she doing there?"

"Having a martini, from what I could make out."

Her mouth dropped. "She *wouldn't!*" She charged toward the door.

Judy turned to me and opened her mouth to say something, then seemed to decide against it. She sniffed and turned on her heels, abandoning me and lurching her way through the crowd, holding her orange juice glass high, looking like a drunk on the prowl.

Suddenly I was alone and uncomfortable. A few people glanced in my direction and whispered to one another. I smiled and nodded back, but by their hostile expressions I guessed that they too were beginning to recognize me from the *Borderline News* segment. I decided it was time to leave. First I did a quick tour of the periphery of the room, checking water stations, instructing banquet staff to clear dirty glasses, and inspecting the canapés that servers were circulating. At the front of the room, I climbed the stage and tapped the microphone to ensure it was in working order.

Hundreds of eyes turned to me expectantly.

Feeling foolish, I backed away and surveyed the rest of the stage, which was empty save for a single banquet chair at the rear. It looked strange there and I considered removing it, but decided it must have a purpose—likely a place for Honica to sit while she was being introduced.

As I made my way to the exit, I bumped into Brenda again. Her face beet-red and fierce, she was tugging a guilty-looking Honica along. Heads in the crowd turned to regard Honica's formidable presence. There were murmurs of admiration, titters of excitement.

"Hiya, handsome!" Honica said to me as Brenda whipped her past.

I nodded at her politely. Clearly, she still couldn't remember my name.

Brenda turned and called out, "Trevor, bring us some coffee. *Immediately!*"

I hastened to the coffee station and filled two cups, then made my way through the crowd to the back of the room, where Honica and Brenda were standing near the rear of the stage.

"I cannot *believe* you were sitting in the *lounge* for all eyes to see!" Brenda was hissing at Honica. "Drinking!"

"I wasn't drinking!" Honica cried. "I was—"

"You can't fool me! Your breath *reeks* of alcohol."

Honica straightened her posture, breaking from Brenda's fierce glare. "Okay, so I had a little nip," she said, flicking her hair back. I offered her one of the coffee cups. She took it and sipped.

Brenda stood back and scrutinized her. "Are you drunk? If you're drunk, I'm going to call this off at once."

"I'm not, Bren! I promise. Believe me, I can slug back more than that." She glanced warily around the room.

"What could *possibly* have possessed you to go *drinking* only minutes before speaking at the opening of *my* conference?" Brenda demanded, her knuckles resting on her hips.

"I was nervous."

"*Nervous?* You?"

Honica bit on her fingernail. "Public speaking scares the hell out of me."

"What?!" Brenda cried. "But you speak in front of millions of viewers each week!"

"That's different," Honica replied, casting another wary glance at the hundreds of expectant eyes watching us. "I'm usually in the studio and I can't see all the people watching. I *love* the camera, but I have this weird phobia about speaking in front of crowds. This coffee is *not* helping." She stared into the cup and handed it to me, then pressed her hand against her heart and winced, as though trying to suppress a heart attack. She took a deep breath and exhaled slowly.

Brenda thrust her own cup at her. "Drink or I'll slap you into sobriety! You might have warned me about this little phobia when I asked you to speak!"

"Don't worry, Bren, I'll be okay. This isn't the first speech I've done. I used to refuse all speaking engagements, coming up with one excuse or another, but I'm starting to accept them now. I've got to start thinking about my next career. Next to Barbara Walters, I'm one of the oldest hags in broadcast journalism. The studio can pack on only so much makeup, and if they dim the studio lights any more I'll be broadcasting in the dark. It's only a matter of time before they replace me with some Britney Spears lookalike half my age. I'm thinking of writing a book, but my agent says I'll have to go on a book tour and I'll need more practice public speaking first."

Brenda's eyes looked ready to pop out of their sockets. "You consider tonight *practice*?"

"No! Of course not. I realize how important this conference is." Honica surveyed the crowd again. "Why does everyone look so hostile?"

"Probably because you've kept them waiting for forty-five minutes," Brenda snapped. "If you screw this up, Honica, so help me, I'll—"

Honica handed me the second coffee cup and put her hand on Brenda's arm. "Don't worry, Bren, I'll do you proud." She pulled a wad of papers from her purse. "I wrote my speech out word for word in case I have a panic attack."

"A *panic attack?*"

I suppressed a smirk.

"Kidding," Honica said, her frightened expression suggesting otherwise. She stuck a knuckle in her mouth and bit down hard.

Brenda stared at the stack of papers. "Exactly how long is your speech?"

"I don't know. An hour or so?"

"An *hour?* Honica, my people have the attention span of gnats. This is a standing reception and there's no booze. I want you up there for no more than fifteen minutes."

"Fine by me. I was just going to tell a few anecdotes."

"Anecdotes? There's no time for anecdotes. Keep it short and sweet. And whatever you do, don't offend anyone. My people are very, very sensitive."

"Right."

"Let's just hope no one saw you in the lounge."

"*None* of these people drink?" Honica turned to me with an expression of incredulity.

"Not the respectable ones," said Brenda.

"It's not as if I'm going to drive. A little drink never hurt anyone."

Brenda's eyes flashed with anger. "Don't you *dare* say that in front of these people! A 'little drink' has hurt many of them!" She turned around to check on the crowd. The room had grown silent, and almost all faces were turned in our direction. "I better introduce you now before they start a riot," she said. "But first take this." She pulled a green ribbon from her purse and fastened it to Honica's dress.

"What is it?" asked Honica, looking down, clearly not pleased with how it clashed with her dress. "It makes me look like a spelling bee contestant."

"Just shut up and wear it," said Brenda, stepping back to look her up and down. "Are you ready?"

Honica gulped and gave Brenda the thumbs-up.

"Wait here with Trevor until I call you up. Don't go near anyone! If they smell booze, it'll be the end of me!"

Honica lifted her fist to her mouth to suppress a burp. "You betcha, Bren."

Brenda climbed the stage to the podium. "Ladies and gentlemen," she said into the microphone, her deep voice booming across the room, "it is my distinct pleasure to welcome you to the Sixth Annual Victims of Impaired Drivers Conference. My name is Brenda Rathberger. I'm the founder and executive director of VOID and the organizer of this year's conference."

The crowd burst into applause.

Brenda had a commanding presence onstage. "What a long way VOID has come in just a few years!" she said. "Very few of you will remember our first conference in Denver five years ago. That's because there were only twenty-five of us at the time. Today, VOID has grown to over three hundred employees, twelve hundred volunteers, and thirty chapters across North America. This week I am delighted to announce that we're expecting over fifteen hundred attendees!"

There was more applause.

I sensed that Honica was swaying a bit beside me, and looked up. She clutched my shoulder and closed her eyes. "Are you okay, Miss Winters?" I asked.

"I think I need to sit down," she said, her words slurred. "I took a couple Xanax to calm my nerves, and I feel kind of dizzy now." She slipped past me and climbed the stage, moving slowly and deliberately, taking a seat in the chair behind Brenda.

Brenda didn't seem to notice her. "The theme of this year's conference is 'Society for Sobriety,'" she continued. "As you know, VOID's primary objective is to eradicate drunk driving from society completely. We will only succeed when *everybody*—family, colleagues, service staff, policemen, legislators, friends, and acquaintances—adopts our policy of zero tolerance. We have an exciting week ahead, with workshops, exhibits, a trade show, panels, and seminars, culminating in our gala dinner on New Year's Eve. The theme of this year's gala is 'Glory Days of Prohibition.' I hope you'll get into the spirit with costumes and props from the roaring twenties. On New Year's Day, our conference concludes with the March for Sobriety though Central Park and a rally at Rockefeller Center. This week, I look forward to collaborating with you to find new strategies and tactics for taking social control of drunk driving. With the support and commitment of everyone in this room, I am confident that before long, drunk driving will be history in America!" Her voice rose to a triumphant cry.

The audience responded with thunderous applause.

Her tone changed then, growing soft. "As many of you know, this week we were forced to make a last-minute change in our agenda due to the tragic hit-and-run death of Mr. Willard Godfrey, the owner of this lovely hotel. I see that a number of you have purchased our Green Ribbons of Hope, which stand for solidarity in the face of adversity. I urge all of you to purchase them in tribute to Willard Godfrey and all the victims who cannot be here today." Brenda was silent for a moment. "After much soul-searching, I consulted the board and we decided to name the late Willard Godfrey our honorary conference chairperson. Although he will be physically absent, his presence will be felt everywhere this week."

The room was completely silent.

I felt myself begin to choke up.

"Behind me is an empty chair," Brenda continued. "This chair is a symbol of the horrific consequences of drunk driving. It contains nothing: a tragic, empty space. A void."

There were gasps in the audience and a few giggles.

Behind Brenda, Honica hammed it up, pointing at herself and mouthing the words, "Me? A void?"

Hysterical laughter broke out across the room.

Still unaware of Honica's presence, Brenda stared into the audience, aghast. Had she said something funny? She glanced down at her dress, looking for a stain, a rip, anything that might prompt such disrespect. She looked back at the audience and glanced over her shoulder, following their gazes.

Honica grinned and waved at her.

I saw Brenda's eyes flash with anger. But when she turned back to the crowd she adopted a good-natured grin. "Well! I'm terribly sorry for calling you a void, Miss Winters."

The crowd roared with laughter.

"I suppose that's a fitting segue to the introduction of tonight's guest speaker," Brenda said, forcing herself to smile as she waited for the crowd to settle. "Replacing a formidable speaker like Willard Godfrey was not an easy task. Tonight, however, I am delighted to introduce a person who in recent years has become a household name. As host of one of the most popular news programs on television, Honica Winters has received numerous awards and accolades. Recently, *Borderline News* was rated one of the top five television news programs in the country. Last night, our speaker proved herself a friend of VOID by hosting a segment on drinking and driving, which was watched by over five million viewers and resulted in unprecedented exposure for our organization. Ladies and gentlemen, please welcome Miss Honica Winters!"

The crowd clapped enthusiastically, cheering and stamping their feet.

Honica rose from her seat, teetering on her heels, and started toward the podium. Halfway there, she tripped and stumbled. Brenda lunged for her arm just as she was about to go down. Honica steadied herself on Brenda's shoulder, thanked her profusely, and then flashed a goofy smile at the audience.

Brenda climbed down from the stage and took her place beside me, her body rigid.

"Good evening," said Honica, adjusting the microphone up to her height. Her voice was higher than usual and a bit squeaky. "Thank you for that introduction, Brenda. I have to admit, I'm a little nervous up here. I've always heard it's best to get your audience liquored up before a speech. But I guess that's not going to happen with this group." She guffawed.

The room was silent.

"How many of you saw my show last night?"

About a third of the people raised their hands.

"For those of you who missed it, shame on you. I mean, come on, I need the ratings." More guffaws. The room remained silent. She sighed and looked down at her notes. "For over a year now, I've been lobbying my producers to do a show on drinking and driving, an issue that's close to my heart. At the same time, I've always wanted to profile Willard Godfrey and this spectacular hotel he built." She spread her arms mechanically, as though rehearsed. "When I found out about this convention, I decided to kill two birds with one stone: to portray Willard Godfrey *and* VOID at the same time. Unfortunately, someone else's stone killed the old bird before I got to him." She stopped as if waiting for laughter

The room was now dead silent.

Beside me, Brenda gripped my arm.

I smiled down at her reassuringly.

Honica continued, "When Willard was killed last weekend, my producers agreed to preempt the scheduled show in favor of a special holiday edition that focused on drunk driving. It was our hope that our show would act as a sobering reminder to viewers about the tragic consequences of impaired driving at a time of year when this type of behavior can be rampant. We hoped it would make people think twice before climbing into a vehicle drunk over this holiday season. We hoped it might even save a life or two."

Heads nodded in approval.

I felt Brenda relax her grip.

Honica paused. "Willard Godfrey was my friend," she said. "I miss him. Like many of you, I'm a victim. When Willard was managing the Plaza and I lived in this city, we used to hang out about once a month. This was before he quit drinking, and we'd sit at the bar together and sling back vodka martinis."

There were murmurs of disapproval in the room.

Brenda's grip tightened again.

Honica shut her eyes for a moment, as if in confession. "I know that may come as a shock to you, especially those of you who know him as a teetotaler, but in my opinion, there's nothing wrong with having a few drinks—it's what happens *afterwards* that is important. Willard and I never, ever drove home. Nobody got hurt and no lives were jeopardized. The point I'm making is that *alcohol* is not the problem, *behavior* is. Drinking is legal. In moderation, it's mostly harmless. I believe it is wrong to equate drinking with drinking and driving. If people simply learn to drink responsibly, to control their actions while under the influence, to stay in their own beds, to resist harmful impulses, to stay out of cars, and to find their way home without endangering the lives of innocent victims, then the world will be a safer, better place. I wish all of you a wonderful conference, and I would like to thank you for watching *Borderline News*."

As the audience broke into applause, Honica flashed a million-dollar smile and stepped down from the stage. On the bottom stair, she tripped, and her body flew forward. She let out a shriek as she landed in the arms of a trio of male delegates.

The audience cried out in shock.

With the help of a few others, Honica pulled herself to her feet and dusted herself off. She covered her mouth and guffawed, bowing and waving at the crowd, then hurried up the aisle, a broken heel making her stagger exaggeratedly.

Beside me, Brenda looked mortified. Her eyes slowly scanned the crowd to gauge their reaction.

Faces turned to glower in our direction.

"Oh god," Brenda said under her breath, "I need a drink."

She turned and fled the ballroom.

13

Chaos in the Universe

Despite the dark cloud of uncertainty that had lingered over the Universe, by Tuesday morning I sensed that things were starting to clear up. On my morning rounds, as I burst through the service door into the lobby, I felt that familiar rush of adrenaline. The atrium's star lights seemed brighter, the chatter of guests was loud and lively, the faces of staff were once again spirited and purposeful. VOID delegates had settled in, and the conference was buzzing—which I hoped would keep Brenda Rathberger out of our hair.

Later that week, travelers from around the world would arrive to celebrate New Year's Eve in New York, culminating in a full house on Friday with New Year's Eve parties across the Universe. Whatever the future held, I was confident that I would remain a dedicated and vital part of the hotel. Should Matthew succeed as general manager, I would support him. Should Sandy convince Cynthia to give her a chance instead—though this looked highly unlikely after *Borderline News*—I would support her. Should Cynthia Godfrey decide to give me the opportunity, then I would give it my best shot.

After my morning site inspection, I decided to inspect the outside of the complex, something I tried to do once a week. I left the hotel by the front doors, passing a group of VOID delegates assembled there, presumably to wait for a ride, wished them a cheerful good morning and descended the left fork of the driveway to the street. Turning left on West Fifty-fourth, I circled the complex to the back, unlocked the gate, and cut across the hotel gardens, passing through the gate on the other side and turning left on West Fifty-third.

The Universe was in excellent order.

As I reached Avenue of the Americas, I spotted Sandy James on her way up the street. I waved to her and stopped to wait, shivering in the cool morning air as she made her way over. Only a slight trace of a limp remained in her step. She was toting a small suitcase in one hand and appeared to be smoking with the other; as she drew nearer, I saw that she didn't have a cigarette but was air smoking. By the anxious look in her eyes, I guessed that she wasn't feeling quite as upbeat as I was.

I glanced down at her suitcase and said hopefully, "Moving back home?"

She shook her head. "I went to pick up a few things."

"Jack still angry?"

She dropped her imaginary cigarette on the sidewalk and stamped it out. "We need breathing space. It's too difficult at home right now. The neighbors are being nosy, people keep making prank calls, my kids stare at me like I'm some sort of evil alien. I need to take refuge in the Universe for a few days and clear my head."

"I understand." As we walked to the hotel, I took her bag. "I tried to reach you yesterday. I was worried when I heard about your mini-bar bill."

She bit her lip. "Right, I had forgotten. I had a party for one Sunday night. I ate everything in sight, including three chocolate bars, a jar of mixed nuts, and an entire tube of Pringles, and opened every miniature bottle of booze and took a sip. I always wanted to do that. I'll pay for it, of course. Actually, I already did in a way. I threw up."

"Sorry I missed the party." At the foot of the driveway, I turned to her. "Seriously, Sandy, consuming the entire contents of a mini-bar is not exactly normal behavior."

She looked at me sheepishly. "I left a bar of Toblerone and the red wine."

"Should I be worried?"

She looked as though she might smile and say something funny or optimistic, in typical Sandy fashion, but instead her face grew serious. She bit her lip again and shook her head slowly, her face contorting. She let out a sob, then covered her face and turned away. "I don't know what happened, Trevor. It's like a domino effect. Ten days ago, everything was wonderful. Then I made an error in judgment, and everything started falling to pieces. I've been exposed as a reckless drunk on television. My husband has thrown me out of my house. My kids are afraid of me, my boss is dead, and everyone—including my own mother!—seems to think *I'm* responsible. What's next, Trevor? I don't think I can take anymore!"

I glanced up the driveway, hoping that the group of guests gathered near the entrance hadn't heard her, and opened my arms to hold her. "Don't worry, Sandy. The worst is over. Hang in there, and before long everything is going to be fine. I promise."

I stood with her for a moment, staring into the morning rush hour traffic, where hundreds of taxis and pedestrians rushed by—everyone too busy to notice a man and woman holding each other, the woman crying on the man's shoulder, and wonder why.

Sandy lifted her head and sniffed. "Thanks, Trevor."

"Anytime. You ready to go to work?"

She nodded slowly, putting on a brave face. "Enough of this! I need to pull myself together." She dabbed her eyes with a tissue and straightened her posture. "It's going to take all my strength and confidence, but I'm determined to do it."

"To do what?"

"To convince Cynthia to promote me to general manager. I'm going to call her this morning."

I was dumbfounded. "In the midst of all this strife? After *Borderline News*?"

"I need this job more than anything right now, Trevor." Taking the suitcase from my hand, she turned and marched up the driveway.

As I hurried to catch up, I heard someone near the hotel entrance shout, "There she is!" A herd of VOID delegates began charging down the driveway in our direction, shouting, pointing, and waving placards. In front of me, Sandy stopped dead in her tracks. I slammed into her, and we both stumbled, nearly falling to the ground.

"Shame! Shame! Shame!" the delegates were shouting.

It took a moment to realize their words were directed at Sandy. Within seconds the mob had encircled us, brandishing posters with slogans written in angry black letters: A LOADED DRIVER IS A LOADED GUN! GOOD MOTHERS DON'T DRIVE DRUNK! and AMAZING DISGRACE! They booed and hissed at Sandy.

I passed Sandy's suitcase to her and stepped in front of her. "People, please! Have some respect!"

"Shame on you!" a young, long-haired fellow wearing a red bandana yelled at Sandy.

A woman I recognized as Judy Gordon from the Chicago chapter cried out, "You should have known better, Sandy James! An executive, a mother—driving drunk! Shame on you!"

The entire group chanted, "Shame! Shame! Shame!"

Sandy cowered behind me, holding her suitcase before her like a shield as the group drew closer, jeering at her and jabbing their posters in the air. I had to get her out of there. Glancing at the hotel entrance, I saw a group of staff and guests gathered there, faces aghast. On the street below, a crowd of pedestrians was observing the spectacle. Reaching for my U-Comm, I paged security, hissing into the microphone for Jerome to come to the front door immediately.

"Our streets aren't safe with people like you!" shouted another woman, lunging at Sandy. "Our *children* aren't safe!"

From the street came a screech of tires, and a New York One news van came barreling up the driveway.

"Shame! Shame! Shame!" the crowd shouted.

I had to get Sandy out of there *now*. I clutched her hand and started pulling her up the driveway, pushing protesters gently out of the way.

Jerome from security appeared at the entrance and came rushing down the driveway. "Break it up, everyone, now!" he shouted. "Please clear the driveway immediately or I'll call the police!" He began shoving people aside, clearing his way toward Sandy.

I pulled Sandy toward Jerome. "Will you please let us get through!" I shouted, trying to control the impulse to thrash a few of them.

We were almost at the entrance when someone cried out, "Hey! Sandy James! Wait a sec! We need to talk to you for a moment!"

We turned to see a female reporter from New York One waving a microphone in the air, a cameraman in tow. We made a last dash for safety, passing through the steel doors just as they were gliding shut. Jerome used his master key to lock them while Sandy and I stopped to catch our breath.

All activity in the lobby had halted, and people were staring at us in alarm. I grabbed Sandy's hand and pulled her across the lobby, up the staircase, and through the administration office, locking the doors behind us.

Once Sandy had calmed down, I went back to the front door to make sure the crowd had dissipated. Jerome had succeeded only in moving the protesters to the street, where three local camera crews and over a hundred spectators were now gathered. He was standing on the sideline, arms folded tightly, watching the protesters through narrow slits of his eyes.

Judy Gordon was being interviewed by the New York One reporter. "The theme of our conference is 'Society for Sobriety,'" she was saying. "If society can't rely on people like Sandy James, a successful businesswoman and mother of two, to set an example by drinking responsibly and staying off the road when she's impaired, then how can we expect the rest of society to behave any better? VOID believes that responsible driving starts from the grassroots. Legislation helps, of course, but not until society as a whole accepts that the consequences of impaired driving are too severe to tolerate *any* amount of drinking before driving will we *really* make a difference."

The camera moved from Judy to a protester who was holding up a sign that said *IS* THERE INTELLIGENT LIFE IN THE UNIVERSE?

I marched up to Judy Gordon. "Would you kindly call your people off? We're trying to run a business here. In the future, I would appreciate it if you would keep your protests off our property and leave our employees alone. And if you intend to call the media, kindly inform me ahead of time."

Judy looked hurt. "We didn't mean to upset you. We really do love your hotel. But this is what we do: we protest. We would never have achieved the success we have today without media attention. We're passionate about our cause. I'm sure you can understand."

Her diplomatic approach was jarring, a sharp contrast to Brenda's bullying nature. "Well, you've upset Sandy James very much, and she's suffered enough as it is. The Universe is not a place for loud protests and politics. It's a place of quiet repose. I simply cannot tolerate any more antics like this."

"Tell it to Brenda Rathberger," Judy said with a shrug. "We're just following orders. She set this whole thing up."

"She did?" I should have known. "Where is she?"

"She had to substitute in a panel for a speaker who dropped out at the last minute. She should be back at the Welcome Center by now."

"Thank you." I turned and marched back up the driveway.

On my way to find Brenda, I received a text message from Matthew requesting my presence in his office immediately. I decided I needed to vent to Brenda first and headed for the VOID Welcome Center.

Brenda was seated behind the desk, talking on her cell phone. A young volunteer with a nose ring sat beside her, regarding her with her mouth open wide.

"I don't care if he's got scarlet fever!" Brenda was barking into the phone. "The seminar starts in an hour, and over thirty paid delegates are registered. I am not going to cancel it! You tell him if he doesn't get his fat ass down here immediately, I'll come over myself and drag him over by the balls. Got it? Good!" She disconnected and turned to one of the volunteers. "Lame-ass!"

"Good morning, Brenda."

She looked up. "Oh. It's you."

"How are things?"

"They're a total disaster!"

By now I was used to her apocalyptic proclamations. "Oh?"

Her face was beet red again, and beads of perspiration had formed on her upper lip; the poor woman was a heart attack waiting to happen. "That's the third speaker who's canceled on me this morning," she said, fuming, as she reached for a cinnamon bun and tore it apart, shoving half into her mouth. "It's all this hotel's fault! People are afraid of being associated with a business that condones drunk driving."

"The Universe does not condone drunk driving," I said tersely.

She folded her arms and grunted.

"With all due respect, Brenda, if you're planning to stage an assault on one of our staff and call the media to catch it on film, I'd appreciate it if you would at least warn me in advance."

"Don't know what you're talking about."

"Oh yes, you do."

"Well, *I* have a request for *you*," she said, meanly mimicking my tone and body language. "With all due respect, if you are planning on coming up with any more dumb-ass ideas to ruin my conference, I'd appreciate it if you would keep them to yourself."

"I'm sorry?"

"Two words: Honica Winters. She was disastrous last night! And you're the one who hooked me up with her."

"I thought she did an okay job."

"She showed up drunk to speak at an anti-impaired driving conference! She might as well have brought a gun to a peace rally! She dedicated her speech to praising drinking, then fell down drunk in front of the entire group of delegates. I couldn't have been more mortified! She's damned lucky she checked out this morning before I got to her. I would have wrung her scrawny little neck. I'm getting it on all sides from my delegates now. If they aren't bitching about this hotel and its exorbitant prices, they're complaining about Honica Winters. *None* of this is my fault, yet everyone's blaming me!"

Beside her, the volunteer made a slight huffing sound.

Brenda turned and glared at her. "Shut up, Megan."

"Yes, well, I'm very sorry," I said to Brenda, knowing it was futile to argue. "I apologize for any part we may or may not have had in the complaints you're receiving."

"Always apologizing. If you got things right the first time, you wouldn't have to keep apologizing."

My blood pressure soared. "Well, I'm terribly sorry for apologizing all the time."

She grunted again, as if proving her point, and turned away, lifting her cell phone to make another call.

Effectively dismissed, I left, rounding the concourse toward the staircase.

"Mr. Lambert?"

I turned to see the volunteer, Megan. "Yes?"

"I want you to know that people aren't complaining about the hotel or even Honica Winters as much as they're complaining about Mrs. Rathberger. She's got a really loyal following, but this week she's been pissing everyone off. I've volunteered at this conference for three years now and she's always a bit aggressive, but this year she's out of control. I think she's gone crazy."

"Is that so?"

She nodded. "The board has put an enormous amount of pressure on her to make this conference a success and to get lots of media coverage. Rumor has it that if she doesn't succeed, she's going to be fired. She doesn't mean to be so rude—she's really a nice person—but things keep going wrong. I think she's on the verge of a nervous breakdown."

"I appreciate your telling me this," I said. "All we want to do is make things easier for her, but there's only so much we can do. If there's anything I can do to make things better, please let me know."

"Thanks. I will."

★ ★ ★ ★ ★

On my way to the administration offices to check on Sandy, I received a call from Matthew.

"Where the hell are you? I told you to get over here ten minutes ago."

"I'll be right there."

On my way to Matthew's office, I ducked in to see Sandy. I was surprised to see a clean-cut young man sitting in the chair across the desk from her, gripping the armrests. She was conducting an interview. As I passed by, she spotted me and broke into a bright smile, waving. I marveled over how quickly she had recovered.

As I turned toward Matthew's office, my U-Comm went off yet again. "Trevor, it's Gaetan. May I ask you to come down to the front desk, please?" He sounded perfectly calm, but I knew him well enough to detect stress in his voice.

"Is it urgent?" I asked. "I'm kind of busy."

"Honica Winters is checking out, and she's asking for you."

"I'll be right down."

Honica was leaning over the front desk, reviewing her bill. Gaetan was standing behind the front desk, a pleasant smile painted on his face. When he saw me, an almost imperceptible flicker of frustration passed over him to warn me that trouble was brewing.

Honica was using a black felt pen to place large X's on items on her bill. "Wrong . . . wrong . . . *wrong!*" she was saying. "Never watched a movie. Never touched the mini-bar. Never went to the lounge." She slid the bill invoice back to Gaetan. "Room rate's wrong too. It was supposed to be comp. You guys running some kind of racket here?"

"Good morning, Honica."

"Trevor! How *are* you?" She hugged me like we were old friends.

As she stepped back I straightened my nametag. "I thought you had checked out already," I said. "Brenda Rathberger said you left early this morning."

Honica's eyes widened. She scanned the lobby. "Does she know I'm still here?"

"I don't believe so. She's busy upstairs."

She sighed with relief. "The woman's a psycho. She left four nasty messages on my phone last night, telling me I've ruined her conference. Then she was banging on my door all morning, but I wouldn't answer. She's so judgmental, such a hypocrite! She called me a shameless boozer!" She held her hand to the side of her mouth and leaned toward me. "*She's* the one who used to be a boozer."

I glanced at Gaetan and back to Honica. "Is there something I can help you with?"

"Oh, yeah. I have to fly back to Niagara for a couple days, and I asked your front desk guy here to make me a reservation for New Year's Eve weekend. Willard sent me an invitation to your Gods of the Universe party a few weeks ago, and I know he *really* wanted me to attend. But this guy"—she pointed her thumb at Gaetan—"says you're sold out. So I asked for you. I know you'll find room for me since I'm such a loyal guest. I'll need one of those Supernova suites if possible, and I'm hoping you can comp it."

With one thousand rooms in the hotel, there was always room to squeeze in extra rooms, even if it meant overbooking, which was definitely the case on New Year's Eve. But I was certainly not inclined to do a favor for Honica Winters. "I'm terribly sorry, Miss Winters," I said, "but we truly are sold out. New Year's is our busiest night of the year."

Honica took a deep breath, as if willing herself to be patient. "Listen, Trevor, I gave this hotel a *ton* of publicity on my show Sunday. I would expect you'd be more appreciative. I know Willard would do it."

"That publicity was dreadful, Honica. You humiliated me and my colleagues *and* this hotel! The damage may be irreversible."

"Are you kidding? The Universe is the talk of the town here in New York and across the country, thanks to me. You can't *buy* that kind of buzz."

"I'm quite sure we *wouldn't* buy it."

"You really want me to stay at another hotel? What if I fall in love with it and decide to move the entire NBC account over? Hmm? I'm sure Cynthia wouldn't be too pleased. Do I have to go to her? Come on, Trevor, don't be such a tight-ass!" Softening her approach, she broke into a great smile and rubbed my arm flirtatiously.

"I'll see what I can do," I said. "But no promises."

"You're a doll!"

"Where's Rasputin?" I asked, hoping the odious little mutt had flushed itself down the toilet.

"Oh, I left him with one of your housekeepers. Hope that's okay. She promised to look after him until I get back. He's such a pain to travel with."

I groaned inwardly. Honica was acutely aware that the ladies in housekeeping were so eager to please they didn't know how to say no. "Is there a problem with your bill?" I asked, glancing at Gaetan.

"Um, yeah. A bunch of charges got mistakenly placed on my account. Can you make sure they're removed? Not that it even matters. VOID is paying for all charges."

"Actually, Miss Winters," Gaetan said, handing me the invoice, "VOID has stipulated that only room and tax charges are to be covered. All incidentals are your responsibility. Based on the strict instructions left by Mrs. Rathberger, I'm quite sure she won't be prepared to pay $112 in mini-bar charges."

"I'm sure she said she would pay *all* charges."

"Brenda is upstairs if you'd like to reconfirm," I offered.

Honica shook her head. "No way. I'd rather just pay the charges. Put them on my credit card, but not the ones I crossed off."

I glanced at the bill. "You didn't use the lounge yesterday afternoon? But I saw you there just before the VOID reception."

Honica stuck a finger in her mouth and bit down. "Oh, right. I forgot."

"And the mini-bar—you didn't consume *anything*?" That would be a first for Honica, though certainly not the first time she disputed the charges.

"I didn't even know where the key was."

I studied her face for a moment. In the back of my mind I could hear Willard Godfrey preaching the Universal Principles. Yet an exception was clearly appropriate.

"Miss Winters," I said. "If you want a room on New Year's Eve, I suggest you pay your bill in its entirety."

Her smile vanished. "Fine," she said with a huff. She reached into her purse to withdraw her credit card.

When I finally got to the executive offices, Susan Medley's desk was empty. I knocked on Matthew's door and opened it.

"It's about time," he said. "Get in here. We need to talk."

I lugged a chair toward his desk. "What's up?"

His face was twitching madly. "I'm very, *very* upset with you right now, Trevor. Why did you allow Honica Winters to get hold of those videotapes?"

"Me? I didn't! Susan gave them to her."

"I know *that*. Susan and I had a very frank discussion this morning. But she said you took the party tape from the staff cafeteria and gave it to her. Why didn't you confiscate it?"

"It's *her* tape. It wasn't mine to confiscate."

"And the parking cam tape?"

"She must have gotten a copy from security."

Matthew was silent for a moment. He placed his elbow on his desk, arched his fingers, and leaned toward me. "It's like this, Trevor," he said. "You fucked up. Seriously. As director of rooms, it's your responsibility to know everything that's going on in this hotel and to ensure confidential material doesn't get into the wrong hands. *No one* should have been given those tapes. You should have taken them from Susan and locked them up. You should have known she was leaking information."

"She's your secretary!"

"Not anymore. I fired her this morning."

"You didn't! But she's been Mr. Godfrey's loyal assistant for—"

"Godfrey is *dead*, Trevor. She deliberately deceived us and sold us out. She had to go."

I nodded slowly. I really couldn't argue.

"I now have both tapes, and they will be in my suite for safekeeping," Matthew said. "A few minutes ago, I sent out an all-staff bulletin warning them that if they speak with the media for any reason whatsoever, they will be dismissed at once." He sat back in his chair and folded his arms. "On Sunday night, after *Borderline News*, Cynthia Godfrey called me at home. She was stunned by the revelations. And furious. She couldn't understand how we allowed such a devastating story to be produced under our noses."

"*She's* the one who gave Honica permission to film here. She—"

"Yes, but *you* are the hotel's designated spokesperson. I relied on you to straighten things out. Instead, you fucked things up more than I could possibly imagine. You lied in front of millions of viewers, making this hotel and your colleagues look like drunken, reckless criminals."

"I think you managed that all on your own, Matthew. I was trying to protect everyone. I can't be held responsible for the video footage. And what about you? You're the one who lied, who said you didn't drive that night. We had to find out the truth on national television!"

Matthew lowered his voice and spoke calmly. "Don't go lashing out now, Trevor. That won't do us any good. I never lied to anyone; I simply did not volunteer certain information to anyone but the police. It was no one's business but my own, and, as the police informed me, the fact that I drove that night is completely irrelevant to the investigation."

"Where did you go?"

"None of your business."

"Obviously you're hiding something."

He sighed. "If you must know, I went out for a drive to clear my head."

"For over six hours?"

"I had a great deal to think about, Trevor. The truth is, the previous night Willard informed me that he intended to promote me to the position of general manager. It doesn't matter where I was, anyway. By the time I drove out, Willard Godfrey was already dead. The rest is none of your business."

I glared at him. I didn't believe him.

"Trevor, Cynthia is so upset over how this situation was handled that she told me to fire you."

I jumped up from my seat. "She *what*?"

"Relax. I convinced her to reconsider. I told her you had made a few very bad mistakes, but your intentions were good. As for Sandy, I wasn't as successful."

I gasped. "She wants Sandy fired?"

"Yes."

"That's crazy! Sandy made a bad judgment call, that's all. She doesn't deserve to lose her job. She's one of the best things this place has going. This is unbelievable!"

"Trevor, please calm down. Sandy James drove home drunk after the staff Christmas party, exercising extremely poor judgment and risking her own life as well as the lives of others. If Sandy had hurt—"

"But you just admitted yourself that you drove! You were just as hammered as she was."

"Trevor, I beg of you, shut up." He waited for me to settle before continuing. "If Sandy had hurt someone—and, of course, we still don't know if she did—the hotel could have been held liable. It might have ruined us financially. Had Sandy informed us of her troubles ahead of time, rather than allowing us to find out along with the rest of the nation, we might have been able to do damage control. But she kept it a secret, and that was her choice. Now this place is crawling with militant anti-impaired driving activists. I understand they staged a rabid protest out front this morning, mauling her in front of TV crews. We can't sustain any more bad publicity, any more scandal, any more confrontation, Trevor. We need to take action to minimize further fallout. I've discussed this issue with Shanna, and she's in full agreement."

"You're going to turn on Sandy like that? Sweet Sandy, who works so hard and does such a wonderful job?"

"I'm really not sure how sweet Sandy is anymore. My regard for her has soured greatly. Trevor, as much as I hate to say it, it's looking more and more likely that she ran down Willard Godfrey."

I stood up and slammed my hands on Matthew's desk. "That's *not* true! She got into an accident, that's all, a little fender-bender a mile away from here. That's how her truck got damaged. That's *all*!"

Matthew closed his eyes, then snapped them open. "Did it ever occur to you that she might have gotten into that accident *intentionally*—to cover up the damage sustained to her truck when she ran down Willard Godfrey? Then she had it fixed right away to get rid of the evidence?"

I stared at Matthew for a moment, then said quietly, "That's ridiculous." I turned toward the door.

"You'll be pleased to know that I've decided not to fire her," he called after me, "but to suspend her without pay until things settle down."

I turned around.

"Police have assured me that an arrest is imminent," Matthew continued. "If she is innocent, she can come back after the conference has checked out."

"I don't support this at all," I said.

"Well, you better get behind it soon. You're the one who's suspending her."

"That's not funny, Matthew."

"I'm serious. I'm not the man to do it, Trevor, you are. I've worked with her for less than a year. She respects you, and you're a gentle, kind soul. If it comes from you, she'll understand. Cynthia herself suggested that you do it. She's very upset with you right now and isn't convinced you're worth keeping on. This is your chance to prove to her that you're decisive, a man of action."

I pictured Sandy's big blue eyes staring at me as I delivered the news. I gulped. "I could never ..."

"Suck it up, Trevor."

"I won't do it," I said.

"You have no choice."

Twenty minutes later, Sandy and I were sitting across from each other in my small office, so close to one another our knees were almost touching. Her sparkling blue eyes blinked. "What is it, Trevor?"

"Uh, well, it's like this, Sandy. Cynthia ... and Matthew ... um, they want you to take some time off until all this controversy dies down."

"You're suspending me?"

"I'm not. They are. I'm just the messenger."

She closed her eyes for a moment, processing the information. Her body lilted to the right, and I was afraid she might topple over in her seat. She opened her eyes. "For how long?"

"Two or three days, maybe more, just until all this mayhem settles. Sandy, I want you to know that I'm completely against this. You have my full support. Whatever you need."

"I guess this wouldn't be the best time to pitch Cynthia on my candidacy for general manager," she said with a grim smile.

"Probably not."

She looked down, suddenly deep in thought, and fidgeted with her hands. "Where will I go?" she asked after a moment, looking up. "I've been living here."

I had forgotten. "Jack won't take you back?"

"Even if he will, I'm not sure it's a good idea."

"You could stay at my place."

She smiled appreciatively and reached over to squeeze my hand. "That's very nice, Trevor. But don't worry. I'll figure something out."

"I'm really sorry about this."

"To tell you the truth, I agree with this decision. I'd do the same thing." She stood up to hug me, and we held one another for a very long time.

"It's been a tough week, hasn't it?" I said. I was trying to be strong for Sandy, but my throat was constricting. "But it's going to get better soon. It has to."

"Let's hope. Say goodbye to your mother for me. Or did she leave already? I saw her checking out at the front desk this morning."

"Mom? No, she's here for two more days."

"I could have sworn I saw her with all her bags. Well, give her my love."

"I will."

★ ★ ★ ★ ★

Later that afternoon, I picked up the phone to call my mother.

"Hotel operator, how may I help you?"

"Jeanine, it's Trevor. I'm trying to reach my mother."

"The computer shows she checked out this morning."

"Checked out? Did she change rooms?"

"Doesn't look like it. She was checked out of the system at 9:43 AM."

I called Gaetan at the front desk, who confirmed that she had checked out with him.

"I assumed you knew," he said.

"Did she say where she was going?"

"No, she didn't say much. But she had a lot of bags with her, and I know a bellman helped her."

I called the front door and spoke with the doorman, George, who remembered putting in her a taxi. "I assumed she was going to the airport," he said. "But she never actually told me."

I thanked him and hung up. Why would she leave New York without telling me? Last night we had gone out for dinner at West in the Upper West Side. She had seemed content and hadn't said anything about leaving early. In fact, we had planned to have breakfast together this morning.

I had forgotten to call her.

Had this been the last straw? Had she become so fed up with neglect that she packed her bags and flew home? The prospect was alarming. She would never forgive me. My sisters would never forgive me. I felt sick to my stomach. How could I have been so insensitive, so out of touch that I didn't see she was angry enough to leave without a word?

I collapsed on my desk and moaned. I was already filled with self-loathing for having allowed Matthew to coerce me into doing his dirty work. Now I had neglected my mother. All week I had treated her like a distraction and a nuisance, a hotel guest I politely entertained but didn't try to get to know too well since she'd be moving on soon. I sensed the walls around me trembling violently, as though the foundation was crumbling and the Universe would collapse on top of me. I felt more alone than I'd ever felt in New York. Abandoned first by Mr. Godfrey, then by Sandy, and now by my own mother. Soon Matthew might be taken away. And Shanna, bitter and tired, was unlikely to stick around for long. Last of all was sweet Nancy Swinton, whom I had suspected had a crush on me but was in fact living with another man. Now she too was leaving, depriving me of the daily kindling I needed to keep our imaginary affair burning.

I would be left alone in the Universe.

"You okay, Trevor?"

Startled, I looked up to see Nancy Swinton standing at my door. "I'm fine," I said tersely.

"You don't look fine. Anything I can do to help?"

My heart ached at the sight of her. Since our chat in room 2112, I hadn't seen her, although I had sought her out on a number of occasions. I had dreaded this encounter, which I anticipated to be businesslike and strained, like two married colleagues who had slept together in a drunken stupor and gravely regretted the indiscretion.

She took a tentative step into my office. "I heard about Sandy. It's really a shame. You want to talk?"

There was a glow about her this morning, as though a halo of warm, white light was emanating from the contours of her body. She came around the desk and stood beside me, resting a tiny hand on my shoulder. Her sweet perfume swirled around my head, making me dizzy. I wanted to place my head against her waist and put my arms around her and hold her tight.

But no. Nancy Swinton could only bring more grief and heartache. Soon she would be gone from the Universe forever. As much as I longed for her, I felt my defenses go up, my emotions retreating, the doors and windows of my internal panic room shutting her out.

She ruffled my hair. "You going to be okay, Trevor?"

I looked up at her, blinking, but said nothing.

"What can I do?" she asked, smiling down at me sweetly, her voice gentle and caring.

"Please just leave me alone," I said, pushing her away.

She stepped back and regarded me in shock. I could see the hurt in her eyes, the humiliation, the anger. She marched out of my office.

I stared at the empty space she had just occupied, then collapsed on my desk and sobbed.

★ ★ ★ ★ ★

When I opened the door of my apartment that night, I smelled paint. My furniture had been moved around, the contents of my closet were piled in the living room, and Mom's suitcases were stacked by the door. I heard the sound of singing in my bedroom and crept around the corner, pushing open the door.

"Mom? What are you doing here?"

She was dressed in one of my old T-shirts and 501 jeans. Paint was splattered on her clothes and face. The far wall, formerly Water Damage Gray, was now a bright blue.

"I'm painting for you, Trevor."

"I thought you flew home."

"Why would I do that? I have two more glorious nights in New York with my wonderful son."

"Then why did you check out?"

She set her paintbrush down in the pan, wiped her hands on a towel, and came to me. "I tried, Trevor, I really tried, but I just don't like it in the Universe. It feels cold and stark and lonely."

Why did it sound like she was telling me she hated my girlfriend?

"I see so little of you," she persisted, "and my time is running out. I thought we could spend these last days together. I thought we could talk."

"There's not much room here," I said, glancing at the mess around us.

"There's plenty of room for me. I'll sleep on the sofa. Don't worry, I know you have to work in the morning. I won't keep you up."

I was so relieved that she hadn't left town in a huff that I didn't mind that she hated my hotel and had moved into my apartment uninvited. Was this another chapter in her book? *My Agenda* by Evelyn

Lambert, Chapter Three: When You Can't Get Through, Move Closer. I realized I didn't care what her intentions were. After a long and difficult day, I was happy to have her company.

"I'm glad you're here, Mom," I said, pecking her paint-splattered cheek.

She blinked and looked away. I saw a smile creep over her face.

"Have you had dinner?" I asked. "You want to go out?"

"I thought we'd order in. Then maybe you can give me a hand fixing this place up."

I was about to tell her I was too tired, but I changed my mind. "Sounds great."

"Oh, before I forget—I ran into Marline Drummond in the spa early this morning, and she invited us to join her and Matthew for dinner in Orbit tomorrow night. Doesn't that sound like fun?"

"Didn't you just tell me you hate the hotel?"

"I don't like *staying* there, Trevor. I don't mind visiting. And I quite like Marline. She's a fascinating woman. And of course Matthew isn't hard to look at. I thought you'd be game. I know how much you like socializing with your colleagues."

Yes, I was about to tell her, *but not Matthew and Marline.* Her eyes were so hopeful that I resisted the temptation to ask snidely if Randall would be coming too. She would be gone in less than forty-eight hours, and I knew I would miss her. I picked up the phone and ordered Chinese food, then retrieved two cans of beer from the refrigerator and sat down on the sofa beside her.

"Tell me *all* about your day," she said.

Once I started talking, I couldn't stop. Mom listened intently. For once she didn't interrupt to ask irritating, agenda-filled questions. She didn't judge me. And she didn't slip in cutting digs or seemingly innocuous questions spiked with guilt and manipulation. She simply listened, nodded in understanding, and urged me to continue. At times she opened her mouth to say something, her face growing serious, as though she had a confession to make, but when I kept talking she seemed to reconsider. I told her the entire history of the Universe, about all my hopes and disappointments and fears. I tried to explain why I was in New York, why I worked so hard, why I didn't mind being alone. I talked straight through dinner and into the wee hours of the morning while we caulked and sanded and painted, reorganized furniture, and mounted prints. I was still talking when, exhausted, she shut off the living room light and said good night.

I went to bed feeling light-headed. The simple act of talking, of being listened to, had been therapeutic. I felt that Mom understood me now. For the first time since the death of Willard Godfrey, I slept in peace.

14

Breathing Space

Wednesday morning, Mom was up early to finish painting, and we sat down for breakfast before I left for work. My day was mostly uneventful. With only three of us remaining on the executive committee, and all of us busy preparing for New Year's Eve festivities, briefings were canceled until the New Year. I ran into Matthew in the morning, and he asked me how things had gone with Sandy. I said it was one of the hardest things I'd ever done, that she had been extremely upset, but that I had talked her through it, and in the end she was accepting and gracious.

"Well done, old boy!" he said, slapping me on the back.

I hoped he would pass this information on to Cynthia Godfrey.

After that, I didn't see Matthew again all day. Shanna was also scarce. The majority of her time was dedicated to hosting a familiarization tour of meeting planners from Japan who didn't speak a word of English; when I passed her in the lobby, she bulged out her eyes in a look of total exasperation. Brenda Rathberger was blessedly tied up in the VOID trade show all day. Nancy was off for two days, to my relief. I felt terrible for treating her so poorly yesterday and couldn't bear the thought of seeing her again. She would be back for a PM shift on New

Year's Eve, then a mid-shift on New Year's Day, and then she would be gone from my life forever, and I could start the healing process.

Every time I passed Sandy's office, I felt sad that she wasn't there but heartened by the hope that she was at home patching things up with her husband. In a few days, she would be back at work, and things would start getting back to normal.

At 7:00 that evening, Mom and I took the elevator to Orbit and were escorted across the restaurant by the maitre d' to Matthew and Marline's table. It was Mom's last night in New York, and I was anticipating her departure with a mixture of sadness and relief—sadness because only now were we getting along, and relief because my daily routine could go back to normal.

Matthew and Marline were sitting at a window table, of course—a privilege shared by Matthew as well as Shanna. As we approached the table, I was alarmed to see them engaged in what appeared to be a heated argument. Marline was shaking her fist at Matthew, her lips moving staccato-like, her expression fierce. Matthew was sitting back in his chair with arms folded, nodding slowly, his face grim, eyes blinking repeatedly. When the maitre d' announced us, their angry expressions vanished. They rose from their seats in tandem, looking delighted—and relieved—to see us.

"Why, Evelyn, how pretty you look!" Marline cried, grasping Mom's hands and air-kissing her cheeks. "What a *gorgeous* dress! Burberry?"

"Why, I believe it might be," my mother replied with false modesty.

"Why, it's fabulous."

Alarmed to see how well the two women appeared to get along, and hoping that all their sentences wouldn't start with the word *why,* I sat down across from Marline and nodded at Matthew. Marline remained standing, likely waiting for Mom to notice her own dress. But

Mom's attention was drawn to something she found immensely more appealing: Marline's husband. He leaned over to peck her cheek, and she blushed like a teenage girl. "I could stare at that handsome, heroic face all night," she had confessed to me in the elevator on the way up. Glancing over, I wondered if that was exactly what she intended to do.

"This is such a treat!" Mom said as the maitre d' placed a serviette on her lap and proceeded to fill our glasses with red wine. "Thank you so much for inviting us!"

"It's a treat for us, too," said Matthew, sucking down the last of a gin martini. By the silly grin on his face, I guessed that he had dipped quite far into the well already. He raised his wine glass. "Cheers."

As we clinked glasses, I was alarmed to see how similar Marline and my mother were in appearance. Though Marline was approximately ten years younger, they were both about the same height, and their bodies were equally razor thin. Both had the same shade of dyed blond hair, cut short and straight, curling up at the back in a modern-day Carol Brady style.

Marline smiled at me over her champagne glass with an unabashedly lascivious expression. She dipped her finger into her champagne flute and dabbed her lips, her tongue darting out to lick it up like a reptile. Fearing she might dab her nipples next, I quickly broke her gaze and turned to my mother, who was gazing lovingly into Matthew's eyes.

Suddenly, I felt like I'd been invited to some sort of sick swingers party.

"This is such a welcome break from all those tedious celebrities and politicians we have to entertain, isn't it, Matthew?" Marline said.

"Hush!" said Matthew, glancing around the room. "This room is *teeming* with tedious celebrities and politicians."

Mom was suddenly on the alert for celebrities.

"Are you coming to our New Year's party, Evelyn?" Marline asked. I turned to Matthew. "You're not going ahead with it?"

"I thought I told you. We really had no choice. Invitations went out weeks ago, and already over three hundred people have informed us they are coming. I consulted with Cynthia, and she's perfectly okay with it."

"Has Cynthia ever said no to a party?" I asked wryly. "I find the thought of holding a party—one that *he* usually hosted—distasteful so soon after his passing."

"To the contrary," Matthew said, sounding defensive, "it's the most appropriate thing to do. Mr. Godfrey loved a party, did he not? Our most loyal guests, our largest clients, and some of the most influential people in New York City are coming. It's an opportunity to show them that all is well in the Universe. To cancel this late in the game might lead them to conclude the contrary, that there is truth to the rumors flying around. This will be the first time Marline and I will host the party. We need to let the world know that the Universe has a new general manager, and it's business as usual."

So that was it, I realized. The party was to be Matthew's debutante ball. "Have you asked Victor Moreno?" I asked, referring to the hotel's director of food and beverage. "This morning he told me he's terribly short-staffed on New Year's. Ticket sales went through the roof after *Borderline News*, and the Space Ball is almost sold out now. Orbit and Galaxy are booked solid, and Stratosphere is expected to sell out by tomorrow. There's also the VOID party in the Saturn Ballroom, and dozens of smaller parties in meeting rooms and suites all over the hotel. It's shaping up to be our busiest day in history."

"Nothing like a scandal to generate business," Marline said with a bemused smile.

"You weren't here last year to see what it can be like on New Year's," I persisted. "It's chaotic. I'm quite sure we can't afford to staff your party."

"It's not *my* party," Matthew snapped, "it's the *hotel's* party. I'd be happy to cancel it, believe me. I'd prefer not even to have to go. But I have Cynthia's blessing, and Shanna's, and I expect you to be there to support us as well. Cynthia said she might even come. Since there was no wake for her father, this will be his tribute, his farewell party—a wake of sorts."

"A wake?" Marline cried. "It better be more upbeat than that, darling, or I won't even show up." She reached over the table and patted my arm. "Don't worry, my dear. I spoke with Victor this afternoon and everything is arranged. Champagne and hors d'oeuvres are ordered, and he assured me he'll have plenty of staff."

"I don't understand where he's going to find them," I said. "We're even short-staffed at the front desk."

Marline looked away and peered out the window, as though something had caught her eye. Matthew lifted a spoon from the table and inspected it. Clearly, they were not interested in further discussion.

Then it occurred to me. "You're not robbing staff from the Drive Me Sober program, I hope," I said, my eyes widening. "That would be very foolish, especially considering who's in-house."

"Why don't you let *us* worry about staffing," said Matthew, "and you can worry about your departments. Fair enough?" He turned to my mother. "Will you be coming then, Evelyn?"

"Unfortunately not. I fly home tomorrow morning."

"Honestly, Trevor," Matthew scolded, "shipping your lovely mother off before the main event!"

"I'd love to stay," said Mom, "but I've already got plans in Vancouver. My boyfriend and I are going out dancing."

I almost spit out my champagne. "You have a boyfriend?"

"Yes, Trevor, I do."

"You never told me that."

"You never asked."

"What about ... Randall?"

"Randall was a fling. My relationship is very casual right now. As soon as he's ready to commit, I'll be ready to commit."

"Good on you, Evelyn," Marline said, raising her glass. "If I were single, I'd be playing the field too."

"You *are* playing the field, darling," said Matthew.

"I'd be dating someone just like your son," Marline said, ignoring Matthew and winking at me. "Such a fine, handsome young specimen he is. And such a work ethic! You should be so proud of him."

Mom gave a half-shrug. "I would think your husband works equally exorbitant hours, if not more, considering you live here."

"Matthew?" Marline rolled her eyes and laughed heartily. "I think I log more hours on this hotel's behalf than he does. Even though I don't get a cent for my work, Willard Godfrey treated me like one of his staff. Being First Lady of the Universe isn't all it's cracked up to be. For example, who's organizing this party? Now that Susan Medley is gone, it's up to me."

I smiled pleasantly and fantasized about reaching over the table and smacking Marline upside the head. She was like a parasite, living off the hotel's food and booze, entertaining friends and relatives on Matthew's promo account, utilizing staff as personal assistants, maids, personal trainers, and chauffeurs, while rarely contributing anything in return.

The waiter arrived to take our orders.

Mom studied the menu, chuckling at the names of various menu items, and placed her order.

Matthew, who always refused to say the names of menu items, said, "I'll start with the oysters and—"

The waiter cocked his head, a faint smile of derision spreading over his lips. "*Which* oysters, Mr. Drummond?"

Matthew's lips tightened. "The Universe is Your Oysters," he replied, his face turning red.

"Of course."

When the waiter was gone, Mom turned to Marline. "But life must be so much simpler now, compared with when Matthew was an astronaut."

"Are you kidding?" said Marline, breaking into a smoker's cackle. "Back then, the only thing I had to do was stare adoringly at my husband. Here I'm trapped in his place of employment. I can never escape! Even in the privacy of my room I can't get away. Chambermaids, mini-bar attendants, maintenance men, room service staff, you name it—they're banging at my door at all hours. I'm constantly under surveillance. I have to watch what I say, how I behave, even what I wear. Willard expected me to look like Jackie O twenty-four hours a day. In September, I pulled on a tank top and cutoff shorts to dash across the street to Starbucks and ran smack into him in the lobby. He took one look at my outfit and tore a strip out of me, sending me back to my room to put on 'something decent,' treating me like I was his slutty little daughter."

"It's none of that man's business what you wear!" Mom cried in outrage.

"He was a tyrant, I tell you," Marline said. "He was very hard on my poor Matthew."

"I must say I've been coming to the same conclusion," Mom said, stealing a worried glance at me. She added, "But Trevor was quite enamored with him."

"He wasn't a tyrant," I said. "He was a perfectionist, a visionary."

"I can't say I miss the old coot—may he rest in peace," Marline said. "I've known the man for years—his wife, Margaret, and I were dear friends—and I never liked how he treated Margaret while she was alive. When Matthew and I moved here, I discovered that he treated his staff in much the same manner—like slaves."

The table was silent. I was determined not to become embroiled in an argument with Marline. Mom was doing her best to be respectful. Matthew was staring out the window, not listening to anyone.

Our appetizers arrived.

Marline said, "Tell me, Evelyn, what happened to Trevor's father? Are you divorced?"

"My husband died many years ago," Mom replied, reaching for her wine.

"What a coincidence," Marline said. "So did mine!"

"Very funny, Marline," said Matthew, sucking an oyster from its shell.

Marline cackled. "No offense, dear, but you haven't exactly been full of life since you started working here." She turned to my mother. "He hasn't been himself since he left NASA. I swear something leaked into his space suit while he was up in space and fried his brain. Or Martians abducted him and gave him a lobotomy."

Mom smiled pleasantly and shifted in her seat. Matthew and Marline were one of those couples who seemed to loathe one another in the company of others, using their guests as outlets for resentment and bashing each other with aplomb, yet deep down were madly in love. I wasn't convinced that the latter part was the case, however.

As we ate, Mom and Marline twittered to each other like birds.

Matthew and I engaged in a stare-down.

He leaned toward me, lowering his voice. "Cynthia Godfrey hasn't been returning my calls," he said. "This afternoon she was showing around a group of very grave-looking people in business suits—not her usual company. When I approached them to introduce myself, she didn't introduce them and seemed very uncomfortable. I fear she's gone ahead and placed the hotel up for sale, and these are prospective buyers."

I shook my head adamantly. "She gave me her word. She promised not to go against her father's wishes."

"Don't be so naive, Trevor. Cynthia's word means nothing. I've tried to convince her that the hotel industry has started to rebound and the good times are just beginning. But I'm not sure I've succeeded. I don't think she's confident in our ability to run this show on our own. Sandy's behavior certainly hasn't helped. And you, Trevor—I'm not getting the support I need from you."

"Matthew, you've been in charge for what—ten days?—and look at all that's happened. You want me to help you make your position permanent? I can only imagine what other horrors would lie ahead."

Marline and Mom halted their conversation and turned to listen.

"I can hardly be blamed for everything that's happened this week," Matthew said, his face twitching. "You're the one who screwed up on *Borderline News*, not me. Meanwhile, I have been doing my best to hold things together. I need your support, Trevor, and I don't feel like I'm getting it. I'm seriously reconsidering my plan to promote you to executive assistant manager."

"Why would I want the position? This week you've forced me to do all your dirty work, and you lied through your teeth about not driving the night of the party. How am I supposed to trust you?"

Marline's ears pricked up. "Matthew lied? About what?"

"None of your business, Marline."

Feeling no obligation to protect Matthew, I turned to Marline. "Matthew failed to mention that he drove his car out of the parkade after the Christmas party, right past the place where Mr. Godfrey was hit. He was content to allow Sandy and Shanna to take the heat."

Marline looked confused. "You didn't know? But he spent the night at your place."

I frowned, thinking I had misunderstood. "At my place? He's never even been to my apartment." I looked over to him. He was biting a knuckle.

"Darling," Marline said, turning to Matthew, an undertone of menace in her singsong voice, "if you weren't at Trevor's, where were you?"

"We're not going to discuss this right now, Marline."

"Fine. But rest assured, we'll be discussing it later."

"I simply need your unqualified support as general manager," Matthew said, turning back to me.

"I'm afraid I can't do that," I said. "How do you expect me to support you when you're such a lousy manager?"

"Trevor, how rude!" Mom cried, casting a look of sympathy Matthew's way.

"It's true, Evelyn," said Marline. "Matthew is a lousy manager. He wasn't much of an astronaut either."

"At least I made it into space," Matthew shot back. "Unlike a certain actress who's barely made it onstage."

Marline gasped. "How dare you!" She turned to my mother. "In fact, I've appeared in numerous plays and Broadway shows. I specialize in Shakespeare and poetry recitals, and often write my own material, so of course I'm very selective about the roles I accept. Recently, I appeared in a Staples commercial and three student films—just for the fun of the art."

"I adore acting," said my mother. "I recently started classes."

"Matthew has no idea how difficult my career is. Yet all along I have stood by him, regardless of what a failure he's been."

"Think about it, Trevor," said Matthew, ignoring his wife. "You're either with me or against me. You know what will happen if the hotel is sold. We'll all lose our jobs."

"You could come home, then!" Mom exclaimed. "You could work at the Four Seasons or join that ValuLuxe hotel they're going to build!"

"Yes, I could," I said, my lips tightening. I turned to stare out the window, not wanting to talk to anyone anymore. The view was facing southeast, and the Empire State Building was looming in the distance. I felt manipulated by the people at the table, pulled in different directions to places I did not want to go.

Our entrées arrived. As we ate, Marline looked up occasionally to glare at Matthew, then turned to smile at my mother and me. Mom raved about the food, but spent most of the time pushing it around her plate, eating little. She barely touched her wine. I regretted that her last night had been wasted in the company of this nasty couple. After dessert, we excused ourselves at the earliest polite moment.

As she got up to say goodbye, Marline got in one last dig at Matthew. "Evelyn, you'll *never* guess what Matthew got me for Christmas! A trip!"

"How wonderful!" cried Mom. "Where are the two of you going?"

"To Ohio!" Marline exclaimed, as though having said Paris. "Except Matthew neglected to buy a ticket for himself, so I get to visit my parents on my own!"

"I would have loved to come," said Matthew, "but there's simply too much going on here right now."

"Two weeks!" Marline cried, clasping her hands together in mock rapture. "Two weeks in Ohio with my octogenarian parents."

"Poor me, I'll be stuck here all by my lonesome," Matthew said, his eyes gleaming devilishly in the candlelight. "It brings to mind our ad campaign: Living Space ... Thinking Space ... Breathing Space."

15

The Dark Side of the Universe

The next morning I awoke to the sound of beeping. My U-Comm was going off somewhere. I opened my eyes and looked at my alarm clock. It was 6:00 AM. In the dark, I fumbled around for the device and shut it off, then stumbled into the living room and flicked on the light, peering into the blue phosphorescent window of the U-Comm.

The message said EGP 555—CALL DUTY MANAGER. *Another* Emergency Group Page? What this time? I was about to call in when my eye caught a movement in the living room. I looked over and saw a pale-faced old woman with wispy gray hair sitting upright on the sofa. She was regarding me with a confused expression.

We both cried out in surprise.

"Mom!"

"Trevor! I must have been dreaming. I forgot where I was." She reached for her blanket and pulled it around her, eyes blinking. "What was that beeping sound?"

"My U-Comm. What happened to your hair?"

She reached up to touch her head. "Oh, dear." Bending over, she began to search the floor around her. "I take my wig off at night."

"You wear a *wig?*"

"I do."

Looking down, I realized I was in my underwear. I darted into my bedroom to grab my robe. When I came back, Mom had disappeared into the bathroom. I called the hotel, and the night manager, Fiona Schwartz, answered.

"It's Trevor. What's up?"

"Have you seen this morning's *Post?*" asked Fiona. She sounded distressed.

"No. Why?"

"You might like to get a copy right away."

"Why?" I felt a pang of anxiety. *What now?*

She hesitated. "Mr. Godfrey is on the front page. Sorry, but I've got to run. The others are calling in. Mr. Drummond wants you in right away."

"I'll be there as soon as I can."

I heard the sound of running water in the bathroom. Opening my front door, I poked my head into the hallway, looking both ways in search of a copy of the *Post*. One was sitting on a doormat a few doors down. I crept down the hallway, snatched it up, and slipped back into my apartment.

The headline screamed at me from the front page: HOTEL MURDER! WILLARD GODFREY BLUDGEONED TO DEATH, NYPD REVEALS. I gasped. Below the headlines, the entire page comprised a full-page photo of a grinning Willard Godfrey. "Hotel *murder*? No fucking way!" I cried out loud.

"Everything okay out there?" Mom called from the bathroom.

"Yeah, just peachy," I answered, tearing open the paper. A few pages in, I found a two-page spread on the Godfrey case. The left page was plastered with photos: a shot of the outside of the Universe at nighttime; of Mr. Godfrey standing in the lobby with Cynthia Godfrey; of Shanna Virani and Matthew Drummond at the Christmas party;

and of Sandy James' now-infamous smiling mug shot. Taking a deep breath, I scanned the copy.

"Trevor, I need to tell you something."

Mom was standing in the bathroom doorway in her pajamas, her wig firmly back in place, her face grave.

"You'll *never* believe this, Mom."

"We need to talk," she said, as though she hadn't heard me. "I've been wanting to tell you this all week, but it's never been the right time. Before I go, I have to tell you."

"Can't it wait?" I said impatiently. "Listen to this: 'Late yesterday, the New York Police Department revealed that renowned hotelier Willard Godfrey, seventy-one, owner of Manhattan's luxurious Universe Hotel, did not die accidentally as originally believed but was murdered. "Autopsy results confirm what we have suspected all along," Detective Owen Lim of Manhattan's Seventeenth Precinct announced in a brief statement. "Willard Godfrey was struck down by a motor vehicle in the Universe Hotel parkade but did not die of these injuries. The cause of death was several blows to the head administered by a blunt instrument shortly after he was run down." Detective Lim went on to explain that from the outset certain evidence pointed to foul play, but only when forensic analyses and autopsy results, which had been delayed by holidays, were released yesterday did they feel they had enough evidence to release details of the case to the public. Asked if an arrest was imminent, Detective Lim refused to comment further, stating only that he was pleased with the progress of the investigation.'"

I looked up at my mother, my eyes wide with disbelief, and thrust the paper into her hands. "Isn't that insane?"

She took it almost reluctantly and scanned the article. "I have to say I'm not entirely surprised. I've been wondering all along if it was foul play."

"Who would want to kill Mr. Godfrey? Everybody loved the guy."

"Not Marline Drummond."

"What, you think *she* killed him?"

"No, of course not." She looked up from the article. "What is Cynthia Godfrey like?"

"Spoiled rich kid. Party girl. Why, you think *she* did it?"

"She is the most obvious suspect. Greed can lead people to do terrible things. I imagine she inherited a fortune."

"She did, but her alibi is air-tight from what I understand. She left the party long before her father was hit. I checked elevator and parkade activity reports myself, and there's no sign of her coming back. Besides, I don't think she's got it in her. She loved her father. She craved his company, used to complain that she never got to see him."

Mom leaned against the back of the sofa, her index finger pressed against her lips, as though determined to solve the mystery right now. "If it wasn't the daughter, then it had to be Sandy."

"It was *not* Sandy," I said, my voice stern. "Maybe it was possible before, when it was an accident, but now that we know it was murder, it's *definitely* not possible. Cassandra James is not capable of murder."

"What if she ran him down by accident, then went back and saw that he was still alive, so she finished him off?"

"Why would she do that?"

"Maybe he was horribly maimed and she wanted to put him out of his misery. That would certainly fit with her 'compassionate' personality."

"Hold steady, Angela Lansbury. This isn't *Murder, She Wrote*."

Mom let the paper drop to the floor and started to pace the room. "Or maybe she did it to protect herself. She was drunk and disoriented, possibly in shock, and she knew if he lived he could identify her. The thought of going to jail was inconceivable. She's the mother of two young children. So she finished him off and fled."

"Enough, Mother."

"People will do terrible things to protect their—"

"Shut up!" I shouted. "Not another word, okay? Sandy did *not* do it. She's a good-hearted, decent person. Stop playing detective! You don't know my colleagues well enough to judge them like this. They are good people."

"Fine. But just because people are excessively polite doesn't mean they're virtuous. In fact, it's often the opposite. How can you trust someone so accomplished at hiding her true thoughts?"

"Will you stop it? I'm tired of your stupid philosophizing."

She clamped her mouth shut, eyes growing wide, and backed away from me, circling around the sofa, as though struck with the sudden realization that I was the killer.

"What are you doing?" I asked, irritated.

"Why are you so protective of Sandy?"

"Because she didn't do it!"

"Do you love her, Trevor?"

"What? Don't be ridiculous. I told you, she's like a sister to me. Besides, she's married."

"People fall in love with married people all the time."

"I love Sandy's work ethic and optimism, but there's no romance there, I assure you."

"I hope you find love, Trevor. *True love.* There's nothing like it. Do you fancy anyone at work?"

"I don't get involved with coworkers, Mom. You know my past. It's far too risky."

"Risk is what love is all about, Trevor. Taking chances. You should be able to love someone without worrying that you're harassing them.

You misinterpreted that girl's feelings at the Park Harbour Hotel and you acted inappropriately, but how did you know she'd be so vindictive? Don't let it discourage you from loving again."

I thought of Nancy, and my heart soared. Of everything I told Mom the other night, I had left that part out. I was afraid to even utter her name out loud. Now I had an overwhelming desire to tell Mom about her. Why hadn't I introduced them? How happy it would have made Mom. "A girlfriend! Trevor has a girlfriend!" she would announce to family and friends when she got home. "And I *adore* her!" Then I remembered the boyfriend, and the fact that Nancy didn't love me, and that I was following the same pattern with her as I had with Rosa. What an idiot I was. Thank god she was leaving the hotel in a few days. I wasn't about to tell Mom about a make-believe romance, a romance that was hopeless, that would only break my heart. My internal panic room kicked into high alert, doors and windows slamming shut, locking emotions inside.

"Did you say you had something to tell me?" I asked, suddenly remembering.

She folded her hands before her and sighed, turning to stare into the bedroom at the bright blue wall. "No."

"Are you packed? We should go."

"Isn't it a little early? I thought we could have breakfast and talk. I—"

"I have to get to work. Matthew wants me in at once."

While she showered and packed her things, I put on my suit, attached my nametag and gave it a good polish, then sat in the living room and flicked on the TV while I waited. News of the Willard Godfrey case was on every local news channel: "Hotelier Murdered!" "New York Hotel Industry Reeling!" "Manhattan Murder Mystery!" I turned it off, unable to watch, and paced the living room.

The walls of my living room were bright yellow now, a bit hard on the eyes and not a color I would have selected myself, but the effect was somehow uplifting. Mom had bypassed the cans of pale gray and dark blue paints in my closet and had gone out to procure brighter colors. "See?" she said to me last night after we got back from dinner, leading me around the apartment. "The living room is the color of sunshine. Your bedroom is the color of blue sky. And the kitchen is the color of roses. How could you ever be unhappy here?" Indeed, the walls were bright and cheerful, all the scrapes and dents gone, and my prints were finally mounted. At last, my apartment looked like a home.

"Ready!" Mom announced, dropping two overflowing Macy's shopping bags by the door.

I helped her on with her coat, lifted her suitcases and shopping bags, and followed her down the hall, dropping the tattered copy of the *Post* back on my neighbor's doorstep.

Outside, the air was crisp and cool, the sky dotted with clouds.

"We'll have better luck on the corner," I said, heading toward Ninth Avenue.

She hurried after me. "Can we share a cab?"

"I'm heading in a different direction."

"I don't mind the detour. We can visit along the way."

I didn't answer. My thoughts were back on the Universe and this morning's startling revelation. I wanted to get there as quickly as possible. At the corner, I lifted my hand to flag a taxi.

Mom stood beside me, deep in thought. "Trevor," she shouted over the din of traffic, "if you don't find love at the Universe, where will you find it? Certainly not sitting alone in your apartment. You don't go out. You don't have friends. All you do is work. Do you want to be alone all your life?"

"What if I do? Just because I'm alone doesn't mean I'm lonely. I told you the other night, I'm content."

"But are you *happy?*"

"Sure."

"You are *not* happy. I'm your mother, I know when you're happy. Tell me, why *do* you spend so much time at work?"

"I told you, I like work. Is that so bad? I suppose I could stay home more often, but why? My apartment is small and empty and depressing, and Jennifer Lopez or Rudy Giuliani aren't going to just show up at the door like they do at the Universe. It's exciting there. People respect me. They need my help. At home, it's just me. It's boring."

"That's because your life is one-dimensional, Trevor. Most people have more to come home to. You've shut everyone and everything out, including your family. Do you know how sad it is to hear you call Sandy James the glamorous sister you never had? To hear you call Willard Godfrey your father figure? Have you replaced me too?"

"Of course not. I—"

"You need to make more room in your life for your family. You need to find a better balance. I don't mean to be so blunt, but really, dear, you need to get a life."

"I *have* a life. I *like* living in New York." I ventured farther into the street, ignoring the cars that swerved around me and honked.

"Careful!" Mom cried, grabbing my arm with surprising force. "You're not *living* in New York. You're only *existing*. When's the last time you jogged in Central Park? Watched a concert at Madison Square Garden? Went to a nightclub in Queens? Wandered through the Guggenheim? Have you ever done these things? Why bother living in New York if you haven't? Why don't you come to your senses and come home where you can be near your family?"

At last, the central theme of *My Agenda* by Evelyn Lambert revealed. "Because I like it here, Mom," I said quietly. "Jesus Christ, thousands of cabs in this goddamned city and you can never get one when you need one. Let's try Broadway." I picked up the bags and marched across Ninth Avenue.

"Listen to me, Trevor!" Mom cried, chasing after me. "You're hiding. Hiding from disappointment and grief and hardship! Hiding in the make-believe world of hotels, where everyone is nice and smiley and life is safe and simple and superficial. But it's not living! You need to face the real world."

I realized that I was wrong in thinking I had a breakthrough with her the other night, thinking she had actually been listening without judging me. In fact, she had listened to my words and stored them up, using them as ammunition in her battle to get me to come home. I refused to listen. My arms were straining from the weight of her suitcases. I dropped them on the street and waved frantically at passing cabs. "Taxi! Taxi!"

Mom grabbed me by the tie and yanked me toward her. "Why are you wearing this nametag on the street? Tell me, *why*?"

"Why do you care? I always put it on before work." Up the street I spotted a young woman climbing from a taxi. I pulled my tie from Mom's grasp, picked up the suitcases, and bolted in that direction. "Come on!"

Mom hurried after me. "Trevor! Wait!"

She caught up with me beside the cab, out of breath. "Who are you besides the director of rooms at the Universe Hotel? Who are *you*, Trevor?"

"Get off the street, crazy broad!" someone yelled from a passing car, blaring his horn.

I grabbed her arm and pulled her off the street. Desperate to get her into the cab and out of my sight, I went to the back of the taxi and banged my fist on the trunk. The driver popped it open. I piled in the bags, then walked around to the door and held it open for her, refusing to look at her.

"Talk to me, Trevor," she pleaded. "Tell me, what are you afraid of?"

"Do you really want to know what I'm afraid of, Mom?" I cried, finally losing it. "I'll tell you what. I'm afraid of failing again like I did in university. I'm afraid of being ridiculed like I was in the film industry. I'm afraid of being rejected by someone I love like Rosa rejected me. And I'm afraid of depending on someone again like Dad and Willard Godfrey. *That's* what I'm afraid of. Do you understand? Do you?"

She regarded me in silence, her eyes welling with tears. She reached for my hand. "Oh, Trevor."

I pulled it away. "*Finally* I have a career I'm proud of, a place where I'm needed and I'm not paralyzed by fear all the time, and *you* won't stop criticizing it! This isn't about me, is it, Mom? It's about you. It's about you being a lousy mother and a walking zombie for twenty years and suddenly waking up and taking an interest in my life. It's about you wanting to make up for lost time, wanting to manipulate my life into something you can be proud of and tell your friends, wanting me to be happy and successful so that *you* can be free of guilt. Well, it's too late. I have my own life now, and you're not part of it. Now get in!"

Mom clutched the side of the door and choked down a sob. "Trevor, please. You don't mean that."

"You getting in or what?" the cab driver yelled, gunning his engine. A line of cars had formed on the street behind us, laying on their horns.

"I love you, Trevor."

"Goodbye, Mom."

She climbed into the taxi and turned to look up at me. "You preferred me as a big, depressed blob on the sofa, didn't you?"

"Please go." I shut the door.

I watched the taxi disappear into a sea of yellow, then turned and slowly made my way up the street.

★ ★ ★ ★ ★

Matthew had organized an emergency meeting with Shanna and me. When I arrived at the Cosmic Bubble, I felt overwhelmed with mixed feelings: despair over the news about Mr. Godfrey; rage toward my mother for the hurtful things she said; and remorse for having put her through such a lousy Guest Departure Experience. I vowed to call her to apologize *and* to solicit her apologies—as soon as I calmed down.

Shanna and Matthew sat slumped in their chairs, arms crossed, looking shell-shocked and worried. A copy of the *Post* sat on the table between them.

"Unbelievable, isn't it?" I said, taking a seat next to Matthew.

Neither Matthew nor Shanna responded.

I wondered if Matthew felt like a caged animal. The investigation was closing in—now an investigation into a brutal murder. He was looking guiltier than ever. To imagine a woman assaulting Mr. Godfrey with a blunt instrument was difficult, if not impossible, particularly gentle Sandy or diminutive Shanna. The prospect of prison, possibly for the rest of his life, must have been terrifying. I felt a pang of pity for him. Eight months ago, when he took the resident manager position, he probably never imagined things turning out this way.

"Matthew," I said, "I know this must be a tough time for you. If there's anything I can do, just let me know."

He turned to me and frowned. "What are you talking about?"

"Well ... not that I'm jumping to conclusions but ... after reading the paper and—"

"Trevor, please."

"—I think you might be in a lot of trouble, and—"

"Trevor," Matthew said again, his voice chillingly calm. "Sandy did it."

I shook my head sadly. "Isn't it time you stopped trying to pin this on her? Isn't it time you faced the consequences of your own actions?"

Matthew's lips parted into a grim smile. He stared down at his folded arms. "Trevor, Shanna and I have been talking. She drove out of the parkade before Sandy, and I drove out after Sandy. Neither of us saw Willard. Now that we know he was murdered, everything points to Sandy. You saw how upset she was when Godfrey announced our bonuses were on hold. When she drove out and saw him standing on the ramp in front of her, she must have lost her mind."

"For god's sake, Matthew, have you no shame?" I turned to Shanna, exasperated. "Tell him, Shanna, tell him we know he did it. He needs to turn himself in."

"Trevor," Shanna said, her voice almost a whisper. "It's time for *you* to stop pointing fingers. We don't want to believe it either, but we have no choice. Sandy James killed Willard Godfrey."

16

Gods of the Universe

New Year's Eve at the Universe.

At 9:00 PM I stood at the front door observing the long line of taxis and limousines, luxury sedans, and SUVs that snaked up the porte-cochère to the entrance. Partygoers spilled out of the vehicles dressed in long, flowing gowns, diamond necklaces and tiaras, designer tuxedos and tails. Others arrived in full costume for the Space Ball, dressed as extraterrestrial creatures and cyborgs, starship cadets and otherworldly creatures, sprouting tentacles and extra limbs, toting lasers and alien babies. It was as though the Universe were holding some futuristic intergalactic celebration.

Despite the activity around me, I felt disconnected from the hotel tonight. I had attempted to help out in other departments, but they were so busy I had only gotten in the way. My attempts to mix and mingle with guests had been coolly received and cut short: no one knew who I was or seemed to care; they were too busy socializing with the people they did know. Feeling like neither employee nor guest, I floated solo across the Universe, a lonely planet searching for a home. I was happy to rest awhile at the front door.

I felt Mr. Godfrey's absence profoundly tonight, but in a pleasant way, as though he were standing on the other side of the doors with me, watching me greet guests as they arrived and nodding in approval. For the past two days I had been obsessing over his death, desperately trying to figure out what happened, contemplating one crazy theory after another. Clearly, Shanna and Matthew had made up their minds that Sandy did it and were unwilling to consider alternatives. This wasn't surprising, considering they appeared to be the only remaining suspects. I had tried to reach Sandy all day, but she hadn't returned my messages. I feared that she hadn't taken her suspension as graciously as I had hoped and was sulking, or perhaps the murder revelation was simply too much for her to bear. Whatever her frame of mind, I hoped she was back at home with her family, enjoying her time away from the hotel. Mom also weighed heavily on my mind, and on several occasions I had picked up the phone to call her, then put it down. I was still too angry.

I was expected at the Gods of the Universe party but looked for any reason to delay my arrival. When traffic at the front door began to ebb, I went inside, weaving through the clusters of people toward the grand staircase. The entire lobby, together with Jupiter Ballroom, Galaxy, and the Center of the Universe, had been transformed into a massive ballroom for the Space Ball, and over twenty-five hundred attendees were expected. On a high stage erected outside Galaxy a seven-piece band was playing pop music, the first of three groups scheduled. The cacophony of music, laughter, and chatter soared into the atrium, rising twenty floors into the air, floating over balconies and swirling through corridors, reaching every door and beckoning every guest of the hotel to join the party.

I took the staircase up to the concourse level, where a different party was being held in every function room: groups of friends, corporate gatherings, and family affairs. Around the outer concourse hundreds of people were mingling, sipping drinks, chatting, posing for photos, kissing, hugging, and leaning over the railing to watch the burgeoning party below. I made my way to Saturn Ballroom, where VOID's Glory Days of Prohibition party was being held, and pushed open the door.

In contrast to the clamor outside, the ballroom was as quiet as a church on Sunday. Hundreds of eyes turned toward me as I entered. The door slowly closed behind me, restoring serenity to the room, and heads turned back to Brenda Rathberger, who was strutting back and forth onstage and speaking into a cordless microphone. The ballroom had been transformed into a 1920s-style cabaret, with round banquet tables draped in black linen and centerpieces of red tea roses. The walls were covered with lush red velvet curtains, and posters from the Prohibition era, preaching the evils of drink and the glories of sobriety, were displayed on easels around the periphery of the room. Dinner plates had been cleared away, and an army of banquet servers dressed in tails was setting up a dessert buffet.

At least five hundred delegates were in attendance, dressed in a range of clothing from three-piece suits and bow ties to denim pants and sweatshirts. A number of men and women wore twenties-style costumes: vintage tuxedos and top hats, knee-length knit dresses and cloche hats. Onstage behind Brenda, a 1920s-style big band quartet stood with instruments poised, waiting for the end of her speech.

"As you all know," she was saying, "the theme of tonight's party is 'Glory Days of Prohibition,' which ties in with our conference theme, 'Society for Sobriety.' In the days of prohibition, society was acutely aware of the evils of drink, and the government took measures to ban it entirely. If only our government were as intelligent today." She looked down at her dress, an ill-fitting flapper costume. "Though I must say fashion has come a long way."

The crowd chuckled.

"I would like to thank all of you for your participation in and enthusiasm for this week's conference. We made good progress this week, I am proud to say, and I was heartened by the unprecedented attendance, an increase of almost twenty percent over last year." She paused. "Yet I cannot say I'm completely satisfied, and already the board has expressed its concern that the conference hasn't been as successful as they hoped. As you know, VOID relies on extensive media attention to get our messages out. While board members were pleased with the coverage we did receive—in particular, the *Borderline News* segment—they were *not* thrilled with its sensationalistic tone. They feel we failed to garner the media attention we truly need if we're going to take our movement to the next level. Tomorrow, we have one last opportunity to get our message out collectively. I urge all of you to attend our closing event, the March for Sobriety, which commences at 1:00 PM at the Grand Army Plaza in the southeast corner of Central Park. From there we will march across the park and down Avenue of the Americas to Rockefeller Plaza, where our Society for Sobriety rally will be held at 2:00 PM. I have invited a number of media to attend and am expecting an excellent turnout. I hope to see each and every one of you there, where we will collectively demonstrate our true passion for our cause.

"In the meantime, please stick around for dancing, followed by VOID's traditional Dry Toast at midnight, then more dancing. Right now, I would like to thank all of you for your hard work and commitment, and to congratulate you for a successful Sixth Annual Victims of Impaired Drivers conference. I wish you a safe, happy, and sober New Year."

Brenda lifted a water glass from the podium and held it up.

The audience cheered, raising coffee mugs, tea cups, mocktails, soft drinks, juices, and water glasses.

As Brenda climbed down from the stage, the band struck up "Tea for Two."

Across the ballroom, people rose from their tables and lined up at the dessert buffet.

I crossed the ballroom to intercept Brenda and caught up with her in line.

"Look at you!" I gushed. "Great costume!"

She groaned and adjusted her shoulder strap. "I feel like a fat, pasty, pre-war hooker."

"How's the party going?"

"Fine."

"Everyone enjoying themselves?"

She gave me a suspicious look. "Yes. Why?"

"Just wanting to make sure." I looked around. "Did Honica Winters come?"

She shook her head and scowled. "When she found out we weren't serving booze, she suddenly remembered she had other plans." She craned her head toward the front of the line, looking anxious, as if afraid the desserts might run out.

"I guess you were as surprised as the rest of us by yesterday's headlines," I said.

"Why would I be surprised?"

I stepped closer to her and lowered my voice. "The revelation that Mr. Godfrey was murdered—that it wasn't a drunk driving accident."

"My theory holds," she snapped. "A drunk ran him down and was too much of a coward to face the consequences, so he—or she—finished him off and fled the scene. It wouldn't be the first time this has happened."

Judy Gordon came hurrying over. "Brenda, everyone's leaving! Look!"

We turned toward the exit, where a number of people were filing out.

"Let them go," said Brenda. "They're tired. It's been a long week. I want them rested up for tomorrow."

"Not everyone's going to bed," said Judy, raising one eyebrow. "Edgar from the Atlanta chapter just took his entire table to the lounge for drinks."

"He *didn't*."

Judy nodded, and turned to survey the ballroom. "I can't really blame him. This party *is* a little dull."

"It is *not* dull!" Brenda cried, gesturing to the dance floor, where a half-dozen delegates were dancing and the band was singing, "*I never knew I had a wonderful wife until the town went dry.*" "Now stop complaining and start mingling. And don't let anyone else leave."

"Fine." Judy walked off in a huff.

Brenda turned to me and sighed. "I guess we've been upstaged by your other parties."

"I wanted to congratulate you for a successful conference, Brenda," I said. "And to thank you for keeping the conference here."

"You're welcome, Trevor." She regarded me for a moment, and I detected a flicker of warmth and tenderness in her eyes, something I hadn't seen since the day she arrived. She looked exhausted, partly defeated, and I felt a flash of sympathy for her. "It hasn't been all bad," she said. "I hope you understand I'm just doing my job. You've been very patient with me and highly professional. I appreciate it."

"Thank you, Brenda. I try. I'm committed to accommodating our guests with whatever—"

Having reached the front of the buffet line, Brenda turned her back on me in mid-sentence and began loading her plate with desserts.

Evidently, our conversation was over.

★ ★ ★ ★ ★

When I arrived at Matthew and Marline Drummond's lavish two-level suite on the sixth floor, the Gods of the Universe party was raging.

I passed my disc across the door scanner, and the front door slid open. The room was so crowded that people spilled into the hallway.

Taking a deep breath, I pried my way in, glancing around nervously and telling myself I would stay only long enough to make my presence known to Matthew. The suite was decorated in the style of ancient Greece, with plaster Roman columns woven with ivy, great Grecian urns painted in gold leaf, and muscled male servers dressed in togas—a tacky theme that could only be the brainchild of Marline Drummond. The guests were dressed in formal attire, tuxedos, ball gowns, and cocktail dresses. A deejay in the far corner was playing loud house music that seemed more appropriate for a rave party.

As I gently pushed my way through the crowd, I was happy to see a few familiar faces—some of the hotel's regular guests and top clients, major suppliers, a few local politicians and businessmen, even a smattering of celebrities. But the majority of guests were Marline's friends, the lackeys and hangers-on I frequently saw in our lounge and restaurants, feeding Marline gossip while she fed them gourmet cuisine and premium liquors.

Across the room, I heard Marline's loud smoker's cackle. She was squeezed into a tiny white dress that was tied at her neck with spaghetti straps, a dress that looked more like an apron. Her back was facing me, and the dress was cut so low that I could see the cleavage of her skinny buttocks. Her limbs bore almost no flesh, only sinewy muscle and skin airbrushed a golden brown. She flitted from social cluster to social cluster, a bottle of Dom Perignon in each hand guaranteeing a warm welcome into all social circles. I watched her replenish flutes, dispensing witty banter, flirting with men and flattering women.

"Trevor, *darling!*" she cried upon spotting me.

Before I could escape in the opposite direction, she was at my side.

"Why, look at how dashing you are in this tuxedo! You look simply edible!" She wrapped her bones around me and stood on her toes to plant a wet kiss on my lips. "Happy New Year, darling!" Her eyes were bleary with champagne. "What's with this nametag? Take it off this instant! You're off-duty now, young man. It's time to party!"

"I'm only here for a few minutes."

"Nonsense!" She pulled the nametag from my lapel and stuffed it into my pocket, her hand lingering there for a moment. Then she turned and snapped her fingers for a waiter. "Bring this young man a glass of champagne at once!"

Within seconds I had a flute in my hands.

Marline lifted her glass and clinked it against mine. "Cheers." The crowd was pushing her toward me, and she was making no attempt to resist. Her tiny little breasts pressed against my upper stomach.

"Where's Matthew?" I asked, stepping back until I hit the wall.

"Who knows?" she said, pulling at one of her dress straps to reveal more pushed-up breast than I cared to see and letting it snap back. "Hiding under the bed, for all I know. He's so hopeless at these things." She moved even closer, a cloud of expensive perfume enveloping me. "Trevor, darling, I've been meaning to ask you about your comment at dinner the other night. Do you recall saying that Matthew had never been to your place before? Well, after dinner I pressed him further. He denied ever telling me he had stayed at your place after the party. But I wouldn't confuse something like that. He's lying."

"Oh?"

"When he got home the morning after the Christmas party, I woke up. It was almost 8:00 AM! He was still in his tuxedo, and I asked him where he'd been all night. He mumbled something about going back to your place for a beer after the party and falling asleep on your sofa. He hadn't been home more than a few minutes when he got your page. I remember him saying into his U-Comm, 'This better be important, Trevor,' and thinking he was being quite rude for just having come back from your place."

I recalled Matthew arriving on P4 in his tuxedo. Hadn't he said something about having fallen asleep in it? "I'll say it again, Marline," I said. "Matthew has never been to my place."

"So I understand. He refuses to talk to me, in typical Matthew fashion." Marline's shrill voice was hurting my eardrum. "He insists that he went out for a drive to clear his head. Considering he left the party around 1:00 AM, it must have been quite a drive. He could have gone to Boston and back." She paused to sip her champagne, then turned and surveyed the crowd, fluttering her fingers at a group of ladies in the far corner. She turned back to me. "He's hiding something, Trevor."

I detected a quaver in her voice and a flicker of fear in her eyes. I gulped and said, "You don't think …?"

She nodded. "A houseman dropped off his tuxedo yesterday, freshly dry-cleaned." Her lips grazed my earlobe as she spoke. "I found an envelope attached to it. Inside were two items they must have found in his pockets: one of his gold cufflinks and a piece of paper with an address scribbled on it."

It wasn't quite the murder weapon I had expected. "An address?"

"Do you know anyone who lives in the Lower East Side?"

I tried to think. "I don't believe so."

She looked disappointed. "I have half a mind to drive there myself and confront the little hussy."

"Who?"

She stared at me point-blank, as though I was being painfully dense. "The woman he's cheating with."

"You think he's *cheating?*"

"What do you think I meant?"

"I thought you suspected he killed Mr. Godfrey."

"What?" She broke into shrill laughter. "Don't be silly, Trevor. Matthew would never murder someone. Sandy James ran him down in a drunken stupor and went back to finish him off. Everyone knows that."

"*I* don't."

"Then you're the only one."

"There you are, Marline!" A heavyset woman with horselike teeth grabbed Marline by the shoulders and whipped her around. "I've been looking for you everywhere! What a fabulous party! Your home is stunning!"

"Why, thank you, Mary. I'm so glad you could make it."

The two women air-kissed, then began chit-chatting like long-lost friends. I took the opportunity to extract myself from Marline's stranglehold. As I eased away, I felt her hand grip my arm tightly.

"Suite 301—179 Rivington Street," she whispered, her eyes intense. "Find out who lives there."

I wandered the party for a half-hour after that, stopping for quick chats with the few guests I recognized, feeling increasingly self-conscious in a room full of people who appeared to be so much more at ease than I was. I felt naked without my nametag but, remembering my mother's nasty remark about hiding behind it, resisted putting it back on.

"Trevor! Hey, how's it going?"

Honica Winters was standing in the crowded open kitchen, sandwiched between two men, her heavily made-up face framed by a massive head of platinum hair. She was waving me over. Having no desire to talk to her, I waved back and headed for the exit. But something I saw out of the corner of my eye made me stop and look back.

Sandy's husband, Jack, was one of the men sandwiching Honica.

What was *he* doing here? Curious, I made my way over.

"Hiya, handsome!" Honica cried, lurching toward me with arms open wide, sloshing pinkish liquid from her martini glass onto my shoulder. She was wearing a bright orange, clingy dress that revealed two brown-freckled boobs almost to the nipples. "Terrific party, hey?" she shouted. She lifted her arms over her head and shook her hips to the music, spilling more booze.

I nodded, trying to smile. The kitchen was too crowded for me to enter, so she stepped out, leaving Jack behind. I saw him sipping San Pellegrino and staring into the living room, looking sober and uncomfortable. He didn't seem to notice me.

"Thanks *so much* for getting me the room!" Honica said. "It's not the suite I hoped for, but I know you were sold out. You're a doll." She wrapped her arms around my head, pulling my face toward her bosom.

"My pleasure, Miss Winters," I said, my voice muffled.

She released me. "You need to loosen up! You're always so stiff and formal."

"Don't worry about me. I'm having a perfectly good time."

She noticed me staring at Jack and turned to pull him over, putting an arm around him. "Hey, gorgeous, do you know Trevor? He's one of the managers here."

"Hey, Trevor. Good to see you."

I glanced at Honica's arm and said, "I know Jack well, Honica. He's Sandy James' husband."

"Isn't he adorable?" She pinched his cheek.

"Forty-five minutes to midnight, people!" Marline shouted up the spiral staircase behind us. "I need everyone to gather in the living room for the countdown in *thirty minutes!*"

"Sandy at home?" I asked Jack.

"She's around here somewhere."

"She's *here?*"

He nodded and rolled his eyes. "There was no way she was gonna stay home tonight. She called a babysitter, pulled on a dress, and here we are."

"That's awesome! I'm so glad you two made up."

He raised his brow slightly and took a swig of San Pellegrino.

"I expect kisses from both of you at midnight," Honica said.

"I'm going to go find Sandy," I said.

"Girl's got balls coming here," said Honica. "Half the people here think she's a murderer."

"Thanks to you," I said.

Jack looked up at Honica, his eyes flashing with anger. "My wife is not a murderer," he said, detaching himself from her arm.

"Relax! I didn't say *I* thought she was a murderer, I said everyone else did. Don't you worry—if she goes to jail, I'll take care of you."

Jack looked supremely pissed off. "I'm getting another water." He turned and pried his way to the refrigerator.

Honica turned to me, her expression suddenly serious. "That man is so intense. He's been trying to bully me into issuing on on-air apology to his wife. As if! Truth is, I'm thinking of doing a follow-up story. Yesterday's news puts an intriguing spin on things." She leaned closer to me and whispered, "That tight-ass detective finally fed me a juicy tidbit yesterday. He told me there were no skid marks at the accident scene. That's one of the reasons they're having a hard time nailing the culprit—there have to be hundreds of different tire tracks down there, and they don't know which of them were made by the perp. So much for the theory that whoever hit him did it accidentally. It was cold-blooded murder."

Her words sent a chill running through me. "Why is the investigation taking so long?" I asked, frustrated by all the speculation; each detail I heard was more disturbing. "Why haven't police inspected all the suspects' vehicles and found a match?"

"Word is, they're baffled," said Honica, now in full journalist persona. "Ever heard of the theory of transference? Basically, when two objects touch, they always leave something behind—paint fragments, clothing, blood, whatever. Whoever killed Willard stole the trench coat he was wearing. Police can't find it, and they can't find the murder weapon. They took samples from the accident scene, but apparently things aren't matching up as easily as they hoped. The body should have made a dent in the vehicle on impact, but they can't seem to find any signs of damage to the suspects' vehicles—except, of course, Sandy's, which was fixed before they got to it."

"Who do *you* think did it?" I asked, almost afraid to know.

Honica opened her mouth to answer but spotted Jack making his way over and clamped it shut. "So, as I was saying," she said loudly, reverting back to her party-girl persona and swilling back the contents of her drink, "I *love* my room!"

I excused myself to search for Sandy.

As I passed the living room, I saw Marline climbing on top of a pyramid of cases of Dom Perignon with the help of two waiters. "Come get your champagne bottles here!" she cried, arms dancing in the air like a conductor. "Gather around, everyone! Only a half hour to a new year!" Below her, the waiters were distributing bottles of champagne, paid for by the hotel, like thirty-cent bingo cards.

I looked everywhere for Sandy—upstairs, downstairs, the terrace, bedrooms, living room, kitchen, den—but she was nowhere to be found. On the terrace upstairs, I paused for fresh air, savoring the calm. The deck was occupied by only about a dozen people, most of them out there to smoke. I leaned against the railing and gazed down at the hotel gardens below, then up to the sky. The moon was out, partially obscured by clouds, casting a dim glow on the terrace.

"Hey, Trevor."

I turned to see a woman lurking in the shadows at the far end of the terrace. Two very thin, very beautiful young women were standing next to her. All were smoking.

"Cynthia? I didn't expect to see you here."

"Yeah, well, I can't sit at home moping for the rest of my life."

I walked over. She was smoking feverishly and shivering in an open Dolce & Gabbana blouse and clingy white leather skirt. A gold lamé belt was draped over her hips. Her model-friends didn't turn to acknowledge my presence, and she didn't introduce them.

"I was going to call you," I said, glancing at the women and wishing I was one of Cyndy's friends. "I felt terrible for you after hearing the news about your father."

Her friends dropped their cigarettes over the railing and excused themselves for the bathroom.

"I knew it all along," Cynthia said.

"You knew he was murdered?"

"Yup." She took a long drag of her cigarette and stared up at the moon for a moment. "I didn't want to go flinging accusations around, but I'm fed up with the pace of the police investigation. I mean, could they be any slower or more stupid? Yesterday, after I read the newspaper, I called them up and told them my theory. They're all over it now." She was talking loudly, not seeming to care that others on the terrace were listening intently.

"What's your theory?" I asked, lowering my voice to a whisper, hoping she would follow suit.

"None of your fucking business."

I gritted my teeth. "Fine."

In the light of the moon, her eyes looked half-crazed. "But I'm going to need to talk to you about something soon, Trevor. Something *big* is going down, and I might need your help."

"Of course. Whatever you need. Can I ask—?"

She shook her head. "I can't talk about it yet. But soon." She dropped her cigarette on the terrace floor and stamped it out with her golden shoe. "Okay, fine, if you really insist, I'll tell you what my theory is. But it's not so much a theory as the real story."

"Go on," I said, deeply curious.

"The night before my father died, I had dinner with him and a few others: Daddy, Roger and Katherine Weatherhead, Daddy's girlfriend, and me."

"His *girlfriend*?"

"I guess you didn't know either. He kept it pretty hush-hush. Well, I'm not about to protect her any longer. She's nothing but a gold-digger and a tramp. She was using my father for his money, was pressuring him to marry her so she could get her greedy hands on his money. At dinner he announced he was selling the hotel, and she got very, very angry. I guess she was banking on inheriting it someday. Secretly,

Daddy had already told me that he was going to dump her. I was so pissed off at her reaction that I whispered it into her ear as she was leaving. She almost dropped to the floor." She sighed heavily, shaking her head. "If I had any idea she was such a psycho, that she would do such a terrible thing, I never would have told her. How was I supposed to know that the next night, after the Christmas party, she would get into her car and run him down, then beat him senseless until he was dead?"

I was astounded. "Who?" I asked.

She dropped her face into her hands and began to sob.

I tried to comfort her, but she pulled away. Around us, a half-dozen people were staring.

The supermodels were back.

"Let's get outta here, Cyn," said the taller one. "This party, like, totally sucks."

"It's *so* ghetto," said the shorter one, folding her arms limply and scowling. "Let's go to Marquee."

Cynthia turned to me. "I gotta go, Trevor."

"What?" I cried. I leaned toward her and whispered. "You can't just leave me in suspense like this! Who was it? Who was your father's girlfriend?"

"Can't you figure it out yourself?"

"No! Tell me, please!"

"Fine. It was Shanna Virani."

17

Stellar Blowout

"*There* you are!"

I was still standing on the terrace twenty minutes later, stunned by Cynthia's revelation, when Marline appeared, hands on her hips like a scolding mother. "Trevor Lambert, stop being such a social moron! I want you to march downstairs this instant and join the party. Midnight is less than twenty minutes away, and I've reserved a big, juicy kiss just for you. If you're lucky, I might even throw in some tongue." She threw her head back and cackled, then disappeared.

The prospect of having to French kiss with Marline gave me ample excuse to leave the party at once. As I descended the corkscrew staircase, I saw Honica and Jack standing in the living room among the others, engaged in an intimate conversation, but no Sandy.

I decided to duck into the bathroom before I made my exit. I headed down the hallway, passing the den to the left and spare bedroom to the right, and knocked on the bathroom door. There was no answer, but I thought I heard a noise inside. I put my ear against the door and knocked again, then tried the door. It was locked.

"Go away!" came a voice inside.

"Sorry!" I retreated down the hallway, but stopped halfway. Was that Sandy's voice? I went back and knocked again. "Sandy, is that you?"

There was no response.

I knocked a third time. "It's me, Trevor. Are you okay? Can you let me in?"

I heard her fumble with the lock, then the door opened a crack. A blue, half-crazed eye smudged with mascara peered out. "Trevor?"

"Sandy? What are you doing? Are you okay?"

She pulled open the door and wrenched me in, slamming the door shut behind me and locking it, then pressing her back against it as though afraid someone might try to bust in. Her eyes were manic. She was wearing a silk mother-of-pearl-colored dress. Her hair was down and uncharacteristically unkempt. Pinned over her left bosom was a large, gaudy corsage, a conglomerate of noisemaker, dried roses, and stars spray-painted gold and lacquered.

"Marline made me wear it," she said, following my gaze. "I know, it's hideous." She unfastened it and threw it in the bathtub.

"What are you doing in here?" I asked. "Are you hiding from someone?"

"I'm hiding from everyone. From Honica and Jack and every damned judging eye out there. Marline was parading me around like a celebrity, introducing me as 'the blond vixen from *Borderline News*.' Matthew is furious that I'm here while under suspension. I came tonight because I couldn't bear to be at home. But now I realize it was a mistake." She pulled herself onto the bathroom counter.

I eyed an empty champagne bottle sitting on the counter beside her. Was she drunk?

"Is Jack still with the bimbo?" she asked.

"Honica Winters? Yes." I sat down on the edge of the bathtub.

"First she ruined my career and my reputation, now she's trying to steal my husband."

"I think Jack is lobbying her on your behalf. I'm glad to see that you two have reconciled."

"Oh, we haven't reconciled. I'm back at home, but things are not good. He came tonight only to make sure I didn't get drunk and try to drive home. We got in a fight on the way over and now he won't talk to me. As far as I'm concerned, he can find his own way home. Maybe Honey will give him a ride."

Outside in the hallway, Marline announced, "Only twelve minutes to midnight, people! Gather round!"

"It's good to see you, Sandy," I said. "I've really missed you."

"I've missed you too, Trevor. And I miss *him* so much!"

"Mr. Godfrey?"

She nodded. "This place isn't the same without him. Being at home these past few days has given me time to reflect, given me a bit of perspective. I spend so much time here, it's crazy. I barely know my kids anymore, barely know my husband. We're like strangers at home. Jack and the kids have this great little symbiotic relationship, and my presence this week has upset the balance. They don't know what to do with me. I feel like I'm imposing. I don't know how to relate to them. All I can think is, 'What's going on at the Universe? What am I missing?' It's like my roles have been reversed; home is work and work is home. Ever feel that way? Ever go into work on the weekend or stay late at night because it's easier than being at home?"

"Of course, but it's different for me. I don't have a family."

"My life is a mess, Trevor. I've been charged with drunk driving, disgraced in front of my family and friends, suspended from the job I adore. The entire population of this country seems to think I murdered Willard Godfrey. If that's not enough to send me into a complete mental breakdown, to add to the stress, Jack and I are broke. We might lose the house. Oh, and I'm a lousy mother. Do you know that I forgot Kaitlin's name the other day? On Christmas Day, when I was introducing her to your mother, for a fleeting moment her name escaped me. My own daughter! My marriage has been deteriorating for a couple of years now, but I've been in denial. But it hasn't been easy to pretend things are fine this week while I've been stuck at home. Jack is a mess. He can't deal with what's happened. He's acting like a sanctimonious bastard. Meanwhile, he's out there flirting with the woman responsible for my downfall."

"You can't blame Honica for everything," I said.

"I know, but I wish I could. God, Trevor, the police have come to see me three times now. I've been trying to keep it together, but I can't do it anymore. I'm tormented by the fear that they're going to arrest me. I'm even starting to question my sanity, to wonder if maybe I *did* do it. Maybe I blacked out and forgot everything. Every night for almost two weeks I've had the same dream. I'm driving home from the party, speeding down this twisted gravel road, and it's so dark I can barely see the road. I'm roaring drunk. Branches are thrashing against the windshield and it's raining hard. I veer around a corner and see a figure on the road ahead, his back to me. I pump the brakes, trying desperately to stop, but they don't work. The truck is flying straight for him. Just before I strike him he turns around, and the moon lights up his face."

I shuddered. "Mr. Godfrey?"

Her eyes closed and she was silent for a moment. "It was Mr. Godfrey for the first few nights. Then it was Jack." She looked at me with horror in her eyes. "The other night it was little Kaitlin and Wesley."

"Oh, Sandy. I'm sorry."

"Last night it was me. The dreams seem so real, Trevor. I wake up drenched with perspiration, my heart thudding, my eyes soaked with tears. I'm tortured by them. Each time, they seem more vivid."

"Why don't you conjure up Honica Winters tonight," I said. "That might make you feel better."

"I'm serious, Trevor. I'm starting to wonder if I'm not dreaming but remembering." She threw her back against the mirror and moaned.

I thought about telling her about Cynthia's remarks. I hadn't seriously contemplated Shanna as a suspect until tonight. But I sensed that Sandy needed to talk rather than listen, so I kept quiet. She sat up and reached for her purse, fumbling around inside, then sat back against the mirror and started air smoking, holding two fingers to her mouth, closing her eyes and inhaling deeply.

"I keep hearing those protesters shouting, 'Shame! Shame! Shame!'" she said. She looked over to me. "Do you ever feel like you're a drunk driver in life? Like you're charging through life, reckless and out of control, so inebriated you can't see things clearly, narrowly avoiding certain obstacles in your path and mowing down others, jeopardizing the lives of the people in the car with you? Ever feel that way, Trevor?" She didn't wait for me to answer. "I'm director of human resources at one of the city's best hotels, responsible for the health and well-being of a thousand people, yet I can't take care of the three people I love, the three people who need me most. Isn't that ironic?"

"I guess so." I thought of my mom's similar comments about my position and my apartment.

She sighed as if I would never understand, then took another drag of her imaginary cigarette and flicked it over my shoulder into the bathtub. "Have you ever been in love, Trevor?" she asked.

I looked up, surprised. "Not really," I lied.

"What about Nancy?"

I felt my heart jolt. "Nancy who?"

"Come on. I see how you look at her. You've been pining for her for months, if not years. Why don't you go for her? I think she likes you too. Tomorrow's her last day, so you wouldn't be violating any of those rules you hold so dear."

I suddenly felt incredibly uncomfortable. "Even if I did like her, she lives with a guy."

"Yeah, a gay guy."

"He's *gay?* How do you know?"

"It's a small world, Trevor." She hopped down from the counter. "I better go." She straightened her dress and checked her reflection in the mirror. "God, my hair's a mess! My makeup's a mess. My life's a mess! I'm one messy girl tonight."

"Yet you're still smiling," I said, my spirits lifted by her revelation.

"Oh my god, I am!" She leaned closer to the mirror and touched her lips. "Look at me! Smiling like some kind of strung-out hospitality moron. It's like I can't turn it off, like my lips are stuck, molded this way." She pulled down the sides of her mouth with her fingers. "There, that's better." She pulled a brush from her purse and started brushing her hair. "I remember when I first started smiling. About fifteen years ago, when I worked as a cocktail waitress in the lounge at the Sheraton Salt Lake City. I was useless at first. I spilled drinks, mixed up orders, and could never balance my float. But soon I discovered the power of a smile. Smiles made my manager forgive me for mistakes, made co-workers like me better, made customers leave bigger tips. I remember getting off work one day, changing out of my uniform and walking home. I caught myself smiling at people as I walked. I had forgotten to remove that one vital part of my uniform. But a funny thing happened: people smiled back. It made me feel good, gave me the illusion that they liked me, that they were happy and I was happy and everything was wonderful. So I kept on smiling. Soon I was smiling everywhere—in the street, on the bus, in restaurants, and at home. I've smiled my way through life, Trevor. Sometimes I catch myself smiling at home for no reason: at the cat, the television, the carpet, alone in bed, at the kids, at Jack. This industry has taught me how to smile when I'm miserable or angry or insulted or humiliated or sick to my stomach. Just like Mr. Godfrey exalts in his book, I've mastered the art of using the Universal Standards of Service in life: I smile, I use eye contact, and I address people by their names. I also use that fourth, unspoken standard that Mr. Godfrey left out."

"Lying."

She nodded. "Pretending everything is fine, even when it isn't. This week has been a disaster, but I've been going about my business like things couldn't be better, smiling and humming and being my usual sunny self. Jack thinks I'm crazy, and I'm starting to wonder if he might be right." She looked at herself in the mirror. "I'm not smiling now." She gasped. "My god, where did all these lines come from?"

I squinted in her direction. "What lines?"

"These *wrinkles*!"

I walked over for a closer look. "You don't have wrinkles, Sandy. Maybe a laugh line or two."

"Laugh lines? Nothing's *this* funny, Trevor. These are trenches!" She pressed her face against the mirror. "It looks like someone clawed my face, like Edward Scissorhands raked his fingers down each cheek! Look, they're around my mouth too! I'm only thirty-eight, Trevor. I'm too young for this! I've never realized they were this bad—probably because I'm always smiling! Whenever I look in the mirror, I smile and make myself go a bit cross-eyed, glossing over my aging face with a self-imposed Vaseline lens." She made herself smile again. "The lines match my smile pattern perfectly. God, Trevor, my face has been ravaged by smiles! Fifteen years in the hotel industry has turned me into an old woman!"

"Sandy, you do not look like an old woman."

She burst into tears.

I touched her shoulder. "Look at me."

"No."

"Look at me."

Slowly, she turned to face me. Her lips were trembling.

"You're beautiful, Sandy."

"I used to be. I'm not anymore."

"You still are."

The sound of her cell phone interrupted us. Sandy wiped her eyes and reached for her purse, flipping her cell phone open. She straightened her posture, opened her eyes brightly, and smiled. "This is Sandy James. How may I help you?" She listened for a moment, and her smile slowly faded. "Did you check her temperature? Is she still throwing up? Oh, dear. No, no, I'll come home right away." She stuffed the phone back into her purse, her eyes filled with worry. "I've gotta run," she said. "Kaitlin's got a fever." She hurried to the door and pulled it open.

Outside, the New Year's countdown had begun. "Ten! Nine! Eight!"

"If Jack ever comes up for air from Honica's cleavage, can you tell him I went home?"

I glanced at the empty bottle on the counter. "Sandy, you're not…?"

But she was already out the door.

In the living room, the crowd was chanting, "Seven! Six! Five!"

I hurried down the hall to stop her, but Marline intercepted me, grabbing me with both arms and pulling me into the living room. I looked back. Sandy had already hurried out the door. Should I run after her? No, I decided, Sandy wouldn't drive. She would take a taxi.

"Four! Three! Two! One! Happy New Year!"

All around, corks popped open, champagne sprayed in the air, people blew noisemakers, hugged, kissed, and cheered. Marline was all over me. She stood on her toes and pressed her lips against mine before I could pull away. I felt her tongue dart into my mouth. My eyes searched the room in alarm.

Out of the corner of my eye, I spotted Jack kissing Honica Winters.

"Ahem."

Honica and Jack stopped kissing and turned to me, startled. Honica lifted her hand to her lips in an "oops" gesture.

Jack wiped his mouth with the back of his hand, as if trying to erase the incident. His face turned red. "Trevor, happy New Year!" he said cheerfully, holding out his hand to shake mine.

"Sandy—your *wife*—had to leave," I said. "Kaitlin—your *daughter*—is ill."

"I'm going to get a drink," Honica said.

Jack looked alarmed. "What's wrong with Kaitie?"

"She has a fever."

He pulled his cell phone from his pocket and dialed home, consulted with the babysitter for a moment, then hung up. "Kaitlin's fine," he said, looking relieved. "She got the same bug Wesley had last week. Sandy left?"

I nodded.

He tried her cell phone next, but there was no answer. "Why would she leave without me?" he asked, looking hurt.

"Maybe she wanted to give you and Honica some time alone."

"It wasn't how it looked, Trevor. I was trying to convince her to recant her story on air."

"With your tongue down her throat? Interesting tactics."

"She jumped on me. I was trying to push her off. I'm not interested, Trevor. I love my wife."

"She really needs you right now, Jack," I said. "You haven't exactly been supportive."

"What about me? Do you know what it's like to have the police show up at your door every second day asking to speak to your wife? To see the fear in the eyes of your kids? To wonder if police are going to take her away and you'll never see her again? I've been terrified, yet she's been flouncing around, smiling and singing, getting up every morning at 6:00 even though she's on vacation."

Vacation? It occurred to me that Sandy hadn't been completely honest with Jack about her suspension.

"She dresses up in her work clothes," he continued, "puts on her hair and makeup, and bustles around the house like it's her office. She sits at the kitchen table for hours, frowning and sighing into her laptop like she's working on a complex corporate document. Yesterday she summoned Kaitie and Wesley to the table, sat them down, and grilled them, asking them their favorite colors and what they want to do when they grow up, telling them to draw pictures for her, like she was conducting a bloody job interview or performance evaluation. It's only a matter of time before a new family shows up at our door and she tells us we're fired. Every day there's something more damning in the news, yet she refuses to acknowledge it. She's been in a good mood since the day I met her, Trevor. It's like living with Annette Fucking Funicello. But it's not real!"

"Sandy's always been an optimist, Jack," I said, feeling protective. "It's part of what makes her so good at her job. I assure you, however, that she is not in a good mood now."

Jack stared at me for a moment, then shook his head. "I'm wasting my breath."

"This will all blow over soon," I said, trying to reassure him. "One day you and Sandy will have a good chuckle about it."

Jack shook his head. "Oh, no, we won't," he said. "She's leaving us."

"She's what?"

"She left once, and now she says she's leaving us for good in the New Year."

"I thought you kicked her out."

He frowned. "*She* walked out the door. I begged her to stay, but she said she couldn't stand being at home anymore. She came back on Tuesday, saying she had decided to take a few days' vacation and wanted to come back for a few days. Yesterday she told me she's about to be appointed general manager and plans to move into the Universe without us."

"She what?"

He wrinkled his brow. "It's not true?"

Clearly, Sandy was delusional. "No, Jack, it's not true."

He blinked a few times. "Then what *is* the truth?"

"You better ask Sandy."

It was time to go home. But as I headed for the exit, I was stopped once again by someone calling my name.

"Pssst! Trevor!"

Shanna Virani was standing in the shadows in the hallway, beckoning me over. She looked tiny and gorgeous in a simple black cocktail dress that was fastened around her neck, exposing her brown, glowing shoulders. I thought of Cynthia's story. Shanna as Willard's girlfriend? It was difficult to imagine, in no small part because they were almost twenty years apart. Shanna as a killer? The image of Shanna wielding a club over her head was almost comical. As abrasive as she was at times, she didn't seem violent. I found it much easier to imagine Matthew doing such a horrific thing.

"Dreadful party, isn't it?" she said, turning each cheek for me to peck them. "Who *are* these people?"

"Marline's friends mostly, it seems."

"Ghastly bunch. I was having a much better time alone in my apartment feeling sorry for myself. Come here, I want to show you something." She took my hand and pulled me down the hallway into the den. There, she stood on her toes and plucked a cassette from the bookshelf. "Universe Holiday Party," she read from the spine. She reached up for another cassette. "Parkade Cam 1." She handed them both to me and gestured to the LCD television on the wall. "Shall we?" Her eyes were wide with excitement, as though they were two of her favorite movies.

"Why?"

"The police have been so hopeless at solving this case, I thought we might do some amateur sleuthing of our own."

I was suspicious. "What do you expect to find?"

"Who knows?" She glanced at the doorway and lowered her voice. "I've been obsessing over who killed Willard. Like you, Trevor, I don't want to believe Sandy did it. I have this idea taking shape in my head, and I'm hoping there might be some sort of clue in one of these tapes."

"Tell me something, Shanna. Were you and Willard—?"

"Matthew! How are you, darling?"

I turned to see Matthew Drummond standing in the doorway.

"What are you two doing in here?" he demanded, glaring at the cassettes in my hands. He marched over and snatched them away. "These are not to be touched by anyone."

"Relax, Matthew," Shanna said. "The party was so boring, we were looking for videos to watch. I know Marline keeps a well-stocked library of man-on-man porn around here somewhere."

Matthew put the cassettes back on the shelf and turned to us. "Now out! Both of you!"

"So *this* is where everybody's hiding!"

Nancy Swinton was standing in the doorway now.

My knees almost gave out. She was in her duty manager uniform but had removed her nametag and let her hair down. She looked utterly magnificent. Gaetan Boudreau appeared behind her, grinning.

Shanna, Matthew, and I stared at them, rendered speechless by their collective beauty.

"Happy New Year, everybody!" Nancy cried, breaking the spell. She went directly to Matthew and kissed his cheek.

"I'm glad you made it," Matthew gushed, stooping down to wrap his arms around her tiny body.

I watched them jealously. I hadn't spoken with Nancy since my outburst three days ago, and I knew she was probably still angry. Now that I knew that her live-in boyfriend was actually a gay roommate, I had a huge incentive to make it up to her. Tomorrow was her last day. Tonight might be my last opportunity to ask her out. I watched her closely, my heart beating rapidly, and plotted my move. I need to get her alone, away from all these people.

When she finally let go of Matthew, she went to Shanna next and hugged her. She had yet to look in my direction. I watched Gaetan hug Matthew, then go to Shanna and peck both cheeks.

Nancy made her way over to me next. "Hi, Trevor," she said, smiling up at me sweetly.

"Hi."

I expected her to slap my face but instead she said, "Do I get a New Year's hug?"

"Of course." I opened my arms and embraced her, filling my nostrils with the wonderful fragrance of her hair. "I'm really sorry about—"

She lifted her fingers to her lips and shushed me. "It's okay."

"How was your night, Nancy?" Shanna asked.

"Crazy! We just got off ten minutes ago." Nancy reached for Gaetan's arm, pulling him closer. "I don't know what I would have done without this guy. We got one page after another."

Gaetan grinned, placing his arm around Nancy.

I reminded myself that he was gay.

"The fun really started when a fight broke out in 2102," Nancy said. "A guest smashed a bottle of wine over another guest's head! Miraculously, it didn't break skin, but I called the police anyway. Gaetan had to break up an orgy in 1113, right, Gaetan? Bet you enjoyed that one. Then the organizer of the function in Neptune called to complain that VOID delegates had crashed her party and were ordering drinks from her host bar. We had to go up and ask them to leave. Then a fight broke out in Stratosphere, but by the time security got there it was over."

"All night we got complaints about the taxi situation," Gaetan added. "There was a huge line."

"Oh, and Brenda Rathberger from VOID caused a huge scene at the front door," Nancy added. "She started screaming at the doorman about the taxi situation, then confronting drivers as they got into cars, accusing them of being drunk and threatening to report them. But by the time I got there she was gone."

"What about the Drive Me Sober program?" asked Shanna. "Weren't they helping with rides?"

"Two drivers just wasn't enough," said Gaetan.

"Two?" I said. "*Five* were scheduled."

Gaetan glanced uneasily at Matthew.

"Marline needed them to work this party," Matthew said, his tone defensive.

"You canceled *three* drivers?" Shanna cried. "That's insane! Well, I'm going to fix it right now. We don't need all this staff up here, anyway." She stormed out of the room.

"Mrs. Rathberger was very difficult tonight," said Nancy. "She was roving the public parking levels and confronting suspected drunk drivers. Gaetan and I tried to find her, but couldn't."

I thought about Sandy. "Did you happen to see Sandy James leave?" I asked.

Gaetan nodded. "About a half-hour ago she was waiting in the taxi queue. But she seemed to be in a real hurry, and I think she gave up. I saw her head for the parking elevator."

I groaned inwardly. Matthew and I exchanged looks of concern.

Nancy and Gaetan proceeded to share stories about their night. As Nancy talked, I stared at her lips but didn't hear the words. I wanted so badly to kiss her. My eyes moved to Matthew. He too was regarding her intensely, eyes glassy, a faint smile on his lips, his face glowing with desire. I felt myself burn with jealousy. So many men were in love with Nancy! I noticed that she put her hand on Matthew's shoulder as she spoke, a gesture I had seen before but it took me a moment to place it. I remembered the morning I found Mr. Godfrey's body, when I came back down to the parkade after taking Brenda up to her suite. Nancy and Matthew were engaged in an intimate conversation, and Nancy's hand was resting on Matthew's shoulder in the same manner. I was suddenly aware of an intimacy between Nancy and Matthew, one that was abnormal and inappropriate for two colleagues.

A terrible thought occurred to me.

I gaped at Nancy, then Matthew, and back to Nancy. My mind raced. The moment I thought of it, everything seemed to fall into place: I recalled them dancing together at the staff party, and their eyes locking during Matthew's speech at the staff meeting. "I have half a mind to drive there myself and confront the little hussy," Marline had said earlier. Where did Nancy live?

It felt like someone grabbed my heart and wrung it like a wet dishrag. I couldn't breathe. I felt dizzy and weak-kneed. I had a vague awareness of the three of them turning to me, of someone calling out my name, but the voice was far away and dreamlike. I closed my eyes and swooned.

Someone touched my face. I opened my eyes and looked down, blinking.

"Trevor?" Nancy said. "Are you okay?"

Matthew and Gaetan were staring at me.

I turned and fled the room.

Desperate to get out of the hotel, I took the elevators to the lobby level and navigated my way through the hordes of people in the lobby, then burst through the sliding doors and outside. As I ran down the ramp, I spotted Shanna speaking with the doorman and four employees in togas, coordinating rides home for patrons. The doorman called out my name, but I ignored him and hurried down to the street, turning toward home.

It was a mild evening for New York, but without my coat I was freezing. Thousands of people crowded the streets, hooting and hollering and shouting New Year's greetings. In the distance, I heard thunder and realized it was fireworks. As I walked, my head began to clear. Were Nancy and Matthew lovers? It made perfect sense. I was heartbroken, but I could only blame myself. How could I have thought for a second that a woman of Nancy's caliber would like someone like me? She wanted the astronaut, the hero who had traveled in space. The married astronaut. How could I respect her if she was fooling around with a married man—a deadbeat like Matthew, of all people? A suspected murderer?

Before long, I was only a block from my apartment. But something made me stop. Did I want to go home? No. I wasn't tired. I didn't want to be alone. I needed to be around people. I needed a drink.

I turned around.

I wandered the streets for almost an hour, searching for somewhere to go but not liking anything I saw. The nightclubs were lined up, the bars full, the restaurants closed. After a few blocks, I spotted the Glittersphere up ahead, sparkling like a great silver moon, beckoning me like a beacon in the sky.

Minutes later, I found myself standing at the entrance to the hotel. My head down, I slipped inside and went directly to the bar in the Center of the Universe.

"Double Scotch, please."

"Coming right up, Trevor."

I drained it, then asked for another. I turned around, leaning against the bar, and observed the crowd. The party was still going strong, the band was playing, and the dance floor was packed. All around me people were celebrating, but no one acknowledged me, no one seemed to notice I was there. I felt invisible.

I sipped my Scotch and watched the crowd.

I spotted Nancy Swinton on the dance floor, and my heart lurched. She was nudging her way through the crowd, pulling Gaetan along with her. They stopped near the middle of the dance floor. Matthew appeared a few feet behind them, and behind him came Marline and a half-dozen others I recognized from the party. Afraid to be seen, I moved closer to the trio next to me and peeked around them.

Nancy turned to Gaetan and they started dancing. Matthew pulled up next to them, leering over as Marline sidled up beside him, raising her arms in the air and shaking her booty. Honica Winters appeared next, shimmying up behind Matthew and resting the back of her head on his shoulder, shaking her shoulders to the music. Marline scowled at her. Gaetan lifted Nancy up, and she threw her head back, laughing, as he spun her around and around.

My heart ached. I wanted to go out and join them, but I was afraid to dance, afraid to face Nancy, afraid to move from this safe, anonymous place at the bar. I turned away, unable to watch.

When I looked back a few minutes later, Nancy was gone. Gaetan and Matthew were dancing with Marline and Honica.

I felt a hand touch my arm.

"You're still here."

Nancy was smiling up at me. Her beautiful lips were pink with fresh lipstick.

"Yeah, well, it's still so busy ... I didn't feel comfortable going home before things settled down."

"Keeping an eye on things from the bar, are you?" she said with a smirk.

"Kind of."

"So you're okay? That exit was a bit strange. I chased after you, but couldn't find you."

"I needed fresh air."

"I hear you. Buy me a drink?"

"Of course." I signaled to the bartender, and she asked for a margarita.

My hands trembled as we sipped our drinks. She chewed on her straw, her cheeks red and flushed, and looked up at me with a bemused expression. I couldn't think of a word to say. Why was she here? Why wasn't she with Matthew? Perhaps Marline had chased her off. I didn't like the thought of being Matthew's stand-in, but the alcohol had rendered me helpless to resist the rapture of Nancy's company. It might be the last time I was so close to her.

Onstage, the band leader announced that the party would be over in fifteen minutes.

Nancy set her drink down.

Oh god, I thought. *I'm boring her to tears. She's going to leave.*

"Want to dance?" she asked.

"Huh? Uh, I, well—I don't really dance."

"It's a slow song. They're easy. Come on."

Before I could protest, she was pulling me through the crowd. Her hand felt small and soft and warm. She steered away from the others to the opposite side of the dance floor. The band struck up a modern version of "Blue Moon." Nancy stopped and turned to me, taking my right hand and placing it on her shoulder, then taking my left hand in hers. I followed her lead, feeling awkward but exhilarated.

We danced.

I was dancing! I could feel the heat of her body and the occasional brush of her breasts. My hand rested on her delicate shoulder. She leaned forward and pressed her head against my chest.

"Great party, hey?" I said.

I felt her head nod.

"The banquets department did a top-notch job," I said.

Another slight nod of her head.

"But look at this lobby, what a mess! I don't know how they're going to turn it around in time for brunch tomorrow. I guess I'll come in early to help. Or maybe I'll stay and help out tonight. Tomorrow's going to be a very, very busy day. We have almost eight hundred check-outs, and food and beverage has about twenty-five-hundred covers. I should probably check with—"

"Trevor?"

"Yes?"

"Can we not talk for a while?"

"Um, sure."

We danced. One song, two songs, three songs, four—and we were still dancing. Under the atrium star lights we were in our own world, and the Universe was revolving around us.

The band leader announced the last song: Train's "Drops of Jupiter."

Nancy nestled up against me as it started to play. I put my arms around her and held her close. I gazed down at her hair, so dark and lustrous under the star lights, emitting its sweet, floral fragrance. I mustered the courage to do something I had longed to do for over a year: I buried my nose in her hair. The fragrance sent me into orbit.

When the music ended, everyone clapped and cheered and started to leave the dance floor, but Nancy kept holding me. I opened my eyes and spotted Matthew and Gaetan gazing at us from the other side of the dance floor.

Nancy pulled away but held on to my finger, gazing up at me with a playful smile. Our arms swung in the air.

"So," she said. "Tomorrow's my last day."

"Is it really?" I said, as if I wasn't acutely aware.

"Are you coming to my birthday party? I'd really love to see you there. I know you said you'd be really busy, but..."

"Of course I'll come. Where do you live?"

"I'm in the Lower East Side."

Suddenly it all came rushing back. I glanced across the dance floor to where Matthew had been standing with Gaetan. Gaetan was gone now, but Matthew was still watching us. I thought I detected an evil, knowing smile on his face. It occurred to me that he had sent Nancy to me, perhaps to call me off his trail or to seduce me into submission. I was being used and manipulated.

"What *is* your address, Nancy?" I asked, my voice shaking.

She smiled demurely. "My, aren't you forward. It's 179 Rivington Street."

"So," I said, biting down so hard on my lip I tasted blood. "You and Matthew..."

She looked perplexed. "Me and Matthew *what?*"

"You're sleeping together."

She dropped my finger as though I had scalded her. "Pardon *me?*"

"It's true, isn't it?"

"How *dare* you!"

"Tell me. I need to know."

"God, Trevor! Why are you so hopeless? What's *wrong* with you?"

She turned and marched off, leaving me alone on the empty dance floor.

18

War of the Worlds

"Yoo-hoo, Trevor!"

The shrill voice pierced my ears like nails grating across a black-board, making my head throb even harder.

"Happy New Year, darling!"

I turned around. It wasn't just her, but *him* too. Sporting dark sun-glasses and pained expressions, Matthew and Marline Drummond were making their way over from the elevators slowly and deliberately, clutching one another like an elderly couple. They were the last two people on earth I wanted to see. After spending all night and morning obsessing over Matthew's involvement in Willard Godfrey's death and in Nancy Swinton's life, I had come to the conclusion that Matthew Drummond was, beyond a doubt, guilty as charged on both counts. How could I have been so naive? Clearly, Nancy and Matthew were having a torrid affair, and she was somehow in collusion with him— was possibly even in the car when it happened. After the party, she could have waited for him, then together they rode down to P5, using his access disc and leaving no trace of her presence. I was certain now that Nancy had been nice to me last night on Matthew's instructions. Now I had three good reasons to loathe Matthew: for killing Willard

Godfrey, for stealing my rightful job, and for stealing my rightful girl-friend.

My expression grew sour as the couple drew closer.

Marline let go of Matthew, leaving him teetering without support, and bustled up to me. "Happy New Year, darling!" she said again, standing on her toes to kiss my lips, thankfully keeping her tongue to herself this time. She removed her sunglasses and turned in a circle, surveying the atrium. "My, what a remarkable transformation! If only *I* could rejuvenate myself like this every day."

Indeed, only hours earlier the lobby had been a catastrophic mess of spilled drinks, torn streamers, deflated balloons, and wobbling, slurring, lurching drunks—Matthew and Marline amongst the best of them. Now restored to its former state of sparkling magnificence, it was crowded with well-heeled patrons who shuttled from buffet tables overflowing with gourmet delicacies, their plates heaping with food, to banquet tables decorated with white linen and calla lilies set up in every conceivable space. On the stage outside Galaxy, a jazz quartet played soft, hypnotizing music that floated through the atrium, providing a dignified, soothing ambience.

"Let's hope they accomplish the same miracle in our suite," Matthew said, catching up and resting his hand on his wife's shoulder. "What a disaster! A dozen room attendants are up there cleaning now. Marline and I couldn't stand to watch. We thought we'd pop down for a bit of brunch."

"My friend Mary had invited us over for New Year's Day cocktails," said Marline, "but, in typical Mary fashion, she's *still* not out of bed."

"Bloody Mary," muttered Matthew. "Why don't you join us, Trevor?"

I shook my head, horrified by the thought. "I'd love to, but I'm far too busy."

"On New Year's Day?" Marline cried. "Don't be silly!"

Onstage, the band struck up "The Girl from Ipanema." Marline cried out in delight and broke away from Matthew, spinning circles on the marble floor. *"Tall and tan and young and lovely,"* she sang, *"the girl from Ipanema goes walking and when she passes each one she passes goes 'aaah!'"* Arching her back, she threw her arm into the air like a Broadway dancer, then stopped abruptly and squeezed her temples. *"God,* that hurts! Darling, why did you make me drink so much?"

"I had nothing to do with your alcohol consumption, my dear. You managed quite well on your own."

She cackled. "I was having *fun,* Matthew, fun! Do you remember what fun is?"

"Not in the remotest."

Marline put her sunglasses back on and hooked her arm around mine, pulling me toward Galaxy. "Come along, gorgeous, don't leave me alone with Grumpy here. We'll have mimosas!"

"I really can't."

"Trevor," Matthew said, "we refuse to take no for an answer. Besides, it's time we had another little chat."

Unable to free myself from Marline's grip, I was dragged along with them. When we reached Galaxy, the host, Clarence, frowned down at the register. "I can't seem to find your reservation, Mr. Drummond."

"Reservation?" Matthew gave a light chuckle, but there was an unmistakable undercurrent of menace in his tone. "I don't *need* a reservation, young man. You may recall I'm the general manager? We'll need a quiet table for three, away from that hideous band and all these"—he looked around and sniffed—*"people."*

"I'm sorry, Mr. Drummond. Brunch is booked solid." Clarence gestured to the lounge. "I've got over fifty people with confirmed reservations waiting."

"Young man," Matthew said, his tone now decidedly threatening, "I'm *not* in the mood for this song and dance. Marline and I were up until all hours entertaining clients. Now be a good fellow and find us a table."

"I'll see what I can do, Mr. Drummond," said Clarence, excusing himself.

"The insolence!" Marline huffed.

"We can't just butt in," I said to Matthew.

He gave me a look of incredulity. "Why not?"

Marline pointed to the far end of Galaxy. "Is that table vacant?"

"So it is!" said Matthew. He held out his arm for his wife. "Shall we?"

I lingered behind to offer an apology to Clarence, but Marline came back and pulled me along like a stubborn mule. The table was set for six. Matthew removed the RESERVED sign and tossed it underneath, gallantly held out a chair for his wife and for me, then sat himself down and flagged a waiter.

"Menus, please. We're famished."

"It's buffet only today, Mr. Drummond," replied Maxim. "Please help yourself."

Matthew chortled. "You can't possibly expect us to line up with all the others."

"I loathe buffets," Marline chimed in. "They're so … *uncivilized*. Like being at some tacky farm wedding."

"Tell the kitchen to whip me up an omelet," Matthew instructed Maxim. "Swiss cheese, red peppers, Spanish onions, shiitake mushrooms, and ham. And bring us a fresh urn of coffee, a carafe of orange juice, and three stiff Bloody Marys." He turned to Marline. "Since Mary is too bloody hung over to serve cocktails, we'll have to make do on our own."

"Brilliant, darling!" she replied, turning to Maxim. "I'll have a plate of fresh fruit with plain nonfat yogurt, no watermelon or apple, a slice of dry whole wheat bread toasted on one side—no butter. And a double espresso."

Maxim turned to me, his eyes filled with contempt. "And you, sir?"

He had called me not Trevor, but sir! After a few minutes with the Drummonds, all the trust and respect I had earned seemed to have evaporated. "Nothing for me, thanks, Maxim."

"And bring me an ashtray," said Marline, pulling a pack of cigarettes from her purse.

As the waiter left, I reminded Marline that no smoking was permitted inside the hotel. She blinked several times, as though I'd spoken a foreign tongue, then stuck a cigarette into her mouth and leaned toward Matthew, who flicked a lighter for her. She inhaled deeply, sitting back to contemplate the cloud of smoke that poured from her nostrils like exhaust fumes from a muffler.

"Didn't you quit smoking?" I asked her.

She nodded. "But I took it up again last night." She gestured in Matthew's direction, indicating he was the reason why, then turned back to me. "You're extremely uptight these days, Trevor," she said. "Why aren't you married? A nice girl would loosen you up. Matthew, doesn't he seem stressed to you?"

"Darling, you wouldn't recognize stress if it hammered you over the head."

"*Me?* I deal with it every day. After all, I live with *you*."

The two smiled faintly beneath their glasses, amused at their own wit.

"You *were* acting strange last night," Matthew said to me. "Whatever possessed you to run out of the den like a teenage girl? Later I saw you mauling Nancy on the dance floor—it was *most* inappropriate, I must say. Whatever you said—or did—to her made her extremely upset. I'm very disappointed, Trevor."

I wanted to leap over the table and throttle him. "I did nothing inappropriate, Matthew," I said.

Maxim returned with a tray of beverages, hands trembling. As he set down a Bloody Mary before Matthew it slopped from the glass, landing on the white linen and seeping into a large, red circle.

Marline looked down and lifted her glasses. "It looks like blood."

Maxim attempted to blot it with a napkin, apologizing profusely, and hurried off.

We sipped our drinks in silence. Matthew and Marline sat facing one another, faces grim, regarding each other through their dark glasses. I pushed away my Bloody Mary, feeling ill.

"Cynthia Godfrey is over there," Marline said quietly, barely moving her lips, her head remaining completely still, as though on surveillance. "Who are those people with her?"

I turned and spotted Cynthia's blond head a few tables over. She was sitting with two men, one large and bull-necked, the other small and pointy-faced, and a heavy-set woman with straight, silver hair. All wore business suits except Cynthia, who was dressed in a mauve angora turtleneck sweater. I remembered her shocking comments from last night.

"Does Shanna have a boyfriend?" I blurted out. "Or did she recently?"

Matthew looked at me. "What a strange question. Why do you ask?"

"Just curious."

Marline was staring at Cynthia. "That sweater makes her look like a big Easter egg sitting in a nest of purple straw," she said. "Clearly, Willard's death is not the only tragedy in that family."

"Will you stop gawking, Marline?" Matthew said, then discreetly lifted his glasses to sneak a look himself. "*Those* people again! She was showing them around the other day. I told you, Trevor, she's up to something. They look like buyers to me—wicked buyers from some odious hotel chain."

I thought of Cynthia's cryptic comment: *Something big is going down.* "I still don't believe she'd do it. She promised to respect her father's wishes, and he would never sell the hotel."

"But that's exactly what he was in the process of doing," said Marline, looking quizzically at Matthew. "Dear, didn't you tell Trevor?"

Matthew's lips tightened. "He wasn't *selling* the hotel, he was bringing in a management company so that he could retire. He was tired of this business, Trevor. He wanted out. This hotel has been bleeding money."

What kind of story was Matthew fabricating now? "Impossible," I said. "The Universe has one of the highest rates and occupancies in New York."

"And the highest operating costs. Do you know how expensive it is to run this place? It costs over a million dollars per year alone to keep the Glittersphere revolving. Godfrey was a great hotel manager but a lousy financier. He finally accepted that this place would never make money as an independent. He was hammering out a deal with Shangri-La Hotels & Resorts of Hong Kong to manage the hotel."

"I don't believe you," I said flatly.

"Why should I care if you believe me or not? Willard told me this himself."

"Matthew had a horrible argument with him the night before he died," Marline said.

Matthew clenched his teeth. "That's not true, Marline."

The meals arrived, putting the conversation on hold.

Matthew cut into his omelet and peered inside, making a face. "I suppose there's no point keeping it a secret any longer. The night before the party, I overheard Willard on the phone with his lawyer, Roger Weatherhead, discussing the takeover of the Universe by Shangri-La. As soon as he hung up, I barged into his office and confronted him. After much cajoling—"

"Threats," Marline corrected him.

"*Cajoling*," Matthew repeated, holding up his hand to silence Marline, "Willard confessed that he was planning to retire in the New Year. The Shangri-La deal was about to be signed. I asked him what that meant for me. He said I might as well know that he was going to promote—"

"Fire."

"—*promote* me, and it would all be announced first thing in the New Year."

"Darling," Marline said calmly, dropping her cigarette into her cocktail glass, where it sizzled out and turned pink, "I believe the word you used when you told me that night was *fire*, not *promote*."

"That is *so* not true, Marline! How do you come up with these things?"

I watched Marline's glass fill with smoke and listened to their banter, wondering where, among all these lies and accusations, the real truth lay. Everyone—Matthew, Marline, Sandy, Shanna, and Cynthia—had his or her own version of events, each slightly—or dramatically—different, and each self-serving in its own way. I was tired of all their lies. I believed my own interpretation of events, and I desperately wanted the police to arrive and take Matthew away so we could all get on with our lives.

"Honestly, Matthew, I'm so tired of your lies," Marline said, as though reading my mind. She turned to me. "That reminds me, Trevor, did you ever find out who lives at that address I gave you?"

"Um..." I was tempted to rat Matthew out but resisted, not wanting to become embroiled further in their domestic dispute or exacerbate the angst and hostility between them, especially while I was seated in the line of crossfire. I would deal with Matthew on my own. "No," I said quietly.

"Marline's stirring things up because she's an angry, bitter woman," Matthew said to me. "Don't listen to a word she says. She's lashing out because she's mad that I'm shipping her off to Ohio tomorrow."

Marline picked up a piece of cantaloupe and chewed on it, ignoring Matthew and choosing to speak directly to me, as though I was a translator or judge. "Then perhaps *Matthew* can tell us who lives there. After all, he spent the night there. Trevor, ask him who lives at the address I found in his tuxedo pocket. Ask him who lives in the Lower East Side at Suite 301—179 Rivington."

Matthew's jaw dropped. He became perfectly still. "I have no idea what she's talking about," he said to me. "As I've said before, I simply went out for a drive to clear my head."

A series of beeps from my U-Comm made me jump. "Excuse me," I said, pressing the speakerphone.

"Trevor, it's Gaetan. Brenda Rathberger is asking for you at the front desk. She says it's urgent."

I got up and excused myself. As enthralling as it was to watch Matthew and Marline lob missiles at one another, I was relieved to have an excuse to run for shelter.

★ ★ ★ ★ ★

As it turned out, Brenda Rathberger was not exactly neutral territory. I could tell she was angry even before I reached her. She was standing at the front desk, hands thrust deeply into the pockets of her parka, her white combat boots planted firmly on the marble floor.

"Good morning, Brenda!" I called out cheerily. "Happy New Year!"

"Same to you," she snapped as though I had uttered an obscenity. Her tan was gone now, and her face was red and blotchy. Her eyes were glowering.

"How may I help you this morning?" I asked, quite sure I didn't want to know.

"I'm here to register a complaint. I would have asked for your general manager, but I have the distinct impression that customer service is not his forte. So I'm coming to you, Trevor."

"Of course. Why don't you come with me?" I steered her out of the earshot of other guests, stopping outside the lounge.

She placed her hands on her hips. "Last night I witnessed some of the most despicable behavior of my career. I stood at the front door of *this* hotel and watched in shock as your patrons, many *stumbling drunk* on booze served by *your* staff, literally *fell* into their cars as your valets handed them their keys and gleefully accepted their tips. There were no available taxis, no designated drivers, and no managers around to supervise. Everywhere in this hotel, the booze was flowing freely and it was *ka-ching! ka-ching!* all night. Why, I even saw Sandy James lurch out of the parking lot just after midnight, probably drunk as a skunk *again!* I reported her to the police immediately."

"You what?" So Sandy *had* driven. I envisioned her locked up in jail, wrists and ankles shackled, weeping uncontrollably. "Brenda, with all due respect, I hardly think the hotel can be held responsible for every patron. People come here to drink, particularly on New Year's Eve. We do our best to ensure they drink responsibly or don't drink and drive, but it's impossible to monitor thousands all at once."

"This is *exactly* the attitude that makes drunk driving rampant in our society," Brenda shouted, her voice booming across the atrium. "No one is willing to accept accountability. Your establishment is responsible for ensuring patrons get home safely. It's the law. Your staff, your managers, this hotel, *and* you can be held personally liable."

"Rest assured, our staff are fully trained to deal with impaired patrons," I said. "They are empowered—and encouraged—to cut people off if they've over-consumed. As for getting home safely, there was a shortage of taxis everywhere last night, yet we took the initiative to implement our Drive Me Sober program to assist getting people home safely."

"With only *two* drivers! One was stuck in traffic half the night taking a group to a party in Williamsburg! *Two* drivers for the *thousands* who spent money drinking here? That's hardly adequate!"

"There were, in fact, five drivers," I said, trying to remain calm. "Three others started at midnight."

"Well, *I* never saw them. I'm appalled by your hotel's insensitive and irresponsible conduct, especially considering seven hundred anti-impaired activists are staying here, spending our money on your facilities. You people are greedy, reckless, and immoral!" She ticked the words off with her fingers as though listing items consumed from the minibar. "'The guest is the center of the Universe'—my ass! *Profits* are the center of the Universe. You haven't heard the last of me, young man. At today's rally, I plan to inform my delegates of this shameful behavior and encourage everyone to boycott your establishment. Upon my return to Colorado, I'll be drafting a letter detailing my observations and forwarding copies to all major media outlets, to every anti-impaired driving organization in the country, and to the mayor, legislators, and the president himself. This hotel will be blacklisted! Then I'll be consulting my lawyers to determine whether you breached my contract, in which case don't expect a penny for this conference."

I was speechless.

Brenda marched off, clomping toward the elevators. Halfway there, she turned around. "You people are out to lunch—*spaced out!* It's time you got back down to earth!" She disappeared around the corner.

I stood there, stunned, telling myself to run after her, but I was unable to move. Were her threats serious? At times it was difficult to tell if she was truly angry or simply pretending to be angry in order to extort further concessions. Had she been building a case all along, planting remarks and accusations and threats to avoid having to pay her bill? Or were her concerns heartfelt? Whatever the case, I was deeply troubled by the accusations; there was far too much truth in them for my comfort. *Greedy. Reckless. Immoral.* Hadn't Sandy used similar words last night to describe her own conduct? How had I permitted Matthew and Marline to downsize the Drive Me Sober program? Had food and beverage staff poured as freely as Brenda claimed? Likely yes—it was New Year's Eve, the most profitable night of the year for the Universe, largely due to alcohol sales. Had the valets handed over keys without restraint? Quite possibly. It struck me that the Universe had been unfairly singled out because it was hosting the VOID conference. We were no different from any other drinking establishment on New Year's Eve.

Were we?

If Brenda followed through on her threats, even greater humiliation would result for the hotel, my colleagues, and me. Since Matthew had hoodwinked me into being the hotel's official spokesperson, it would be up to me to explain our actions to the media and to the public. What could I do to stop her? Mr. Godfrey had often told me never to let a problem fester, never to let an upset guest leave angry. "They become terrorists," he said, "spreading stories like biological weapons, embellishing them, recruiting soldiers to help spread the disease, and destroying the hotel's reputation. If we let it get that far, we're helpless to defend ourselves. *Never* let it get that far, Trevor."

I needed to disarm Brenda Rathberger as quickly as possible.

I hurried across the lobby and stepped inside the elevators. Mona wished me a Happy New Year, then rocketed up to the seventy-first floor. When I arrived at Brenda's suite, there was no answer. Deciding she must have gone to the VOID Welcome Center, I hitched a ride with Mona to the concourse level.

There, I found the desk dismantled. Megan, the volunteer, was packing things up. "You just missed her," she said as she loaded supplies into a box—including stacks of notepads, pens, stationery, water glasses, and mint dishes stamped with the Universe logo. "Everyone went to Central Park."

Damn. I considered chasing after Brenda, heading her off at the entrance to the park or showing up at the rally, but a vision of Brenda flogging me in front of hundreds of rabid protesters made me reconsider. I decided to wait until she returned and try talking sense into her then. *She was all talk anyway,* I told myself. She was harmless. There was plenty of time to win her over. Lord knows, I had done it before.

I decided I should fill Matthew in. But Matthew and Marline's table in Galaxy was now occupied by a large Japanese family. Cynthia

Godfrey and her brunch companions were leaving. Cynthia was leading them to the exit, lovingly stroking her angora sweater. Turning away before she could spot me, I hastened toward the elevator and tried to page Matthew on my U-Comm. There was no answer—not surprising, since today was a holiday. I picked up the house phone and tried his suite, but there was no answer there either. Returning to Galaxy, I asked Clarence if he knew where the Drummonds had gone.

"I heard Marline say something about a Bloody Mary," he said. Mary's. They must have gone there for cocktails.

I went to the front door and asked George if he'd seen them.

"Their car drove out a while ago," he said, gesturing to the parking ramp. "Marline was driving. I didn't see if Matthew was with her."

As I walked back across the lobby, my mind wandered to the previous night, when Shanna had proposed we watch the videos in Matthew's den. Why had she been so eager to see them? Did she really think there might be a clue there? Matthew's reaction when he walked in was swift. Why did he care if we watched them? What was he hiding? Maybe the truth lay in those tapes.

I took out my master key disc and regarded it thoughtfully.

To be sure that no one was there, I knocked several times on the door of the Drummond suite. Then, checking both ends of the corridor to make sure no one was around, I waved my disc over the scanner. The door glided open with a swoosh, and I slipped inside. It swooshed shut behind me.

I stopped and listened. There was dead silence in the suite. The housekeeping department had worked its magic; the suite was immaculate, all props removed, every piece of furniture restored, every surface gleaming. I turned left, passing beneath the spiral staircase, and headed down the hallway.

The door to the den was slightly ajar. I gave it a push and peeked in as it swung open. Slowly, the television revealed itself in the corner, then the desk, the leather chair, the edge of the sofa, and two feet...

Two feet!

I froze. The door continued to swing, and a pair of gray trousers came into view, followed by a wrinkled white shirt, untucked, and the back of Matthew's head.

A low, guttural snore rose from his body.

I turned to flee. But as I did, I spotted the videocassettes sitting on the bookshelf where Matthew had placed them. I stopped. In a matter of seconds I could dash over and grab them, then be out the door before Matthew was any wiser. I could replace them later or, if I found anything of interest, take them directly to the police. I stood contemplating the move, my heart pounding.

Matthew was deep asleep.

I took a tentative step into the room. He stirred on the sofa and smacked his lips, mumbling something somnolent and incoherent. I stopped and waited for him to settle again, then resumed my journey across the carpet, halting with each step to check on him.

The cassettes were now inches from my grasp. I reached up and—

Riiiinnnnggg!!!

The telephone! It was on the desk, only inches from Matthew's head. I froze, unable to move, one eye on Matthew, the other on the telephone.

Riiiinnnnggg!!!

Matthew stopped snoring. I envisioned him rolling over and opening his eyes, catching me tiptoeing across his den. How would I explain myself? I had to abort the mission. Slowly, I began to back out.

Riiiinnnnggg!!!

My back struck the edge of the door.

Matthew rolled over and opened his eyes.

I jumped behind the door, wedging myself into the corner, and pulled it tightly against me, willing myself to disappear. Had he seen me?

The phone stopped ringing. There was absolute silence.

I waited, praying for him to go back to sleep or to get up and leave.

After about a minute the snoring resumed, first softly, then increasingly loud. I breathed a sigh of relief. Slowly, I pushed the door away from me, cringing as it creaked. Matthew's torso came into view. He had rolled over, and was facing me now. He looked peaceful and innocent, curled up with his fists tucked beneath his chin like a little boy. I edged my way around the door. One little peep from me and his eyes might flutter open.

Suddenly, I heard the swoosh of the front door.

My heart leapt. I hurried back to my hiding space.

There was a click of shoes on the marble floor. A woman's heels. Marline? As they drew closer, I caught a whiff of exotic perfume. The aroma was unmistakable.

Shanna Virani.

What was *she* doing here? I peeked through the crack in the door. Sure enough, Shanna was tiptoeing down the hallway, eyes wide, looking frightened and guilty. Was she here for the tapes too?

The front door swooshed open again.

Shanna halted in her tracks. Her eyes grew wide and her mouth opened to form an O. She darted into the bathroom at the end of the hall, where I had found Sandy last night.

This time the footsteps were heavy and brisk. A man. But who? A houseman? I peeked through the opening and caught a glimpse of a tall, dark figure with broad shoulders making his way down the corridor. Men's cologne hit my face as he passed into the den. I gripped the door handle tightly, curling into a standing fetal position, bracing myself for discovery. With three others now in the suite, the odds of getting out undetected had rapidly deteriorated.

"Hey," said a voice, deep and resonant.

I heard movement on the sofa and Matthew's groggy reply. "Oh, hi. I must have fallen asleep." There was a loud yawn and stretch. Then silence.

I waited, puzzled. It seemed odd that two men were alone in a room and neither had uttered a word. Who was it and what were they doing? I heard the rustle of clothing. And then...a soft moan. And another unmistakable sound: the smacking of lips.

What on earth?

"You looked so hot last night I wanted to jump you," I heard Matthew say.

"You should have. I was waiting."

"I think my wife is onto us. She got your address somehow. I think I left it in my tux."

"Maybe that explains why Trevor accused Nancy of sleeping with you."

"Nancy and me?" Matthew chuckled. "Tell your crazy roommate to mind her own business."

"Don't laugh. She's really upset about the whole thing."

My hand flew to my mouth. The accent was unmistakably French. Gaetan Boudreau. *He* was Nancy's roommate? Suddenly everything started to become clear.

"Hmmmm..."

"Ooohhhhh…"

I had to get out of there. A shadow passed over me, and I peered through the crack in the door. Shanna was retreating down the hallway, holding her shoes above her head as though in surrender. Halfway down, she froze, then scurried back to the bathroom.

To my amazement, the front door swooshed open again.

"Yoo-hoo, Matthew!" came Marline Drummond's voice.

Uh-oh.

From the sofa I heard a sharp intake of breath, followed by a flurry of activity.

"Mary went back to bed, she's too hung over," Marline cried out in a singsong voice, the sound of her heels drawing closer. "Bloody Mary!" She cackled. "I thought we could have a little chat, darling. Are you ready for that? It's time for the truth!"

Marline burst into the den.

There was a moment of absolute silence.

"What the hell is going on here?"

"Marline! It's not what you—"

"What are you doing? Oh. My. God!"

"Marline, please! We were just—"

Marline's shrill voice was inches away from me. "I can't *believe*—I *don't*—I—Oh. My. *God*! You're a *ho-mo-sex-u-al*, Matthew?" She enunciated each syllable as though it were an obscure medical term. "A *ho-mo-sex-u-al*! Well! No *wonder* you're so hopeless in bed! All this time I thought it was *me*! And you, you—you … *French whore*! Get out! Both of you! Get out this instant!"

"You don't understand! We were just—"

"Just what? Having a meeting? Shirtless?"

"No! I … We…"

"Shut up! Shut up! I don't want to hear any more lies! You bastard! Get out! Get out!"

There was a slap.

"Ouch! Marline! Calm down!"

Sounds of a struggle ensued, punctuated by grunts and curses.

Beep! Beep! Beep!

Everything came to an abrupt stop. A U-Comm was going off somewhere.

Alarmed, I glanced down at my belt and breathed a sigh of relief when I saw it wasn't mine.

"Marline, please!" said Matthew. "Get off me! My U-Comm is going off. Gaetan, grab it from the desk, will you?"

"It's an EGP," Gaetan announced.

An Emergency Group Page ... that meant mine was next! I fumbled for my device, frantically searching for the *off* switch. It was too late.

Beep! Beep! Beep!

I covered it with both hands, trying to muffle the sound.

"Where's that coming from?" said Matthew. "Is it yours, Gaetan?"

"No. It's coming from behind the door."

Oh, shit. I pulled the handle tightly against my chest, delaying the inevitable. Four hairy fingers curled around the door and pulled. I tugged harder, knowing it was futile. Another set of fingers curled around and pulled with full force. I lost grip, and the door flew open.

Gaetan, Matthew, and Marline stood gaping at me. "Trevor?" all three cried in unison.

Beep! Beep! Beep!

This time it wasn't mine. And it wasn't Matthew's. It was coming from the bathroom.

"Who now?" Marline marched into the hallway and kicked the bathroom door open.

I glanced at Matthew and Gaetan. Matthew's hair was ruffled, his belt loose. Gaetan was clutching a shirt against his bare chest.

"*Shanna!?*" Marline exclaimed. "What are *you* doing here?"

Shanna emerged from the bathroom with an expression of indignation, as though Marline were the intruder and not she.

"*Both* of you?" Matthew cried. "What in god's name are you up to? Why are you in my home?"

"I came for the cassettes," I confessed.

"Me too," Shanna said haughtily, her eyes moving up and down Gaetan's muscled torso.

"And why, pray tell, do you want to see them so badly?" Matthew demanded.

I glowered at him. "So I can prove once and for all that *you* killed Willard Godfrey."

"Me?" Matthew cried, emitting a derisive laugh. "You seriously think *I* killed him? Is this why you've been behaving like such a jackass, Trevor?"

"Matthew was ruled out as a suspect a few days ago, Trevor," said Shanna. "Detective Lim himself told me that Willard was hit by an SUV or a truck." She turned to Gaetan and looked him up and down again. "Clearly, Matthew has something else to cover up."

Gaetan pulled on his shirt and started buttoning it up.

"I was never seriously considered a suspect, Trevor," said Matthew. "You silly fool."

All heads were nodding, even Marline's. I turned to Shanna. "An SUV ran him down? One like yours, Shanna? Tell us, why are *you* so eager to get these tapes?"

Shanna's eyes fluttered. "Let's just say I'm curious." She pushed her way past Marline and marched across the room, pulling both cassettes from the shelf. "Now, if you don't mind, I have to go. I've been paged."

"Oh no, you don't," I said, blocking her path. I held out my hand for the cassettes.

Hugging them against her chest, she hissed at me. "Out of my way!"

I lunged for them. Shanna swung them out of my reach. Her elbow struck the edge of the bookshelf, and both cassettes flew into the air, landing on the floor. I scrambled to my knees and snatched them up.

"You people are shameless!" Marline cried. "Get out, all of you!"

Beep! Beep! Beep!

It was Matthew's U-Comm again.

"Jesus, the EGP, I forgot!" I set down the cassettes and pulled my U-Comm from my belt. "'EGP 555—Call Nancy Swinton,'" I read aloud. I punched in her extension.

The others waited, arms folded, staring at the floor in embarrassed silence.

"Nancy, it's Trevor. What's up?"

"My god, Trevor, it's crazy! Come as quick as you can! There's a riot in the lobby! The VOID group has stormed the Universe!"

19

The Cosmic Bubble Bursts

Gaetan, Shanna, and I left Matthew and Marline behind in their suite to "have a chat" and hurried down to the lobby. By the time we arrived, the riot was over. We found Nancy Swinton standing just outside Galaxy, gazing at the destruction around her in disbelief.

The lobby looked like a war zone. The lounge had received the brunt of the rampage; almost every piece of furniture was broken. Outside Galaxy, the great white Christmas tree had been razed, and a half-dozen banquet tables had been flattened by its weight. The display cases in the front of the lobby had been smashed to pieces. Already, a group of hotel employees had started to clean up. A half-dozen police officers wandered the ruins, sifting through the debris.

"It all happened so fast," Nancy said as she guided us around. "In a matter of seconds, about a hundred protesters swarmed in and destroyed everything in sight."

A commotion drew our attention to the front door. Honica Winters was trying to get past security.

"But I *am* a guest!" I heard her cry. "Let me in!"

We hurried over.

Honica's camera crew was right behind her. "Jerome," I said, "you can let Miss Winters in, but not the camera or the crew."

"Thank you," she said with a huff, pushing past Jerome. She turned and called out the door to her crew. "Go get more exterior shots. I'll be back in a sec." She walked in and looked around, her eyes growing wide. "My god, they did all this? I knew they were angry, but this is insane!"

"Were you at the rally?" I asked.

She nodded, still gazing around in amazement. "It started out so peacefully! Everyone gathered in Central Park, then we marched to Rockefeller Plaza for the rally. Brenda was spirited but mostly well-behaved until we reached the plaza, then she started yelling into a megaphone, accusing the crowd of losing the war against drunk driving. Everyone was chanting 'Save a life! Don't drink and drive!' and she was punching her fist into the air. Then she started ranting about the Universe, about the irresponsible behavior she witnessed last night, about how reckless and immoral all its staff are. The crowd went into a frenzy. 'We must take a stand!' she cried. 'We must show the Universe, show the world, that society will not tolerate enablers of drunk driving. We must storm the Universe!' She leapt off the stage and charged down Avenue of the Americas, motioning for everyone to follow. At least a hundred people did, yelling and waving placards and stampeding like elephants. I tried to keep up, but they were too fast."

"I was in the back office when they got here," Nancy said. "George paged me from the front door when he saw them charging toward the hotel. By the time I got to the lobby they were everywhere. They used signs like swords and sledgehammers, hacking and slashing everything in sight. Guests were scrambling over one another to get out. I called 911, then we did our best to get guests and patrons out of harm's way. The protesters took off when the police arrived."

I decided that Honica had heard enough and thanked her, steering the others away. "What about Brenda Rathberger?" I whispered to Nancy. "Where did she end up?"

"I saw her run up the staircase a few minutes ago," Nancy replied, pointing toward the upper concourse. "A couple NYPD officers went after her."

We wandered over to the circle of shattered display cases, their contents scattered across the lobby. Only the replica of the Universe at the center of the circle remained standing, its pedestal stooped over like a crippled old man. Crushed papier-mâché planets littered the floor. The space suit lay draped over the *Endeavour* shuttle model like a collapsed astronaut. We made our way along the edge of Galaxy, stepping around overturned chairs and banquet tables, and smashed plates and glasses.

"The tree would have killed the people sitting at these tables had they not fled seconds before it fell," Nancy said. "Miraculously, no one at all was hurt."

"Thank god for that," I said, shuddering to think of what could have happened.

We walked the length of the tree, regarding it sadly like a fallen soldier. Its gold star decorations had exploded upon striking the marble, covering the floor with a powdered glass like golden snow. I kept sneaking sidelong glances at Nancy, but she refused to look me in the eye. Though clearly rattled, she was businesslike and demure. I wanted to establish eye contact with her to reassure her that I understood everything now, that I was desperately sorry for my behavior. But she kept her eyes trained on the ruins around us.

We picked our way to the Center of the Universe, where cocktail tables and chairs had been toppled over and smashed to pieces. Anti-impaired driving signs were strewn everywhere, spiked into the backs of overturned furniture, stretched along the carpet, slapped up against walls: SOCIETY FOR SOBRIETY ... GET UNDER OUR INFLUENCE! ... A SOBER WARNING ... THE LIPS THAT TOUCH LIQUOR SHALL NEVER TOUCH MINE. A twelve-foot banner bearing the words INTOXICATED UNIVERSE in angry red letters had been draped along the bar. We stopped and stared at it for a moment, then continued our tour.

The Cosmic Bubble appeared to have exploded, sending fragments of glass in all directions. Only a barren metal carcass remained. Inside, the boardroom table was still intact, as though patiently awaiting its next meeting.

Nancy's U-Comm sounded, and she excused herself. Gaetan followed. I watched her bustle across the lobby to the front desk, then pulled my eyes away, feeling dejected—and rejected. I turned in a circle. The Universe was in ruins. How brokenhearted Mr. Godfrey would have been.

The sound of a struggle caught my attention. Two NYPD officers appeared at the top of the grand staircase and began dragging Brenda Rathberger down the stairs. Handcuffed and hysterical, she was writhing and protesting and struggling to free herself. "Get your hands off me, you brutes!" she shouted. "I'm innocent!" As they dragged her past Shanna and me, she tossed her head in our direction, twisting her neck and bulging her eyes demonically. "*Those* are the people you should be arresting! *They're* the criminals!"

Shanna called out to her politely, "Checking out, Mrs. Rathberger?"

"Shanna, please," I said, turning to chase after Brenda. "Brenda! Why did you do this?"

The officers halted.

Brenda turned to me, suddenly calm, then burst into tears. "I—I did it for... for F-Frederick!" She turned to one of the officers and growled, "Let go of me, you beast!"

They carried her out the door. I followed them and watched as they pushed her into a cruiser. Honica's crew descended upon the cruiser as it drove down the ramp. On the street below, crews from various local TV stations were arriving from all directions.

Shanna came up behind me. "Oh, god," she said upon seeing all the cameras.

"Yikes," Matthew Drummond said, having come up from behind. He was fully dressed now, a sheepish look on his face.

"Everything okay upstairs?" I asked.

"Let's just say that when Marline finishes her rampage, our suite will look very similar to this lobby."

"My god, look at all the camera crews!" cried Shanna. "What should we do?"

"I think we've learned our lesson about avoiding the media," said Matthew. "Shall we?"

"Let's do it," I said.

Taking a deep breath, I made my way down the ramp toward Honica Winters and her crew. Matthew headed left down the driveway to another crew, and Shanna headed right.

"Remember the three Cs?" I called out to Matthew.

"Of course," he called back. "We care. We're concerned. We're cooked."

That night, the telephone jolted me out of sleep.

"Hey, I just saw you on the news!" Cassandra James cried. "There was a *riot* at the Universe?"

"Kind of." I quickly filled her in on the day's events. "Can you believe it, *Matthew* and *Gaetan?*"

Sandy hesitated. "Actually, I've known about them for a while. Gaetan came to see me last week because he was afraid he was jeopardizing his employment by seeing Matthew. He said they hooked up after the Christmas party and have been seeing each other since. I told him that yes, definitely, he was jeopardizing his employment, but more importantly, what about Matthew's marriage? Then I went to Matthew and advised him to cease seeing Gaetan immediately. Obviously, he didn't listen. Poor Marline. She must be a wreck."

"She is. How was I on TV?"

"Um, well, not bad ... um, but not great, either. I saw you on New York One. You seemed kind of nervous, to tell you the truth. It wasn't all your fault—the reporter sensationalized the whole incident. But you might want to get some more media training if you plan to do more interviews."

I was shocked. I had expected her to say "fantastic." Sandy always said everything I did was fantastic. If this was part of a new, brutally honest, non-smiling persona, I wanted the old Sandy back.

"Yeah, well, it's not easy being on the firing line."

"Believe me, I know."

"Hey, how's Kaitie?"

"Oh, she's fine now, just a little fever, that's all. But guess what? Driving home from the party, I got pulled over. A cop took me into the station for a Breathalyzer test! I think someone reported me."

"Oh no, Sandy."

"They kept me there for two hours. I was frantic. I was so worried about Kaitie."

"Did you pass?"

"The Breathalyzer test? Of course. I didn't have a drop to drink. Believe me, I've learned my lesson."

"But … I thought—that champagne bottle on the bathroom counter…"

"You thought it was mine? It was there when I got there. I think Marline guzzled it down while going for a pee."

"Thank god. How are things at home?"

"Good!"

I knew better than to take this comment at face value. "Honestly?"

"Actually, they *are* good. After we put Kaitie to bed, Jack and I stayed up all night and talked. We're trying to work through our issues. We're going to get counseling. Bottom line is, we still love each other very much. We're committed to making it work."

"Does he still think you're on vacation and are about to be promoted to GM?"

"No. I came clean on that part too."

"I'm so glad, Sandy."

"It helps that the police have stopped badgering me. I think they've finally accepted that I didn't do it. They must be harassing someone else. Matthew's taking the heat now, I guess."

"Actually, Matthew's off the hook. Apparently he never was considered a serious suspect. It's down to Shanna now. Somehow, all along she managed to keep under the radar, but she won't be able to escape suspicion now. You'd never guess what Cynthia told me." I filled her in on our conversation. "I still can't believe it—Shanna and Willard, lovers!"

"Oh, I knew about that too."

"You did? How the hell are you privy to all this gossip? And more importantly, why didn't you tell me?"

"I'm director of human resources, Trevor. It's my job to know these things—and to keep them confidential. Actually, I walked in on the two of them a few months ago and found Shanna sitting on Mr. Godfrey's knee and nibbling on his ear."

"Too much information, Sandy."

"So you really think Shanna did it? She's definitely got the temper. You better be careful, Trevor. For all we know, she'll come after us next. She definitely won't like you snooping around. Leave the sleuthing to the police. Promise?"

"I promise."

"Hey, I'm coming back to work on Monday! Cynthia called and asked me to come in for a meeting. Now that the VOID conference is over, I'm hoping she'll distribute our bonuses."

"The conference wasn't exactly a success, Sandy. They held a riot in our lobby. Brenda refused to pay, and she's threatened to sue us."

"Even so, I feel really optimistic about things now."

I didn't have the heart to tell her that I feared that the worst was yet to come. I wished her good night and went back to bed.

The telephone rang again a few minutes later. To my surprise, it was my sister, Wendy.

"Wendy, how are you?"

"Pregnant."

"So I heard. Congratulations!"

"Listen, Trevor, I just talked to Mom, and she's really upset about her visit. What happened?"

"Nothing! She tried to push her agenda on me, and I resisted. The usual."

"Did she tell you about …?"

"About what?"

She made a growling sound. "I can't believe it! She promised she would."

"What are you talking about, Wendy?"

"Nothing. Forget it."

"Come on, you're freaking me out."

"It's nothing, Trevor. Ask Mom."

"Fine. I will."

There was a moment of uncomfortable silence.

"Hey, Wendy? Did you and Janet have a good time here in the summer?"

"Yeah, why?"

"Mom said you didn't like the way I treated you or something."

She hesitated. "You weren't the same, Trevor. You seemed ... distant. You didn't have much time for us. You were so into your job, and not much fun, and ..." She hesitated.

"And what?"

"You made us feel like small-town hicks. Like you were embarrassed by us."

"Oh god, Wendy. Did I? I'm sorry."

"Don't worry about it. We're big girls."

"Maybe I was reacting to how you and Janet made me feel."

"How?"

"Pretentious. And phony."

"We did? I'm sorry, Trevor." She was quiet for a moment. "What happened to us, Trevor? We used to be pals. Then you moved away and you barely even call me anymore."

I was sitting by the window in my bedroom, the only window in my apartment, and craning my neck, my head almost upside down; it was the only way I could see the sky. Sometimes I stuck my head out and looked up just to reassure myself that I was still on earth, like a prisoner staring longingly into an empty field, knowing he won't walk on it for many years but comforted nonetheless. The sky was clear tonight. I could see a star, a lone star that was so unusually bright it might have been a planet. It seemed to grow in intensity suddenly, almost flashing. What *did* happen to us? How had I become so distant from my baby sister, whom I had always loved and protected?

"I don't know, Wendy. I've been busy."

"Yeah, well, we're all busy, Trevor."

The rest of our conversation was brief. She sounded distracted, and I was grappling with this newfound clarity, this horrific realization that I had abandoned my baby sister, just like Mom abandoned us after Dad died. I had shut her out, shut everything and everyone out. When Mom said it, I didn't want to listen, didn't allow it to get through, and didn't want to believe it. Shanna said similar things to me, and I hadn't listened then, either. Now, with a simple question, my sister had jolted me into consciousness.

What *was* I doing in New York, so far from my family, with no friends and no hobbies and nothing to enrich my life but work? What happened to *me*?

Who are you, Trevor? I heard Mom ask, her voice pleading.

You're vapid, I heard Shanna say.

I glanced around my apartment. Mom had left it spotless, the cupboards stocked with enough supplies to survive Armageddon, the walls freshly painted in bright colors, the prints mounted. Even the air smelled fresh and pleasant. I realized that she had removed the dead cactus from the corner and replaced it with a robust-looking fig tree.

Having failed to refurbish my life, Mom had settled with refurbishing my apartment. Perhaps she hoped the rest would follow. She herself had undergone such a dramatic transformation in life. Maybe I *could* learn a thing or two from her. I glanced to where my copy of

Refurbish Your Life! sat unopened. Was there was more to this book than I wanted to acknowledge?

I picked it up and turned to the first page.

20

The Cosmic Dust Settles

Early Sunday morning, unable to sleep, I got up and went to the hotel.

The lobby was dead quiet. It had been two weeks to the day since my fateful journey into the bowels of the Universe with Brenda Rathberger. In that short period, my entire world had been turned upside down. I circled the lobby, regarding the destruction around me as though looking at my own life. The Center of the Universe, the nexus of activity in the hotel, was now a barren wasteland, its broken chairs and tables carried away, leaving faded shapes in the carpet like outlines of murdered bodies. The steel beams of the Cosmic Bubble had been picked clean of glass, leaving an empty carcass slouched over the boardroom table. In the front lobby, nine faded circles in the marble floor marked where the display cases had once stood. The center display case remained intact, stoic among the ruins, its pedestal and brass plate now bent back into place. I took out my handkerchief to polish the brass plate.

A voice startled me from behind. "'Dedicated to the late Margaret Bains-Godfrey, the center of my universe.'"

I turned to see Marline Drummond standing behind me, hands folded before her, her head slightly bowed, as though paying respects at an altar. She was dressed in a full-length sable fur coat and hat, a red leather purse slung over one shoulder, and was clutching a pair of gloves. Her face was serene and devoid of makeup.

She stepped forward and ran her fingers along the inscription. "What hypocrisy," she said.

I regarded her in surprise. "Hypocrisy?"

"Poor Margaret wasn't the center of his universe. This hotel was."

I stared down at the inscription. "But don't these words express the purest form of love?"

"The purest form of *guilt*, my dear," Marline said. "Have you ever read "Ozymandias"? It's a poem by Percy Bysshe Shelley. A nomad comes upon a huge monument lying in ruins in a barren desert. He reads the words inscribed there." Assuming a theatrical pose, she deepened her voice and bellowed, "*'My name is Ozymandias, King of Kings. Look on my Works, ye Mighty, and despair!'*" She relaxed her stance and turned to me expectantly.

I gave her a blank stare.

"The poem could have been written about Willard Godfrey," she explained, gesturing to the tunnel of balconies above, to Galaxy, to Jupiter Ballroom, and to the Center of the Universe. "Willard Godfrey was like Ozymandias. He didn't build the hotel for Margaret, he built it for himself, with her money, as a monument to his ego. He resented her for not giving birth to a son, an heir, and he resented Cynthia for not being male. He hoped the Universe might make him immortal. But in the end, it means nothing. This is just a building, a hotel like hundreds of others. Like the Hilton before it, one day it will be replaced with another phallic symbol of another man's ego. Willard would have died a happier man if he had dedicated his time and effort to his family. Maybe he wouldn't have died at all."

I studied Marline's face, wondering if she was projecting her own problems onto Mr. Godfrey. She turned to watch a luggage cart rumble toward us from the elevator.

"Ah, here come my belongings."

The bellman, Felipe, nodded to us as he passed. The cart was wobbling, weighed down by Marline's suitcases, at least a half-dozen Louis Vuitton knockoffs. I noticed that the iron globe, the symbol of the Universe, was missing from the top of the cart, leaving its chrome support bars hanging loose.

"Felipe," I called out, "why are you using a broken cart?"

"Three carts were broken in yesterday's riot," he replied. "Maintenance retrieved this one from the repair cage. The globe is missing, but it works okay."

I remembered the cart that I had pushed into the repair cage on P4 before discovering Mr. Godfrey's body. It was probably the same one. I sighed, irritated that someone would put it back into operation before it was fixed. "Tell maintenance to find that globe and replace it at once," I called after Felipe. I turned back to Marline. "I apologize for the intrusion yesterday."

"Don't mention it, Trevor. I hope you got what you came for."

"The cassettes? No, I left them there."

"Then Shanna must have taken them. They're gone."

"Really?" *Damn her!*

"Mrs. Drummond, your car is here," George called out from the front door.

"Come, walk with me," Marline said, taking my arm.

Outside, a silver stretch limousine idled in the driveway. The driver stood at attention by the door.

Marline reached for my hands and squeezed them. "Take care of Matthew, Trevor. He's going through a lot right now. He's mortified by what happened, outed like that in front of his colleagues. God, I was so blind! I had no idea what he was going through. After we left Houston he changed dramatically, but he had been so depressed about being booted out of NASA I assumed it was more of the same. Little did I know what other issues he was dealing with."

"Matthew got *booted* out of NASA?"

She nodded, looking around to make sure no one was within earshot, and pulled me closer. "For the record, he retired, but he was forced."

"Why?"

"His shuttle trip was disastrous. The mission was fairly routine: to bring supplies and equipment to the International Space Station. Matthew was one of three crew members scheduled to do space walks. Despite countless hours of training, when the time came to leave the shuttle and walk in space, he refused to get out. He proved to be completely useless to the mission."

"What happened?"

Her face assumed a wistful expression. "He's never been able to explain. Maybe he panicked. Maybe he saw the face of God. Or maybe he saw an alien. Perhaps he was simply too afraid."

"Mrs. Drummond," said George. "It's almost eight. You don't want to miss your flight."

"Damn right I do!" Marline retorted with a cackle. "I'm going to Ohio, for god's sake!"

I walked her to the limousine. "Did you and Matthew work things out?" I asked.

She laughed bitterly. "If you call uttering threats and insults working things out, then I suppose we did. He called me an overbearing shrew and I called him a two-timing faggot, then I hurled a vase at him. He's lucky I'm a lousy shot. But you might want to send someone up to fix that window." She threw her head back and cackled, as if this were the funniest thing she'd ever heard. Then she grew quiet. "As hard as I tried, I could never make him happy. Maybe Monsieur Le Hottie will have better luck."

She opened her arms and gave me a long embrace, then lowered herself into the limousine. "I wish you the best, Trevor. Now that all this cosmic dust has settled, you should see things more clearly. Learn from Willard Godfrey's errors. Work isn't everything, my dear. Family, health, friends, good shoes, and killer abs—those things are far more important. As for me, I'm checking out of the Universe and back into reality."

The driver closed the door. I stepped back onto the curb to wave her off.

The window glided down. "I hate to sound like a modern-day Copernicus," she added, "but the fact is, this hotel is not the center of the universe. Life is too transitory here. You meet someone in the health club one day—like I did your mother—and strike up a promising friendship, then the next day they check out. Never have I been surrounded by so many people, yet felt so lonely."

I nodded, understanding.

"How *is* Evelyn, anyway?" she asked.

"She's good."

"You talked, then, before she left? She told you?"

Not this again. "Told me what?"

Marline looked thunderstruck. "Call her," she said. "Talk to her."

"Why?"

"Promise me."

"I promise."

The limousine rolled into motion. "Goodbye, my sweet. I'll miss you."

"Goodbye, Marline."

She turned and stared straight ahead, jaw set, expression poised, like the seasoned actress she had never become. As the window glided upward, I saw a single tear roll down her cheek.

The limousine took off like a rocket.

A half-hour later, I knocked on the door of Matthew's suite. He answered wearing a Universe bathrobe over blue silk pajamas. He was unshaven and haggard and did not seemed pleased to see me.

"What is it, Trevor?"

"Can I come in?"

He hesitated, then stepped back and gestured for me to enter.

As the door glided shut behind me, I sensed a change in the atmosphere. A high-pitched whistling sound was coming from the living room. I walked over to the window, where a perfect oval hole had been carved in the glass by the vase Marline had thrown. In the gardens below, the vase was lying among the rosebushes, the sun's reflection making it glow like a fallen meteor. Air was rushing in, infusing the hotel's oxygenated, chemically scented air with the cool, pungent air of the city. I crouched down, breathing through the hole. Although faintly foul-smelling, it was somehow preferable to the air inside the hotel.

I heard a great sigh behind me.

Matthew was slumped on the curving, purple Contessa Banquette sofa, scratching his beard, looking confused and mildly demented.

"You okay, Matthew?" I asked.

He shrugged and grunted, then heaved himself from the sofa, as though wanting to escape the spotlight of my gaze. On the end table was a photograph of Marline. He picked it up and regarded it thoughtfully. "*Yours forever—love, Marline,*" he read aloud, turning it over in his hands, flipping it so that she was smiling upside down. The words were written in black felt, movie star-style, like the photograph he kept facedown in his office. He looked up. "How many husbands get airbrushed, autographed headshots of their wife for Christmas?"

I shrugged. "Not many, I would guess."

"She sent copies to all her friends in a mass mail-out that rivaled the Reader's Digest Sweepstakes. She had so many of them. Her agent refused to send them out, said she looked too young in them, that it was misleading." He sighed. "Poor Marline." A startled expression came over him. "My god, have I ever used those two words together before? Has anyone?"

He set down the photograph and lay on the sofa, curling into a semi-fetal position. "After years of bullying and abusing, Marline is finally a victim herself. A victim of my reckless, philandering behavior, of my lies and deceit." He turned over onto his back. "She didn't deserve this, Trevor. Beneath all the sass and brass, deep down, much further down than she allows most people to go, is a vulnerable, insecure, lovely human being. She's the only person in this world who truly loves me. I've hurt her and humiliated her and broken her heart."

I took a seat in the loveseat across from him. "I'm sorry, Matthew."

"What a coward I am! I've been lying to her for years. I couldn't bring myself to tell her the truth. I couldn't bear to admit it to myself."

"That you're gay?"

He sat up on the sofa and turned to me, his mouth falling open in indignation. "I am *not* gay!"

"Oh…I thought—"

"I mean, well…I admit to having certain tendencies…But…I'm not. Not…well, you know…"

"Not gay?"

He collapsed back down. "Oh, I don't know! I've felt certain attractions for years, but they always subsided over time. Only a handful of times did I act on them. Afterward, I felt such shame and self-loathing it took months to recover. But it was different with Gaetan. I was intrigued the moment I set eyes on him. I saw him almost every day, and rather than subside over time my feelings grew stronger—so strong I couldn't ignore them. At the Christmas party he slipped me his address. I was terrified but incredibly excited. The booze emboldened me. By the end of the night I was in such a frenzy of lust I didn't think twice about driving. In the morning, I woke up horrified and skulked home. That's when you paged me. And, well, the rest is history."

"Marline had no idea whatsoever?"

"Not at first. She has always chosen to believe everything I say, to question nothing. Perhaps she lived in denial. When the truth started slapping her in the face, left-right-left—when my lies became so big and outlandish that she couldn't possibly swallow them anymore—she started to ask questions, to make inquiries. She was miserable living here, in this prison of a hotel, stuck in a relationship with someone who never touched her. She must have realized she had nothing left to lose, so she started seeking the truth. We had pretended we were happy for years, but we weren't. I carried on blithely, determined to live a normal life. At NASA, even whisperings of such tendencies could have ended my career. It's part of the reason I left."

"Marline told me you were booted out."

He lifted his head and looked at me angrily, then lay back down. "That was the other part." He was silent for a moment, contemplative. "Something happened up there, Trevor. I endured months and months of intensive training, but nothing could prepare me for the epiphany I experienced. As we entered orbit and circled the earth,

I looked down and saw how small it was, how insignificant, a blue marble in the cosmos. I thought about the millions of people down there, no larger than atoms on this marble, and how self-important we all are. In the great scheme of things, in the realm of the universe, we couldn't be less significant. In a hundred years we'll all be dead. No one will remember us. No wonder Godfrey built this hotel. He left a legacy."

"So you never got out of the shuttle?" I asked, unable to contain my curiosity.

"Space is the most inhospitable environment a human being can endure, Trevor. A tear in my space suit would have led to the most painful death imaginable. Air would be sucked from my lungs, my blood would feel like it was boiling in my veins, my internal organs would seize. I used to think it ironic that Godfrey chose to call his hotel the Universe, considering what a hostile and lonely environment space is. Yet I've since come to the conclusion that the name is perfect.

"When it came time for our spacewalk, I clung to my seat like a schoolgirl on a Ferris wheel. My colleagues tried to coax me out, but I refused to budge. I was incapacitated by my epiphany. Finally, they gave up, and everyone had to cover for me. After we landed, I was stripped of my astronaut status, given a desk job, and later, when Honica Winters started snooping around, forced to resign. NASA kept a tight lid on the story, but somehow Honica got wind of it and came knocking on my door. By then I had been outcast by my colleagues, and I felt bitter and dejected. I was desperate to talk to someone, *anyone*, about what happened, to tell my side of the story. So I agreed to be interviewed.

"When the cameras started rolling, Honica was ruthless. She attacked me for being a coward, for reneging on my civic duties, for wasting millions of taxpayers' dollars. Every question she asked made me hate myself even more. I was reduced to a blubbering fool. Fortunately, NASA managed to strong-arm the network into killing the story. But the damage was done. I spent over two years as a recluse, unable to leave my home, refusing to talk to anyone. I was depressed and suicidal.

"It was Marline who saved me. She allowed me to wallow awhile, offering me nothing but love and support, never prying about what happened up there. She hasn't always been so nasty; living with me, trapped in this Universe, has aged her and embittered her. After two years of listening to my whining, she told me my time was up and slapped me back to life. She called Willard Godfrey and pitched him on the idea of installing me as resident manager. Godfrey thought it was brilliant. This job saved my life, Trevor.

"But soon after I arrived, I discovered how little I knew about the business. At first I was eager to learn, but Godfrey had no interest in relinquishing his authority. He had hired me as a publicity stunt, a figurehead, and treated me like some sort of trophy wife with nothing to offer but a heroic past and a photogenic face. I grew to loathe him. After years of staying in five-star hotels as a guest, being doted upon and pandered to and treated like a hero, the transition to hotel employee wasn't an easy one. I felt out of my element. The only thing I looked forward to was my monthly Stargazers lectures.

"I'm a scientist, Trevor. I think logically. I frankly don't care about the comfort and well-being of others. Scientists are trained to question everything, to speak our minds, yet in the hotel business you suppress anything remotely unpleasant. From day one I've fantasized about telling a guest, just one guest, to go fuck himself. That's not normal, is it, Trevor?"

"Not really. We all want to lash out sometimes, but we take pride in our work. We're eager to please."

"I find it astounding how seriously people in this business take their work, more seriously than many of the scientists and astronauts I've worked with—people who are advancing humankind and exploring the universe!"

"Hotels aren't entirely frivolous," I said, offended. "They provide a place for people to rest and sleep and relax, to work and study and meet."

"Yes, of course. At first I wrote this business off as painfully simple. But I've grown to realize that it is a science of sorts, albeit a baffling one."

"Remind me again why you want to be general manager?"

"When Godfrey died, I saw an opportunity to step into a truly challenging role."

I stared at him pointedly. "As opposed to being fired?"

His eyes flashed with anger. "Godfrey didn't *fire* me, Trevor. He told me that my future was in the hands of Shangri-La Hotels, and that they didn't see a place for me in the new order. I had every intention of convincing them otherwise. I knew I would shine once I was out from under Godfrey's shadow. Behind all the smiles and handshakes, all the feigned concern and encouraging words, I strongly believe that Willard Godfrey was an evil man. We were all just pawns in his pursuit of greatness. He created this idyllic environment, this refuge in the center of this mad city, so clean and safe and happy, with exquisite food and fine wines, populated by wealthy, civilized people and far removed from poverty and pestilence and war. But the key difference was that we were not his guests, we were his employees. 'Eat here, drink here, and sleep here,' he told us. 'But don't ever leave.' With the paltry sums he paid us, how could we? How could we ever hope to live this lifestyle outside the hotel? He trapped us, imprisoned us, seduced us. As an outsider, I've managed to resist total submission, but you, Trevor, and Sandy, and even Shanna, your lives revolve around this place. You're slaves to the Universe. Outside of work you have nothing, no hobbies, no true friends, no functional relationships. Life outside the Universe is just one big void. Godfrey robbed you of your lives and your souls. Thank god somebody stopped him."

"Jesus, Matthew. Aren't you being a bit dramatic?"

"You don't see it that way?"

"I'm happy here."

"Are you?"

"Why does no one believe me? Okay, maybe I'm not happy, but I'm content. I'm not sure I even know what happiness is." I got up from my seat and wandered to the window. The whistling sound had stopped, as though the air inside the Universe had been fully replenished.

"You want to know what happiness is?" Matthew asked.

I turned to him. "Yes."

"Happiness is Nancy Swinton. Don't let her go, Trevor."

Nancy's last shift was to start at 3:00 PM. I waited all afternoon in my office, pressing the "check messages" button on my computer every few minutes to distract me, unable to focus on anything more engaging. At 3:12, allowing just enough time for Gaetan to complete the pass-on and go home—or up to Matthew's suite for more shirtless romping—I made my way down the staircase and crossed the lobby.

My heart was pounding.

She was standing in the front office, lost in thought. I was shocked to see that her hair was set free, unencumbered by the requisite fastener.

She turned when I knocked on the door frame, and her eyes lit up. "Trevor! I was hoping you'd drop by today."

"Yeah, well, I was in the neighborhood."

"Today's my last day."

Her expression was radiant, not sad and desperate like I might have hoped. "Nancy, your hair..."

Her lips parted into a playful smile. "You like?" She reached up to toss her hair, twirling around on the floor, first in one direction, then in the other, making it bounce on her shoulders like she was in a shampoo commercial.

I was completely disarmed. "Uh, N-Nancy, you're supposed to—it's against Universal..."

"Oh no, it's the hair police!" she shouted, cowering away from me mockingly. "Please don't bust me!"

"Nancy."

"You don't like it?"

"It's beautiful, but—we have rules to uphold... It's distracting."

"What are you going to do, fire me?" she asked, moving closer, a playful, defiant look on her face.

"I'd really prefer you tied it up."

"You're serious?" Her expression grew exasperated. "Trevor, it's harmless. I haven't dyed it pink or shaved it or fashioned it into dreadlocks. It wouldn't hurt you to let your own hair down from time to time. Do I look unprofessional?"

"No, but—"

"Will guests be offended?"

I sighed. "No."

"Then get over it. It's time this place—and you in particular—stopped being so uptight. *This*"—she whipped her hair side to side—"is my parting statement."

I didn't know what to say. She looked so carefree, so liberated, so utterly gorgeous that I couldn't even pretend to be upset. I felt a smile creeping over my lips. I tried to fight it off but couldn't.

Nancy sat down and frowned at the computer screen. "Brenda Rathberger came by the desk a few minutes ago and asked if we would waive her room charge for Saturday night, since she wasn't there."

"Where was she?"

"In jail."

"Right."

"I told her I'd have to check with you. Can I charge her?"

I sighed. "Comp it."

"Really? You're a lot nicer than me. I guess that's why I'm leaving the business. Are we going to press charges?"

"That's up to Cynthia. I suppose it will depend on whether Brenda follows through on her threat to sue us."

Nancy began typing into the computer. "Honica Winters leaves tomorrow too."

"Oh, thank god! At last, everything will be back to normal."

She stopped typing. "Except for one thing." She turned to me.

Our eyes locked. I experienced a moment of utter rapture, as though our souls had connected. Then panic set in, and I broke away. The intimacy was too much. My internal panic room kicked into alarm mode. I wanted to flee from the office, but I forced myself to stay.

"Nancy, I want to apologize ... I didn't realize you and Gaetan were roommates. I thought that maybe ... that Matthew was—"

She stood up and placed two fingers on my lips, silencing me. "I understand," she said, her voice a whisper. She regarded me with her bemused smile, smiling not only with her lips and eyes but with her entire face. Even her hair seemed to smile the way it cascaded over her shoulders and around her breasts.

"It's been such a … such a difficult couple of weeks," I said, my lips nibbling at her fingers. I stopped talking, embarrassed. I looked up to the ceiling, inhaling her lovely floral scent. "I've been so confused and scattered. I've wanted to tell you that—but I can't, you know, we work together and it's against the rules, and it's so risky, and—"

"You talk too much, Trevor," she said softly. Our eyes met. Her gaze, so self-assured and soothing, deflecting each neurotic impulse I sent in her direction, calming me, allowing me to hold my stare and revel in the moment. I felt the locks on the doors inside me unbolt, windows open tentatively, sunshine pour in.

I took her hands in mine and kissed her fingers. I wanted so badly to tell her I loved her.

The sound of my U-Comm broke the spell.

"Excuse me," I said, pulling it from my belt.

Nancy stood up and composed herself, looking embarrassed, as though we had just made passionate love. She started to tie her hair back into a ponytail.

My hands were trembling as I fumbled with the device. I had forgotten how to use it. At last I located the receive button. "Trevor Lambert here." My voice was boyish and squeaky.

"Trevor, it's Shanna. Are you alone?"

I glanced at Nancy. She got up to leave, but I put my hand up to stop her. I plugged in my earpiece.

"Yes, Shanna. What is it?"

"I was wondering if you might come over."

"Come over? Where are you? In your office?"

"I'm at home."

"You want me to come to your *home*?"

"Yes. Please." She sounded distraught.

"Is everything okay?"

"I need to show you something. It's very important, Trevor."

"Okay." She gave me her address in Gramercy Park, and I hung up.

Nancy was placing personal items into a cardboard box.

"Nancy, I have to leave. I'm going to see Shanna."

"Is that a good idea? Everyone's saying she's the one who killed Mr. Godfrey. What if she's dangerous?"

"Shanna? She's harmless."

She looked worried. "Let's hope."

I walked over to her and gently pulled the fastener from her hair, letting it fall free.

She looked up, her face turning scarlet.

Embarrassed, I broke her gaze and went to the door. I stopped and turned around. "Hey, I thought... I thought we could get together some time. Maybe have dinner?"

"Here? At the Universe?"

"No. Somewhere else. Anywhere else."

"I'd like that."

"I'll call you." I hurried out of the office.

Nancy. Loves. Me.

21

Solar Eclipse

A taxi dropped me off in front of a stately six-story brick building on Irving Place in Gramercy Park.

As I made my way up the stone steps, shivering in the cold afternoon air, it occurred to me that I might be walking into a trap. If Shanna *had* killed Mr. Godfrey, which was looking increasingly probable, she could be unstable, maniacal, or possibly homicidal. What if she was luring me off-property to chop me into little pieces and feed me to her cat? The prospect seemed outrageous, but still a chill ran down my spine. Reminding myself how petite she was, and that her personality was much more overpowering than her might, I found her name on the directory and pressed suite 401. The building was lovely, located in a beautiful neighborhood, but, as with Sandy, I had always imagined Shanna living in something far more grand—a large townhouse with high, wrought-iron gates and a butler, perhaps.

Shanna's voice came through the intercom. "Who is it?"

"Trevor."

When she opened her apartment door a few minutes later, not only did she look pleased to see me, but she surprised me by opening her arms for a hug. A quick check confirmed that there was no gun in her hands, no knife or blunt instrument in the vicinity, save for a black umbrella in a ceramic urn near the door. In fact, she was wearing oven mitts and an apron smeared with cookie dough. Her hair was braided to one side, and she wore no makeup. She looked different out of business attire—younger, less severe, and more at ease. Certainly not violent or menacing.

I followed her down a narrow hallway with a vaulted ceiling painted in gold leaf into a small living room furnished with a Persian rug, red velvet divan, and matching sofa. A series of large canvases featuring Far Eastern landscapes was mounted on the walls. The furniture was antique and oversized, as though she had downsized from a larger home. It felt odd to be in Shanna's home after seeing her every weekday for five years yet knowing almost nothing about her personal life. The apartment was unexpectedly girlish, with Kewpie dolls, crystal figurines, and bundles of dried flowers covering every surface.

"Have a seat," she said. "Can I get you something to drink? Wine? Tea? Water?"

"Water, please."

While she was in the kitchen, I wandered over to the mantle. Between two tigers carved in rosewood was a framed photograph of a boy and girl in their late teens. Like Shanna, the girl had big black hair and the boy had a big-toothed smile. Her children, I assumed.

Shanna returned with a plate of cookies and large bottle of San Pellegrino. "Sit," she said, handing me a glass. I sat down on the divan and she lowered herself to the floor, sitting cross-legged and cupping the water glass with both hands like hot tea. She offered me a cookie.

I took one and went to bite into it, then stopped, suddenly suspicious. "When you said you hadn't baked in twenty years, is this the last thing you made?"

"It's not that bad, is it?"

I took a bite. "It's actually quite good." The cookie was hard but tasty, with oatmeal, carrot shreds, and walnuts. It occurred to me that she might be trying to poison me, so I waited until she selected one for herself, seemingly at random, before I took another bite.

"I'm sure you're wondering why I asked you to come," she said. "I want to show you something." Reaching for the remote control on the coffee table, she turned on the VCR. I recognized footage from the staff Christmas party—the people and their clothes, but not the scene. It was dark and chaotic. "The bus ride home," she explained, pressing *reverse*. "Susan Medley was so drunk by then she could barely hold up the camera." As the tape rewound, employees stepped down backwards from the bus and walked backwards into the hotel. Even in reverse they looked inebriated, their movements wobbly and comical as they back-stepped across the lobby. The camera panned the lounge, which was crowded with people.

"Here," said Shanna, stopping the tape and pressing *play*. "Give it a minute; I didn't stop it in time."

The tape began to play, in forward mode this time. The same group was in the elevator, descending from the Observatory. I recognized Manny from Housekeeping, Liz from Accounting, Jeff from Maintenance, and at least two others besides Susan. They hammed it up for the camera, making obscene gestures. The camera turned to the glass wall and pointed down to the lobby, moving up the great white Christmas tree and lingering on the gold star on top. The image went blurry as the elevator reached lobby level and the group spilled out. Susan lagged behind the others, zooming in on Liz's hand as she squeezed Manny's backside.

"Isn't Liz married?" I said.

"So is Manny. Pay attention now. Watch closely."

The camera panned the lobby, stopping briefly to catch two waving night desk agents, then moved over the display cases in the front lobby and ventured into the lounge—the same scene I had watched in reverse.

"What am I looking for?" I asked impatiently.

"Shush!" she said, pressing *slow*. The tape inched forward, frame by frame. "Watch closely ... *there!*" She pressed *pause*, freezing the screen, and stood up, hurrying to the television set. She pointed at the upper right corner of the screen with a long, lavender fingernail. "Look! Look who's sitting in the lounge!"

I stood up and squinted at the screen. A woman was seated alone at a table in a dim corner of the lounge. She wore dark glasses, a fur coat, and a scarf wrapped around her head like a movie star from the sixties. She was holding a glass of amber liquid to her lips and appeared to be licking its side.

"Cynthia Godfrey?" I said.

"Indeed!" She turned to me, eyes wide with intrigue. "I'm positive it's her."

I glanced at the digital clock in the lower right corner of the screen. It said 12:13 AM. "It couldn't be. She was long gone by then. Besides, she was wearing a different outfit, a floor-length baby blue gown."

"She changed."

I stared at her blankly. "I'm not following."

"Cynthia went home and got changed, then came back to the hotel. Here she is, hiding in a dark corner of the lounge by herself, observing the activity in the lobby."

"So? It wouldn't be the first time she hung out in the lounge. She often waited for her father there."

"Which is precisely what she's doing. Look at her! She looks positively evil. And she's in disguise!"

I peered at the TV. Indeed, there was something diabolical about her expression, but she was too blurry and far away to recognize for certain. "So what if it *is* her?"

"Think about it, Trevor. What if none of us—not me, not Sandy, not Matthew—have been arrested because none of us ran Willard down? What if a fourth vehicle got onto P4 undetected?"

"I've been trying to figure out how that could have happened myself, but I've seen the activity reports. No one else went down there, Shanna. Police themselves said there's no sign of break-in."

"I'm not talking about a break-in."

"I don't get it."

"Let me tell you a story, Trevor." Leaving the tape frozen on the image, Shanna sat down on the floor, assuming a meditation position. "As you know," she began, "I started at the hotel only a few weeks before you. I had never worked with Willard Godfrey, had never even heard of him, but he had heard of me, and he poached me from Claridge's in London. We worked well together from the beginning, and we became great friends. Then, to my utter amazement, just over a year ago, we fell in love."

"I know. Cynthia told me."

"She did?" Shanna looked alarmed. "When?"

"At Matthew's party."

"What else did she tell you?"

"Let me see ... oh, she said that you killed Willard Godfrey."

"Of course she did."

I was surprised to see Shanna break into a smile. She certainly wasn't acting like a killer. I decided to hear her out, but I was starting to wonder if she had concocted a complex story that somehow framed Cynthia and had invited me over to convince me it was true. After listening to others' lies for two weeks, I could no longer trust anyone.

"I wasn't attracted to Willard at first," she said, continuing her story. "After all, he was almost thirty years older than me."

The difference was less than twenty years, but I let it go.

"Our relationship evolved very, very slowly. First I felt only admiration and respect. After his wife died, I felt tenderness toward him, but no love. Behind all the smiles and charm and sunny optimism, Willard was one of the saddest, darkest, loneliest people I had ever met. About two years ago I was surprised by a little spark inside me, a flicker of intrigue that caught momentum and grew into a flame. It was only about a year ago that things started to really heat up. We began seeing one another regularly. It was essential to keep our relationship secret, what with all his preaching about 'Universal Values,' but it wasn't easy. For the first time in years, I discovered I was happy. And so was Willard. About three months ago, we grew tired of hiding our relationship. Willard was finished with the hotel business. His perspective on life had changed. He thought he had accomplished his dream in building the Universe, but he had sacrificed so much, and he had grown to regret it. He wanted to salvage what life he had left to live."

She glanced at the mantle, to the photo of her children. "Sometimes we become so consumed by work that we forget we have a home. Then suddenly there's no home to go to. Bantu and Eliza refuse to speak with me. Before the divorce, we all lived together in London, happily, I thought. But I spent so much time at work I didn't realize that my husband had stopped loving me. He met someone else who had all the time in the world to give him the love and adoration he craved. One night I came home from work and they were all gone. After that, the only thing that kept me from wallowing in complete misery was my work.

"Meeting Willard helped me to remember how wonderful love could be. We planned to elope, to go traveling, and to enjoy life."

I remembered Shanna telling Brenda that she, too, had lost her husband. Now I realized she had been talking about Willard Godfrey.

Shanna continued. "He wasn't ready to let go of the hotel entirely, so he started to negotiate a deal with Shangri-La Hotels to take over management of the property. In the weeks prior to his death, he hammered out a deal in which all executive staff would be given an option to stay on for at least one year or to take a one-year buyout. He planned to sit down with each of you and convince you to take the buyout. He thought it would be the perfect opportunity to do something like what we planned: to take a sabbatical, to stop and enjoy life for a year, to evaluate our priorities and perhaps take a new direction."

"So that's why he set up those meetings with us? That's what he meant by 'The Future'?"

She nodded.

"Then which of us did he plan to appoint to general manager?" I asked.

She closed her eyes for a moment. "None of you. That he was leaving up to Shangri-La—and of course they would bring in one of their own."

I nodded, feeling hurt.

"Try to understand, Trevor. Willard considered you a strong candidate, but in the end he decided you weren't ready. It came down to dedication and work performance. You weren't lacking in these areas, you were *over*performing in them. He realized too late that the best managers find balance in their life. In the long run, all work and no play leads to burnout, something he had experienced personally. He didn't want to set you up for the same, nor did he want to entrust the management of his beloved Universe to someone who would be burnt out in a couple of years. He planned to discuss this with you at your meeting on January 3, at which point the Shangri-La deal was expected to be wrapped up, and you would be given your options. But he died before anything was signed."

"If you knew this all along, why didn't you tell us?"

"I was going to, but I was so wound up, so completely devastated by his death, that I feared if I let even one string loose, if I tried to talk to any of you, I would unravel completely. Besides, it was pointless. I knew Cynthia would do whatever she felt like. I tried to talk to her several times, but she wouldn't let me near her." Shanna sipped her water and smiled sadly, her eyes misting. "The night before he died, five of us had dinner in Orbit—Willard, Cynthia, Katherine and Roger Weatherhead, and me—to say farewell to the Weatherheads before their cruise. At dinner Willard announced his plans to elope with me. Roger and Katherine were thrilled. Cynthia was furious. She already felt abandoned by her father, and not without reason, and this was too much for her to bear. He had cut her off only months prior, refusing to give her money until she stopped partying and found a real job, and now he was taking off with someone else, leaving her alone and broke. If he were to remarry, her entire inheritance stood in jeopardy."

"Cynthia said Willard was going to break up with you, so you killed him."

"Did she really? How intriguing." Shanna got up and plugged the parkade cassette into the VCR. "Now watch this," she said.

As the tape began, I recognized the black-and-white footage from the parkade camera that had been played on *Borderline News*. Shanna pressed *rewind*, providing commentary as the tape played backwards. "That's Matthew driving out last ... Here comes Sandy ... and here's me. Ignore that car, and that car—they go to the pay booth—see? Okay, watch this next one." She stopped the tape, freezing the frame on a black SUV with tinted windows, what looked like a Jeep Liberty. The clock in the corner of the screen said 1:03 AM. Unlike the staff cars, this one pulled up to the pay window. The license plate had been removed. The tape rolled frame by frame. An arm draped in fur poked out the window, handing the cashier a bill. The cashier missed it, and it floated to the ground. The driver opened the door and leaned down to snatch it up.

"Look!" cried Shanna.

It was difficult to see clearly, but I could make out that the woman was wearing dark glasses and had a scarf draped around her head.

"*That*," Shanna announced triumphantly, freezing the frame, "is Cynthia Godfrey."

I stood up and went to the TV. The image was grainy and black-and-white, and it was impossible to identify anyone for sure, but there was no doubt it was the same woman from the lounge. "But Cynthia drives a Mini Cooper," I said.

"She must have borrowed a friend's truck or rented one. Here's my theory, Trevor. After finding out that her father was going to marry me, she became desperate. If I became his wife, she could lose her entire inheritance. She was well versed in our Christmas party traditions, having attended every one of them in the past, so she cooked up a plot to kill her father—and possibly even to frame one of us in the process. When she drove out the first time, around 10:00 PM (I have that on tape too), in her Cooper, she used her parking pass to ensure there was a record of her leaving. She went home, changed, got the SUV and came back, but incognito this time. I can show you her arrival if you like, at around 11:30 PM. She didn't use her pass, but took a ticket like other visitors so she wouldn't be recorded. Then she used her remote control to get down to P5, knowing this activity wasn't monitored. She parked her truck on P4 or P5 and went up to the lounge to wait for the party to end and her father to leave."

"She used a pretty lame disguise," I said.

"It was probably intentional. She didn't want to alarm her father, so she dressed like she was going out clubbing, knowing her father had never understood fashion. When she saw Susan and the others come down to take the last of the shuttle buses, she knew the party was over and we'd be right behind them to see them off. At that point she probably went up to her father's office and waited for him. When he arrived, she took the elevator down with him, letting him use his own pass to ensure there was no record of her presence. While he was loading presents into his car, she hurried down the ramp to get her truck. She pulled around the corner and waited until he was an easy target. Then she floored it. *Bang!* She stopped and went back to make sure he was dead, but he was still alive. Working quickly, since she knew the rest of us would be driving out in a matter of minutes, she found something to use to finish him off, then sped away. The gates aren't monitored, so there was no record of her coming back. When she went to pay, she was probably shaking so violently she dropped her money, and as such was caught on camera."

I was so riveted by her story I had stopped breathing. My mind raced. "What do you think she used on him?" I asked. "Maybe if police found it they could swab it for her fingerprints."

Shanna shrugged. "I have no idea. Maybe she brought a sledge-hammer with her, or maybe she found something down there."

"The luggage cart!" I cried out suddenly.

"What? You think she lifted a luggage cart over her head and—"

"No. The iron globe screwed to the top. When I went down with Brenda Rathberger, I saw a luggage cart. It was missing the globe. I pushed it into the maintenance cage, thinking it was left there for repair. She must have unscrewed it. My god, she used the symbol of the Universe to murder her father!"

"But where is it now?"

"Probably at the bottom of the Hudson."

Shanna reached over and clutched my hand, her long nails digging into my skin. "She killed her own father, Trevor. She stole his last precious years, eclipsed his life just as we were about to sail off together into the sunset. We have to make her pay."

"We will," I said. "I promise."

Late that night, I was lying on my sofa trying to concentrate on *Refurbish Your Life!*, struggling over yet another of Kathy McAfee's bad renovation metaphors, when the phone rang.

"Trevor, it's Cynthia Godfrey."

My heart almost stopped. What did she want? She had never called me at home before. Had she somehow found out about my conversation with Shanna? Was she going to come after *me* now? But she didn't sound sinister. She sounded upbeat and friendly—which was alarming in itself.

"Cynthia, how are you?" I asked, trying to control my breathing.

"Can you talk? Are you alone?"

"I am."

"I want to give you the heads-up about what's going down tomorrow morning."

"I'm listening."

"I've sold the Universe to ValuLuxe Hotels & Resorts."

"You *what?*"

"I can't deal with all this crap anymore. I'm only following through with my father's wishes."

"But your father wasn't going to sell the Universe, Cyndy, he was going to hire Shangri-La to manage it."

"That's bullshit! Who told you that?"

I didn't answer.

"Remember a couple of weeks ago when you told me it was your dream to become general manager of the Universe?" she asked. "I was listening, Trevor. I like your passion. And I trust you. I've made a deal with ValuLuxe to keep you on as head of the transition team from the Universe side. They want somebody around who has the respect of staff and knows the operation inside out. I told them you are the one. You're going to be general manager, Trevor. What you always wanted!"

"Really? Me?" My pulse was racing. "But what about the others?"

"You mean like Matthew and Shanna?"

"And Sandy."

"Um, all executive staff are going to be replaced with ValuLuxe people. Wait until you meet them, Trevor, they're a really impressive group. The head of the transition team is Debbie Schmidt. She's a sharp cookie and a totally amazing person. They do takeovers like this all the time. One night a hotel's a Marriott, the next morning it's a ValuLuxe. You'll *really* like working with them."

"But I really like working with the current team. They'll all be fired?"

"If you're not interested ..."

"What's the alternative?"

"You either stay and help with the transition or you go with the others."

"I'd be fired, just like that?"

"It's their condition, not mine. I went to bat for you, Trevor. I convinced them to keep you around."

I sighed and pondered the offer. "I'll be their puppet."

"Okay, fine, I'll call and tell them you're not interested."

"No! Let me think about it."

"There's no time to think, Trevor. It's happening tomorrow morning, and I need to call Debbie back right now to tell her if you're interested. Just tell me yes or no. If you say yes they'll have the paperwork ready for you in the morning."

I thought about my colleagues. Fired, all of them! How could Willard Godfrey have ever wanted that?

"What about buyouts?" I said. "Are they getting taken care of?"

"Absolutely."

My mind raced. Would they think I had sold them out? Just this morning, Matthew told me he loathed the hotel industry. And Sandy? She herself said she needed to be at home to work things out with Jack. And last week Shanna had confessed to me that she had lost her passion and was only biding her time until early retirement. Why sacrifice my career for these people whose hearts weren't in their work? I was tired of being pushed around by everyone, being so concerned about their needs and aspirations. What about my aspirations? To be general manager was my lifelong dream. Trevor Lambert, General Manager! Only by staying on could I ensure Mr. Godfrey's legacy continued. It was my duty, was it not? Without me, who would be there to protect it? And what alternative did I have if I refused the position? I'd be out of work. I'd have to return to Vancouver.

"Trevor, what is it? Yes or no?"

"I'm thinking."

Of course, there was the small detail of Cynthia Godfrey being a murderer—assuming Shanna's theory was correct. Now that I was speaking to her on the phone, my conviction was beginning to waver. She didn't sound like a murderer. I wondered again if Shanna had cooked up the whole story to protect herself. Deep down, wasn't Cynthia really a nice person? She said she liked me, she trusted me, and she had gone to bat for me. That was more than I could say about the others. Maybe I was wrong about her. Even if Shanna was right and Cynthia was guilty, she'd be arrested soon, and the hotel would be sold, which meant that she'd have nothing to do with it anymore. So I wouldn't be reporting to a murderer. My job would be secure. And once I proved myself to ValuLuxe—

"*Trevor.*"

"Okay. I'll do it."

"You sure?"

"I'm sure."

"Great. I'll have Debbie draw up the papers, and we'll see you in the morning."

After I put down the phone, I thought hard for a long time, trying to convince myself I was doing the right thing, that I wasn't being a turncoat. *You can't please all people all of the time,* I told myself. Tomorrow would be difficult and uncomfortable, but once it was over, things would get easier.

And I would be General Manager of the Universe.

Satisfied, I picked up *Refurbish Your Life!* again.

Annoyed with chapter one, I flipped ahead to chapter two. "When I first found out I had cancer," wrote Kathy McAfee, "I was afraid to tell my family. They were busy with their own lives and I didn't want to be a burden. So I kept it to myself and—"

I put the book down. A chilling thought occurred to me.

I picked it up and read the passage over: "…I didn't want to be a burden…" Was this Mom's big secret? Was this the reason she carried this book everywhere she went? Suddenly I couldn't breathe.

I reached for the phone and dialed my mother's number.

"What news did you tell everybody but me?" I demanded as soon as she picked up the phone.

There was a long pause. "I tried to tell you, honey, but you didn't give me a chance."

My throat was so dry I could barely speak. "Tell me *what?*"

"I have cancer."

"Oh god. Are you going to die?"

"No, Trevor, I'm not going to die. I had it a few years ago and they managed to kill it with chemotherapy, but it's back now. They're going to remove one of my breasts on Thursday. I'll go through another round of chemo, and that should be the end of it. It's really nothing, Trevor. I don't want you to worry."

I ran my fingers through my hair. "How do you feel?" Sobs like hiccups began lurching up from my stomach.

"I feel great, actually."

"You went through this a few *years* ago and didn't tell me?"

"You were so involved with opening the hotel that I didn't want to distract you. I was afraid you'd feel obligated to come home, and you were so excited about your new life in New York. I made the girls swear not to tell you."

"And this time?"

She sighed. "I didn't want to upset you."

"You spent your entire visit trying to upset me! This would have been the ultimate trump card, Mom, the perfect device to guilt me into coming back to Vancouver. I can't believe you didn't use it!"

"I want you to come home for the right reasons, Trevor, not because you're worried about me or because you feel guilty."

"Are you okay, Mom?" I asked. "Tell me the truth. Are you going to be okay?"

"I'm going to be fine, dear."

"Is that why you wear a wig? Is this what you mean by 'I got a haircut'?"

"My hair never grew back properly, so I kept the wig. Losing my hair was the best thing that ever happened to me, Trevor. Ironically, cancer made me start living again. I'm going to lose my hair again, but I don't mind. I have my life."

"I'm so sorry, Mom. I'm such a terrible son."

"You're a wonderful son."

"I'm reading *Refurbish Your Life!* That's what made me realize something was wrong."

"I'm glad, dear. I wish I could tell you I was reading *Universal Values,* but I'm not."

"I'll come home for a visit soon, Mom. I promise."

"I look forward to that."

"I'll check back in with you before Thursday."

"Don't worry, dear. It's really not necessary. I know you're busy."

I hung up and threw *Refurbish Your Life!* across the room, putting a fresh dent in the yellow wall.

22

End of the Universe

The Cosmic Bubble having burst, Monday morning's briefing was moved to Pluto boardroom on the concourse level. The hotel's smallest meeting room was aptly named; located in a remote part of the concourse level, in a room with no windows, poor lighting, and almost no ventilation, it was tiny and dark, and always felt cold.

"From the Center of the Universe to Pluto," Matthew quipped as he joined Shanna and me. "How fitting, considering our fall from grace."

As we settled in, Sandy James appeared in the doorway, beaming. "Hi, guys!"

How refreshing it was to have her back. We all got up to hug her.

"We missed you, Sandy," said Shanna.

"Hasn't been the same without you," said Matthew.

Matthew went to shut the door and turned to us, his face grave. "I thought we should have a chat before Cynthia gets here. I had a brief conversation with her last night. She didn't come right out and admit it, but I'm quite sure she plans to announce that I'm to be permanently installed as general manager."

"Bravo, Matthew!" Sandy cried, clapping her hands.

I turned to her in surprise. Hadn't she informed me she expected Cynthia to install *her* as GM? Had her ambitions changed that quickly, or was she faking it? Either scenario was unsettling, considering what was really about to take place. I turned back to Matthew, feeling the color drain from my face.

"I wouldn't be so quick," said Shanna, glancing at me. Clearly, she was not pleased that the limited time we had before Cynthia arrived had been hijacked by Matthew. "Trevor and I—"

"Let me finish, Shanna," Matthew said. "I also insisted she distribute our bonuses, since the VOID conference was an outstanding success, aside from the small riot, that is, which I informed her wasn't our fault. She assured me that yes, we will be getting checks today."

He nodded triumphantly and sat down, assuming an expression I recognized from his pre-shuttle publicity photo: *Yes, I'm a hero.* Little did he know that by "check," Cynthia meant severance check. His arrogance was appalling. I felt a glimmer of delight in the knowledge that, in a matter of minutes, his smug expression would be wiped clean from his face, to be replaced by one like that of his post-shuttle photograph: *Yes, I'm a failure.* In an instant, I felt terribly guilty for the thought.

Sandy squealed with delight. "I was thinking," she said excitedly, "today is January 3, the exact day Mr. Godfrey had scheduled our meetings. Cynthia must be simply following through with his wishes, just like we hoped all along. She's getting things back on track!"

I decided that Sandy *was* expecting Cynthia to promote her, and was either pretending to support Matthew or had resigned herself to supporting whatever decision was made. I wondered how long her smile would last once Cynthia arrived.

My god, where were these wicked thoughts coming from? The ghastly reality of the situation was taking its toll on me, I decided, turning me into an evil person. I wanted the deed done as quickly as possible—and, I hoped, as privately as possible. Surely Cynthia didn't intend to make a group announcement? I trusted she would take them away one by one and wield the hatchet somewhere out of sight, without my having to witness the slaughter.

"Let's hope she's not following his wishes to a *tee*," Matthew muttered, glancing over at me with an expression of alarm, likely recalling that there had been no place for him in Shangri-La's takeover plan. He stood up again. "I want you all to know that as general manager I intend to respect your expertise *and* your history here. Rest assured, I will—"

"Matthew," Shanna interrupted, losing her patience, "save the acceptance speech for later, okay? We don't have much time, and Trevor and I have some extremely important news." She went to the door and opened it, peeking into the hallway to ensure no one was in the vicinity, then closed it and turned to face us. Locking her fingers together at her waist, as though about to give a formal presentation, she glanced at me for a signal to begin.

I bit my lip and nodded slowly. The realization that Shanna was about to announce that Cynthia Godfrey was a murderer, when only minutes later I intended to stand up and accept her offer of the general manager position, was most distressing. Should I abort her speech before the damage was done?

I stood up. "Shanna, maybe we should wait—"

Shanna held up her hand. "Please, Trevor, allow me." She turned to Sandy and Matthew, who were regarding her intently.

I sat back down, resigned to allowing the day's events to play themselves out without my interference.

"Last night," Shanna said, "Trevor and I had a little movie night at my place. The featured videos were Susan Medley's Christmas party tape and the parkade camera tape, both riveting productions that I highly recommend you watch at the earliest opportunity. They're full of twists and turns and startling revelations, and there's a surprising ending that had Trevor and I on the edge of our seats."

Shanna proceeded to highlight our discoveries and subsequent conversation. Her story was punctuated by cries of disbelief from Sandy and nervous throat-clearing noises from Matthew.

"So," she concluded, glancing at her watch and picking up the pace, "we are certain that Little Miss Peroxide Godfrey murdered her father to secure her inheritance and went to great lengths to cover her tracks—framing us in the process, possibly even intentionally. I called Detective Lim this morning to fill him in and he was *very* interested. Although he didn't divulge anything, I got the distinct impression that his investigation had been heading down a similar path. He did tell me that they had noticed the mystery Jeep Liberty on the tape and have been trying to trace its ownership. He promised to check things out at once."

"I'm shocked," said Sandy. "How could Cynthia murder her own father? What kind of sick—?"

"I knew she did it all along," said Matthew.

"What?" I cried. "You suspected Sandy all along!"

"I certainly did not! I always knew our sweet little Sandy was innocent." Matthew reached across the table and squeezed her hand.

"So did I," said Shanna, smiling at Sandy fondly.

Sandy flashed them an expression of gratitude.

I couldn't believe my ears. If it had been up to them, Sandy would have been locked up two weeks ago.

"So ... what do we now?" asked Matthew.

"We wait," said Shanna. "We go along with whatever she has up her sleeve. We don't want to spook her and cause her to flee. We act as though we suspect nothing at all."

At that moment there were four loud raps on the door. We exchanged frightened glances, as though they were our death knells. We stood up one by one, inhaling deeply.

Matthew went to the door and opened it.

Cynthia Godfrey was standing there. "Matthew," she said with a curt nod, elbowing past him.

"Cynthia. Lovely to see you," Matthew replied in a similar manner.

Cynthia nodded to the rest of us and placed a silver briefcase on the end of the boardroom table. She was dressed in a charcoal-gray pinstripe suit, her blond hair tied back and freshly bleached. Her look was unusually corporate, save for the absence of a blouse or bra beneath the blazer, which was unbuttoned almost to her navel. She looked like a strip-o-gram dressed as a businesswoman.

Someone pushed open the door behind her, and in walked a heavy-set woman I recognized as one of Cynthia's New Year's brunch guests. Roughly fifty years old, she had straight gray hair cut perfectly angular and thick bifocals. A long, gold chain holding a cross hung around her neck. Nudging beside Cynthia, she plunked a tan pleather briefcase on the table and stared at the wall at the opposite end of the room, her expression severe. I knew this must be Debbie Schmidt from ValuLuxe Hotels & Resorts, and I shifted on my feet. Contrary to Cynthia's claim, she did not look like "a totally amazing person." She looked cold and unfriendly.

Cynthia began speaking, a slight tremble in her voice. "As you know," she said, staring down at the table, "my father was in the process

411

of selling the Universe prior to his death. I am here to inform you that the sale is effective immediately."

My colleagues gasped in unison.

"But you promised me you wouldn't!" Matthew cried.

"Your father wasn't *selling* the hotel," Shanna hissed. "He was hiring a management company!"

Cynthia closed her eyes for a moment, as if willing herself to be patient. "This is Mrs. Debbie Schmidt, leader of the transition team and vice president of operations with ValuLuxe Hotels & Resorts."

"*ValuLuxe?*" cried Shanna. "You've *got* to be kidding."

Cynthia stepped back from the table and folded her hands before her, staring down at the floor.

"Good morning, people," said Debbie, her voice deep and no-nonsense. "I represent ValuLuxe Hotels & Resorts, and I'm from our head office in Dallas. As of midnight last night, this hotel is owned and operated by my company. The name has been changed to the ValuLuxe Hotel New York."

"It's not called the Universe anymore?" said Sandy, looking as though she might burst into tears.

"But ValuLuxe is a chain of crappy discount hotels!" Shanna cried.

A thin smile of tolerance passed over Debbie's lips. "ValuLuxe is not a chain of discount hotels but a group of fine hotels that provide luxury at an affordable price. However, this is not your concern. The owners have determined that the present executive committee is not suited to the ValuLuxe brand, vision, and value system. Effective immediately, your positions are terminated."

Sandy gasped.

Shanna clutched her heart.

Matthew mouthed the words "What the *fuck?*"

"I have your letters and final paychecks here," said Debbie, opening her briefcase and withdrawing a stack of envelopes. "Matthew Drummond?"

"Here!" Matthew said, stepping forward like a meek schoolboy and holding out his hand, looking away as though anticipating a strap.

Debbie thrust the envelope into his hand. "Shania Verainy?"

"That's *Shanna Virani*," Shanna said with a huff, marching up to Debbie and snatching the envelope away.

"Sandy James?"

I looked over to Sandy. Her lower lip trembling, eyes blinking, she made her way around the table to take her envelope.

"Susan Medley?" said Debbie.

"She was fired last week," I said when it became apparent Matthew wasn't going to offer any information.

"Very well." She snapped her briefcase shut. "The new executive team will be meeting with all employees this afternoon at 1:00 PM to announce the change in ownership. At that time, we will inform them that you are no longer employed with this hotel. We will extend our gratitude for your service and dedication. You are now required to turn in your communication devices, nametags, and hotel identification. You will be escorted to your offices to collect personal belongings. You are not permitted to make phone calls or to use computers or communication devices. Once you are escorted off-property, you are not authorized to return for at least six months."

"But I *live* here," Matthew said.

Debbie nodded. "We have arranged temporary accommodation for you and your wife at the Plaza Hotel. Movers will be here to pack your belongings later this morning."

Matthew regarded her for a moment, his eyes filled with hatred, then looked down at his letter. Sandy and Shanna were also reading their letters. With no letter of my own, I glanced at Cynthia anxiously, wanting it all to be over as quickly as possibly. She was rubbing her arms and shivering in the corner.

Matthew looked up from his letter. "There must be a mistake. I've been paid only six weeks' severance."

"Me too," Sandy said.

"And me as well," said Shanna, throwing her letter at Debbie. "This is bullshit! Willard Godfrey negotiated options for all executives to stay on for a year or accept a generous severance package that included *a full year's pay.* And he wasn't working with a chain of fleabag hotels. He was working with Shangri-La!"

With the air of a schoolteacher, Debbie Schmidt explained, "You have been paid severance according to employment standards. The sale of this hotel was negotiated by Cynthia Godfrey and her lawyers, not by Willard Godfrey, whom I believe is dead."

"My father never signed the Shangri-La deal," Cynthia piped in.

Debbie grabbed her arm and urged her forward.

Cynthia glanced at her. "Oh yeah, I wanted to thank you. My father always appreciated working with you. But I'm not a hotelier like my father. I hope you understand." She stepped back again.

Shanna stared daggers at her, struggling to keep from lashing out.

Debbie tilted her head to the side and nodded sadly, as though Cynthia had just delivered a heartwarming speech. She pulled her briefcase from the table. "Three gentleman are waiting outside to escort you to your offices, then off-property. Please follow me."

My heart was in my throat by now. I held my breath, silently urging them to go.

Shanna turned to me and frowned. "What about you, Trevor? Where's your letter?"

Sandy and Matthew turned to me too, their expressions puzzled.

"I, uh—" I glanced at Cynthia, then at Debbie. "Um..."

"Trevor Lambert has been asked to stay on," said Debbie. "We plan to appoint him interim general manager and leader of the transition team from the Universe side."

"*What?!*" all three cried in unison.

"You knew about this?" Shanna exclaimed in outrage.

"I... well—"

"You *knew* this was going to happen?" Matthew cried. "And you didn't say a word?"

Even Sandy was glowering. "How could you turn on us like this, Trevor?"

Suddenly I could hear VOID protestors shouting in my ears, "Shame! Shame! Shame!" I gasped and gazed helplessly at my former colleagues, unable to utter a word in my defense.

"Come along, people!" Debbie shouted. "No time for chitchat!" She opened the door and gestured impatiently.

Outside, three grave-looking men in dark suits were waiting.

One by one, Shanna, Sandy, and Matthew filed out, shaking their heads, refusing to look me in the eye. I felt my heart turning inside out. My dear colleagues, my friends, my universe! Would I ever see them again?

Debbie closed the door. "Well! That wasn't too bad, was it?" she said. She reached over the table to offer her hand. It was cold and clammy. "Nice to meet you, Trevor Lambert. I'm very much looking forward to working with you. Now, let's talk turkey." She opened her briefcase and pulled out a thick, legal-size document, sliding it across the table. "Kindly read this and sign on the bottom," she said, glancing at her watch. "We don't have much time."

I looked down at the document. I lifted the pen and glanced at Cynthia. She was so cold now that her entire body was trembling; she looked like a heroin junkie in need of a fix. She nodded at me, looking impatient. I looked over to Debbie, who was watching me intently. Her lips parted into a smile, revealing a set of gray teeth.

I put down the pen. "I'm sorry," I said. "I've made a terrible mistake. This isn't in *my* future. I quit."

I marched out of the room, leaving Cynthia and Debbie staring after me in shock.

A few hours later, Shanna, Matthew, Sandy, and I were sitting in the Oak Bar at the Plaza Hotel, enjoying our newfound freedom and our second martini. At first, they had treated me icily. I apologized profusely, pleading temporary insanity, and they agreed to forgive me. After that, our conversation was spirited, full of proclamations of eternal damnation for Cynthia, vows of revenge against ValuLuxe Hotels, and declarations of lifelong allegiance to one another. But as reality sunk in—it was the beginning of a new year, a Monday morning, and we were out of work in New York City—we grew quiet and pensive.

"I wish that bloody detective would call me back," Shanna said, picking up her cell phone again. "What if Cynthia flees?"

"Why don't I call the hotel to see if I can find out what's going on?" I offered, reaching for my U-Comm. But there was nothing on my belt; my U-Comm was gone, along with my nametag and identification. No longer was I Trevor Lambert, Director of Rooms at the Universe Hotel. My entire identity had been stripped from me. The realization was frightening.

"Here, try this." Shanna handed me her cell phone.

I dialed and waited.

"Good afternoon, the ValuLuxe Hotel New York. How may I help you?"

I almost dropped the phone. "Gaetan Boudreau, please," I muttered, covering the mouthpiece to tell the others what I'd just heard.

"ValuLuxe doesn't waste any time," said Shanna. "They're notorious for hostile takeovers and midnight move-ins. Group firings are their specialty. I've heard stories of them herding three hundred staff into a ballroom and firing them en masse."

Sandy choked on her olive. "Don't tell me that's what they plan to do with *our* staff?"

Gaetan came on the line. I handed the phone to Matthew.

"Gaetan, is Cynthia Godfrey still there?" Matthew asked. "Good. Call us at once if you see her leaving. And if anyone needs us"—his defeated tone suggested this was unlikely—"we're in the Oak Bar at the Plaza." He asked him what was happening at the hotel, listened for a few minutes, and hung up. "The hotel is buzzing with rumors," he told us, "but no one seems to know what's going on. They assumed we'd been fired when those ValuLuxe thugs paraded us across the lobby and out the door like outlaws being run out of town."

"I'm terrified they're going to do the same thing to our staff," said Sandy. "What can we do to stop them?"

I thought of all the employees I had worked with at the Universe over the years. Their jobs were their livelihood. They had mouths at home to feed, college tuition to pay, debts to pay off. How many would be thrown out on the street? Would it have made a difference if I had accepted the position? No, I decided. Likely I would have been forced to do the dirty work, to fire them myself.

"You can be quite sure they'll let go a whole whack of them," said Shanna. "But probably not today. They usually start from the top and work their way down over a period of a few months, weeding out executive staff, then department heads, and finally line staff—whoever they feel won't fit in with their corporate culture."

"I've fired hundreds of people in my career," said Sandy, "but I've never been fired myself. Now I understand what it feels like. I think I hate myself."

A waitress approached our table. "Another round?"

"Why not?" said Matthew. "It's not like we have anything better to do."

Shanna watched her bustle away. "I wonder if they're hiring," she said. "She probably makes more money than the director of sales anyway."

"They're closing this hotel down," Matthew said, "converting it to condos."

"Good riddance." said Shanna. "This place is a dump. Drove me insane when we lost business to it."

"My room hasn't been renovated since the First World War by the looks of it," said Matthew, who had checked in to his new home before joining us.

"I can't imagine working anywhere but the Universe," I said.

"They've done us a favor," Shanna said, sitting upright and sprucing her hair. "Who wants to work for a motel chain?"

"I never cared much for the hotel business," said Matthew. "I might as well tell you now that I've been offered a position as instructor in the Space Program at the University of Tennessee. I've decided to accept it."

"Matthew, that's amazing!" Sandy cried. "I'm so happy for you!"

"Congratulations," Shanna said. "A smart move on your part, I must say. You never showed much aptitude for the hotel industry."

"I can't argue with you there," Matthew said. "If Cynthia had promoted me I planned to accept the position, then, as soon as arrangements were finalized with the university, I was going to tell her to take the job and shove it."

I understood now why Matthew had been so candid about his disdain for the hotel industry; he had no intention of sticking around.

Our drinks arrived. Sandy sipped hers and smiled at everything and everyone in the room, clearly feeling the effects of her third martini. I looked down at her palms and saw that they were fully healed, save for a constellation of tiny scars like pink stars.

"I was planning to resign too," she blurted out.

We regarded her in surprise.

"Jack and I have decided to sell the house and move into an apartment to free up some money," she explained. "We're going to take some time off to focus on our relationship and to spend more time with the kids. It's going to be a challenge financially, but this is more important to us than anything right now, and we'll make do. I'll go back to work part-time in a few months, maybe as a consultant."

"Well," said Shanna, "since it's true confessions time, I might as well tell you that I too have been planning to resign, though not as soon as you—within the next year, I hoped. I'm moving to LA to be closer to my kids. I am going to try and rekindle our relationship. It's far too difficult from this side of the country."

"All of you?" I cried, regarding each of them in turn. "You were all planning to leave the Universe? I gave up a general manager position, my lifelong dream, when *none* of you were planning to stick around?"

"Now, Trevor," said Shanna, "you wouldn't want to work for that horrid company anyway. That Debbie woman is a nightmare; I've heard horror stories about her. You'd be selling your soul. Besides, they wouldn't have kept you on for more than a month or two. They like to keep at least one senior manager around to help with the transition, someone who will help them gain the trust and confidence of staff, then hang him out to dry with the others."

419

Matthew lifted his glass. "I propose a toast to our new lives."

The others cheered and clinked glasses.

But I didn't share their enthusiasm. Unlike them, I didn't have an exit strategy. I had nowhere to go, nothing to do, no friends, no family, nothing here in New York. Last night's conversation with my mother had been hovering over me like a dark cloud all morning.

"I'm going to fly home," I said, surprised by my own words. "I'm going to spend some time with my family." Suddenly I felt a sense of liberty. I could do whatever I wanted now. I was free to make whatever changes I needed. I could refurbish my life.

"Bravo, Trevor!" Shanna cried. "Let's drink to the end of the Universe and the start of a new universe, *our* universe!" She looked at me and winked, and we all clinked glasses and cheered.

"Shanna, there you are!"

A tall, distinguished man hurried across the bar toward us. It took me a moment to recognize Roger Weatherhead, Mr. Godfrey's attorney and good friend. I hadn't seen him since running into him and his wife prior to their cruise.

"Roger!" Shanna exclaimed, rising in her chair. She opened her arms to embrace him. "It's so good to see you! When did you get back?"

"Just last night. I've been looking for you all morning, Shanna. A gentleman at your front desk told me I might find you here."

Shanna's hand moved to her heart. "Have you heard the terrible news?"

Roger nodded, his face grim. "I'm still in shock. There were a half-dozen messages waiting for us when we got back. Poor Katherine hasn't stopped crying."

"Tell her to call me and we'll talk," Shanna said. She turned to us. "Have you met my colleagues?"

"Yes, I believe I have."

We stood up to shake hands.

Roger pulled up a chair and sat down, placing a manila folder on the table. He glanced at our drinks. "Martinis on a Monday afternoon? So this is life after Godfrey? I want to work for you too, Shanna."

"We don't work at the Universe anymore," Shanna said. "We were fired this morning."

"Fired?" cried Roger. "How could that be?"

"Cynthia sold the hotel," Matthew said. "The new owners let us go."

"That's impossible," said Roger, picking up the envelope and tearing it open. "Shanna, do you remember when we all had dinner together, the night before Katherine and I left?"

Shanna nodded slowly. "Yes."

Roger withdrew a sheet of stationary and handed it to her. "I guess Willard never got a chance to tell you. After you went home, we stayed in Orbit and had a long discussion. He loved you so much, Shanna. He was worried about Cynthia. Since he cut her off, she had been acting strange, almost psychopathic, and had threatened him with violence on several occasions. He knew she was furious about your plans to elope. He asked me to help him draft a new will. Katherine witnessed it. I was supposed to meet with him the next morning for breakfast—I still needed his signature on the Shangri-La management contract—but he didn't show up, so I put all the papers in the hotel's safe deposit box. Cynthia can't possibly go through with the sale, Shanna."

"But why?"

"Because Godfrey left you the Universe."

23

The Big Crunch

While Roger went to his office to contact the attorneys representing Cynthia Godfrey and ValuLuxe Hotels, Shanna, Matthew, Sandy, and I hurried back to the Universe.

Jerome from security was guarding the front door.

"Sorry, I can't let you in," he said, crossing his arms defiantly. "They said I'd be fired if I did."

"You have to!" Shanna cried, bullying him. "I insist! Now get out of our way!"

Matthew stepped forward, speaking through his teeth. "Jerome, I'm warning you, if you don't—"

But Sandy elbowed Matthew and Shanna out of the way. "Please, Jerome," she pleaded, regarding him directly in the eye and flashing a sweet smile. "We need your help. We're here to stop this hotel from being sold illegally. Could you just turn your back for a minute and let us slip in, please?"

Jerome swallowed hard. He glanced over his shoulder. "Okay, but I never saw you." He stepped aside.

Thanking him profusely, we hurried in.

I stopped to ask Jerome if Cynthia Godfrey was still around.

"She's in the ballroom, I think," he replied.

Inside, the lobby was quiet. Most employees were gathered in Jupiter Ballroom, leaving a skeleton staff to run the hotel. Across the lobby, I saw the last few employees trickle into the ballroom. The great doors swung closed.

Shanna picked up her cell phone and called Detective Lim again.

Sandy whispered, "What do we do now?"

"Let's split up," I said. "Matthew—you and Shanna can wait here for the police. Sandy and I will go to the ballroom to keep an eye on Cynthia."

Shanna stuffed her phone into her purse, her eyes bulging. "I just talked to Detective Lim. He said they got a search warrant for Cynthia's townhouse this morning. Guess what they found in her basement? A big iron globe wrapped in a bloody trench coat." She buried her face in her hands.

Sandy went to her and held her.

"My god," Matthew remarked, turning to me. "Cynthia's even dumber than I thought."

Shanna composed herself. "The police are on their way. We better get to our posts."

Sandy and I hurried across the lobby toward Jupiter Ballroom. As I passed the Center of the Universe, I glanced inside and was surprised to see Brenda Rathberger sitting by herself. I recalled that today was her scheduled day of departure. Not wanting her to see me, I looked away and kept walking.

Sandy and I slipped into Jupiter Ballroom.

Over six hundred employees were gathered in the ballroom. The room was buzzing. Heads turned in surprise at the sight of Sandy and me. People whispered our names. Onstage, Cynthia Godfrey was standing near the podium, preparing to speak. Behind her, four chairs were occupied by Debbie Schmidt and three of her colleagues. Before they could spot us, Sandy and I hurried to seat ourselves, Sandy veering right and I left. A few rows down the aisle, I ducked into a seat and slid down, trying to look inconspicuous.

"Hey," said a deep voice next to me.

I froze and turned slowly in my chair.

Gaetan Boudreau was grinning at me. "Glad to see you back, Trevor. I hope you're here to put an end to this nonsense."

"I'll try my best."

Onstage, Cynthia coughed into the microphone. "Good afternoon, everyone. I'm—well, I think most of you know who I am. I'm Cynthia Godfrey, daughter of Willard Godfrey."

There were a few claps in the audience, notably from the chairs on the stage behind her.

With an embarrassed laugh, Cynthia continued. "We have some exciting announcements for you today. I, uh, I guess I'll get right to it ... okay. So. As per my father's wishes, the Universe Hotel has been sold."

There were gasps in the audience.

Cynthia looked down and read from her notes in a monotone voice. "The hotel has been purchased by ValuLuxe Hotels & Resorts. Effective immediately, I no longer own this hotel nor do I have any association with it whatsoever. I would like to thank all of you for your hard work. My father loved you very much and couldn't have run this great hotel without you. Now I'd like to introduce to you Mrs. Debbie Schmidt, vice president of operations with ValuLuxe Hotels & Resorts and leader of the transition team."

The room was dead silent as Debbie stood up and made her way to the podium.

Cynthia stepped down from the stage and stood off to the side, against the wall.

"Hello, all you fine people," Debbie said, putting on her glasses and flashing a crooked smile. "We are excited to share a few of the changes we have in store for this magnificent hotel. There will be wonderful opportunities for all of you. First, I would like to inform you that this hotel is no longer called the Universe Hotel. It is called the ValuLuxe Hotel New York. The Universe Hotel name is in the process of being removed from all signage, stationery, and promotional material. You are forbidden to use any name other than the ValuLuxe Hotel New York from this point forward. Violation of this rule will result in discipline up to dismissal."

There were murmurs of discord in the ballroom. Heads turned toward me. I could only shrug helplessly. Afraid of attracting further attention, I shrunk down in my seat.

"As I'm sure you will understand," said Debbie, her tone softening, "a change in ownership means a change in executive management. We have therefore accepted the resignation of your executive management committee: Matthew Drummond, Shanna Virani, Sandy James, and Trevor Lambert."

Cries of disbelief broke out across the room. More heads turned in my direction. Up ahead to the right I saw Sandy sitting among a group of housekeeping staff, her blond hair rising up from a sea of black, looking highly conspicuous. I prayed she wouldn't be spotted by the ValuLuxe people.

"We would like to thank these individuals for their hard work and dedication," Debbie continued, "and we wish them the best of success in the future. Now I would like to introduce you to your new executive team. First, it gives me immense pleasure to introduce your new general manager. This brilliant, dynamic gentleman is a relative newcomer to the hotel industry, having moved from a prominent funeral chain in Arkansas to ValuLuxe Hotels & Resorts' headquarters in

Dallas as chief financial officer just two years ago. He has an impressive reputation for whipping money-losing companies into shape. We are confident he will work these wonders with this hotel. Ladies and gentlemen, I am delighted to introduce Mr. Edward Jonestown."

A bald-headed, hunched-over man rose from his chair and made his way laboriously across the stage with the use of a cane. He looked to be at least seventy-five years old, possibly as old as eighty, and moved not half as quickly as the spry old Mr. Godfrey.

Debbie walked back to the group of ValuLuxe executives and whispered something to them, pointing in Sandy's direction. The two males stood up abruptly and hurried down from the stage, marching toward Sandy. I saw her slink down in her seat, but in seconds they were on her. A struggle ensued involving a half-dozen room attendants who formed a protective barrier around her. The men proved stronger than they looked. They pushed the attendants away and lifted Sandy from her chair, dragging her up the aisle.

"Good afternoon, all you fine people," Edward Jonestown said from the podium, his voice laced with a thick southern drawl. "How y'all doing? I know you've experienced a whole lotta changes these past two weeks, but I'm here to tell you things are gonna get better from this day forward. We're gonna bring some real Southern, no-nonsense hospitality to this hotel..."

Craning my head, I saw the two men reenter the ballroom and scout the rest of the room. Onstage, Debbie was pointing in my direction. I leapt to my feet and scrambled up the aisle and out the door.

Outside, I searched frantically for somewhere to hide. Shanna and Matthew were no longer in the front lobby, and Sandy was nowhere to be seen. I spotted Brenda Rathberger in the lounge. Behind me, the ballroom door swung open and Debbie rushed out, her eyes searching the lobby. Two of her colleagues spilled out behind her. I sprinted toward Brenda and dove onto the sofa next to her.

Brenda shrieked.

"Shhh!" I cried, burrowing into the sofa to hide.

"You scared the life out of me, Trevor! What on earth—?"

"Don't let them see me!"

"Who? Honica Winters?"

"No. The ValuLuxe people. Is Honica still here?"

"She's around here somewhere. We had breakfast together, in fact. You'll be happy to know we've resolved our differences."

"How nice for you. Is a heavyset gray-haired woman with glasses lurking around out there?"

"Yes. She's heading toward the front door."

"Don't let her or the men in dark suits see me." I turned over onto my back and tucked my hands behind my head to make myself comfortable, thinking I might be there for a while. "And tell me if you see Cynthia Godfrey come out of the ballroom," I said.

"Aren't you a bit old to be playing hide-and-seek?" She reached for a punch glass on the table and slurped it down, suppressing a burp. "This Astronomical Punch is so tasty!" She set the glass down and wiped her mouth with the back of her hand. "I'm glad you dropped by, Trevor. I went looking for you at the front desk this morning, but they said you were off. I wanted to apologize. I've been such a cow. While I was in jail, I had some time to reflect. I've been under a great deal of stress, as you know. There were many, many problems with the conference, but I suppose I can't blame them all on you."

I turned on my side, facing her, pleased to hear her finally accept some blame. "Thank you, Brenda."

"It's all the board's fault. *They're* the ones who made me book the conference here. They should have trusted my instincts. Of course, now *I'm* the scapegoat. The chairman fired me this morning."

"He didn't."

She nodded. "He said I'm too radical for their tastes. He didn't like the fact that I started a riot and was thrown in jail. Yet my actions got him exactly the results he's been demanding all along: the riot was featured on news programs across the country. Thanks to me, Victims of Impaired Drivers attracted more media attention than MADD could *ever* hope for." She sighed. "I make no apologies for my passion. I've worked my *ass* off for this organization, night and day and right through Christmas and New Year's, for six years straight. And this is how they thank me." She huffed. "I hate those bastards on the board, all of them!"

The server, Alexandra, arrived at the table and gave me a strange look. "You okay, Trevor? Can I get you anything?"

"I'm not here."

"Whatever you say." She turned to Brenda. "How about you, Mrs. Rathberger? More punch?"

"Don't mind if I do."

"Another double shot of rum?"

"Please."

As Alexandra hurried off, I shot up in my seat and regarded Brenda. "You're *drinking?*"

She sighed. "Yes, Trevor, I'm drinking. I haven't had a drop of booze in almost two decades, but I've been craving one since the day I set foot in this cursed hotel. After all I've gone through these past two weeks, I've earned a drink. So don't go judging me—you, of all people! Don't think I can't smell booze on you now—again! You might want to get some help for your little problem, Trevor. As for me, I'll be back on the wagon tomorrow. Booze and I are like gas and matches. Put them together and *boom!*" She threw her hands out.

I glanced at her drink. "Then maybe you shouldn't ..."

"Don't tell me what I should or shouldn't do!" she roared, her eyes flashing ferociously. "I can do whatever I goddamned want!"

I lifted my hands in surrender. "All right. I'm sorry." Suddenly regretting my choice of hiding place, I lifted my head and looked around. Debbie was still patrolling the lobby, along with one of her colleagues. I was stuck here for now. I collapsed back down. "So what will you do now?" I asked Brenda.

She shrugged. "Who knows? Work was my life. I'm nothing without it. I have nowhere to go."

"I know the feeling."

"Yeah, you seem like a hard worker too. We have more in common than you might think, you and I. We're both passionate about our work, perfectionists, and extremely dedicated."

Except you're crazy and I'm not, I thought.

Alexandra dropped off another Astronomical Punch for Brenda, and she dove for it.

"Your cause is so much more worthy than mine," I said. "You're saving lives. I'm fluffing pillows. Despite your questionable tactics, I really do admire you, Brenda."

"No, you don't!" she barked. "You think I'm a fraud!"

"No. Honestly, I think—"

"I *am* a fraud! Nothing but a lying fraud!"

I recoiled. So this was what she meant by gas and matches.

"Wanna know why I got into this industry?" she yelled. "Wanna know why? *Really* why?"

I was quite sure I didn't.

"Because of *guilt*, that's why!" she answered for me. "Twenty years ago I was broke, single, and depressed. I had nothing to live for, and I was incapacitated by guilt over my past. All I did was drink. It was the only thing that eased the pain. One day a minister at church got fed up with my self-pitying and said, 'Brenda, why don't you volunteer for an anti-impaired driving organization? Maybe you'll find redemption.' So I got a job fundraising for MADD. I discovered I had a knack. After that, I started putting my life back together. I stopped drinking. Getting involved in this industry was the best thing that ever happened to me. It gave me a sense of purpose. A while later, I left MADD and started up VOID. There's been no turning back since then."

I was relieved to see that she had calmed down. "Did you find redemption?" I asked timidly, afraid of setting her off again.

She was quiet for a moment. "As a matter of fact, I did. I never talk about this, Trevor; no one knows the real story. But now that I've been fired, I suppose I don't have to keep it secret anymore. Remember how I told you a drunk teenage girl killed my husband?"

"Yes."

"Well, that drunk teenage girl was me."

I stared at her, speechless.

"Frederick and I had been married only one year when it happened. We didn't have much money, but we adored one another and he treated me like a princess. On the night of our anniversary, he took me to a restaurant in the fanciest hotel in Denver. I had the best meal of my life. We were celebrating, so we had lots to drink: a cocktail each and a bottle of champagne before dinner, a bottle of wine with dinner, and coffee with liqueurs at dessert. When we finished, Frederick asked the waiter to have the valet bring up his car. We stumbled outside, giggling and fooling around, and the young valet—he couldn't have been older than sixteen—handed Frederick the keys and accepted his tip. We got into the car. Frederick leaned over and gave me a big, long kiss and told me he loved me, that he hoped we would be together forever."

Brenda paused and sipped her punch. "On the highway, I kept teasing Frederick and tickling him. He was laughing and tickling me back. I tried to get my hand under his shirt to pull at his chest hairs, but he kept slapping my hands away. I bolstered my efforts and climbed on top of him while he was driving. We thought we were invincible back then. I didn't realize I had blocked his view. He drove right into an oncoming truck."

She turned to look at me, her eyes wide, as though reliving the accident. "Frederick died instantly. The driver of the other truck, a thirty-two-year-old farmer and father of four young children, died too. A small fire started in the engine of Frederick's car. The car was so banged up I was trapped. It took emergency personnel almost an hour to get me out. That's how I got these scars." She pointed to her face. "I wear lots of makeup and bronzing lotion to cover them up."

I realized then that her blotchy complexion was more than just a fading tan. I wanted to take her hand and pull her toward me, to hold her. But she had wrapped her own arms around herself as she spoke, binding herself up tight, leaving no room for me to get in.

"I'm sorry, Brenda," I said.

She released her arms and reached for her drink. "Do you understand now why I'm so distrustful of fancy hotels? That hotel in Denver empowered a sixteen-year-old boy to hand us our keys, to make a decision that led to the death of my husband and another man, that destroyed my life and the lives of that man's four children, his wife, and the rest of his family. Of course, Frederick and I share the greatest responsibility. But hotels and restaurants must stop being enablers.

I simply cannot stand by and allow these things to reoccur over and over again. Do you understand, Trevor?"

"I understand."

She drained her drink and set it down. "Sorry to unload on you like that."

"Not at all."

"Cynthia just left the ballroom."

I lifted my head and peeked over the sofa. Cynthia was standing outside the doors, looking around, her face anxious. I crouched down again.

"I'm not fond of that young lady," said Brenda. "When I saw her at the car rental counter at the airport I thought I recognized her from *People* magazine, but I couldn't be sure. She was giving the agent such a hard time, something to do with damage to her vehicle, and caused such a fuss that even I was embarrassed. The poor young agent kept calling her Miss Roberts, so I thought I was mistaken—until I saw her here."

"You saw her at the airport? At a *car rental* counter?"

"I thought I told you already. Speaking of which"—she glanced at her watch—"Oh my! My flight departs in less than two hours! I better get going." She jumped to her feet and opened her purse, fumbling around for her wallet, and almost fell back down.

I reached up to steady her. "Drinks are on me."

"Why, thank you, Trevor."

"You need a taxi?" I asked, forgetting that these things were no longer my concern.

"No. I'm all set."

I signed the bill to my promo account and got up with her, thinking I'd better get out of there before the server realized my signing privileges had been canceled. I reached out to shake Brenda's hand. "Friends?"

"Best friends," she said. "Come visit me in Colorado sometime."

"Maybe I will." I watched her wobble across the lounge toward the front door, then turned to look for Cynthia. She was still lurking around the entrance to Jupiter, pacing back and forth, apparently waiting for the meeting to break. I decided to head to the front door to see if Detective Lim had arrived.

Outside, Matthew, Shanna, and Sandy were standing at the foot of the driveway, watching anxiously as a team of workers took down the Universe Hotel sign. On the pavement beside them was a large neon ValuLuxe Hotel sign. I was making my way toward them when I heard someone call out my name. I turned around.

Honica Winters was standing at the entrance, holding Rasputin in one arm and a carry-on in the other. A pink bow was tied to the dog's head. "I'm leaving now, sweetie," she called out to me. "Thanks for everything!" She hurried up to me and smooched my cheek. "Is that Matthew down there?"

"Yes, but he's not really—" But she was already on her way down the driveway. "Careful!" I called out to her, eyeing her spiked pumps. "It's icy!"

No sooner had I said this than Honica's feet flew out from under her. Rasputin pounced out of her hands, landing on the pavement with a yelp. Honica hit next. Then the suitcase landed, bursting open, its contents flying in all directions.

I hurried over to help her to her feet.

Matthew rushed up the driveway and stooped down to gather up her belongings.

Honica was furious. "Fucking driveway! Fucking hazard! Fucking hotel! I could have *broken* my leg! I have half a mind to sue, Trevor.

433

Where's my puppy? Rasputie? Come here, baby! You poor little thing!"

Rasputin was nosing through her belongings. His jaw clamped onto a big white towel, and he dragged it down the driveway.

"Rasputie, no!" Honica cried. "Get back here this instant!"

He trotted back up the driveway and circled around us, letting the towel fall at Matthew's feet.

Matthew crouched down to pick it up. "Honica, is this one of the hotel's towels?" He turned it over, revealing the hotel logo stitched into the seam.

"How'd that get in there?" Honica cried. "Rasputin! Bad dog, bad!"

"And this?" said Matthew, squatting down to pull a bathrobe stitched with the Universe logo from the pile.

Honica crouched down to pick up Rasputin by the scruff of his neck, holding him in front of her face and waving a finger. "Rasputin, how many times have I told you not to steal other people's belongings?"

"Shall we charge them to your account?" Matthew asked wryly.

"What? No! I don't even want those crappy things," Honica said. "Take them. Bad little dog!"

Rasputin growled at her.

There was a honk from the top of the driveway. I looked up to see a red SUV parked at the front door.

"That's my ride," said Honica, lifting her hand to wave. "I'll be right there!" She turned to Matthew. "Listen, I'm hoping to come back in a week or so to do a follow-up story on the Godfrey case. This time I want to focus on Cassandra James, how on the outside she's this happy-go-lucky hotel executive, but on the inside she's a ruthless killer." She didn't notice Sandy coming up from behind. "I'm thinking of a 'Victim or Vixen?' theme, where viewers wonder if she really did it until the very end, then we show her behind bars. I assume she'll be arrested by then, if police ever get off their fat asses and solve this case. So what do you say?" She slapped Matthew on the back. "Can you put me up for a few nights? I'll need a suite, of course, since I'll have interviews and paperwork to do, and I'm hoping you can …" She noticed Sandy standing beside her, and her voice trailed off.

Matthew turned to regard Sandy, then looked back at Honica. His eyes were fierce. "Honica?"

"Yes?" said Honica, eyes fluttering.

"Why don't you just go … just go … f-fu—" He stopped. "Why don't you go find your own accommodation," he said. "You're not welcome at the Universe anymore."

Sandy stepped in front of Honica so that they were eye to eye. "And while you're at it, why don't you go fuck yourself, Honica Winters."

Honica's jaw dropped. "Why, I never! How rude! Come on, Rasputin. Let's get out of here. We don't need these people. We'll stay at the Four Seasons from now on. They appreciate us there, don't they?"

Rasputin whined as Honica marched up the driveway.

I hurried after her, intending to go back into the lobby to check on Cynthia. Then I noticed who was sitting in the driver's seat of the red Nissan Xterra parked there, and I halted.

It was Brenda Rathberger.

Honica was climbing into the passenger's seat of the SUV.

I banged on Brenda's window.

She rolled it down. "Hi, Trevor. What's up?"

"You're *driving?*"

"I, uh, well … the truck's only insured in my name, and I need to return it."

In the passenger's seat, Honica sniffed. "I smell booze." She turned to Brenda. "You haven't been drinking?" Her eyes grew wide.

Brenda covered her mouth and suppressed a burp. "Maybe you should drive, Honey."

There was a loud honk behind us. A NYPD cruiser sped up the driveway, lights flashing, and came to a screeching halt behind Brenda's truck. Detective Lim and his partner jumped out.

Just then, Cynthia came rushing out of the hotel. When she saw the police car, she turned and ran back into the lobby.

"I'll go after her!" Matthew yelled, rushing up the driveway. Shanna hurried after him.

Within seconds, Shanna came running back out. "She took the elevator to the parkade!"

"You go down to the parkade," Detective Lim shouted to his partner. "I'll head her off at the top of the ramp." He jumped back into the cruiser and leaned out the window. "Get that truck out of my way!"

I turned to Brenda, who had undone her seatbelt and was about to climb out. "There's no time!" I cried. "Pull out now! You can switch drivers on the street."

Brenda froze, eyes bulging in panic.

Behind us, Detective Lim laid on the horn. "Move! *Now!* Police orders!"

"Here she comes!" Sandy cried, pointing at the parking ramp.

Cynthia's Mini Cooper was charging up the ramp, tires squealing.

Brenda started the truck and gunned the engine. The vehicle lurched into motion and rocketed down the driveway. Cynthia's car reached the top of the ramp and fishtailed onto Avenue of the Americas.

Brenda's truck was heading directly into its path.

"Watch out!" I shouted.

It was too late.

The Xterra crashed into the Cooper, causing an ear-splitting crunch of metal and glass.

24

A New Universe

Six months later, Sandy, Shanna, Matthew, and I gathered at Vandenberg Air Force Base just outside Santa Barbara, California, for the launching of Mr. Godfrey's remains into space.

Only a symbolic portion was to be sent up, about seven grams of powdered Godfrey encased in an aluminum capsule similar to a lipstick container. It would be accompanied by forty-nine similar containers, each bearing the partial remains of men and women who had paid the Final Journey Corporation scads of money to make space their final resting place. Mr. Godfrey and his fellow passengers would orbit in space on board the miniature spacecraft for up to ten years before gravity and physics pulled the capsule back toward earth. Upon entering the atmosphere, the capsule would burn up like a shooting star, sending the dust floating back to earth.

The rest of Mr. Godfrey's remains were buried in a cemetery in Southampton, next to his daughter, Cynthia, and his wife, Margaret.

The blast-off was somewhat anti-climactic, little more exciting than watching a teenage boy send a homemade rocket flying into the neighbor's garden, except that this rocket shot straight upward in a cloud of smoke and fire and kept going until it disappeared into the clear blue sky.

"Farewell, Mr. Godfrey," Sandy called out.

"Rest in peace, my love," said Shanna, waving a handkerchief in the air.

Matthew only gulped. Perhaps he was reliving his own launch experience.

I had long since come to terms with the death of Willard Godfrey and no longer resented him for making plans to transfer management of the hotel to another company without telling me. That Shanna had honored his intentions and bestowed the three of us—Sandy, Matthew, and I—with close to a year's salary helped me to forgive him and granted me time to ponder my next career move. Now, nothing but fond memories of Mr. Godfrey remained. I knew that no matter where I went in my career, I would take with me everything he taught me. His death had forced us to step outside of our lives, to reevaluate our priorities, to question why we measured our self-worth by our jobs. Now, six months later, we were all in a better place.

After the launch, as the late afternoon sun began its descent, we drove back to the ValuLuxe Santa Barbara Resort to say our goodbyes. Sandy and I were spending the night at the hotel before flying home—she to New York and I to Vancouver—and Shanna and Matthew were leaving that evening, Shanna to Los Angeles to see her son and daughter, and Matthew to West Hollywood for "a bit of fun" before returning to Tennessee.

The valet brought up Shanna's rented Jaguar convertible, and we took turns hugging her goodbye before she climbed into her car.

"You need directions?" I asked Shanna, leaning over the door.

"Always the host," Shanna said with a smile, donning a pair of oversized Prada sunglasses. "Thanks, darling, but I know exactly where I'm going." She reached for a book on the passenger's seat and held it up. "Have any of you seen this yet? It came out last week." It was a copy of *Borderline Nuts,* Honica Winters' tell-all about the zany, cutthroat broadcast journalism industry.

None of us had.

"Is it any good?" Sandy asked.

Shanna turned her thumb down. "The *New York Times* calls it 'as deep as a teenager's diary and half as interesting'—and they were being generous. NBC executives are not amused, either. An entire chapter is dedicated to the Godfrey case. It's a fascinating read, but I'm sorry to say that none of us come out smelling like roses. Fortunately, most of her wrath is reserved for Brenda Rathberger."

"Likely Honica hasn't forgiven her for that horrific accident," Matthew said. "Poor little Rasputie. He'll never pee on a hotel carpet again."

"How is Mrs. Rathberger, anyway?" Sandy asked. "Has anyone kept tabs on her?"

"I have," I said. "She and I have become friends, in a strange sort of way. She's almost fully recovered from her injuries, but she'll always need a cane. Her case goes to trial in a couple of months. She's hoping the judge will be lenient in light of her anti-impaired driving work. She and two girlfriends are about to launch a new organization called Spouses Against Drunk Driving, or SADD. She says they plan to take a less radical, more conciliatory approach, but I'm not sure that's in her nature."

"From MADD to VOID to SADD," said Shanna. "The poor woman is destined to be miserable all her life. Couldn't she have created an acronym like FUN?"

"I don't think 'FUN' quite captures the tragic consequences of drunk driving," Sandy said in a scolding tone. Her court-ordered sentence to complete 250 hours of community work with Mothers

Against Drunk Driving had turned her into quite an anti-impaired driving advocate.

"I suppose not," said Shanna. She turned to me. "I meant to ask you, Trevor, how is your mother?"

"Much better now," I said. "She's still recovering from chemo, but the doctor says the cancer is all gone—for now, at least. She's in a state of absolute rapture over Nancy and me having moved to Vancouver. I'm afraid we'll come home to find she's converted our second bedroom into a nursery. We just bought a condo, and now that her energy is returning she's intent on refurbishing it while we're in Europe."

The night after the attempted ValuLuxe takeover, I called Nancy to ask her out. Over dinner she confessed that she had harbored a secret crush on me for quite some time, but was disturbed by the amount of time I spent at work. The next day I flew home to spend time with Mom, and when I returned I convinced Nancy to move to Vancouver with me. We'd spent almost every day together since.

Shanna pushed her sunglasses over her forehead and squinted at me. "Don't tell me you're settling in Vancouver permanently?"

I shrugged. "Maybe."

I didn't tell her that I'd just accepted a job managing a hotel in Vancouver. I hadn't even told Nancy yet. My new job would start as soon as we returned from our vacation.

Shanna studied me for a moment. "You know, I met with a headhunter the other day to see what kind of job prospects there are for me in LA. The sale of the Universe promises to make me scandalously rich, but I'm not about to retire. He told me about a fabulous new boutique hotel in Hollywood called Hotel Cinema. He asked if I might be interested in the director of sales and marketing position. He also inquired about candidates for general manager. I thought of you immediately. He was quite disappointed to learn you've retired from the hotel industry."

"He was interested in *me?*" I said, flattered.

She nodded eagerly. "It's going to be very stylish and hip, but the owner wants a more conservative type to manage it, someone like you with traditional hotel training and extensive operations experience."

"Someone vapid," I said.

Shanna smirked. "I told him I wasn't interested, but if you were in charge I might change my mind. Wouldn't it be fun to work together again? They're sparing no expense in building this hotel, and they're already planning splashy, star-studded launch party."

I nodded slowly, breaking into a grin. "Sounds intriguing."

"*Trevor,*" Sandy said, clearly distraught, "you told me the hotel business wasn't for you anymore."

"Don't be silly," said Shanna. "He was *born* to manage hotels. Trevor, darling, I know I told you at Christmastime to get out of the industry while you can, but those were the words of a grieving, embittered woman. Now that I've reconnected with my children, I don't regret my life for a second. One simply needs to find balance. You can't possibly pass up a life of travel and adventure at this young age."

I glanced at Sandy. She was leaning back against Shanna's car, arms crossed, a disapproving expression on her face. I turned to look for Matthew, curious to know his thoughts, but he had wandered off to chat up the handsome young doorman.

Shanna reached into her purse and handed me a business card. "When you get back from Europe, at least give him a call and hear what he has to say."

I took the card and slipped it inside my pocket.

Shanna gunned her engine, causing Sandy to jump away from the car. "Farewell, my friends. Keep in touch!"

I watched her car disappear down the road into a cloud of dust.

Matthew sauntered over. "I've decided to stay in Santa Barbara for dinner," he said, glancing over at the doorman, who was staring down at his feet. "It's such a handsome town, I hate to leave."

"So you and Gaetan are finished?" Sandy asked.

Matthew nodded. "He dumped me the second I told him I was moving to Tennessee. Can't blame him, really. I don't think there are more than a handful of homos in the entire state. I'm becoming so desperate I've started to ogle women again."

"How *is* Marline?" I asked.

"Oh, fine. We've become quite close again, if you can believe it. She's still in New York, pursuing her acting career. In fact, she just landed the role of Blanche DuBois in a modern-day adaptation of *A Streetcar Named Desire*. Talk about typecasting!" He chuckled, then let out a heavy sigh. "Well, I think I'll go inside and have a drink while I wait for Justin to get off. Care to join me?"

"No, thanks," I said, taking Sandy's hand. "We're going for a walk."

We said our goodbyes, and Sandy and I made our way around to the rear of the hotel, where a path lined with palm trees meandered through a verdant garden. We walked in silence until we came to a white gazebo that appeared to be a small wedding chapel, and sat down on a bench next to it. I sneaked a sidelong glance at the gazebo, which seemed old-fashioned and quaint but somehow claustrophobic. Darkness had descended upon the hotel grounds, and above us the moon was bright and almost full. One by one the stars were blinking on.

"They look like the star lights at the Universe, don't they?" said Sandy.

I murmured my agreement, but in my eyes they couldn't have looked more different. On my last visit to the hotel, I had stopped for a drink in the Center of the Universe, and everything had seemed smaller to me, less awe-inspiring. The star lights had lost their sparkle; they seemed artificial and illusory, like a gaudy Vegas display. Tonight, the stars in this universe were real and wondrous, infinite in number and glimmering with hope and possibility.

I put my arm around Sandy. "How's everything in your world?" I asked.

"Wonderful," she said. "Between my volunteer work at MADD and consulting for Shanna, it's enough. The rest of my world revolves around Jack and the kids. I couldn't be happier." She turned to me and broke into a smile. "And I truly mean it this time."

"I'm so glad," I said. Her smile was different tonight; less forced, more natural. In the light of the moon, she was even more beautiful than I remembered.

"And you, Trevor, are you happy?"

I turned to look up at the sky again and pondered the question. A shooting star appeared to my left and began traveling slowly across the sky. I watched it in awe for a moment, then realized it was an airplane. "I can't wait to get back to Vancouver," I said. "I can't wait to see Nancy again, and to spend time with my mother and my sisters and my nieces and nephews. So yes, I suppose I'm happy."

"Then you've found your universe?"

I watched the plane float gently downward, heading toward the Los Angeles airport, where it would unload its passengers, refuel and reload, and take off again. "Part of it, yes," I said. "A big part, but not all. I think Shanna's right. I was born to manage hotels. But something tells me I'll always be a lonely traveler in life, searching for my place in the universe, the consummate host who never quite finds his own home."

THE END

Acknowledgments

Thank you to Carrie, Bonnie, and Suzanne for your feedback and encouraging words, to Christof for your understanding and support, to Mom for your brilliant editing, and to my agent, Jodie Rhodes, for believing in this novel.

About the Author

Daniel Edward Craig began his career in the hotel industry in Toronto in 1987, and has since worked for eight luxury hotels in Canada.

Originally intending to pursue diplomatic service, he has studied international relations, modern languages, film, screenwriting, and acting.

Currently, Mr. Craig is the general manager of Opus Hotel in Vancouver, famous for the celebrities that frequent it. Under his leadership, Opus has gained an international reputation for exemplary service, cutting-edge marketing, and unique design.

In his leisure time, he likes to keep in shape both physically and mentally. He travels extensively, being particularly passionate about hotels, having stayed in—and managed—some of the best in the world.

Read on for a sneak peek at

Murder at Hotel Cinema

★ ★ ★ ★ ★

A FIVE-STAR MYSTERY

by

Daniel Edward Craig

Opening night at Hotel Cinema.

I stood on the periphery of the pool deck, enjoying a moment of peace in the warm summer air. Everywhere I looked I saw famous faces and beautiful people, the jet set of Hollywood. They were crowded around the pool deck, spilling out of the cabana rooms, wall-to-wall in the restaurant, dancing around the DJ booth in the lounge. What a change from three days ago, when the city inspector had arrived to find little more than a dusty construction site. By some miracle—or perhaps money had exchanged hands—Tony Cavalli, the son of the hotel's owner, had finagled an occupancy permit. When he made the announcement, an enormous cheer had erupted from staff. Then exhilaration quickly turned to panic. Only seventy-two hours remained to prepare for a full house and a splashy, star-studded opening party.

Yet somehow we made it. Now, catching my reflection on the surface of the swimming pool, I detected a glimmer of satisfaction in my eyes. There was even a trace of—what was it again?—oh yes, happiness—or at least the memory of happiness. This was my third opening, the first as general manager. Inevitably, it's a chaotic experience rife with impossible deadlines, delayed furniture and equipment, incompetent contractors, overbearing owners, and overstressed employees. And all this even before the guests arrived bringing a new set of challenges. The guests were here now, and much work remained to be done. But tonight was a time to celebrate. My core management team was solid, and I was feeling hopeful about the future. The hotel, a costly renovation of a motel on Hollywood Boulevard destroyed by fire in the seventies, was ultra-luxurious and small: 124 rooms with modern, stylish décor. Surveying the crowd around me, I knew it was going to be hot. And I was living in Los Angeles, where the weather was sunny, the people were gorgeous, I drove a convertible BMW, and all my troubles were behind me. Life was good.

And then the moment was gone.

Tony Cavalli lumbered across the pool deck toward me, a pissed-off expression on his face. "Where the hell is she?" he demanded.

"Who?"

"You know who. Chelsea Fricks. She's goddamned late."

"She's not here?" I asked, feigning surprise, even though I, like most of the guests, was keeping a vigilant eye out for her. I glanced up at Penthouse Suite 1. Five floors up, it occupied the southwest corner of the U-shaped building, overlooking the far end of the swimming pool. The balcony walls on each level were made of smoked glass and underlit by red lighting. "I don't see much life up there."

"I'll kill her if she doesn't show," Tony said, also regarding the suite. He caressed his black goatee nervously, eyes blazing, fueled by his manic personality and, I suspected, copious amounts of cocaine. He was stylishly dressed tonight, almost handsome. His soft, round belly and bull neck were concealed beneath a tailored black Versace suit with elaborate swirls of purple stitching on the lapels. His shirt, like his teeth, was impossibly white, reflecting a soft orange glow from the fire basins at the corners of the pool deck. Clearly, his girlfriend Liz Welch, the hotel's interior designer, had dressed him. "It's 11:15," he said, checking his Cartier watch. "People are getting antsy. If she doesn't show up soon, we're gonna lose them."

Officially, the party had started at 8:00 PM. But this being Los Angeles, for the first hour servers had stood around holding trays of champagne and staring at one other across an empty room. In the meantime, hotel guests arrived one after another in limousines and luxury cars, many of them local residents eager to be the first to experience the much-anticipated Hotel Cinema. By 9:00 PM, every available room was occupied, and the first party guests began to trickle in. Mortified to be the first, they drifted into dark corners, clutching cocktails and waiting. The trickle soon swelled into a steady flow, and by 10:00 PM, the time Chelsea Fricks was scheduled to appear, the lobby, restaurant, lounge, and pool deck were overflowing with guests.

It was no surprise she was late. Reputedly, she had once shown up for a photo shoot three full days after call time. Her appearance tonight had been negotiated in excruciating detail through Moira Schwartz, her snarling pit bull of a publicist. Chelsea was obliged to appear for no more than fifteen minutes. She would pose for an official photo, and, if she felt inclined, would mingle with guests.

Although she lived in Bel-Air, Moira demanded the penthouse suite for Chelsea and two adjoining rooms for herself and Chelsea's boyfriend, Bryce Davies. They were leaving for a film shoot in Lima the next day and wanted to go straight to LAX. She also negotiated complimentary limousine transfers, meals, and incidentals—like a bottle of Jack Daniels to be waiting in the suite for Chelsea's arrival. The fee was $150,000.

Tony had balked at the price, but Moira was defiant. "Do you have any idea what a photo of Chelsea is worth these days? If that hare-brained publicist of yours does her job properly, it'll be printed in every tabloid, every entertainment magazine, every fashion rag in this country. It'll put your little boutique hotel on the map." Ultimately Tony caved, but only because he was desperate. After several disastrous attempts at breaking into the film business, first as screenwriter, then as director, and finally as producer, he concluded that his only hope of getting into Hollywood's inner circle was to own a hot hotel. If André Balazs could date Uma Thurman and Jason Pomeranc could call J. Lo a close friend, then Antonio Cavalli could have the stars fawning all over him too.

So far, his plan seemed to be working, save for one small detail: his guest of honor was a no-show.

"Think she's up there?" Tony asked, folding his arms and glaring at the penthouse suite.

"Hard to tell," I said. The balcony was dark, but a light was on in the living room. The sliding glass door was ajar, and the wind had coaxed out the diaphanous curtain, whipping it around in the breeze. I opened my mouth to tell Tony that Miss Fricks had called me from her room a couple of hours ago, but changed my mind. He would insist on knowing every detail. I couldn't possibly tell him that she had called to complain. Or that she had sounded hysterical, possibly unstable. After listening to her rant, I apologized profusely, promising to address the situation at once. Then I made the mistake of asking when she expected to join the party so I would know when to have her room turned down. "Whenever I fucking feel like it," she growled and slammed the phone down.

"Why won't she come down?" Tony whined. He began pacing back and forth in front of me, teetering precariously on the edge of the pool. *One little push,* I thought. "She's in breech of her contract. I could sue. You know, that conniving bitch Moira called me earlier to try and weasel out. She said Chelsea's 'exhausted.'" He sneered as he said this, putting air quotes around the word. "You know what it means when the publicist says her client is 'exhausted'? It means she's been partying nonstop for weeks. 'Don't even think about it,' I told her. 'I planned this entire fucking party around Chelsea. I put her name on the invitations.' She'll be here, all right. She better be here." He stopped and looked at me pleadingly. "She's coming, right?"

"Of course she is."

"Tony, there you are!" A tall, over-tanned, well-preserved man with permed blond hair who looked vaguely like Barry Manilow rushed up. "How's it hanging, you handsome devil?"

"Marlon Peters, how are you, you fucking homo?" Tony cried, breaking into garrulous laughter. He opened his arms and gave him a man-hug, slapping him hard on the back.

"Congratulations on this fucking fabulous hotel!" Marlon gushed.

Tony's eyes lit up. "You like it?"

"It's amazing, Tony. It's almost too hip for me. But what's up with the name? Hotel Cinema? How *bourgeois*."

"You don't like it? See, I've always thought of hotels as theater, right? Contemporary hotels are just like modern cinema. Problem is, employees seem to think they're the stars. It's all about how cool they are, how beautiful they look, how much you should tip them—you know? Hotel Cinema's different. Our guests are the stars. Employees are crew and supporting cast. We provide the soundstage, the props, the styling, the beds—whatever our guests need to give a flawless performance. Each day, every guest lives out a different story. Maybe it's a drama, a romance, a comedy, an action-adventure, a chick flick, porn—you name it. Hotel Cinema. Get it?"

"Oh, I get it all right," Marlon purred, a bemused expression on his face. "You just better hope it's not a tragedy. But seriously, your staff is absolutely delightful. I checked in an hour ago— Morris and I thought we'd spend the night, rather than risk totaling yet another Ferrari—and they couldn't have been more hospitable."

"I only hire the best," Tony said, puffing his chest. "And I treat 'em real good."

I smiled and nodded in agreement, even though they were both ignoring me. The truth was, Tony could take credit for only a handful of hires. They were all relatives or friends or relatives of friends or friends of relatives—all uniformly incompetent. As for the rest of staff, he treated them like crap.

"Obviously everyone underestimated you, Tony Cavalli," said Marlon, lifting his martini glass to cheer him. "You're a genius hotelier."

Tony beamed. "Thank you, my friend."

Realizing I wasn't going to be introduced, I sidestepped away and searched the crowd for a familiar face. Besides employees, I knew only two of the invited guests: Shanna Virani, the hotel's director of sales and marketing, who was there to schmooze, and my mother, Evelyn, who was visiting from Vancouver. I hadn't seen Shanna since the party began. Could she have left already? I certainly hoped not. As for my mother, I had tried to talk her out of visiting this week, warning her I would have no time to spend with her. But she was a willful woman. She wasn't exactly a wall-flower either. An hour earlier I had watched her work the crowd like a seasoned politician, walking straight up to famous actors, world-renowned directors, movie moguls, talk-show hosts, pop stars, and supermodels. "Hello, I'm Evelyn Lambert," she would tell them, and quickly added that she worked as head nurse at a hospital in a suburb of Vancouver, as though her title held equal billing with theirs. "And who are you?" She considered herself far more important than the people around her, and she was probably right. As a nurse, she saved lives, comforted sick people, helped to stop the spread of disease. But this was Hollywood, where people in show business were gods, and everyone else was the audience. They were courteous to her, but not interested.

Unable to spot Mom or Shanna, I peered up at the penthouse again. It was too loud on the pool deck to hear anything, but this time I saw movement in the living room, flickers of shadow and light, as though someone were dancing. A tremor of excitement passed over me. At only twenty-three, Chelsea Fricks was one of Hollywood's hottest stars. Her face adorned current issues of *Vanity Fair*, *Details*, and *Glamour*. She was relentlessly pursued by tabloids, where photos of her and her on-again, off-again boyfriend Bryce Davies commanded top dollar. Each week a new rumor appeared in the tabloids: "Chelsea Cheats on Bryce with Chauffeur!"; "Chelsea Joins Ku Klux Klan!"; "Chelsea Adoption Scandal!" But the press wasn't all bad. She was revered for her acting talent. Only two weeks ago her latest movie, *Blind Ambition*, premiered to rave reviews. Already there was Oscar buzz about her portrayal of real-life Stephanie Greene, the American diving champion who, despite going blind, went on to win a gold medal in the 1996 Olympics. Chelsea Fricks was larger-than-life, a star to the stars—young, gorgeous, talented. Would I get to meet her? What would I say? Our telephone conversation had not gone well, but I was willing to forgive her. The burden of celebrity must be more than she could bear at times. A cutting remark, an unfair accusation, a phone slammed in the ear—it was my job to absorb such abuse, and try to make things better.

Maybe she'd take a shine to me and . . .

I halted my train of thought. After almost a year, the memory of Nancy was too raw. Besides, it was beneath my dignity to become giddy over an actress. I was an adult, a respected hotelier, not an eleven-year-old boy. In my career, I'd met movie stars, heads of state, billionaire philanthropists, royalty, rock stars, and CEOs of major corporations. Few people fazed me anymore. Yet every once in a while, someone got through, made me quiver with anticipation, rendered me into a stammering fool. Why Chelsea Fricks? She was a spoiled, bad-ass party girl with a volatile temper and, if one were to believe the tabloids, semi-sociopathic tendencies. Yet, beneath that brash exterior, I sensed a sensitive, vulnerable person. She was a nice girl from a suburb of Portland. Her fame had been explosive, and she probably didn't know how to handle it.

Tony was back. "I know how to get her down," he said, breaking into a devilish grin. He rubbed his hands together as though warming them in the fire. "She loves the spotlight, right?" He pointed at a floodlight illuminating a palm tree next to us. "Let's smoke her out!"

Partly wary and partly amused, I watched as Tony lugged the contraption toward the edge of the pool, bumping people with his backside, wheeling over toes, prompting cries of protest. At the edge of the pool, he stopped and circled around the light to calculate the best positioning, his toadlike body hunched over, arms swinging back and forth like Quasimodo. Crouching down, he maneuvered the device until a beam of light struck the west wing of the building. He guided it upward to the fifth floor and along the row of balconies to the penthouse suite. The balcony was now illuminated by a bright circle of light. Through the sheer curtain, the animated movements inside the suite became more pronounced.

Tony chuckled to himself. "This'll get her out!"

A number of partygoers stopped talking and turned to watch.

"Cut the music!" Tony shouted. "Cut the music!"

The music stopped. More partygoers turned their attention to the balcony, assuming this was Chelsea's planned appearance. She was notorious for grand entrances and childish pranks. She would step onto the balcony, give an Eva Peron-type wave and air-kiss, perhaps regale us with a song from her soon-to-be released album. A platform would magically appear to transport her down to the pool deck. The crowd quivered with anticipation, their faces flickering with blue light from the pool. The pool, treated for effect with a biodegradable blue dye, looked like a great phosphorescent iceburg. How inviting the cool water looked on this sweltering July night. I lifted my head to the sky. How would the party look from the heavens? A blue pool surrounded by manicured, pedicured, coiffed, surgically enhanced and Botoxed people clutching cocktails, their heads all craned in the same direction. The sky was clear and bright, lit up by hundreds of stars, some so faint they were barely perceptible, others so bright they might be planets. The moon, svelte and luminous, outshone all other entities in the sky. *Much like Chelsea Fricks,* I thought.

Next to me, a large, elegant woman in a snug silver dress flicked a cigarette butt into the pool. I watched it sizzle and spin as though in protest, then fizzle out, surrendering to the water. I glared in her direction, but she was staring up at the penthouse suite intently, a mixture of hope and curiosity in her eyes, even a trace of envy. A buzz was traveling through the crowd; people were spilling onto the deck from the lounge and restaurant.

But the spotlight remained empty.

Growing impatient, Tony lifted his fingers to his mouth and let out a loud whistle. "Hey, Chelsea!" he shouted. "Come on out! We're waitin' for ya!"

There were chuckles in the crowd, murmurs of excitement. The movements inside the suite seemed to gain momentum. I heard a female voice shouting. Then a scream. A woman rushed onto the balcony and leaned over the railing, checking the pool. It took me a moment to recognize Chelsea. She was wearing a black bra and panties.

"Bravo!" cried a man, whom I recognized as a director. Brett Ratner?

Several others began clapping.

Chelsea scrambled onto the railing, teetering on top. There was a collective gasp from the crowd. Glancing over her shoulder, she let out a shriek and leapt off the railing. Her arms flailed in the air, as though she were trying to flap her way to the pool, then came together in a clumsy swan dive just before she struck the surface. She disappeared underwater.

The splash sent the crowd stumbling backward. Immediately, they rushed forward again, peering into the pool, waiting for Chelsea to surface.

"It's a prank!" the butt-flicking woman next to me shouted. "A publicity stunt for her movie!"

There were sighs of relief, moans of disapproval, gasps of outrage. A few people began clapping. The woman next to me began laughing hysterically. It was a prank. It had to be. The crowd broke into applause.

Yet Chelsea didn't surface.

I was deeply troubled. I knew something they did not: Chelsea had landed in the shallow end.

Pushing people out of the way, I rushed around the periphery of the pool, stopping at the edge where Chelsea had landed. My eyes searched the pool. A few feet away, near the center, I spotted her body morphing in the blue waters. Fumbling for the two-way radio clipped to my belt, I switched it on and shouted into the mouthpiece, "Trevor to Comm Center. Call 911 immediately. There's an emergency on the pool deck. Someone's fallen from the balcony into the pool."

The reply came instantly. "Ten-four, Trevor. Calling right now."

I tossed the radio down and pulled off my tuxedo jacket. Across the pool, I caught a glimpse of a short, heavyset man staring into the water with a lascivious grin. Chelsea had been under for at least thirty seconds, yet he and the others still expected her to surface, to take a bow. Some were beginning to get nervous. Yet no one made a move to rescue her. As I prepared to jump in after her, I considered whether the butt-flicking woman might be right. Was it a publicity stunt? Chelsea was in the midst of a publicity junket for *Blind Ambition*. What better way to draw attention to the movie than to arrive at a party by diving off the balcony of her suite? No wonder no one was jumping in after her. Who would ruin designer clothes and perfect hair to be the butt of a practical joke?

As the hotel manager, I couldn't afford the risk. I dove into the pool.

The water was colder than I expected. My hands struck the bottom hard. I opened my eyes, blinking rapidly to regain my vision, and searched for Chelsea. The blue dye stung like iodine. I spotted her pale body floating a few feet away and kicked toward her. Swirls of purplish liquid swelled around her, as though she were bleeding. An image of Nancy came to me. How many times had I envisioned this same scenario—frantically swimming out to sea in a vain effort to save her? I grabbed Chelsea's arm and pulled her toward me. Her head swung in my direction. Her eyes, brown like Nancy's, were open. I felt a rush of relief. She was conscious. But her blank expression and the swirls of liquid seeping from her back and abdomen gave me reason to doubt. Wrapping my arms around her torso, I planted my feet on the bottom of the pool and pushed upward.

The crowd cheered as we broke the surface. The water was shallow enough to stand in. I heaved Chelsea over my shoulder and made my way to the edge of the pool. For a petite girl, she felt heavy. I expected her to struggle, to break free and to climb onto the edge of the pool to take her bow. But she lay limp in my arms, not choking or gasping for air or moving. Either she was a brilliant performer or she had passed out.

A dozen hands reached out to pull her from my arms. I let her go, watching her head loll backward as though her neck was made of rubber. Her eyes stared back at me, then disappeared as they placed her on the deck. Her skin was an odd shade of blue. I looked down at my own arm and saw it too. The blue dye. My white shirt was now pale blue in color. Placing my hands on the edge of the pool, I pulled myself out, ignoring the proffered hands.

A houseman hurried over with a big white towel for Chelsea. A man placed it over her body. The houseman then brought me a towel too. I thanked him and mopped my face, dried my eyes, and pulled it around my shoulders, feeling a sudden chill. Turning to regard where Chelsea lay, I saw that she had disappeared behind a swarm of people.

"Is there a doctor here?" a woman shouted. "This woman needs attention! Anyone? Please!"

There were murmurs among the crowd.

"I played a doctor on *House*," said a man to my right. "Does that count?"

No one laughed.

I tried to pry my way toward Chelsea to offer assistance but stopped when I saw Arte McLachlan, the hotel's director of security, pushing his way through the crowd.

"Hotel security!" he shouted. "Let me through! I can help."

I breathed a sigh of relief. Arte was a former paramedic. If anyone could save her, he could.

I bent down to pick up my radio.

Above me, I heard a cry of anguish. Looking up, I saw a dark-haired woman leaning over the balcony railing next to Chelsea's suite, gazing down with an expression of horror. I recognized Moira Schwartz, Chelsea's publicist.

"Oh my God!" she cried. "Chelsea!"

A man appeared next to her. Bryce Davies. "Hold on, baby!" he cried. "I'll be right down!"

They disappeared.

I reached for my radio. "Trevor to Comm Center. Is an ambulance on the way?"

"Affirmative," came the reply. "Has Arte McLachlan arrived on scene?"

"Affirmative." By now, more than three hundred people had crowded onto the pool deck. "Paging all security staff," I yelled into the radio. "We need everyone cleared from the pool deck *now*." I began herding people out of the way. Inside, people were pressing their faces and hands against the floor-to-ceiling windows of the lounge, looking anxious as they tried to see what was going on.

Turning around, I caught a glimpse of Chelsea's pale-blue face. There was a large welt on her forehead, likely from striking the bottom of the pool. As people were cleared from the area, her towel-covered body came into view. Arte was squatting over her, administering CPR. Her long, honey-colored hair was splayed around her head. She looked like Botticelli's Venus, having decided to lie down for a nap. Her head was turned away from me, her neck unnaturally twisted. Suddenly, her chest heaved. I experienced a moment of joy. It happened again. Then I realized the motion was from Arte's attempts to revive her.

A woman beside me was sobbing. I took her by the arm and led her inside, trying to comfort her along the way.

"Where the hell is the ambulance?" she cried.

"It's on its way," I assured her.

As we reached the doorway, Bryce Davies burst past us. "Out of my fucking way!" he cried, shoving me.

I stumbled back and turned to watch as he rushed across the deck to Chelsea's side.

Moira Schwartz was right behind him. "Move, people! Move!" she shouted.

Bryce grabbed Arte by the shoulders, wrenching him away from Chelsea. "What the fuck you doing, man? You some perv or something?"

I rushed over. "He's trying to save her!" I pulled Bryce out of the way. "He's certified in first aid. Please give him room."

Bryce turned and lifted his fist at me, but let it drop. He turned to Chelsea. With a cry of anguish, he fell to his knees. "Don't die on me, Chelsea baby!" he cried. "Don't leave me. I love you! I'm sorry! I'm so sorry!"

Moira let out a great sob and collapsed beside him, clasping her hands in prayer.

"Out of the way, please!" shouted a security officer. "Emergency personnel are here!"

I turned to see two paramedics rushing over. Directly behind them came two Los Angeles Police Department officers.

The crowd cheered.

Arte stood up and backed away to make room for them. Spotting me, he came over.

"Is she going to make it?" I asked.

He shook his head slowly. "She's already dead."

www.MidnightInkBooks.com

From the gritty streets of New York City to sacred tombs in the Middle East, it's always midnight somewhere. Join us online at any hour for fresh new voices in mystery fiction, book club questions, author information, mystery resources, and more.

Midnight Ink promises a wild ride filled with cunning villains, conflicted heroes, hilarious hazards, mind-bending puzzles, and enough twists and turns to keep readers on the edge of their seats.